NOT READY

DOROTHY BERTSCH

PublishAmerica
Baltimore

ISBN: 1-60563-082-9
PUBLISHED BY PUBLISHAMERICA, LLLP
www.publishamerica.com
Baltimore

Printed in the United States of America

For Sally, my daughter-in-law,
for her encouragement and hours of fine-tuning

And to my husband Fritz and my son Kirk
for their belief in my ability

ONE

INDECISION

The noise was deafening. Strobe lights were flashing. Jarred out of our sleep, we looked at the clock. Five in the morning! A continuing series of loud and jolting, raucous sounds were coming from the fire alarm high on the wall above our heads, accompanied by flashes of light like those from a high speed camera.

"Now what the hell is this all about?" Jeff muttered as he climbed out of bed and struggled to pull on his brown-corded pants, a red bandana handkerchief hanging half-way out of a rear pocket.

Bleary-eyed, I sat upright in bed, brushed wisps of graying hair from my face, and watched Jeff pull a short-sleeved knitted shirt over his bald head and chubby chest. "I'll walk out to the parking area in front of our building, Jeanie. See what's going on," he told me, shoving his bare feet into a pair of brown leather moccasins.

When I heard our apartment door slam shut I knew Jeff had left, and I flung the sheet and light-weight blanket aside and hurried into our walk-in clothes closet. The hanger swayed on a rod as I grabbed my Chinese happy coat. Then I hurried into the dining room slipping my skinny arms into the coat's wide, silky sleeves and wrapping the sash around my waist. My fanny on a chair, I drew up my knees and propped my feet on its front edge. Not as young as I used to be when I could sit on my feet, I thought. The blare continued to vibrate through the entire apartment, and I clasped my hands tightly over my ears. Positioned like that, I glanced at the flowers in the tall cut-glass vase on the dining room table. The vase was sitting directly over the center seam where we'd removed a leaf. It must have been vibrating a titch, too, for I could see the water trembling

5

around the stems of the pink carnations Jeff had brought home from Publix yesterday. "To celebrate our move into our new abode," he'd said. I concentrated on the phenomenon occurring in the vase as I sat there and waited.

Jeff returned in jig time and the door slammed shut again. He motioned toward the parking area and said, "Two fire trucks and an ambulance out there. Rotating flashers 're casting weird reflections on the walls of the next building. Firemen in hard hats and black rubber boots striding about carrying emergency equipment." He stepped out of his moccasins and wiggled his toes.

We had been in this two-bedroom two-bath apartment, residents of Sandycreek Terrace, for only two weeks and were just starting to feel *settled in.* At least Jeff was. *I* wasn't so sure this was where we belonged, here in this continuing care retirement community. It hadn't been my idea, you see.

Exactly how did Jeff and I arrive at this point? How did we happen to be living in this CCRC? I'll tell you. The decision started with a not-too-congenial discussion between us after we had attended a cocktail party at Sandycreek Terrace one afternoon. The affair that day, hosted by the establishment's marketing division, was our last visit to the facility. The first contact made by Sandycreek Terrace had been an invitation to attend a luncheon. A few months later, we'd accepted an invitation to a brunch. And now the cocktail party we'd attended today.

Mailed to us, the invitation was enclosed in a pink envelope. I'd casually looked at the front of a glossy folded card with a photo of a white-haired, smiling, elderly couple framed by a background of leafy trees, blooming flowers, and a manicured lawn. Then I'd opened the card, and inside on the upper half I'd read:

You are invited to a complimentary cocktail party at Sandycreek Terrace
No obligation to listen to a presentation about our brand new apartments
Learn how you can enter the warm and exciting world of Sandycreek Terrace and enjoy all the benefits of continuing care
Don't miss this one-in-a-lifetime opportunity!
Limited number of apartments available
Monday, September 11, 2003 4:00 p.m. at Sandycreek Terrace, Jupiter, FL

The lower half read:
Incredible spacious completely new and utterly well-designed apartments
Balconies and fabulous view
New fitness center, pool, and spa
Fine dining by a Certified Executive Chef
Luxury amenities and fun activities
Services that free your time
Health care on campus if you ever need it
Call 772-561-0000 to say you're attending our cocktail party

I'd handed the invitation to Jeff when he'd come onto the lanai where I'd deposited the mail and was sorting it there on one of our two glass-topped tables. He'd lowered his glasses from atop his bald head, quickly read the invitation, and said, "Might as well take advantage of free drinks and food, Jeanie. I think that's a pretty nice place. Don't mind seeing it again and hearing their pitch."

I'd agreed to go after some hesitation, thinking it unfair to take advantage of the establishment's hospitality when we were not intending to move there. At the time, I wasn't aware of Jeff's serious consideration of the virtues of living in a continuing care retirement community, and this one in particular. I would need more time to know him completely, as completely as anyone knows anyone, that is. Six years of marriage hadn't been long enough. (As I looked back on forty-seven years of living with my first husband, I realized I hadn't known him completely before he died.) Even though I knew Jeff as a forthright, out-spoken, kind, considerate, and conscientious man, I was yet unable to read his mind, to know how strongly he felt about such a move—out of our lovely many-roomed house with its two-car garage and large front and back yards into a CCRC, lovely as *it* was. And I had to admit Sandycreek Terrace appeared to be an upscale living arrangement option for retired people, if that type of living suited one's fancy.

Each time we had approached the grounds of Sandycreek Terrace, a uniformed attendant at the guard house had leaned his head out the open window and said, "Your name, please, sir."

Jeff had told him.

The guard had read down a list of names on a clipboard, nodded, and said, "Go straight ahead, Mr. Metz. Your car will be parked for you," and handed Jeff a slip of orange paper to place on the dashboard.

On each visit, as we'd passed white stucco cottages and condominiums, all with red tiled Spanish-type roofs, we were favorably impressed by their architectural features and the abundant well-designed landscaping. Each time, we'd followed a winding drive past a quaint gazebo painted white and a sculptured bridge curving over a large pond, like a Venice venue without gondolas. I'd watched the water, silver in the sun, as it rose from three fountains. From two, spears seemed to shoot straight up about ten feet toward the sky and immediately cascade down like numerous sparkling ribbons entering the pond. From the third fountain located in the middle, water spewed forth much lower and broader like a forever blossoming flower dropping its petals to form a huge diamond ring in the water around it. We'd driven past more white cottages before arriving at a large building with a sign proclaiming it was Sandycreek Terrace Club House. Our car doors opened by an attendant in khaki, we'd stepped out onto a walkway of decorative concrete blocks, flower-filled planters gracing its edges and flanked by two rows of tall white pillars. Double glass doors would swing open automatically as we'd step across the carpeted approach. The foyer was so spacious as to be almost overwhelming. Live plantings were spaced along glossy marble floors and birds sang from immense split-bamboo cages. Through another set of glass doors we could see a spread of Irish-green lawn and the glittering ocean inlet.

Today, as before, we were greeted by marketing personnel in black gabardine suits and white silk blouses, nylon hose and black high-heeled pumps. I had selected a deep-blue Patchington suit for myself and convinced Jeff to wear a sport coat, coordinating pants, and white dress-shirt. No tie. I would have preferred he wore a tie for I thought men looked professional when they wore ties. But he'd informed me more than once, "I stopped wearing ties when I retired."

Residents who served on the welcoming committee greeted us as well. "Nice to see you. Nice you could come," said one male resident of medium-height dressed in a dark-gray suit, white shirt, and red-printed tie as he advanced, shook our hands, and escorted us to a table in the spacious dining room. I blinked in the brightness from the sun shining in two long window-walls and from the light pouring down from sparkling chandeliers. Again we were impressed by the table setting—white linen-like cloth and large white napkins, shining flatware, and shimmering stemmed water-glasses. After seating us in cushioned chairs, the resident host said, "Any time you're ready just go up to the cocktail table and help yourselves. Order drinks of your choice."

No sooner were we seated than Jeff said, "Might as well go up and see what they have to offer."

As we ventured up to the cocktail table, we realized this cocktail party equaled and perhaps surpassed the other two events we'd attended. "Look Jeff!" I said. "Look at the huge ice carvings! They tower over this immense hors d'oeuvre table. I've never seen so many hors d'oeuvres!" My eyes swept over the lay-out of shrimp, crab legs, oysters on the half shell, pate', cheeses, deviled eggs, finger sandwiches, a great variety of crackers and chips, and more delicacies. Cocktails of choice were unlimited! Jeff took particular note *and* advantage of that. When we left the tantalizing table about six potential residents remained. Or maybe they were just guests like we were, there out of curiosity.

With our cocktails and platters of appetizers, we went back to our assigned table where we joined a fine-looking elderly couple already seated. The thin gray-haired woman wearing a satiny saffron-colored dress like I'd seen in an *Appleseed* catalogue coyly said, "We're residents here. I've lived here for five years, and last year Peter and I were married here. Here in the Palace by my minister. Peter was a resident, too."

Peter smiled and nodded.

The female resident continued after helping herself to a plump pink shrimp she first dipped in bright-red cocktail sauce. "We love it here. It's a wonderful place to live. And there is so much to do! We're busy all the time!"

"Shrimp are rather small," Jeff joked, a twinkle in his blue eyes while he watched the woman manage another large morsel.

"Oh, you're joking, aren't you?" she said, looking hard at Jeff. "The shrimp are always this size here. Always big."

Jeff said, "Our marriage is relatively recent, too. Older than yours, however."

"How long have you been married?" Peter wanted to know.

"Six years, Jeff and I said in unison.

"Where do you live?" the pleasant little old lady asked, looking at Jeff and then at me.

"We live in Pine Gardens. Do you know where that is?" Jeff asked her.

"I've heard of it, but I've never been there. I lived in Admiral's Cove before I came here. I liked it there but I don't miss it at all."

"What is it you're so busy doing?" I asked the lady in the Appleseed dress.

"Why we have exercise classes and card games and book reviews and symposiums and Bible study and dinner parties with entertainment and dancing...I'm sure I've forgotten something. Something's going on all the time!" she said, folding and unfolding her napkin.

She was continuing to tell us about a recent party they attended when, from somewhere in the room, we heard, "May we have your attention everyone, please."

At that point, we listened respectfully to brief presentations by the Marketing Director and the Executive Director both lauding limitless attributes of the facility and answering questions about buy-in agreements. I raised my hand and asked, "What is the capacity of your skilled nursing care unit?"

"We have fifty-five beds," The Executive Director answered.

"And you have a state license and federal certification?"

"Oh yes, of course," he said, confidently. "Our last inspection was six months ago. We're fully licensed and certified. In fact, our facility is staffed with a greater number than the state requires."

As we were leaving the dining room, Jeff said, "Holy smokes! I was afraid you were going to ask how well they did on their last inspection, Miss Surveyor."

"Well, I wanted to ask how many deficiencies they had, but I thought that would be cruel. He probably wouldn't want to admit to having any deficiencies." I giggled.

"You surveyors always found deficiencies, didn't you? You nurses were expected to probe until you found some, weren't you?" Jeff asked with a grin and a knowing look on his full face.

"Of course we looked for them. But no facility ever operates without *some* deficiencies," I said, thinking back to those days I surveyed nursing homes, usually as part of a team of registered nurses for the larger facilities.

When we walked out the main door, Jeff said, "That cocktail party was exceptionally nice." I agreed wholeheartedly.

We were back from the cocktail party relaxing on the lanai of our Florida house when Jeff started the disturbing discussion by remarking, "Nice place! I think we should consider living there."

Living there? I couldn't believe my ears. "Jeff, you can't be serious!" I said, suddenly sitting upright and looking him straight in the eyes. It wasn't meant to be a statement, of course. It was a question, and I wanted an honest answer. Did he really want to move from our beautiful free-standing house in a country club community where we'd lived happily for six years? Move from this house he'd bought and where we'd moved after getting married, both of us widowed? Move into that Sandycreek Terrace place in Jupiter?

Jeff turned his attention to me and my question and said, "Yes, Jeanie, I am thinking seriously about moving to a continuing care community. Maybe not Sandycreek Terrace. There are others. We can look around." He smiled and patted me on the knee.

I stared at his smile. He had a nice smile and smiled a lot, and his thin lips never revealed his teeth. "But Jeff," I began, ignoring the smile and gesture of affection and frowning at him. His smile disappeared and his expression grew serious. I continued, "I thought we were doing just fine here. I like living here in Pine Gardens. I like this large house, the lanai with its whirl-pool tub, the two-car garage, the fruit trees in the back yard, and the neighborhood. We have friends here, and I like going to the Club. We've belonged to the Club for a long time. Separately and together. I've belonged since I bought the town house, and you've belonged since you bought your condominium apartment. Our church is practically next door!"

He arched his thin eyebrows and horizontal lines creased his forehead.

"We'll make new friends wherever we go, Jeanie. We're not using the Club much any more. We don't play golf any more. And we can come back here to church. We won't move *that* far away." He leaned toward me, tapped the table with an index finger, and continued, "It's too much work here. When we moved here six years ago I didn't have this back problem. I hadn't had that cervical surgery. I can't take care of this place any more! I can't climb up and repair the pull cords on the ceiling fans or change an overhead light bulb without practically falling off the ladder! Damned if I like to admit it, but I can't pick all those oranges and grapefruit any more! After all, I am *almost* eighty-three years old!"

"Well, I *am* eighty-three years old," I said, straightening my spine to its fullest and speaking emphatically. "But I don't feel that old. The dermatologist said, 'There are old eighty-three year olds and young eighty-three year olds, and you, Mrs. Metz, are a *young* eighty-three year old.' That's what he said." I heaved a sigh and kept on spouting off. "We can get somebody to come in. Hire a young person to come in and do the things you can't do any more. Like we have Lefty cut the grass and trim the bushes." I hesitated, gathered my thoughts. "Oh I know how you feel about spending money, Jeff. You being half-Dutch and your family's poverty during the Great Depression. My Scottish blood has always made me frugal, too. But we have enough money. You said yourself we should spend it. Not save it for our children who make more money than we ever dreamed of." I peered at him for his concurrence.

He said, "That's another issue. If we stay here getting older and older, maybe not sick or needing nursing home care, our children will feel obligated to care for us. They'll want us to live with them. I don't want that. I don't think you do either. If we're in Sandycreek Terrace or some other CCRC, they'll be relieved of that burden. We'll be giving them the best gift we could give them. Peace of mind. They'll be happy we're in a safe and caring environment."

I hadn't thought of that angle. But after a quick reflection, I was sure I'd never be so old I couldn't take care of myself, self sufficient as I'd been for many years. I shook my head. "You haven't convinced me."

He was frowning, fiddling with the glasses he'd removed from atop his head but not saying anything so I continued, "You know how I feel about living in a place like that. When I worked as an RN surveying facilities for state licensure and federal certification, I never inspected a CCRC. But I did inspect and license nursing homes and assisted living facilities. Never, never did I plan to live in one!" My fist hit the table.

I saw Jeff flinch. Of course he knew all about my career, knew before he married me. I knew he admired me for my achievements and, in a way, understood why I objected to moving into a facility that provided assistance.

He came back with, "I understand. I understand, Jeanie. But we have to be practical. We're not getting any younger, and some day we'll need care, and I want to be prepared for that day whenever it arrives. If we go now, we can enjoy the service, the activities, all they have to offer. We'll be free to do what we want. No responsibilities." He shifted in his chair and fingered the invitation to the cocktail party still lying on the table.

I didn't want to be unreasonable, wanted him to know I understood his limitations, but I persisted. "What about those long-term care insurance policies you bought? You've had one for ages and you bought one for me even before we were married. And you continue to pay the yearly renewal fees. If we go into a CCRC, we're not going to need them. It's like throwing money down the drain!"

Jeff wasn't going to give up either. He repeated what he'd said to me in the past when I claimed buying insurance was like throwing money away. I didn't believe in insurance even though my father had made a fine living being an insurance agent and managing the three offices he opened to handle the increased business. And my dear husband did repeat, "You buy car insurance, don't you? You may never need it. But if you have an accident, you need it! You need long-term care insurance every bit as much as you need car insurance. In my book, you need it even more. We may very well be able to have it apply to care we might need some day at Sandycreek Terrace." He sighed, changed his position again, and rubbed his hand over his bald head, his blue eyes holding mine.

My fingers out-spread on the table, I said, "We should find out if it applies in their nursing home unit or if the homecare part of the policy applies in a resident apartment. We don't need it now. But you're right. We may need it some day."

"Nobody gets out of here alive," he said and was fond of saying. Well, maybe he wasn't exactly fond of saying it, but he repeated the statement often, usually when someone died—a friend, a neighbor, a relative. And it was the truth even though I hated to hear it. He continued to enlarge on the subject. "Without a doubt, should we live long enough, some day we'll need assistance in daily living. Can't you see you're human, and you're not going to be eighty-three and in good health the remainder of your life, Jeanie? You have a pacemaker now even though you claim it amounts to nothing more than a band aid." He ran his hand over his head again. picked up his glasses from the table, fiddled with them, then continued, "This place is different from the facilities you had anything to do with, Sweetie. This is independent living. Just like living here in this house. Give it some thought, Honey. We don't have to decide this minute. But it's time we started being waited on, have our dinner prepared and served to us. All we have to do is call maintenance to come and change a light bulb or fix an appliance. Have the house cleaned and the flat linens washed. Have a maid make the bed with clean sheets every week. We can afford it. Yes, the kids do have enough money. We should spend what we have on ourselves!"

He gave me one of his best smiles. "Your hair's especially pretty today. Golden silver with the sun shining on it. And it always stays perfectly in place." He replaced his glasses, the temples firm against the sides of his head but never quite reaching all the way around his ear lobes. Then he pulled his pocket knife out of his pant's pocket and started to open the mail lying on the table.

I was tempted to tell him *flattery will get you nowhere*, but this conversation didn't lend itself to humor so I pursued, "That's just it. If we go there, we'll be waited on hand and foot and get stiff from doing nothing. And no one! No one but *I* will ever make our bed!"

Jeff looked up at me from the pile of mail. "That's fine. You go ahead and make our bed, Honey, but stop wrinkling your forehead. It's not becoming."

At that point, Honey got up and left the room.

Two

Stress

The discussion about moving into a continuing care retirement community arose again several days later when Jeff opened the lanai door and stumbled in from the back yard. He looked at me sitting there hemming a pair of slacks that were too long. "I have the oranges picked. The ones I reached with the picker and the lower ones I picked by hand," he told me. "The raccoons can have the rest. The highest ones. They've already helped themselves to a few. I had to throw them over the fence. Those raccoons suck out the insides and leave the rind practically intact so you think you have a perfectly good whole orange until you have it in your hands. Then you find out it's a hollow shell. Clever little devils!"

I smiled, knowing what he meant. I'd seen and felt one of those empty oranges the other morning.

"But I'm bushed!" he said as he sank down onto a wicker chair and grunted loudly. "I can't possibly tackle the grapefruit tree. And it's loaded!"

"You called Joe to help you last year. Gave him as many as he wanted to take home after they were picked."

Jeff shook his head and said, "He's having trouble with his hip. Can't walk without a lot of pain, Dolores told us the other day."

"Oh that's right. Maybe you could ask Lefty the day he's here to trim the shrubbery," I said, making another attempt to solve the grapefruit dilemma.

"Look, Jeanie," Jeff said, his voice serious, his hands folded in front of him. "I've had enough. I'm ready to sell this house. Retire from these property problems. These responsibilities. Relax. Enjoy being waited on.

15

Do some writing. Work on my stamp collection. I want you to agree to go to that continuing care retirement community."

I could see his shirt above his shorts was saturated with perspiration, and he seemed short of breath. I realized I had no choice. I was defeated in my efforts to keep on living in this single-family house. I had to agree to move into that CCRC. He'd made up his mind. I knew I couldn't change it. I had tried, but to no avail. Resigned, I asked rather weakly, "To Sandycreek Terrace, you mean?" Then I had to say, "It *is* a lovely place. It's providing that *Aging in Place* concept my old profession calls it these days."

So after Jeff had showered and made us each a cocktail, we sat at our glass-topped wicker table on the lanai before dinner. We clicked our glasses and kissed as we always did to demonstrate our devotion and then started a serious discussion about moving.

Jeff said, "The facility is offering two entrance plans: the Extensive or Return of Capital contract and the Modified at a lower fee and no return of capital."

After reviewing the pros and cons of the two plans at length, we decided on the Modified contract, Jeff saying, "Why pay more to have ninety percent of our money returned when we're dead? Our children won't need the money. They'll be taken care of by the provisions in our wills. Besides, they're all making more money now than we ever dreamed of making."

"True," I agreed. "And both plans have lifetime nursing care at exceptionally low rates. And you think those health care insurance policies you're paying for might apply?" Well maybe they would, but I doubted it. I also doubted my sanity, agreeing to move into Sandycreek Terrace. I clenched my teeth, gripped my hands into fists, and heaved a deep sigh.

As Jeff and I sat there finishing our drinks and talking about the ramifications of our move and all the details involved, I suddenly realized I would have to accept my own individual financial responsibility to enter and live in this continuing care retirement community. I would have to pay my share of the breath-taking cost of the apartment, including the initial payment to hold the unit, and also the monthly maintenance fees.

This I would be obliged to do in order to satisfy my part of the financial agreement Jeff and I had made when we married six years ago. This financial arrangement had been determined in view of the fact that we both had fair-sized incomes, Jeff more than I.

At the time, that decision had been difficult for me to accept. I guess I hadn't thought through that phase of another married life before Jeff and I repeated our marriage vows. Oh I had assets due to my father's business opportunities and having worked much of my adult life. But Jeff's portfolio at least tripled mine as he'd had retired military income and successful business ventures, and he'd worked hard and been frugal. We'd both saved and cautiously coveted our wealth, such as it was. Since Jeff's income was much more than mine, he had said it would only be fair to share our joint expenses in proportion to our assets.

My first marriage back in the forties had been entirely different. We'd started with little money in the bank and shared income and expenses and financial obligation.

Were all second marriages different from first marriages when it came to finances, I wondered? Certainly they would be different if children were involved. Jeff had four children and I had three. At the time of death, Jeff's assets would go to his children and my assets would go to mine. I had no difficulty understanding that, and I wholeheartedly agreed.

Even so, the decision this evening was again difficult for me to accept. I felt nervous, a tingling up and down my spine, my stomach nauseous. Could I afford it? Could I afford to live in this CCRC? Doubt clouded my mind. Concern whirled. I'd always been in control, guarding my assets with religious fervor, saving and never spending more than I could pay for at the end of each month. Now I would have to withdraw a sizeable amount from my trust account to pay my share of this new living arrangement. I needed some counseling, some reassurance.

"I'll feel better if I consult my stock broker friend," I told Jeff at the end of our conversation. "I'm afraid if I withdraw the buy-in amount now, and if the maintenance fee is withdrawn each month, not enough will be left in my account to gender an income to continue to pay the monthly maintenance fee."

Jeff didn't seem to think I had anything to worry about and said, "Sure,

Jeanie. Go ahead and call your stock broker if that will give you peace of mind."

When I called my broker friend the next day he assured me ample funds were available for the buy-in amount required. Yearly income from interest and dividends would more than cover my share of monthly fees. I breathed a big sigh of relief. Nevertheless, I was squeamish. What if maintenance fees rose exorbitantly? What if stocks plunged? What if one of my children was in desperate financial straights? I really wasn't a *what-if* person, but these thoughts did cross my mind. Surely Jeff would step forward if I couldn't pay my share. He'd as much as said so once, hadn't he?

That decided, on October 8, 2003, Jeff's eighty-third birthday incidentally, we drove to Sandycreek Terrace, and, once inside, were directed to the marketing office. There we were met by Virginia Friedman, the Marketing Director, a tall smartly dressed woman, probably in her late thirties or early forties. We handed her the required physician's statements attesting to our health status. "Thank you very much," she said. "I'll be giving these to Amanda Murray. She'll have a few questions for you."

At that very moment, a solidly-built rounded woman of medium height entered the office and smiled broadly at us. She extended a chubby hand when Virginia introduced her as the Manager of Independent Living Assistance, and then Virginia promptly left the room.

"Please have a seat," Amanda Murray offered, glancing at the physician statements and nodding toward the wicker chairs positioned around a round maple-wood table at one end of the room. After we were seated she seated herself and smiled again, a genuine smile from a friendly middle-aged woman, I decided. "I'll want to talk to both of you alone," she started and then asked, "Which of you wants to be first?"

We looked at each other, and I said, "You be first, Jeff. I'll go look at the relief map of the complex. It's out in the foyer. I noticed it when we entered."

"We won't be very long, Mrs. Metz," Amanda said, getting up, escorting me to the door, and closing it behind me.

Before long, Jeff came out of the marketing office and I went in to sit with Amanda at the round table. "Just a few questions for you to answer, Mrs. Metz," she began. "Tell me. What is your current address, Mrs. Metz?" I gave her our present address. "And can you give me the date? Today's date? The day and the month and the year."

I answered without hesitation.

"Now the president of the United States. Who is the current president of the United States, Mrs. Metz?"

I recognized these questions as the time, place, and person orientation test questions used in the health profession to test the mental status of patients. After I answered, she brought out a pencil and small piece of paper, drew stick figures of two houses diagonally positioned from each other. She showed me her drawing and then took it away.

"Now I need you to count from fifteen back to one." I did that successfully, and was then asked to spell the word *initially* backwards. After I complied again successfully, she gave me a blank piece of paper and a pencil. "Will you please draw the picture I drew for you a few minutes ago?" she said.

I'm no artist. Far from it. My mother had painted beautiful birds and flowers. Prompted by her, I'd taken an art class in college and was lucky to pass with a C grade. That career ended before it began. Nevertheless, stick figures shouldn't be that difficult, should they? Pencil in hand, I made an effort to reproduce Amanda's drawing and didn't do badly. At least the result suited Amanda Murray. After asking about my children and career, she appeared satisfied, thanked me, and opened the door for Jeff to enter.

At the same time Amanda left, Virginia reentered. Now we were sitting with the Marketing Director about to sign documents allowing us to occupy an apartment for the rest of our lives. Yes, it would be for the rest of our lives I suddenly realized. Until that very moment, I hadn't thought of it that way—for the rest of our lives. I had thought of it as just another move, like the many moves I'd made throughout my life in the Pittsburgh suburbs and elsewhere in Pennsylvania and also on the Florida Treasure Coast. This was just another move, I had told myself. But perhaps deep within my subconscious I knew this move would be my last and Jeff's last. It would be the last move for all the people who moved into Sandycreek Terrace. We might eventually move again, be housed in Park Place, Sandycreek Terrace's euphemistically-named nursing home that I called Final Phase, in jest. But the move would be internal, at a time we needed that level of care. I shuddered at the thought of a move into Park Place alias Final Phase. Into any nursing home for that matter. May that time never come!

I thought back to the reason my mind was so dead set against nursing homes. It came from twenty-three years experience working in nursing homes. My first position was director of nursing of a two-hundred and forty-eight bed facility. After that I was a state surveyor, inspecting nursing homes to determine their qualifications for state license renewals or initial state licenses and for federal certifications. Then I accepted the position of director of nursing of a one-thousand-bed state owned and operated skilled nursing facility. Before I moved to Florida and surveyed nursing homes out of a West Palm office, my last position in Pennsylvania was supervisor of inspectors of assisted living facilities in the western region when these facilities were required to be licensed for the first time. I wanted no part of living such an undesirable life as I'd seen in nursing homes and assisted living facilities, being dependent and at the mercy of others, some capable and caring, some not. That was not living!

But now here we were sitting in cushioned wicker chairs at the round maple-wood table in the brightly lighted marketing office. Virginia Friedman was saying, "We do have an apartment available like the type you prefer. It's a first-floor apartment with two bedrooms, two baths, Florida room, dining and living room with the entrance close to the kitchen. You said you wanted to enter near the kitchen." We had specifically wanted that configuration so we could enter and carry our groceries directly into the kitchen and not have to carry them through the entire apartment.

Virginia then started to explain, "A number of amenities are included in our arrangements. You will receive one full banquet-type meal per day, weekly housecleaning of your apartment, a high order of twenty-four-hour security, and be entitled to participate in a host of activities."

While she talked I was looking at her blond coiffeur, not a hair out of place, and at her smart black silk suit like a Sacs Fifth Avenue creation, the skirt now riding above her nylon covered knees. By comparison, Jeff and I had dressed casually in slacks and short-sleeved knitted tops.

It seemed this marketing director sat much taller than we, almost appearing to tower over us at the table, especially over me. Being tall, she would sit tall. I had long legs but I wasn't tall, so I sat short. Jeff's legs were short but his torso long, so he sat taller than I. Short like that, I eyed the chocolate mints in green foil-wrapping tempting me from a shallow ceramic bowl in the center of the table. Don't give in, I mouthed, tearing my eyes away from calories and chocolate addiction. I crossed and uncrossed my skinny legs and glanced over at the wall where framed floor plans of apartment options hung side by side.

Now Virginia was explaining the two options of legal and financial agreements between Sandycreek Terrace and prospective residents. "We offer the Extensive or Return of Capital contract and the Modified at a lower entrance fee and no return of capital." These were the contracts we'd already heard described at presentations given at the three invitational events we'd attended. They were also identical to the ones we'd discussed at home. We both nodded and told her we had decided on the Modified contract.

As Virginia sat with pen posed above two documents facing us, we each signed. Then Jeff handed his check over the table to her, and I bravely handed her mine of an equal amount, thus holding the apartment for thirty days.

"You might like to have these floor plans of your apartment and pictures of furniture drawn to scale and so identified," Virginia Friedman said, offering us the papers she was explaining. "You can cut out the pieces of furniture that match *your* furniture and place them on the floor plans. They'll help you in arranging your furniture in your apartment."

We thanked her, and our business completed, we left the office aware we had little time to prepare for our move into Sandycreek Terrace.

Three
The Move

We made good use of the floor plans of our apartment and the sheets of paper with pictures of furniture drawn to scale and given to us by Virginia Friedman. By now we'd decided to make the guest bedroom a den to hold Jeff's large desk, our computer set-up, a small bookcase, and extra chairs. We measured our furniture, cut out paper furniture of the same dimensions, and placed them on the floor plans with the exact measurements of our rooms. The exercise was fun, like playing paper dolls. Not all the furniture would fit, of course, as the apartment was much smaller than the house. We would have to sell or give away our guest bedroom suit and patio furniture and remove the leaves from the dining room table. We complimented ourselves on doing a fine job, even though the furniture would fit with absolutely no room to spare.

That done, we were faced with the job of packing dishes, glassware, pots and pans, linens, and all the artifacts displayed, especially the china on the hutch and the many objects in the étagère. I dreaded this move. But bless Jeff, the move turned out to be a relatively smooth endeavor. He called his son and then one of his daughters and simply said to both, "We need help moving."

I knew they must be busy with their own lives but, lo and behold, the day before the moving van was scheduled to arrive, son Fred flew into West Palm airport from Norfolk, and daughter Susan flew there from Louisville. They met, rented a car, and arrived at our house late afternoon. Both Susan and Fred gave me a hug. I felt like a child enveloped in Fred's big frame, his head towering over mine.

"You look great, Mom," Susan gushed, appraising me with smiling eyes.

I was finally getting accustomed to having three of Jeff's children call me *Mom*, and I accepted the new title with a fond feeling. They'd dubbed me with this title from the very beginning of our marriage. Their children called me *Grandma*, and the endearment seemed to come naturally.

Not so for Jeff's youngest daughter nor for my three children. I don't believe my son and two daughters ever expected me to remarry, at least not at age seventy-eight! My son had said, "I thought you were getting along just fine on your own, Jean." He'd called me by my first name ever since he'd married Sally. Perhaps because *she* called me Jean. At any rate, I'd gotten accustomed to *Jean* and would have been surprised to hear Kirk call me *Mother*.

Jeff told me his son had suggested to him that we wait a few years to get married and just live together for awhile. I realized many of the younger generation cohabitated some years before getting married. But Fred and his wife had been high school sweethearts and had done no such thing. Why suggest that for us? Didn't he understand that, common and acceptable as that present practice was, our generation, for the most part, frowned upon it? Besides, Jeff and I didn't have that many years left to enjoy a married life together.

My children called Jeff *Jeff*. Jeff's youngest daughter called me *Jeanie*. I understood. I wasn't her mother, and Jeff wasn't my children's father, and that was that. Whatever they all chose to call me and Jeff was fine with us.

After hugs and kisses, conversation with Fred and Susan was non-stop. Dinner was late, and *the kids*, tired from an early rise and the trip, needed sleep. We put Susan in the guest bedroom and relegated Fred to the extra-large living room couch that had belonged to Jeff. (I'd sadly sold my couch to the woman who bought my condominium apartment.)

Large boxes took up floor space literally everywhere on the living room floor. Fred looked at his designated bed, yawned, and, giving Jeff a mischievous side-glance, said, "Say, Dad, did you purposely make it difficult for me to get into bed? What's in all these boxes, anyway?" he wanted to know.

"Do you think we just loafed before you two came? Holy smokes! For days Jeanie and I have been wrapping dishes and glassware in newspaper and packing them very carefully in these boxes I confiscated from Walgreens. We've labeled all the boxes. See that box?" Jeff pointed to one

23

by the television. "It's full of Japanese teapots, trays, saki bottles, and punch bowls. We wrapped them in newspaper and packed them like we did the china dishes. Jeanie's father gave her the bone china. Brought it from Canada. I bought the Japanese items in Japan during the big war." Jeff continued, pointing to another box at the foot of the couch. "In that box are silverware and books. In the box in front of that chair are the contents of the bathroom cabinets and drawers and clothes closet shelves. All but our hanging garments. Do you want to know what's in that box at the end of the coffee table?"

"No, no. I've heard enough. Let me get to sleep," Fred begged and laughed.

"I'm gonna tell you anyway," Jeff said, a twinkle in his eyes. "In that box is stuff we stored in the overhead storage area in the garage. I climbed up those steps for the last time! The very last time!" he emphasized.

What he didn't tell Fred was that we'd given duplicate excess bedding and towels to grandson Kasey who was visiting one weekend. Or that we'd sold furniture and given pots, pans, dishes, and canned goods to our church to bolster their upcoming rummage sale. We'd done the best we could to decrease the moving load.

The *kids* were up early the next morning eager to get started with their assignment. After breakfast while Jeff and I gathered items from the tops of dressers, chests, desks, and small tables in our two bedrooms and the den and packed them in yet another large cardboard box, Fred and Susan concentrated on the kitchen cabinets and refrigerator yet to be tackled. They chatted away, emptying drawers and shelves. "Hey Dad," Susan called out. "Why do you have four tins of cinnamon, three cans of dry mustard, two big boxes of salt and three little ones? You planning on opening a store?" She laughed through her chewing gum.

"Get lost," Jeff joshed. "When I can't find what I want I buy another. Stuff gets pushed to the back out of sight. Sometimes I buy two if they're on sale."

"O. K. Have it your way. But what happened to frugal Frank? Don't mind if I make a pun out of your middle name, do you, Dad?" She laughed again and said. "You certainly don't need all of them. You'll never use all these if you live to be a thousand. I'll throw out the half empty ones." She continued to crack her gum and help her brother stack dishes and glasses and pots and pans on counter tops. Tall as he was, Fred easily reached items on the top shelves, and as they worked together, they laughed and joked, probably about more of our odd assortment of *keepers*. I was amazed how quickly counter tops were cleared and contents methodically packed into more liquor-store boxes.

That completed, Fred asked, "What's next? What do you want us to do now?"

"The garage," Jeff responded and led the way into the garage where Jeff pointed to the many items stacked on ceiling-to-floor shelves.

"Better move out the Caddy and Volvo first," Fred said, holding out his hand for the keys. To leave room for the moving van, he parked the Volvo behind the Caddy in the driveway. With our blanket permission Fred and Susan started pitching items from the shelves onto the concrete floor in a corner of the garage. Through the air flew articles we never really needed but had kept, *just in case*. "What are you doing with this old rusty metal sprinkling can?" Fred asked. Then he laughed and said, "How about this length of flattened garden hose? You saving it to jump rope, Dad? And this bent fruit retriever is worthless. Out she goes!"

"You don't want this, Mom, do you?" Susan asked, heaving old wrinkled Christmas wrapping paper and used ribbons and bows into the trash container. "You gonna use two vacuum sweepers in your new place? How about leaving one here to sweep up after the movers leave? And just take one with you?"

Jeff heard that suggestion and interjected, "We don't even need *one* where we're going. A maid comes in every week. She'll sweep with her own machine."

"We'd better take one, just in case," I said. "And the tank type one. I must have the tank sweeper."

"O. K., Mom. You got it!" Susan promised me, while Jeff shook his head and rolled his blue eyes.

In short order, the kids decreased the contents of the many garage shelves to a mere arm-load. By then it was early afternoon, and we thought we might get a bite of lunch. Just then Susan spied the moving van pulling into the driveway and called out, "Here come the movers!"

Two muscular men came walking through the garage and through the open door into the living room lugging huge boxes. "Where are your clothes closets? We'll take care of your hanging clothes first," they informed us. While they tackled that job, we family members loaded linens from the linen closet into one of their large boxes. Then we packed dry and canned goods from the pantry.

When the movers started to load furniture onto the van, Susan said, "Mom, you and Dad go on to Sandycreek Terrace to be there when the movers arrive. Tell them where to put everything. Fred and I'll stay here and sweep up after they leave. We'll be along shortly."

So instructed by the younger generation, Jeff and I were in the apartment when the movers arrived, and we directed them to place each piece in the exact space we intended in all the rooms. After the movers left, Jeff stood back, looked around, and exclaimed, "Holy smokes! Look at this place! The furniture fits in just as we'd planned, Jeanie!"

"I know," I said, pleased with the result and also a little surprised.

"It's been quite a day, hasn't it? Are you tired, Honey?" Jeff asked, sounding concerned.

"Not too tired. I guess the adrenalin's still flowing. I'm so thankful for Fred and Susan. They've been great! Worked really hard! They're probably exhausted."

"They're good kids," he agreed. "And they're young."

About then, Fred and Susan waltzed in our open door. "Here we are! We're gonna go to work putting away the stuff in the boxes marked *kitchen*. Put it into your new kitchen cabinets," Susan said, walking into the kitchen and looking around. "I like this kitchen better than the one at your house. Everything's white. And it's bright! I didn't like those dark wooden cabinets in your old kitchen."

She was screwing up her face, and, surprised at her reaction, my eyebrows shot up and I said, "Oh really?" I had long bushy eyebrows that I'd inherited from both parents. My father's had been long and curling, and my mother's bushy like John L Lewis's.

I told Susan, "I thought those darker cabinets were neat." Then I looked at my watch. "Golly, we need to go to dinner! They stop serving dinner in the dining room in a half hour!"

"You, two, get changed and go," Fred urged. "Susan and I aren't wearing the proper clothes for eating in *that* dining room. Besides, we want to finish this job."

Susan waved her arm saying, "I second the motion. Go!"

"What about you two kids?" I asked, worried about their dinners.

They laughed, and Fred said, "With all this food that came over from the house, we'll make something. Don't you worry."

"Be sure you do that," Jeff said as we stepped over boxes, went back to our new bedroom, pulled out something appropriate from the two boxes of hanging clothes, changed, and hurried over to the Club House.

"Shall we have a drink first?" Jeff asked me as we approached the lounge and bar.

"I think we deserve one, don't you? Certainly! We deserve one!" I smiled in anticipation of sitting and sipping a cocktail.

Jeff ordered our drinks and, carrying them, we followed a hostess to a table, passing a group of staring strangers already seated in the dining room. We ordered, ate, and then filled with tossed garden salad, crusted wahoo, potatoes au gratin, creamed broccoli, and German chocolate cake, we returned to the apartment. Fred and Susan were lounging at the dining room table, talking and laughing, faces flushed, each holding an empty glass. Susan looked up and said, "We're about ready to go to our motel rooms in town. Do you want us to do anything else before we leave tonight? We'll be back tomorrow for a few hours before our planes take off."

"You've done plenty! More than enough!" I said, and then I remembered. "Oh wait. There is one little thing I'd like you to help me with. I bought two panels of lace curtains to hang at the kitchenette window. Rather than vertical blinds. I thought lace curtains would look pretty, let in plenty of light, and provide privacy as well. I know they're too long."

Susan seemed to understand and said, "Sure, Mom. Fred's tall. He can hold them up, and we'll measure them."

I went to the Caddy where I'd left them since the day I'd purchased them. Susan unwrapped a panel and handed it to Fred. "Here, Fred, hold this up to the ceiling so I can see how much they need to be shortened to just reach the sill."

He dutifully took the lace panel and followed instructions. Susan eyed the curtain where it reached considerably below the sill. "You're right, Mom. They're too long. Need to be hemmed up about four inches. Give me some pins, a needle, and thread, Mom. I'll hem them in the motel room tonight. Won't take but twenty minutes."

"Oh, Susan! Are you sure?" I said, amazed at her willingness to undertake such a task after all she'd done today. All I needed to know was the amount I'd have to shorten them. But she stood waiting, so I went to my sewing box, gave her the materials she requested, and off she and Fred went to the motel.

After they left, I snickered and motioned to an empty wine bottle on the counter top next to the sink. "Did you see this, Jeff?"

Jeff chuckled. "Yep, I noticed. They deserved it. I'm glad they helped themselves. They needed some R and R."

Four

Unpacking

The next few days Jeff and I unpacked boxes. But before we removed our hanging clothes from the large vertical ones furnished by the movers, or before we put *anything* in our bedroom closet, Jeff went to Home Depot and bought racks and brackets and installed them. Then we filled Mother Hubbard's cupboard with our clothes, suitcases of various sizes, and boxes containing numerous items until there was no room to spare.

Again I realized how fortunate Jeff owned many tools and knew how to use them. Through our few years together I'd been amazed at his expertise, his talent to construct and repair almost anything we needed. He'd learned much building a sail boat in his father's garage, beginning its construction when he was only thirteen.

Come to think of it, when I was half that age I was sewing at my maternal grandmother's knee, so to speak. I had no siblings to vie for her attention. That dear old German lady started me with quilt patches and then taught me how to make clothes using a Butterick pattern. I made a cape for my oldest cousin who was in college and then made clothes for myself when *I* went to college.

I was lucky to have daughters for I had fun making sister dresses for them when they were little. And I made a sport jacket for my hubby, one so finely finished and tailored it was admired by all his male friends. I'd graduated to making slipcovers for our couch and two chairs, ones that made the furniture look like they'd been newly upholstered. I'd also made draperies for the living and dining room windows, all in our first little house. Sewing was enjoyable for me, and I was pleased that every item looked professionally made. My cousins? None of them, or my mother, could sew a stitch, it seemed. I had a given talent for sewing and was blessed in the same way Jeff was blessed with his carpentry skills.

The next two evenings, we still continued to step around a few boxes to get dressed in required attire for dinner—a sport coat and dress slacks for Jeff and a country-club-style outfit for me. "Not going to get me to wear a tie. I quit wearing ties when I retired," Jeff said, getting ready for dinner the fourth night and lifting a brown tweed sport coat from the back of a dining room chair. It had *hung* there since the first night we'd gone for dinner in the Sandycreek Terrace dining room.

"Yes you've told me about your love affair with ties," I said while I helped him into his coat since his left arm refused to locate the sleeve opening. Even though I was resigned to never seeing him wearing a tie to dinner, I said, "Some male residents wear ties. I think they look very nice. I like getting dressed for dinner. What we're required to wear is appropriate for the lovely dining room and for the lounge. All the residents look very nice, dressed as they do. I'll have a difficult time keeping up with some of the women."

"Not you, Sweetie. Not with your wardrobe. Have you noticed how your clothes take up three-fourths of the room in our bedroom closet?" Jeff looked at me with his eyes purposely forced wide open, causing two horizontal lines to crease his forehead as he waited for me to respond.

I knew he intended to be humorous so I frowned and cocked my head, posturing to rebut his accusation. I taunted, "I appreciate your giving me the racks on two sides of our closet, Jeff dear. But do you realize all *your* sport coats and jackets are hanging in the den closet?"

"Hmmm," he said, and we walked out of the apartment to go to dinner.

By week's end we were mostly unpacked, the contents where we wanted them and in some acceptable order. I said to Jeff, "Do you realize management offers all new residents the help of two employees four hours a day for two days to help with placement of belongings. We could have requested that service, but we opted not to have it. Didn't seem necessary, did you think? Why direct someone and then stand there and watch them do what we could do ourselves?"

"I agree. We done good all by ourselves." He chuckled as he has a nice habit of doing.

It was an early morning of the third week we were residents of Sandycreek Terrace that the shrieking alarm, blinking blinding lights, and continuing loud blasts frightened us and sent Jeff out of our apartment to investigate. Now that he was back with little to tell me, I kept my ears plugged with my index fingers and shouted to him, "Did you see any smoke? Smell any smoke? What should we do, Jeff?"

"No smoke. I'm dialing the front desk again. Didn't get an answer when I phoned them before I went out," he called back to me, lunging for the phone. He grabbed the receiver from its base and said in a loud voice, "What's going on? What's all this about? The blasts and the flashing lights. We can't stand it!"

He listened then dropped the receiver onto its cradle. "All the night receptionist said was everything will be turned off shortly. We're not to leave the apartment. I want to know what's going on!"

Of course he wanted to know. A retired Navy Captain, a Pearl Harbor survivor, chief engineer of a destroyer, and veteran of many crises at sea. He was accustomed to being in charge in tense situations. In his second career, he was a high school principal. Always in charge.

After what seemed like an hour, the noise ceased and the lights stopped flashing. The phone rang. Jeff picked up the receiver, listened, and turned to me. "It was the night receptionist telling us the fire was a false alarm. We're to relax. And we may leave our apartment whenever we like. Guess I'll do that after we have breakfast." Jeff looked at his watch. "The supermarket should be open by then. We're about out of food. What would you like for breakfast, Jeanie?"

"Do we still have raisin bagels? And cream cheese? If we do, that's what I'd like. And orange juice and a cup of herbal tea, please."

"Believe we do. And the queen shall be served what the queen requests." He bowed low, casting his eyes at me still sitting at the dining room table.

I giggled. "You're silly, Jeff."

I enjoyed having a chef. After cooking for a family of five for many years, I was happy to be relieved of this wifely and motherly duty. At the start of our marriage when Jeff offered to cook every meal if I would do the clean-up, I jumped at the opportunity. Who wouldn't? Not that I

31

particularly enjoyed cleaning-up, but I'd seen how Jeff cleaned. Because of my nursing background, especially my six years of sterile technique in the operating room, I realized I was a harsh and certainly not impartial judge. Now that we were at Sandycreek Terrace, Jeff only had to prepare breakfast and lunch while I put dishes into and took them out of the dishwasher and cleared counter tops. Once a week, maid Marigold arrived and gave the kitchen a thorough going over.

Ready to go to the store, Jeff asked me, "You want to go along?"

I declined even though I usually went with him. He could choose the food he was going to prepare.

While Jeff was gone, I could putter around the apartment. I was eager to unwrap the many saki bottles and arrange them on the four glass shelves separating the living room from the Florida room. And I wanted to align books in the bookcase below the glass shelves. In fact, I had a desire to evaluate the entire apartment. Although some apartments were larger than ours and some smaller, we'd chosen this two bedroom two bath arrangement on a first floor which provided us with a much-desired fair-sized patio. Of course our choice had also and largely depended on affordability.

With Jeff at the supermarket, I was alone for the first time since we moved in. I sat down, looked around the apartment, and started unwrapping saki bottles. Here I was in this place, a place I vowed never to be. Oh, it wasn't a nursing home or an assisted living facility of course. It was independent living, as Jeff had said. That's what it was called. Independent living. The skilled nursing unit was in a connecting building, and assisted living was provided in independent living quarters, residents' needs evaluated and arranged for by Amanda Murray. Even though these independent living units were lovely places, this wasn't life in a house with a yard on a street with other houses and neighbors of all ages who pretty much kept to themselves.

We had many neighbors here, but we saw them more often. Much more often. When I looked out our kitchenette window through the lace curtains or when I walked out our apartment door I often saw them walking along the corridor. They came out of their apartments that were lined up along the corridors like motel rooms at the Best Western. I saw these neighbors at the mailboxes, at the front desk, in the lounge and library. In the dining room we sat like we would sit in a public restaurant except every evening the other people there were always the same people. All the residents looked old, most with wrinkled faces. Any women whose hair wasn't white or gray had their beauticians giving them a dye job every month.

Jeff always complimented me. "You don't have any wrinkles, Jeanie. And your hair always looks great. Always stays in place."

It was true. When I looked in the mirror I couldn't see any wrinkles on my face, a feature I inherited from my mother. But I saw aging lines, of course. Not the least becoming. If I smiled, this feature faded somewhat. I minimized the lines under my eyes by wearing rimmed prescription glasses so the lower rims would practically obscure them. The lines on my forehead I covered with bangs brushed sideways.

The bathroom mirror was fairly friendly. It didn't show these undesirables that much. But the full-length mirror on the linen closet door was unforgiving. I avoided looking into it or stuck out my tongue at it when I passed it. Away from mirrors, I never thought about my facial flaws. In some photographs, snapshots, mostly, I didn't look my age. My younger daughter said I never aged. Bless her! Jeff thought I was beautiful, and that was all that mattered to me.

What Jeff said about my hair was true. I was very fortunate. I had a head of healthy hair. Many female residents complained that their hair was thinning. They asked me who my hair dresser was, where I went to have my hair styled. The truth was I only went to a beautician to have my hair trimmed, a dry cut every six weeks to keep it fairly short. Fine in texture but thick, my hair had a slight wave and tended to curl on the ends. Although it was gray, it had high lights, almost blond in the sunlight and in bright over-head lights. Never did I use hair spray. I hated that sticky stuff that felt like a board when it dried.

Many residents depended on canes, walkers, and motorized scooters. At mail boxes they leaned on them as they inserted keys and retrieved their mail. Those with walkers placed their mail on the seats; scooter drivers dropped their mail into attached baskets. Into the dining room they surged like a sea of seniors with ambulatory aids. When these residents sat down to eat their wheeled devices were either walked or driven by hostesses to a designated place away from the dining room out of sight. They were brought back to the tables when their owners finished eating.

Would the sight of these devices and their frail owners grasping their handle bars always bother me? Would living in close proximity to the same people day in and day out always make me uncomfortable? Would I always feel like I was living in a commune? Was this the price one paid for the benefits of twenty-four-hour security, planned activities, services, scheduled transportation, fine dining, a fitness center, an outdoor heated swimming pool, and health care when needed? Was it?

Then I had to smile, remembering my surveying days. We surveyors, eight of us, would sit at our desks in the state office completing licensing and certification reports of the nursing homes we'd inspected the week before. We'd check deficiencies, write explanations to substantiate our determinations, include recommendations for improvement of resident care or physical plant or both. Occasionally we'd talk across our desks, usually to confirm a regulation, infrequently to make a personal comment. One day I called across the desk to one of my co-workers, "Do you know what I recommended in that last nursing home I surveyed last week? During the exit interview? I suggested they institute a policy requiring all residents be removed from their wheelchairs in the dining room and helped into chairs at the tables. I told them residents should eat normally in regular chairs at a table. I said this would give the residents some exercise getting in and out of their wheelchairs and changing positions."

"What did the administrator say to that recommendation?" my co-worker asked.

"She just looked at me with a blank face."

"Well I think that's a good idea. I'm going to make that recommendation during my next survey," she said and bobbed her head up and down.

So here in Sandycreek Terrace my recommendation was being followed. Imagine that! I continued to reminisce about my job as a state surveyor. All at once I smiled again remembering our lunch conversation one day. A co-worker had surveyed a nursing home the day before and had found twenty deficiencies. "Never, never do I want to end up in a nursing home!" she said.

A chorus of "Neither do I!" followed.

"I'd rather die first. I'll kill myself if any one of my kids decides that's where I belong. Committed!" a newly-hired surveyor said.

"I know a sure way we can all prevent that from happening," someone said.

The rest of us looked at her.

"When we're old and retired we should buy a boat. All of us get in it and shove off. Out onto the high seas. No government regulations. No inspections. Away from snoopy surveyors."

"Not a bad idea!" I said. "Fill it with food and booze and have a good old time."

"Let's make it a yacht!"

"Yes, let's make it a yacht!" (To buy it or steal it wasn't decided.)

"What happens when the food and booze runs out?"

We'd jump overboard, we decided. Oh where were all my co-workers today?

I got up and started to place fourteen sake bottles, evenly separated, on each of the four glass shelves. Then I stepped back and surveyed my effort. The bottles stood in measured rows like decorated toy soldiers at attention.

After arranging books on the shelf below, I heaved a deep sigh. Yes, I'd given in to Jeff's desire for us to move and become residents of a continuing care retirement community. I knew once he made up his mind there was no changing it. The matter was settled, a done deal the day we had that not-to-compatible talk on the lanai in our house.

We *did* visit three other facilities. One was The Devonshire, a large, many storied, elaborately decorated facility housing many residents. We felt it too cold, as in unfriendly, and with a prevailing, overwhelming, upscale atmosphere. Another was simply an assisted living facility where residents had individual apartments. A third was also assisted living with only one large room and bathroom per resident or couple with a common dining room serving three meals a day.

Once decided, Jeff had moved quickly to finalize the contract, calling the Marketing Director, telling her of our decision, and arranging for an appointment to see her. He never wasted time in matters of this kind. It had been the same six months after we'd met. Three times before that he'd said, "If I asked you very nicely, would you marry me?" Each time I'd laughed, not taking him seriously, thinking he night ask me *nicely* the next time. And I'd answered, "Yes." One day we'd gone to the jewelry store *just* to size my finger, and he immediately asked to see diamond rings. When we left the store, a glowing, sparkling, sizable diamond on my finger, I was walking on air, feeling just like Cinderella at the ball.

He'd made a quick decision when he bought our house. We'd determined he'd move from his apartment into my apartment after we were married. But, when we visited friends who lived in a free-standing house, he'd called a realtor the very next day and asked to see single-family houses. We'd looked at two, and he'd bought the first one that day.

FIVE

FRIENDS

Jeff had just gotten home from the supermarket, groceries plunked soundly on a kitchen counter, when Fanny Porter was at our door with a bottle of wine in fancy foil wrapping. "You're going to love it here," she assured me smiling, her short, tinted-blond hair stirring in the balmy breeze.

We knew Fanny from Rotary Club meetings. Her first husband and Jeff were former District Governors of Rotary—Jeff in Michigan and Fanny's husband in Wisconsin. Since moving to Florida, both men had been members of the Jupiter Rotary Club and attended their weekly meetings regularly. Jeff always took me to the meetings with him, and I'd become acquainted with Fanny when she, herself, had joined Rotary. After her husband's demise, she continued to attend and enjoy the meetings. Before long, however, she announced she was moving into a retirement village, and she no longer attended the meetings. The *village* turned out to be Sandycreek Terrace where Fanny, we learned, had become friendly with a male resident. Most friendly, I'd say, considering they were now married. I can't say I was surprised because Fanny was a vivacious, attractive blond with a nice figure.

Fanny refused to sit down but stood just inside the open door and cautioned, "When you meet Clyde, don't talk about Rotary. He hates to hear me talk about Rotary. I can't even mention it! So remember, when you meet him, say nothing about Rotary."

"Is he jealous of your first husband?" I asked, incredulous.

Her mouth tightened. "I don't know. I don't know what it is. When I told him we should have dinner with you he said he wouldn't want to because you knew me from Rotary."

I thanked her for the wine and promised we'd say nothing about Rotary when we met Clyde. After she left, I said to Jeff, "Isn't it strange how Fanny cautioned us about her husband and Rotary? Is it possible for people in their eighties...or maybe she's only in her seventies. No matter. Is it possible to be jealous of a deceased spouse at our age? It sounds childish to me."

"Maybe jealousy has no age limit. I guess people's nature doesn't change that much through the years," Jeff speculated and shrugged.

I looked at him a moment. Would I want him to talk much about his deceased wife? No, I wouldn't.

I opened the dry sink in the kitchenette and placed the bottle of wine on the bottom shelf along with the other liquor bottles. Then I turned to look at the groceries Jeff had bought. "I smell cantaloupe. You bought a cantaloupe, didn't you, Jeff?" I closed my eyes and took a deep breath.

"Two. I bought two. They were nice and ripe and on sale. Got salad makings, too. Gonna make a tuna fish salad for lunch. If that's all right with you." His eyes opened wide questioning me.

"Sounds wonderful. And you don't have to ask me. Anything you prepare is fine with me," I replied, grinning at him. I just wasn't that fussy an eater as long as the food had little or no spices added. And no fat, wasn't greasy. Food, like cooking, wasn't one of my big interests. Sewing, as I've said, was my forte.

Because of diminished vision, I hadn't sewn for years except to mend and alter. At the house, we'd handled the window dressings professionally. Here in the apartment, the need for window treatment was minimal. The living room and dining room had no windows. We'd hung the lace curtains at the kitchenette window. At the Florida room's two window panels and door, a pale pink vertical blind had been in place when we moved in. In order to provide plenty of daylight for writing, we'd decided not to cover the den window. That had left the bedroom window to dress. We'd ordered a vertical blind installed there. Since the bedroom drapes and cornice we'd had in our house at our bedroom window matched our pink-and-aqua printed bedspread, I'd wondered, could we possibly move them to the apartment? I hated to give up the set. Would they fit? To find out, I'd done some measuring and decided maybe, just maybe they would fit in the space available. I called a decorator I'd used before and presented him with the problem. With some adjustment, expertise, and magic mastering, the decorator had performed the task.

After we'd completed the window treatments, all we needed was a comfortable place to eat breakfast and lunch. We didn't care for the bar arrangement between the kitchen and the dining room, nor did we like sitting on stools to eat. We'd gone to Home Depot and purchased a small maple table that we'd placed in front of the lace curtains at the kitchenette window.

Even though we didn't have nearly as much room as we enjoyed in our house and the apartment was crowded with furniture, we figured we were in pretty good shape. That's what we'd thought, but before long, I found a problem. I kept bumping into the glass top on the dining room table every time I walked through the dining room into the living room. After I appraised the situation with a critical eye, I said to Jeff, "All our furniture fits perfectly except for this glass top on the dining room table. Look! It extends out too far into the room. Too far! I keep bumping into it!"

"Why do we need the glass top? I don't think it's necessary since the tabletop's lacquered," Jeff said, eying the top.

"But I like it," I said, defensively. "I like the color. It's smoked. It came with *my* dining room table. The one we decided to put in the Florida room." I looked out to my round amber-stained wicker table. The top had been very pretty with the wicker design showing through the glass top.

"Then put it on that table." Jeff chuckled as if settling the matter.

I shrieked, "No! We can't do that! My table in the Florida room hardly fits as it is. And it already has a glass top. A smaller, clear glass top. Don't you remember? We took that glass top from the patio table because the smoked glass top made the table too large to fit in the Florida room. That's why the smoked one's on this dining room table."

"Oh for God's sake! Well, I guess you're right. Then we'll give it away," Jeff said, clapping his hands together with finality. "Baring this glass top though, we done good!"

"Yes, we done good," I agreed, grinning at our grammar.

Since we couldn't possibly continue to have that glass top on the dining room table sticking out like an open drawer and bumping into it all the time, I decided to call the Goodwill. The person who answered my call sounded pleased with my donation offer and said he'd send two men that very day since the top was very heavy. Jeff immediately called the guard at the gate. "We're expecting the Goodwill truck this afternoon. Please direct the driver to our apartment."

That afternoon, a man, only one, arrived at our door. He frowned at the glass top. "Can't take it without the table, too," he grumbled and abruptly left.

"I'll call the desk and see how we can get rid of it," Jeff offered. "Maybe somebody here could use it or take it off our hands."

I nodded. I still hated to part with that glass top, almost changing my mind. How lovely it had looked on my pedestal-based table in my condominium apartment, and it was mighty easy to glass wax and keep shiny.

I wasn't far from the phone when Jeff dialed the front desk, and I heard the receptionist say to Jeff. "You'll have to talk to maintenance. I'll connect you." After a pause a man's voice addressed Jeff's query with, "I'll send someone over."

Before long our bell chimed, and two men were at the door. Both were middle aged, of sturdy build, and dressed in the kaki uniforms worn by all maintenance and security personnel. One man had sparse, short, brown hair; the other was balding with a blond pony tail. "We're John and Matt," the brown-haired man introduced in a pleasant voice and twisted grin. "I'm John. This is Matt," he said, motioning to the man with the pony tail. "What can we do for you?" He looked at Jeff and then at me. Matt kept his eyes lowered.

"Hi fellas," Jeff greeted them and pointed to the dining room table. "We want to get rid of this glass top. Can anyone use it?"

John scratched his head. "I doubt it. We'll take it off your hands though. Employees here are given a chance to take second-hand items residents decide to dispose of. But, without a table, I doubt any one will want the glass top," he said.

"What will happen to it if no one wants it?"

"Trashed," John answered Jeff. "So you want us to take it?"

Jeff nodded emphatically. John looked at me for a joint approval. "Yes," I uttered with a sigh.

"O. K. Matt, you grab one side. I'll grab the other," John directed.

"Right on," Matt said, opening his mouth for the first time and walking to the far side of the table. As his large hands started to lift the glass, he groaned, "Heavy son of a gun. Maybe too heavy for you, John."

"Sure, sure. You think you're stronger than I am? Get off it."

The two men bantered back and forth as they lifted the glass top clear of the table. "Set it down! Set it down!" John instructed.

After an edge of the top was on the carpeted floor, Matt said, "Roll it! Roll it! Do I have to tell you how to do everything?"

With the glass top in tow, the two uniformed men went out the door, their jesting voices trailing off. "Very funny pair," Jeff commented, laughing as I was, and closing the door solidly behind them.

The next evening, there we were sitting eating with Fanny Russell, now Fanny Porter, her husband, Clyde, and a female resident we didn't know. I'd been surprised when Fanny phoned and asked us to join them for dinner. Had her husband changed his mind about eating with Rotarians? Then I wondered if the other resident, Bessie Richards, was there as a buffer, to divert any conversation away from Rotary. During the initial conversation, we learned Bessie was single, had moved in the same time as we, and lived in our building. From then on throughout the entire meal, Fanny and Clyde directed their conversation toward her, and I felt like an outcast. But Bessie seemed nice enough, and I was now convinced she was invited so Clyde wouldn't possibly be drawn into a Rotary discussion.

Actually Fanny wasn't the only person we knew here. Pam and Ben Butcher came to Sandycreek Terrace two months prior to our moving in. They'd lived at Pine Gardens, too, in one of the condo apartments on the other side of the tennis courts. Ben had been our condominium association's first president.

After seeing us at the cocktail party given by Sandycreek Terrace's Marketing Department, Pam had called us at our house in Pine Gardens. "We saw you at the cocktail party. Ben and I live at Sandycreek Terrace now. You should come here to live. You'll enjoy it," she'd said. Because of the large number of residents residing here, I doubted we'd run into them very soon.

As with Jeff and me, this was Ben and Pam's second marriage. When Pam was twenty-one and pregnant she'd contracted polio and had a decided limp when I first met her as a single person. Never would she marry again, she told me. Never would she wash a man's underwear again! Soon after that proclamation, she and another single female resident took an around-the-world trip. Not long after they returned, I saw Pam sitting in the club house lounge talking to Ben Butcher a number of times. Was it true she would never marry again?

Ben was also single by then, his wife deceased six months. As predicted, marriage was rumored about the complex. Before long, condo residents were invited to a wedding reception at the club house. All guests watched the newly-weds dance the first dance together, Ben assisting Pam in her efforts to follow, hindered by her noticeable limp. When the dance ended everyone cheered and clapped.

Ben had lived in Cleveland before retiring to Florida. It never ceased to amaze me how some men became millionaires because of the careers they chose. Not physicians and attorneys. That I understood. But men like Ben. He was an accountant employed by a large automobile dealership. One day in the dealer contract he discovered the company was entitled to large bonuses when a certain number of sales were reached. The company had been overlooking the claims to these bonuses. Realizing other dealers may be doing the same, overlooking their claims, Ben went into business for himself. He went around to individual automotive dealerships and offered to recover their losses for fifty percent of the profits.

Some weeks after we moved into Sandycreek Terrace, Pam invited us for cocktails at their apartment in a four-story structure called Inlet Building. We had never been in that building, and I was surprised to find it was much like a huge hotel. When we entered through double doors we were immediately in a large lobby furnished like a sitting room. Aside from lamps, couches, upholstered chairs, coffee table, and television set, it contained a computer. A coffee maker and paper cups sat on a small table in a corner. We walked through this room into a carpeted hallway that led to a number of apartments. Residents had decorated their apartment doors with wreaths, swatches of artificial flowers, and various trinkets. Many had placed jars and vases filled with greenery and various floral arrangements on the carpet to one side of their doors. Large framed pictures decorated the walls on either side of the hallway. We walked along until we found an elevator and rode it to the third floor. The Butcher apartment was much larger than our apartment in the two-story Sentinel Building, and it had a view of the inlet from a large picture window.

When we got home after dinner in the Club House I said to Jeff, "Pam and Ben's apartment makes ours look little, doesn't it? And theirs has a wonderful view of the inlet. It would be nice to have a lobby like that, too." I was impressed. Maybe I was a titch jealous.

Jeff said, "It is very nice. But I like our apartment better. I like having an entrance to the outside right from our door. Not having to walk inside and go up and down an elevator. I like being on the first floor and having a patio. None of those apartments in the Inlet Building have patios. Or any place to sit outside. I like our arrangement much better. And I wouldn't want to pay more for an apartment in the Inlet Building. I'm satisfied right here."

I mulled over this rationale but made no comment.

The following week, we invited Pam and Ben for cocktails at our apartment before dinner. Several nights a week we continued to eat dinner together in the dining room. Ben, a large rotund man with reddish balding hair, was usually very quiet, smiling but not talking much during our conversations, adding a one-syllable comment now and then. When we all lived in Pine Gardens he was quite talkative, as I remembered. Pam was still chatty, but she was suffering increasing latent symptoms of polio and appeared smaller than ever, using a cane indoors and a wheeled walker outside their apartment.

"Say," Jeff remarked, flipping on the light as we stepped into our apartment after eating dinner with the Butchers one evening. "Do you realize we haven't played cribbage in a coon's age?"

"I was just thinking the same thing. I don't believe we've played since we moved in here. Why don't we start tonight? I remember where we put the cribbage board. In that space below the desk." I hurried over, bent down, and pulled out the pegged board and a deck of cards. Jeff was walking toward the kitchen, so I carried the board and cards to the kitchenette table, turned the board over and proceeded to remove the four pegs secured in a tiny tunnel on the back. I read the inscription in the center of the board and smiled. There, neatly indented, were the initials of a high school and the date the shop students had presented their work of art to Jeff when he was their high school principal.

"Wasn't it great of your students to make you this cribbage board, Jeff?"

"Yes. They were good kids," Jeff said, chuckling. Then he removed his coat, hung it on the back of a dining room chair, took off his shoes and socks, and pushed them under another dining room chair with his bare feet.

I watched this disposition of his clothes. I was becoming accustomed to the dining room being a partial clothes closet and was determined not to be a nagging wife. Peace and harmony, I thought. That was important and what we both strived for. I would tidy the apartment when we expected visitors or when maid Marigold was due.

"I'll get a tablet," Jeff said. "Have to keep score so I can mark down my winnings tonight."

"I believe you're talking entirely too prematurely. It's *my* winning score you'll have to mark down." I laughed and drew out a chair, scraping it along the tiled floor.

Jeff laid the tablet on the table and pulled a pen out of the pocket of his short-sleeved shirt. No matter what kind of shirt he wore, it was short-sleeved and required a pocket to hold a pen and his glasses case in a position for instant removal of his glasses.

The cribbage game had become a habit of sorts. For about six years, after dinner or during cocktails before dinner, we'd played one game of cribbage almost every evening. Jeff introduced me to this game. I'd been a rummy player, taught well by my father, and rarely lost. I found cribbage to be fun even though it was, for the most part, a game of chance, the luck of the draw. Apparently I had beginner's luck because, after several months of playing, I was ahead twenty-six points. As we continued to play, by the end of a year Jeff was ahead *thirty-six* points. Much cribbage-talk went along with the game, making it even more fun.

Tonight, over a third of the way through the game with Jeff's foremost peg ahead on third street, I said, "You're gonna skunk me! How dare you skunk me!"

I noisily shuffled the deck and dealt the next hand, after the cut. We played it, and the cards were face-up to be counted. In an accusatory tone, Jeff said, "You forgot to deal me a decent hand!" He counted, "Fifteen two, fifteen four, there are no more."

My turn to count. "Fifteen two, fifteen four, fifteen six, the rest don't mix." I picked up the crib. "Nothing much here. Just a pair for two."

At the end of two more deals Jeff had counted his hand and was looking across the table at me and saying, "You're in position."

I dug my fists into the sides of my waist, pursed my lips, and replied, "How can you say I'm in position? Your peg's still way ahead of mine."

"Not enough ahead. Wait 'til you count your hand *and* your crib. You'll be in position."

"No, no! You're in position, I tell you." I counted the cards lying face-up, picked up the crib, counted a total of twenty-one and moved ahead.

"Holy smokes! See there! You *are* in position now," Jeff said, rubbing his forehead.

And so the bantering went throughout the game.

Six
Befriending

A few days later we had a phone call from Judith Schreiber inviting us to their cottage for cocktails before dinner that very evening. I remembered when this friendly petite woman with a short gray bob had introduced herself to us in the lounge. The few times I'd seen her she was wearing a short-sleeved calf-length dress, noteworthy because few women wore dresses, short or long, preferring, it seemed, to wear pants suits or slacks with long-sleeved dressy tops. That was my choice as well. Judith apologized for the short notice, but, having no plans to eat with the Porters or Butchers (the only residents we knew) and after checking with Jeff, I accepted.

We followed Judith's directions, driving from the parking circle in front of our building, down a mile stretch of paved road past car ports and then past the guardhouse to a row of white stucco cottages. The cottages were identical, enhanced by grassy-green lawns and flowering shrubbery.

After we located Schreiber's cottage, we pulled into the driveway and parked. Then we walked down a recessed entrance and were met at the door by Peter, Judith's husband. I was instantly entranced with his western European accent and impressed by the way he graciously ushered us into their spacious living room.

Judith, demure as I remembered her and again wearing a calf-length short-sleeved dress, appeared immediately behind Peter. "I'm so happy you could make it on such short notice," she said in her friendly alto voice. "We've been wanting to have you visit. We like to make the acquaintance of all new residents."

"We're certainly pleased to be invited," Jeff said, smiling broadly, and I uttered my pleasure as well.

Peter approached me and asked, "Where would you like to sit, Jean?"

I glanced around and suddenly realized another couple was sitting on a couch on the far side of a cocktail table. Several upholstered chairs were available but Peter was at my elbow saying, "Come over here. We've saved this chair for you."

He was propelling me to a chair resembling one made for an African queen—wicker, with cushioned seat, extremely high back partially padded, and bedecked with an overhead canopy. "Oh my," I exclaimed, "You want me to sit in this fancy chair? It's made for a queen, I believe."

"And you will be queen tonight," Peter said in his profoundly European accent, his slight figure bowing and gray eyes smiling at me.

I attempted to seat myself in this large lavish low-seated chair in a lady-like fashion. Then as I looked straight ahead across the room I found I was facing a large picture window. Through it I could see a large pond and water shimmering in the setting sunlight. Judith disappeared, and Peter introduced us to the couple seated on the couch. "This is Betty Howe and Ralph Wilson," he said.

Jeff addressed the male guest. "Will you please repeat your name?"

"What was that you said?" The brown jacketed slight figure on the couch leaned forward.

Jeff spoke in a loud voice, "I didn't catch your name. Will you please repeat your name?"

"2241," the man said, whereby both Jeff and I stifled a laugh.

Betty Howe turned toward him and said, "He's asking for your name, Ralph."

"Ralph. Ralph Wilson," he said and was immediately plagued with a prolonged coughing attack to which Betty apparently was accustomed as she made no move to be vaguely alarmed.

Peter mixed and served us drinks of our choice, but he served my vodka martini straight-up in a martini glass. Since I always drank my martini over oodles of ice in a cocktail glass, I found this particular drink filled to the top of a tall stemmed martini glass difficult to manage. With no table close by, I had to hold the glass continuously without being able to put it down between sips. I was concerned that I would spill the drink or, worse yet, drop the stemmed glass.

Judith reappeared carrying a large platter of hors d'oeuvres. Now I had double trouble trying to hold the martini glass steady in one hand and help myself to hors d'oeuvre with the other. The aromatic appetizers were warm and delicious. One was a melt-in-your-mouth crabmeat twist and the other a cheese twirl equally tasty.

"These are marvelous, Judith," I said. "Did you make them from scratch?"

"Yes, I did," she said, rather bashfully. "My own recipes."

"They are excellent! Very good! I'd like to have your recipes for these if you'd share them," I said, knowing some women guarded their recipes and didn't share them.

"I'd be happy to," she said.

As we munched, sipped, and talked, Jeff and I learned Judith had been on *News Week's* editorial staff in Washington, DC some years ago. Peter had been a United Nations staff person and was well-traveled, his accent from being born and educated in Austria. Marriage to Judith was his second. Peter was Judith's first. To a limited degree, Jeff and I talked about our careers. Neither Betty nor Ralph divulged their past history and, in fact, engaged in very little conversation. We were to become well acquainted with them in the future.

At home after having dinner in the dining room with the two couples, Jeff grabbed my arm. "What's your name?" he wanted to know, flashing me a grin.

"2241," I answered, laughing. "But we shouldn't make fun of people with hearing disabilities, Honey," I added.

"No, of course not. But I thought that was priceless! Hilarious! And if we don't laugh, we'll cry. Obviously the hearing aid he was wearing wasn't doing him much good."

"Yes, obviously," I said. "I thought Judith and Peter were a delightful host and hostess, and Judith served such delicious hors d'oeuvres. Made them from her very own recipes. She said I might have the recipes. But I forgot them."

"You'll see her again, and you can ask her for them," Jeff said, taking off his coat and draping it in a lop-sided fashion on the same dining room chair he chose every evening. Later, I'd change the way it hung and make sure the shoulders fit neatly over the back of the chair.

He was starting to take off his shoes when I said, "Their cottage was lovely. Has more room than our apartment and has a yard. I'd like that. Wouldn't you?" I didn't give him time to answer but continued voicing my thoughts. "Living in a cottage would be like living in a single-family house on a street in a neighborhood with other single-family houses except it's on the grounds of a CCRC, gated and bound by the policies of management. And of course residents in cottages see the same people in the dining room every night. They see the canes and walkers and scooters. Just as we do."

"So what's wrong with that?" Jeff wanted to know, arching his eyebrows and peering at me. "They're all nice people. We're free to come and go as we please without a care in the world. Our apartment gets cleaned every week. Burned-out light bulbs get replaced. Dinner's prepared for us. We eat in a lovely dining room. How could we have it any better? I'm very satisfied here. Wouldn't want to be anywhere else." He looked at me askance and blinked his blue eyes.

"I guess you're right," I had to say so I wouldn't sound negative. But how could I feel positive when the sight of ever-parading canes, walkers, and scooters still bothered me? Or how could I not be annoyed when it seemed we were living permanently in a motel, passing other people's apartments every time we walked to the Club House? How could I get accustomed to living in close quarters with the same people all the time, many crippled, hunched over, and shuffling instead of walking? And all old. It wasn't that I was unsympathetic. I'd spent most of my working life being responsible for the care of people in poorer health than these residents. Some day I'd be in the same predicament, probably. Maybe worse. But until then must I pretend I loved living here? What about other residents who seemed as physically able as we? The Schreibers, the Porters, the McKees across the corridor, and there were many others I'd seen, of course. Were they happy and contented living here? They appeared to be because everyone, male and female, even the most physically disabled, smiled and spoke when they passed in the corridors. Everyone was friendly and seemed to be in a good mood. I spoke and was friendly, too. Did anyone else feel like I did?

The next people to befriend us were the McKees, Stuart and Ruth, our neighbors. Several days after we had moved in, Ruth had seen us outside and had practically insisted we come into their apartment to see their layout. They'd chosen their apartment pre-construction and had been able to make several desired changes in the standard plan. Since they never used the tub in the master bathroom, Ruth showed us how they'd strung a rope lengthwise from one end of the tub to the other close to the ceiling to hang clothes to dry, ones that shouldn't be dried in an electric dryer.

A week later, the Mc Kees invited us to their apartment for cocktails and hors d'oeuvres before dinner. They asked Emmett and Ellen Gorman as well. "To give you an opportunity to get to meet some nice people," Ruth had said when she phoned to invite us.

I enjoyed Ellen as she'd been a seamstress as I had, and we conversed about fabrics and where to buy clothing in West Palm. Ruth interjected in her rather loud monotone voice, "Not on Worth Avenue in Palm Beach, God forbid! Palm Beach Gardens Mall is the place to shop. That's where I go. Or I go down to Fort Lauderdale where we used to live. Salesgirls there know me, and I get good service. That's where you should go." She spoke as though she had the ultimate knowledge about where to buy clothes on the Treasure Coast.

"How long have you lived in Sandycreek Terrace?" I asked Ruth, wondering if she and even Ellen really liked living here.

"Five years. The same as Ellen and Emmett. Here, have some more cheese spread and crackers and more nuts." She pushed the hors d'oeuvres platter my way.

The three men were huddled together talking. Men always seemed to choose seats together, and converse about subjects rarely of interest to most women. I suppose the same could be said of women. This evening, I heard the men talking about fishing and boating, where to do both, and the different boats they'd owned. I heard Jeff talking about the boat he'd started to build as a teenager in his parents' garage. The voice coming through the loudest belonged to Ellen's husband, Emmett. It had a distinct twang that carried. After hearing his voice this evening, no matter where we would be sitting in the dining room, if Emmett was present we would recognize his twang resonating over the prevailing din of dishes and conversations of other diners.

NOT READY

Ruth dominated the female conversation, her distinct monotone more or less commanding our attention. Her hair style also commanded my attention. Never had I seen a style quite like it except in grade school perhaps. Every single strand of hair was pure white and straight, like it was steam-ironed. From a center part, bangs lay across her forehead like Cleopatra's, and the rest was cut short and perfectly even starting in front of her ears and proceeding around her neck. When cocktail time ended and we all walked over to the dining room in the Club House, I was walking directly behind her and was mesmerized by her hair. It methodically rose and settled back down with every determined step she took.

Several days later, Stuart McKee, who was chairman of the Health Care Committee and now knew about my nursing background, phoned. In his slow soft voice he asked, "Would you serve as a member of the Health Care Committee? We need more members on the committee. It meets the third Wednesday of each month in the conference room behind the library."

Of course my response was affirmative. I rather anticipated this offer having learned about resident committees from Amanda Murray the day we signed our contract. I still remembered her pretty round face, broad smile, and rather matronly figure and how she engaged in a few informalities and then requested private sessions with Jeff and me. At the very beginning of my interview, I'd realized she wasn't only the Manager of Independent Living Assistance. She was also the staff person who determined if prospective residents qualified with required physical capability as well as mental alertness for entrance into Sandycreek Terrace. When she'd asked about my family and career I'd given a shortened version of my nursing background. She'd beamed and exclaimed, "Mrs. Metz, you would be an excellent addition to the Health Care Committee!" So I'd been looking forward to attending my first meeting of the committee.

A limited number of residents ate their main meals mid-day in the dining room, mostly single women and a few single men. The majority of residents chose to go for dinner between five and six-thirty. We

51

considered even that time too early. But the dining room closed at eight, the generally socially accepted starting time by our standards. When we addressed this subject to several residents they informed us the closing time was established for the benefit of dining room and kitchen staff, many of whom were high school and college students needing to get home to study. We certainly couldn't fault that. Forget any notion of eating later!

Each evening before dinner, our cocktails concocted to order by a female bartender, we sat in the lounge at one of the small round tables talking together when we weren't eating with the Butchers. Being invited for cocktails and dinner by seasoned residents seemed to be a thing of the past now that we weren't the new kids on the block. Every other Saturday night we listened to the grand piano centrally located in the lounge. Those nights were called *Happy Hour Nights* when drinks cost slightly less and a paid pianist played our-kind of music from five to seven. On rare occasions, a couple paused where we were sitting and asked if they could join us while waiting to be seated in the dining room. After introductions, the conversation usually consisted of an exchange of information about our former residences in Florida, where we originated in the United States (few if any were native Floridians), careers pre-retirement, and often numbers of children and grandchildren, plus where they lived.

"I'm a Dutchman, a dike-jumper," Jeff always said. Sometimes he added, "If you're not Dutch, you're not much." A number of residents were former Michiganders but usually from a town near Detroit, not from the western side of the state. Jeff would respond, "I'm from the civilized side of the state. Holland." Of course he said this in jest to preempt a laugh from Michiganders who were aware of the notorious reputation of Detroit.

When people said they were from Pennsylvania my ears perked up, and I exclaimed, "I'm a Pittsburgher!" Then sadly I found out they were from Philadelphia or Scranton, always from somewhere in the eastern part of the state. Never a Pittsburgher!

While conversing in the lounge, residents sometimes decided to join at a table for dinner. All in all, it was a very social time. While working in nursing homes, I'd learned meal-time was the high light of a resident's day. I must say it was true here, as well.

One evening while we were sitting in the lounge before dinner, Jeff and I became friendly with Donald and Doris Jordan. Doris, hair tinted blond and worn short, was about my five-feet-three height and maybe a little heavier than my hundred and twenty pounds. She was a retired RN, too, and we related well although her hearing deficit made communication difficult. One day a week, she volunteered blood-pressure-screening duty for the American Red Cross. Slightly built and somber faced with a somewhat gray complexion, I thought, Donald had been a manufacturer of a small auto part in great demand by auto makers and thus had traveled extensively on business. The few times we ate with them, we enjoyed their company.

During *Happy Hour* one evening, residents were gathered around the piano, singing. We were joining in from our seats in the lounge when we heard a beautiful tenor voice above all the others. The voice belonged to Donald Jordan. We listened intently admiring his amazing voice. When Donald and Doris's daughter, a Presbyterian minister, visited she played the piano in the lounge, and we'd have the pleasure of hearing Donald sing. From time to time as the spirit moved her, a resident by the name of Sarah Grant sat herself down and played our-era songs by ear amazingly well. At these times, many of us residents with the inclination to blend our voices, on key or off, joined in singing. But Donald's voice was the one that stood out loud and clear and beautifully.

We soon learned Donald had colon cancer. The news saddened Jeff and me, and then I remembered the facial grayness I'd noticed when I first met him. His enthusiasm for singing continued regardless of his diagnosis.

SEVEN

VOLUNTEERING

Some mornings Jeff made homemade waffles for breakfast. This was waffle morning, and I sat at the small maple table in the tiny kitchenette waiting for him to free the waffles from the iron. The table was the only piece of furniture we'd bought after we moved in. All the other furniture had belonged to either Jeff or me and was now considered ours. I glanced up and smiled at the colorful rooster in the tapestry hanging on the opposite wall, glad I'd purchased it in Portugal years ago. Behind me above the dry sink, we'd hung a painting of the Jupiter Lighthouse we'd brought from the house. I smiled again at bare-footed Jeff, his ubiquitous red bandana half hanging out of his rear pants pocket as he served me a plate of golden Belgians.

"Thank you, Honey," I said, still smiling at his trade marks. "Aren't your feet cold?"

"Never cold," he answered, glancing down.

And I guess they never were. In the house, he walked around barefooted all the time. Only immediately before he went outside did he don socks and shoes. Some day I felt positive he'd enter the Club House dining room in slacks, shirt, sport coat, and bare feet.

Waffles enjoyed, Jeff opened the morning Palm Beach Post and read me the headline about CEOs of large corporations and their billion dollar incomes. The article also compared salaries of renowned ball players to those of President George's salary. "That's one thing that can't be legislated. Salaries companies pay their employees," Jeff said. Then he turned to the funny page he also read religiously. He started to laugh. "Listen to this, Jeanie. Dennis's friend Maggie says, 'I'm mad at you, and

I'm never going to speak to you again.' Dennis looks sky-ward with folded hands and says, 'Thank you, God!'"

"Oh here's Family Circus. Two little kids are sitting in the theater watching a ballerina on a stage standing on her tiptoes, arms reaching upward. The little boy's mouth is open, and he says, 'What's she trying to reach?'"

Jeff read much. He read all the correspondence that came in the mail and every printed word in all his many weekly and monthly magazines. In addition, he was always in the process of reading a book or two. He piled much of his reading material on the counter top of the sink in the guest bathroom. Considering the jam-packed magazine rack and the numerous magazines and books on the counter top, the guest bathroom could qualify for a mini library. At the very least, it was his reading room that he some times used in the middle of the night. He laid claim to the guest bathroom so I could have privacy in the master bath, bless him. He was easily amused and frequently chuckled. When I heard him laughing out loud or chuckling at something that he was reading I couldn't help being amused myself.

At the second Health Care Committee meeting I attended, one of the members reported she was continuing to visit residents in Park Place, the nursing home unit. I offered to join in these visitations. Amanda Murray, the attractive matronly Manager of Independent Living Assistance, was one of three department heads attending the meeting. She leaned forward to look at me sitting at the other end of the conference table and spoke up, "Mrs. Metz, I suggest you talk to Mr. Valenzuela, the Administrator of Park Place. He may be able to use you in some other capacity besides visitations because of your experience."

I thanked the woman who remembered my nursing background and promised I'd contact him. Then she gave a report of her department's activities for the past month as did the other two department heads, the Director of Nursing and the Admissions Director.

When I got back to the apartment I told Jeff all about the meeting. "Gonna put you to work, aren't they?" he said, chuckling.

The next day when I approached Mr. Valenzuela on the phone with my offer to volunteer, he advised me to contact the Social Worker of Park Place. So I did that and received a most welcome response. "I'd be delighted to have your help! You have no idea how far behind I am with my work. Any help will be most appreciated! I can use you several days a week. What days are convenient for you?"

We arranged days and times for me to report. The first day I was scheduled to volunteer, my feet itched to be back in familiar territory, to play a role in a nursing home. I walked along the corridor, past apartments, mailboxes, Grecian fountain, the Palace, and through the Club House to the walk connecting to Park Place. The walk was flanked on one side with a white trellis and with white and dark pink impatiens blooming on either side the entire length of the walk to the door leading into the nursing center. I knew my way to Park Place since, at my request, I'd had a tour of that facility after the invitational brunch Jeff and I had attended. Ever the surveyor, I wanted to have a look at and smell of their nursing home unit.

Believe me I was duly perplexed when I cast my eyes on the flowing shoulder-length white hair of the Social Worker clad in an equally-flowing red-printed shift. Where was the professional Social Worker? I'd never seen one like this in my many years of contacts with Social Workers.

After thanking me profusely for coming to her aid, she assigned me to Xeroxing multiple-page packets of admission material for Medicare, Medicaid, private pay, and life care potential residents. In Park Place, residents were categorized under one of these four identifications.

I learned Medicare residents were independent living residents of Sandycreek Terrace admitted to Park Place after they'd been hospitalized for at least three consecutive nights and needed skilled care. As beds allowed, people who lived in the community and qualified for Medicare coverage in a skilled nursing facility were also admitted as Medicare residents. Continued stay as Medicare residents required periodic certification by an attending physician. The number of Medicare-covered days of stay was based on the resident's need for continued therapy and skilled nursing care in a skilled facility as long as the resident was improving to the point of being able to be discharged home. This was determined by an attending physician. Nursing and therapy departments played a consulting role.

Private pay residents were former Medicare-covered residents in Park Place, admitted from the community, whose Medicare-eligible days had expired and who stayed on, needing extended care. Private pay residents were also people admitted directly from home, not having been hospitalized but needing nursing care. These two types of residents who were not covered by Medicare paid out of pocket for their care in Park Place. When their funds, with the exception of a federally-designated minimal amount, were exhausted they qualified to be Medicaid residents.

Life Care identified those who were Sandycreek Terrace residents, had been admitted from a hospital as Medicare residents and, when their Medicare coverage expired, still needed care in the nursing unit. Life Care residents were also Sandycreek Terrace residents admitted directly from their independent living quarters when they needed skilled or intermediate short-or long-term care as prescribed by their physician. Some, but not all, improved to the point of being able to return to their former living quarters. Pay for Life Care residents' care was in accordance with their Sandycreek Terrace contracts.

A physician was on staff at Park Place. He was the Medical Director, as required by the federal regulations, and was the attending physician for all the residents. Although some residents would have preferred to be under the care of their primary physicians, few physicians practicing in the community had time to follow their patients residing in nursing homes.

When I went to Park Place the third day the Social Worker was no longer employed. Why wasn't I surprised, given her unprofessional appearance? Much more was at stake, I imagined. Several weeks later, I reported to a newly-hired part-time Social Worker. Dark eyes snapping, vivacious, and excited about her new position, this well-dressed social worker handed me satisfaction questionnaire forms that, when completed, would be reviewed by the Administrator or Director of Nurses and then placed in residents' medical records.

With these forms in hand, I sat in residents' rooms and filled out the forms with answers given to me by the residents. Some residents were satisfied with all the care they received—meals, nursing care, cleanliness of their rooms, activities, and courtesy of staff. Others objected to lack of activities. One ninety-nine year old painfully thin white-haired resident claimed, "I may be old but I'm very alert. My mind is as good if not better than anyone employed here. See here," she said demanding my full attention. She flung the bedding aside, raised both legs high in the air, and said, "You see! I'm physically fit! Spry as a spring chicken! I'm just old, that's all. Now go ahead! I'll answer your questions."

When I read them aloud one by one she complained her room was dirty, the cleaning mops were filthy, the food was unfit to eat, the nursing care was non-existent, and she wore her own night-clothes because facility gowns were gray with dirt as were the bed linens. I concluded this resident would not have been satisfied if the walls were gold-plated.

"I'm delighted you have come to talk to me," she stated at the end of my questioning. "You're the first intelligent and sensible person who has ever come into my room! I'd like you to come back anytime."

Tongue in cheek, I smiled as sweetly as I could then left having documented all comments, or should I say all complaints, on the form.

I thoroughly enjoyed talking to the residents, especially the spring chicken, and looked forward to the next day I would continue with that assignment as I had completed but one-third of the questionnaires. That was not to be. The new part-time Social Worker had taken it upon herself to finish my pleasant job.

My next assignment given to me by this part-time Social Worker was monitoring and taking minutes of resident family meetings she intended to hold. I was to be in complete charge of these meetings, I was told. For the first and only such meeting I attended, the Social Worker arranged for it to be held in an empty room, its customary purpose I knew not. She had dietary bring in a large pitcher of fruited punch, assorted cookies, drinking glasses, and napkins. The two and only two family members who showed for the meeting were generously greeted by the Social Worker who introduced herself. Even though I was standing right there, I was ignored. So I introduced myself and explained who I was. The Social Worker served refreshments to the two family members and helped herself, but again ignored me. I made a vague attempt to take minutes.

Several mornings later, Mr. Valenzuela phoned and asked if I had time to meet with him. "I'm finalizing our application for eligibility to receive the JCAHO Gold Seal Award. I could use your expertise."

"Be glad to," I answered, eager to see what this was all about. I knew about the Joint Commission Accreditation of Healthcare Organizations and its accrediting program for hospitals and nursing homes but not it's Gold Seal Award.

I located Mr. Valenzuela's office opposite the business and accounting offices and knocked on the door.

"Come in, come in," he said, striding forward and shaking my hand. He went to his desk, picked up a packet of papers and said, "Here are the pages I'd like you to review."

I sat down at an empty desk with the packet. As I started to read, I immediately realized his Spanish was interfering with English grammar in this application. "May I make some editorial notes as I read along?" I asked him.

"Absolutely. That's what I want you to do. I have other copies. Please, please feel free to do that."

A very frank and courteous man. And down to earth. I was pleased and continued to read, finding many grammatical errors to be corrected. Since I'd toured Park Place and noted some outstanding creative features about the dementia wing in particular, I inserted a comment. I wrote about the family photos posted on the walls next to the doors of residents' rooms enabling a resident to identify her own room and not wander into the wrong room and disturb or alarm another resident. A big black dog was posing in one of the photos, a child in another, and a house was the familiar object in still another. I wrote about the long activity room containing many games, arts and crafts, books, fish tank, and bird enclosure. This room had two doors, one at each end of the long room, enabling residents to walk about freely, entering one door and exiting the other. A large bulletin board centrally located and changed daily (rather than weekly as on other wings) listed the day's activities in large print for the benefit of staff as well as residents. My intention was to point out to award reviewers the advantages provided to dementia residents residing in Park Place.

Then I read that at least two letters of recommendation were required to accompany the application. One was already enclosed with the packet and was written by a Dr. Tom Price, one of the residents, according to his address. Although I looked for another letter, I couldn't find one. Then I wondered a little about this Dr. Price. Later I would know him quite well. "You'll need another letter of recommendation," I said, looking over at Mr. Valenzuela seated at his desk on the other side of the office.

He looked up at me and asked with a pleading smile, "Will you write it?"

I couldn't refuse, and frankly I was eager to comply.

With a copy of Dr. Price's letter that I requested, I went home and wrote what I considered a winning letter of recommendation, if I do say so myself.

"What are you doing?" Jeff asked me just as I had completed the letter on the computer and taken it out of the printer.

"Would you like to read this? It's a letter I've written to accompany the application being sent to JCAHO for the Gold Seal Award. For Park Place."

EIGHT

THANKSGIVING

Thanksgiving 2003 was upon us, and, as in other years, we'd been invited for turkey dinner by our long-standing friends Chick and Betty Hahn. They lived in Pine Gardens where we lived before moving to Sandycreek Terrace. When we went to the Hahn's for dinner we'd be going back to our former residential community for the first time since we moved away. How would I feel? Could I go there and not wish I were still living there?

As we drove into the entrance, past the familiar gate house and onto streets even the Caddy should recognize, nostalgia gripped me. I blinked back the tears as I looked all around. I grabbed a quick glance at the old club house before we turned and parked in front of the Hahn house I knew so well.

I'd always admired their house with brown shutters slanting diagonally out from the windows and the front entrance recessed beside the two-car garage. No bell but a knocker was attached to the frame left of the door. Regardless of the time of day, fast friends would jiggle it and push open the door. From somewhere inside the house, Betty would always call out, "Come on in!" Then she'd hug her friends and insist they sit down and have a drink.

I'd been in the house so often, stayed overnight a number of times when I'd come down from Pennsylvania to check on my rental property close by. I loved the large living room with its functional fireplace, gas logs always burning in cool weather and a grouping of three comfy couches facing it.

Through two large picture windows and a glass door on one wall, one could look out to a long porch that had been attached to the back of the house. How many hours Betty and I had spent talking about how to dress those windows! Should they have a cornice above connecting the two wide windows? Should she buy curtains or drapes? Should the fabric be plain or have a design, be a thin nylon or lacy material, the color white or ecru?

The backyard reached to the banks of a fair-sized man-made pond, water spouting from a fountain in the center. On their bank, Chick had constructed a small dock on which he sat and fished and smoked his pipe.

As we got out of our car with the package of rolls Betty had asked us to bring, other friends were parking cars and going into the house carrying casseroles, covered platters of food, and laden liquor-store bags. We were all following the tradition of other years—Chick and Betty furnishing the turkey, mashed potatoes, stuffing, gravy, and pumpkin pie with guests bringing appetizers, side dishes, salads, dinner wine, and rolls. Inside everyone hugged and kissed after depositing their donations on a kitchen table.

I'd worn an ankle-length skirt and was glad I had when I saw the festive attire of the other *girls*. As usual, Chick urged us to make our own cocktails at the wet bar, and, chattering away, we concocted our drinks and found seats in the living room or out on the porch.

I chose the porch and sat there looking across the pond, my fingers traveling up and down the smooth, flowered, vinyl-covered cushion beside me. On the opposite side facing the pond loomed the two-story condo housing my old apartment. I studied it for a moment and wondered about the single woman living there now. When Jeff and I married, I'd sold it to her, she eager to live there, I sad to leave it. I'd heard neighbors liked her and that she'd done a fine job of decorating *my beloved apartment*. Lost in the past, I forced a smile as I talked to my friends.

Throughout the cocktail hour stretching into two hours, guests mulled around conversing and wending their way to the dry sink for another drink and to side tables to pick at the hors d'oeuvres. Topics of conversations varied from personal health issues, to recent trips, to the country club bar room's new seating arrangement and addition of a small dance floor and popcorn machine. From time to time, several of us girls went into the kitchen to help Betty.

Even though it seemed longer to me, we'd moved from Pine Gardens only one month ago. I was happy to be with old friends again, and I wasn't surprised when many posed questions to Jeff and me. "How do you like Sandycreek Terrace? Are you glad you moved? Don't you miss living here? We think about you every time we pass your house."

The inflection in their voices gave me, and Jeff, too, I imagined, an impression they were expecting us to acknowledge dissatisfaction with our move and our new digs.

Uncertain as to how I would answer, I let Jeff do the talking. He said what I knew he would. "We love it there! Should have moved sooner. *You* should move there. You'd *love* it!"

Ignoring, almost scoffing at Jeff's jubilance and his sales pitch, one after the other replied, "We're not ready."

Just then, Betty announced dinner was served, and we all chose seats at two pre-set tables, light flickering from tall tapered candles. As usual, Chick said Catholic grace, and we started passing the sumptuous wonderfully-smelling food filling the two tables.

On the way back to Sandycreek Terrace, Jeff lamented, "Those people will never be ready. Most are as old as we are. Not in that great physical shape. But they'll *never* be ready! And they'll wait until it's too late for them to pass entrance requirements. They'll be crippled and crotchety. They should move now while they can enjoy all the amenities."

I sat quietly beside him while he drove the Cadillac. I knew exactly how our friends felt. Hadn't I felt like that? A few hours ago when I was sitting on the porch looking out across the pond I'd been homesick, quite homesick. Many years before I knew Jeff, I'd sat on my apartment patio and looked out at that very same pond. I'd written most of my book on that patio. I'd swum in the pool a few steps away. My daughter and granddaughter had visited there. What memories! But those days were gone. Now Jeff and I lived at Sandycreek Terrace where I didn't feel at home. Not yet. Maybe never?

When we moved into Sandycreek Terrace just before Halloween, the indoor planting areas outside the library and along the sides of the tile floor leading into the lounge and dining room were overflowing with multiple pumpkins, scare crows, and corn shocks. Tables in the dining room were decorated with miniature pumpkins and small ears of Indian corn. We'd missed the Halloween party being unaware of it. And of course we hadn't been present for the Thanksgiving dinner which we heard was a buffet with a lavish menu. Now in the Weekly Bulletin we read that the twelfth anniversary of Sandycreek Terrace would be celebrated with a semi-formal dinner dance held in the Palace.

We didn't know pre-registration for all parties and other such special functions was required. As a result, by the time we learned about sign-up sheets at the front desk and looked at the ones marked *Anniversary Party*, many of the listed tables were completely filled with residents' names. Apparently many residents had arranged far in advance to sit together. Of necessity, we signed our names in two empty spaces for a table where only single women's names appeared. Poor Jeff would be the only male. "I don't mind," he said. "I'll break down and wear my black suit, red bow tie, red cummerbund, and red printed vest Susan made for me. And with my harem, I'll be the envy of all the men!"

I was glad he was such a good sport, but I didn't believe anyone would envy him. I decided to wear my long black silk skirt and a white sequined top. When we walked through the automatically opening door from the corridor we were in a small foyer. People were pouring into another swinging door to the left. We followed the elaborately dressed crowd and were led by a dining room hostess to the center of the room to a table already occupied by six female residents. The room was large like an immense auditorium with a stage and fair-sized dance floor. On stage in front of a shimmering gold colored curtain, a three-piece band strummed a warm-up tune.

One of the women at our table looked at us and said, "You're new here, aren't you?"

"Yes,, we are," I said. "We moved in the end of October."

"We all moved in four years ago," she said, glancing around the table at the other women. "We've been friends ever since."

Another resident, the one sitting next to Jeff, smiled, nudged his arm, and said, "If you want a drink before the server gets around to our table, go to that bar over there." She pointed to the right.

"I'll just do that," Jeff said and left the table.

Now the resident turned to me. "That's the Terrace. Where the bar is. It's a separate room, but for big social affairs, the wall that separates it from the Palace slides open to make the Palace large enough to accommodate the crowd. Have you eaten in the Terrace?"

"No, we haven't," I replied.

"The Terrace is an informal restaurant where breakfast and lunch are served daily from eight in the morning until two in the afternoon, Sundays excepted. Residents can choose to eat indoors or on the patio at umbrella-covered tables. The pool's in full view from the patio. From any meal in the Terrace, residents are permitted to take home containers of their uneaten food. That's a practice prohibited in the main dining room, you know."

I nodded.

She laughed and continued, "It seems management fears food taken from the dining room will be forgotten, will be stored until it's tainted, and then, when a resident eats it she'll get sick." She laughed again. "Management must think Terrace food won't spoil."

"Doesn't make sense," I said. Then a little confused, I asked, "Why is this room where we're sitting called the Palace and the small restaurant, which is another room, called the Terrace, and yet on the outside of the building the lettering is *The Palace*?"

"That doesn't make sense either, does it? But that's just the way it is." She smiled.

We enjoyed the women at our table, ate fancy food, danced, and had a great time. Jeff danced only with me, but I wouldn't have objected had he danced the light fantastic with other women, especially those who had no mate and who sat there all evening like wall flowers at a prom.

It seemed all such events started at five and ended by eight. Home early, Jeff removed his fancy regalia and his shoes and socks and we sat down to our usual game of cribbage in the kitchenette. The present on-going score was twenty in Jeff's favor. "I guess I'll be a loser again tonight. You're on a winning streak," I said, resigned to another loss.

The game began. Jeff's foremost peg was ahead, then mine was, then his was. Now we were both on fourth street, I barely, Jeff with only three moves to go to win. I hadn't a chance. He had the game sewed up, I felt sure. Since he was dealing he'd have that added advantage of possibly cutting a Jack with a guarantee of pegging one. (The dealer always pegs one. That was a proven cribbage fact.) With no hope, I picked up my hand. I counted eighteen! The cut wasn't a Jack but a card that gave me a total of twenty-six! I couldn't believe it! I held my breath while Jeff paired my three and moved his peg two holes ahead. "One more move, Jeff, and you'll win the game." I said. But I had another three to follow his three and laid it down, giving me six moves ahead. That's all I needed! I had the count to go out! I masked my excitement, kept a solemn face, laid down my cards, and moved my peg home!

Jeff sat there dumbfounded. "I can't believe it!" he exclaimed. "I just can't believe how lucky you are, Jeanie! We'd better take you to Lost Wages."

Because of increasing back pain, Jeff was finding it difficult to walk the distance from our apartment down the length of our corridor around the Palace building and the area inside the Club House to the dining room. We'd only been married a year when he'd had extensive surgery on his cervical vertebra. Now an inoperable lumbar spinal stenosis was exacerbating, and only Celebrex relieved the pain, and that only temporarily.

"I'm going to start taking the facility transportation to get to dinner and back," Jeff told me. "I understand it's available during dinner hours from five until eight-thirty."

"I might as well go along with you," I said, even though I had no difficulty walking the distance to the Club House and then some. "I think we have to call the desk so the receptionist can notify the driver what time to pick us up. I'll do that, Jeff. Is six o'clock all right? We usually go at six." I looked at him for his agreement.

He nodded. "Find out the transportation pick-up point, too, Jeanie."

I called and the receptionist said, "Transportation will pick you up at the entrance to your building. At the circle. If you're late, they'll be back. You can sit on the benches to wait."

We became accustomed to watching for the approach of the white Lincoln Continental with a green Sandycreek Terrace logo on the side. It veered around one side of the circle, around the planted area filled with a grouping of trees and a bed of bright red flowers, and then it stopped at the entrance. After we boarded, sometimes finding one or two other residents already seated, the vehicle circled around the other side of the planted area, out to the road, and then to the Club House.

Liza was the driver Monday through Friday; two different men drove Saturdays and Sundays. Liza was a case, to say the least. If we weren't at the entrance at the exact minute of our scheduled pick-up time, off she would go to return ten to twenty minutes later, depending on the time of the next scheduled pick-up. As the receptionist had said, a cast-concrete bench provided seating during waiting-time, but not when it rained unless one enjoyed getting wet.

Liza liked comfort. She was obese, black skinned, and had short curly hair that was sometimes black like a black Scotty dog, sometimes blond, sometimes henna red. Never did she relinquish the driver seat to assist a resident board or dismount. In cool weather, the car's temperature was unbearably heated to her satisfaction even though she was garbed in a wool jacket buttoned high, a scarf wound around her neck, and a tassel cap pulled over her ears. Her chewing gum cracked to the tune and timing of the parson's voice delivering his sermon on the car's radio. Although Liza portrayed an unfriendly attitude, she did answer when spoken to. In an attempt to soften her up, we asked her questions but found our efforts hopeless. Both male drivers were very pleasant. They smiled, responded to our questions, and engaged in further conversation. One of the male drivers always got out of the car to open the door for us; the other man sometimes did; lazy Liza never. Often she demonstrated a cough and sniffling nose. I turned my head to avoid breathing in what she was breathing out.

This means of getting to the Club House for dinner worked fairly well except that we were rushed at times to make the deadline, a matter of urgency when Liza was driving. After a time, I decided to walk to get exercise. And I have to admit it was a relief not having any more contact with loser Liza.

When we walked into the lounge one evening, we noticed Doris Jordan coming to dinner alone. I stopped her. "Where's Donald?" I wanted to know.

"He's at home. He hasn't come to dinner all week. He just isn't hungry."

"Oh Doris, I'm sorry," I said, remembering his colon cancer diagnosis and patting her arm.

She acknowledged my concern with a quick nod and a blink of her sad eyes. "He's been complaining lately. To be expected." Eyes filling with tears, my nurse friend shook her head and walked away.

Jeff was close by listening. "That's a shame, but that's the way it goes," was his comment.

Approximately a week and a half before Christmas, we arranged to have dinner again with Pam and Ben Butcher who had also lived in Pine Gardens before coming to Sandycreek Terrace. We were to meet at the lounge bar at six. The other times we'd eaten together, they'd arrived before us, and this evening we expected to see the Butchers in the lounge when we arrived. Since they weren't there yet, we ordered drinks and sat down to sip them and wait. After a time when Pam and Ben still hadn't arrived and because employees seemed to know all residents by sight and name, I went to the bar and asked the female bartender if she'd seen the Butchers.

"No, I haven't seen Mr. and Mrs. Butcher as yet, Mrs. Mertz," she said, addressing me as all employees are instructed.

After fifteen more minutes of waiting and supposing our friends had forgotten our arrangement, we decided to go into the dining room. Ben and Pam still hadn't arrived by the time we finished dinner. The next morning, I phoned Pam.

"Oh, Jean," she answered, her voice quaking, "Ben's in the hospital! I didn't have an opportunity to call you last night. At four-thirty yesterday afternoon I was in the kitchen, and Ben was reading the newspaper in the living room when I heard a noise. I called to him but he didn't answer. When I got to him his eyes were rolled back and he was drooling."

"Oh dear," I interrupted and asked, "A stroke?"

"Yes. I pulled the cord. Security came immediately. And then two nurses from Park Place. They dialed 911. Paramedics were here in ten minutes. He's in ICU. I'm going there now."

"Is there anything we can do? Take you to the hospital?"

"No, but thanks. My daughter's here. She'll take me."

Jeff watched me place the receiver in the cradle and stood there in his bare feet waiting to hear the news. "It's Ben," I told him. "He's had a stroke, and he's in ICU."

"Damn," was Jeff's response as he turned and went back into the den where he'd been sending an e-mail to Susan when he heard me talking to Pam.

I'd made the call on the phone stationed on the counter top of the half-wall separating the kitchen from the dining room. Now I looked at the dining room table swarming with French stamps. Among the stamps were an open collectors' stamp book, stamp tongs, and a pair of eye glasses. I knew Jeff would return to his absorbing hobby as soon as he finished his e-mail to Susan. I would then have access to the computer to work on my nursing home article. When completed I planned to query the nursing magazine editor who'd previously published two of my continuing education course modules on nursing homes.

I sat down at the table and waited, and, as predicted, when Jeff was finished with his e-mail to Susan he came into the dining room. He looked at me and asked, "Have you seen my glasses? I can't find them. I thought I might have laid them on my desk when I went into the den but they're not there. I looked in the bathroom but they're not there either. I don't know why I can't keep track of my glasses." I giggled and pointed. "They're right where you left them, Jeff. Here on the dining room table. I don't have that problem, you know. My glasses are attached to my ears all the time except when I go to bed." Of course he knew that.

He was always losing his glasses mainly because he only needed them for fine print. Often they were on top of his bald head. The other personal item he often misplaced was his favorite pocket knife. He'd told me that pocket knife was a Barlow knife like the one Mark Twain chose for Tom Sawyer, the knife famous for its reference as Tom Sawyer's *Genuine Barlow Knife*, admired by Huckleberry Finn and Nigger Jim. Jeff used his Barlow knife to open the mail, slice apples, cut threads, and for many other immediate needs. And he treasured it.

When he lost it I often found it in the pocket of the last trousers he wore. Before I washed his clothes, I always checked his shirt and pants pockets. I'd find store lists, store receipts, match clips, handkerchiefs, a piece of hardware, and sometimes his Barlow knife.

The next evening I phoned Pam. She answered immediately. "The neurologist examined Ben. Read the MRI. He's had a bad one. He'll never be able to talk again or swallow. And the test showed massive hemorrhage in the brain which will only increase, he tells me."

"Oh Pam, how awful!" I exclaimed. "Please keep me posted. And if there's anything…"

"I will," she promised, her voice cracking.

Several days later, I phoned Pam for an update.

"Ben's been moved to Hospice," she informed me. "But I'm having a terrible time."

"How so? What's the trouble, Pam?"

"A daughter of Ben's. The one who lives in Pompano. She wants heroic measure taken to keep her father alive. Revive him! And she claims I'm having her father poisoned. With rat poison!" Pam paused.

"My heavens, Pam! That's ridiculous! How could she say such a thing? What kind of a person is she anyway?" I was flabbergasted.

"This daughter's a dietitian in a nursing home. She thinks she knows it all. She never wanted her dad to marry me in the first place, or to sell the house he owned in Cleveland. She never talks to me, and she's always been mean to me. His other daughter lives near Cleveland. She's never been friendly either, but she's never been mean."

"Gee, Pam, what are you going to do?" What was she going to do?

"I wish my sons were here. At least one of them. The closest lives in South Carolina. He hasn't been able to come because he has pneumonia. My other son lives in Hawaii. But my daughter's been here a lot. She lives close by, you know."

The next time I talked to Pam, Jeff and I were in the lounge waiting to have dinner. I saw her sitting at a small round table by herself, her walker abandoned, next to a wall. Concerned, I walked over and sat down. "How are things now?" I asked her.

"I'm overwhelmed with records and papers. Ben never kept them in any order. But I'm delighted with Hospice. They're so wonderful! Ben's getting such good care."

"Is there any change in his condition?" I studied her face.

"No. No change. No response. He's almost comatose." She frowned, sighed, and rubbed her forehead.

"And what about his mean daughter? You said she might sue."

"The Hospice social worker wants to have a conference call with me, Ben's daughter, and herself to get things out in the open and come to some resolution."

That sounded like a good solution to me but Ben was dead before the conference could take place. He died at one-fifteen in the morning on December twenty-second, nine days after his stroke. Pam was thankful death occurred before Christmas, she told me.

The next evening as we walked toward the front desk on our way toward the lounge, we saw a single red rose and white baby breath in a vase on the desk. "Why the rose?" we asked the evening receptionist.

"Mr. Butcher died," she said in a soft serious voice.

"Yes, I know. What has that to do with the rose?" I questioned.

She glanced up at me from her sitting position behind the desk and explained, "It's customary, when someone dies here, for a rose to be placed on the desk in memory and to alert everyone. When you go down the hall toward the library you'll see, across the hall from the bank office on the semi-circular table that usually holds a plant." She stopped to answer the phone and then continued, "You'll see a framed photograph or a brief history of the deceased, or both, and perhaps an announcement of a memorial service. Residents and usually a few staff members place bereavement cards and notes on the table for family members."

"How nice," Jeff said, and smiling slightly, I nodded in agreement.

No memorial service for Ben was being planned here or in town. Ben's body was being sent to Cleveland for burial.

To myself I said, "So this is life and death at Sandycreek Terrace! What's next? Who knows what's next?" That's what I've always said when thinking of the hereafter. Now that I was living in this establishment where so many people were vulnerable, I realized death would be a frequent occurrence and so would illness, falls, and deterioration of mind and body.

NINE
MEMORY

Here in this continuing care retirement community or CCRC, as healthcare professionals called it, especially those specializing in gerontology, Jeff and I were but two members of a *family* of 230 people. I'd heard residents say we were a family, but I didn't consider the residents my family. I felt as though I were still here on a part-time temporary basis. Most residents acted as though Sandycreek Terrace was their home, but I had no way of knowing how they really felt. I didn't know any of them well enough to ask and get an honest answer. Some residents seemed to have close ties with other residents; some appeared to be merely acquaintances. But we all spoke when we passed on our way to meetings, the library, meals, or wherever we were headed. Sometimes we'd stop and engage in short conversations. Everyone was friendly, usually always saying, "Hello. How are you?" The employees greeted the residents the same way.

As yet, Jeff and I had not made what you would call close friends. We'd met many residents but didn't really know them. Perhaps more time was needed or quite possibly we never would really know them. Certainly not like I knew Chick and Betty Hahn.

With that in mind, one day I interrupted Jeff engrossed in his stamp collection hobby. "Honey, we haven't been called lately to eat with anyone in the dining room. After our first few dinner invitations by seasoned residents, no other invitations have been extended. I feel as though we're being ignored."

Jeff put down his stamp tongs, moved his eye glasses to the top of his bald head, and looked up at me, a quizzical frown spreading over his face.

"We've been invited to people's apartments and to Schreiber's cottage for cocktails and then eaten dinner with all of them."

"Yes, I know. But that was when we first came. And then we had the McKees and Gormans for cocktails. But I'm talking about lately," I persisted.

"Well go ahead and call someone to eat with us. No harm in doing that, is there?" He turned back to his stamps and lowered his glasses.

"I suppose not," I said hesitantly. "But, Jeff," I continued, staring at the back of his head and then down at the multitude of foreign stamps that were unrecognizable and of no interest to me. "A number of couples seem so friendly and eat together often. Haven't you noticed? Lately we've met several seasoned couples that come to the later dinner hour as we do, and I'd like to eat with them. But they've made previous arrangements to eat with other couples, it seems. They probably aren't interested in eating with new residents like us. In the beginning we were invited just because we were newcomers. Seasoned residents were trying to be nice. Welcome us."

Jeff turned around, moved his glasses back onto the top of his head, and glanced up at me again. "Nonsense. We're not being excluded, if that's what you're thinking. Many residents knew each other before they came to Sandycreek Terrace. Where they lived in some adult residential community here in Jupiter. In Johnathan's Landing and Frenchman's Creek. A couple lived at Admiral's Cove. Some of them knew each other and were friends up north before they ever moved to Florida. I've heard them talking. It's time they made new friends. Us. Give someone a call. Call several and fill in the calendar."

"I'll think about it," I said, frowning, not totally convinced, and watching my husband go back to his hobby. I did think about it, but I knew how friends of long standing were. It was only natural for them to arrange to eat together frequently and to sign up for the same tables for parties. It reminded me of the time long ago when my family moved to a different town, and I attended a different high school where I knew no one. Most of the kids had known each other since first grade and had formed cliques.

"Honey," I said, standing in front of him now. "It isn't as though I don't enjoy eating alone with you. I like sitting at a two-top by the window, always a little vase with a pretty bouquet of live alstroemerias. Where we can look out on the Inlet and see that deserted boat stranded on a strip of land because of some past hurricane. I like looking at those red flowering bushes by the veranda. The bougainvillea. You said they couldn't live up north because of the frost. And we always have something to talk about. I do like just the two of us to eat alone. I don't want you to misunderstand."

"Of course not. I understand, Sweetheart," he said in a low sexy voice, like Humphrey Bogart talking to Lauren Bacall. Every once in a while he mimicked Bogart just to make me laugh.

Fortunately Jeff was a very outgoing person and engaged in conversation with all the residents we encountered in the lounge while waiting for dinner. Some evenings he told his Dutch stories. He had a captive audience when, in his Dutch dialect, his Dutch brogue, he told the story about Pete and Yake.

Tonight we sat with our cocktails at a round table in the lounge with two other couples waiting to be called to dining room tables. The conversation lagged and Jeff said to me, "Shall I tell my Pete and Yake story?"

"Yes, go ahead," I prompted, knowing he didn't need my permission.

As the two couples turned to listen, he leaned forward and began. "Pete and Yake verked at the Vest Michigan Furniture Factory. They valked to verk together every morning. Vone morning, Pete vasn't dere. The next morning, Yake said, 'Pete, you vasn't here yesterday. Ver vas you?' 'I know I vasn't here,' Pete said. 'I had the back door trots.' 'Vell,' Yake said. 'You voodn't believe vhat happened. A car drove up beside me. It vas a Cadillac. Had no top on it. A beautiful blond vas behind the veel. She said, 'Yakie, Vood you like a ride to the Vest Michigan Furniture Factory?' Vell, I hain't never had no ride to verk. She reached down and pulled up a bottle of vine. 'Vood you like a drink, Yakie?' she said. Vell, I like a little drink. She headed out toward the voods. She vasn't going to the Vest Michigan Furniture Factory at all. She stopped the car. Took off all her clothes, mind you. And she said, 'Yakie, you can have anything you vants.' Vell, I had to think about that. So after a vile, I said, 'I think I'll take the Cadillac.'"

The listeners laughed, but I said, "Wait, you haven't heard the best part."

Jeff continued, "Pete said, 'I think you vas right, Yake. Dem clothes voodn't have fit your vife anyvays.'"

The couples laughed louder and then rose and followed the hostess who'd been waiting to seat them while they listened to the end of the Pete and Yake story.

Even though Jeff and I weren't being invited to eat dinner with couples we thought we'd like to know better, we knew their names, and I recognized them even with my poor vision. My bigger problem was learning names and recognizing faces of the many other seasoned residents and those just moving into Sandycreek Terrace. Was I starting to have a severe memory problem? No, this just had to do with meeting too many people in too short a time.

My memory was intact. Not like the residents in the incident told us by the female bartender one evening. Jeff started a conversation with her by asking her, "What is your name?"

"My name is Amelia, Mr. Metz," she said.

How staff recognized new residents and learned their names so quickly was a mystery to me.

"And where were you born?" Jeff asked while I wondered why he was pursuing this line of questioning.

"Venezuela," she replied, much to my surprise.

Jeff said, "I figured somewhere in South America from your appearance. Dark hair, dark eyes, pale complexion. Smooth skin. You speak fluent English."

She smiled at Jeff and explained, "I've been here in Florida since I was three. What would you like to drink, Mr. Metz? The usual?"

"Yes. Mrs. Metz will have a Vodka Martini on the rocks with a lemon twist, and I'll have a Manhattan, extra sweet. Make it look like root beer. And no garbage, please. That means no cherry, no orange peel, no garbage."

"I understand. I believe yours is on the rocks, too, Mr. Metz?"

"That's right."

All this time I was observing short plump Amelia standing behind the bar, her chubby hands spread open on top of the bar as she looked at Jeff asking her personal questions and then giving her our drink order. Her white blouse tucked into her black skirt spanned her breasts. White pearly buttons down the front struggled to hold the blouse together. To complete her uniform, a black band circled the blouse's stand-up collar and ended in a flat bow under her chin. She wore her very black hair pulled back behind her ears and tied with a black ribbon to form a mid-length pony-tail. An artist would have enjoyed painting her.

As the resident standing beside me walked away with her drink, I said to Amelia, "Can you tell me the name of that person? The resident you just served a gin and tonic? I know I've met her, but I can't remember her name. I've met a lot of residents, but I'm having difficulty remembering their names and even recognizing their faces. You know, they should have a memory class here, like they have physical exercise classes. To help us old folks with our memories."

Drinks made and placed on cocktail napkins, Amelia looked over the bar at me and said with a sober expression, "They *did* plan to have a memory class here, Mrs. Metz. Planned one a year ago. They hired a psychiatrist to teach it. A qualified psychiatrist well known for his memory classes. They announced it. Posted it." She paused before she said, "But no one remembered to go."

"Is that right?" I said, amused. I turned to Jeff. "Did you hear that, Jeff? They tried to have a memory class here. Advertised it. But nobody remembered to go. Isn't that funny?"

"I guess *you* would have remembered to go?" he said, head cocked.

"Oh course I'd have remembered to go! You might have forgotten," I jested back, "But *I* wouldn't have forgotten."

Two days later, I was reminded of memory problems again when I was having my hair trimmed in the beauty salon just down the hall from the dining room. When I first learned a beauty salon existed in the Club House I decided to give it a try. I'd been quite pleased.

Ethel was the middle-aged friendly beautician manning the salon, and now she was about to trim my bangs when a male resident walked into the shop. She looked up and said to him, "Mr. Trimble, your appointment's next week. Not today."

"Is that right?" the resident placidly said, not even questioning, just accepting, and walked out.

Curious, I asked Ethel, "Does this happen often? Residents not remembering when they have an appointment with you?"

"Yes, it does happen quite often with some residents, Mrs Metz. Some residents can't remember much of anything. Some I have to call the day of their appointment to remind them."

"Is that right?" I said, amused again but amazed that any of the residents had such poor memories. Then I turned my attention to the photograph of a baby stuck in the corner of the mirror in front of the beauty chair where I was sitting. "Is that your grandchild?" I asked.

She beamed. "Yes, and I have another on the way."

TEN

CHRISTMAS

Chairman Stuart, our neighbor across the corridor, phoned one day. "Jeanie," he began. "The resident who's been serving as secretary of the Health Care Committee is resigning. She's been writing the minutes in long hand. She can't type. Since all committees must now submit copies of the minutes of their meetings to the Resident Council, she feels she can't do an adequate job with our minutes. Would you serve as secretary? You do type, don't you?"

"Yes, I type on the computer keyboard, and I'll be happy to be secretary," I answered. I knew the Resident Council was entitled to committee meeting minutes since the Council was the governing or representative body and spokesperson for the Resident Association, made up of all the residents.

"Who called?" Jeff wanted to know.

"That was Stuart McKee. He wants me to be secretary of the Health Care Committee. I told him I would. He says the Resident Council is to get copies of the minutes from every committee meeting. About this Resident Association, Jeff. It only meets annually. And in the meantime, the Resident Council speaks for the residents who are all members of the Resident Association. How do you think this organization started here at Sandycreek Terrace and why?"

Jeff leaned back in his chair and started to explain in his professional manner. "It's my understanding the owners of Sandycreek Terrace, based on their experience at the older CCRCs they own, requested such a resident organization be formed. In order to have communication with the residents. The owners wanted to keep in touch with residents'

78

concerns. They probably instructed the Executive Director to meet with several male residents he considered qualified representatives of the majority of the residents. And he outlined an organizational plan the owners wanted these men to adopt. We weren't here then, but I understand that's what happened."

"What about the by-laws? There's a copy of them in the material Virginia Friedman gave us," I said.

"I imagine the Council wrote by-laws, probably according to the plan outlined by the owners and presented through the Executive Director. The many committees here were formed to discuss relative issues and concerns and make recommendations. And thus we have the Health Care, Landscaping, Food and Beverage, Housekeeping, Maintenance, Security, Decorating, Finance, Library, Marketing, and Social Committees. All the committees that function now. Probably started with a few committees and then more were added as needed. Committee chairmen can make recommendations to the Resident Council, and the Council can take concerns and suggestions to management. To the Executive Director, that is. But he makes the decisions and sometimes consults the owners for a final decision. The owners hold the purse strings. And there you have it! The political scene here like everywhere else.

"Who was the first chairman of the Resident Council? Do you know?" I asked.

"He died before we came here, but his photograph is on the wall in the Palace as well as photographs of succeeding chairmen. They serve for two consecutive years. Somehow a nominating committee is appointed, and, from the slate of candidates, a co-chair, secretary, and treasure are elected by the votes of the resident population attending the annual Resident Association meeting. I believe the co-chair steps into the chairman seat at the end of the chairman's two-year term. At least that's the way it's worked so far."

That made sense to me, and I said, "I guess we're lucky to have nice owners. And it's to their advantage to keep us residents satisfied. We're the ones who sell this facility to our friends and other contacts in the outside world. If we like it here, we make positive comments about

Sandycreek Terrace. Word of mouth is the best way to bring in new residents. What do you think of Raymond Watson, the resident who chairs the Resident Council now?" I asked.

"Seems like a nice capable guy. Did a good job at the annual Resident Association meeting we attended, didn't you think?" Jeff said.

"Yes he did. He's a handsome dude. Tall and handsome. Always dressed in an expensive-looking sport coat and tie when we see him and his wife in the lounge before dinner. His wife's tall, too, and beautiful. She's a beautiful woman, but practically blind, I understand. She's always immaculately dressed in a tailored suit. And her blond hair's always styled in a pony tail tied with a black scarf. She carries herself with perfect posture, like a soldier." I immediately straighten up. "Have you noticed how her hand's always resting on his arm? I wonder how she manages to choose what to wear? Maybe he selects her clothes and helps with her coiffeur."

Christmas on its way, Jeff brought out several boxes containing Christmas decorations from a hall closet where we'd stored them when we moved in. He opened one of the boxes, dug out a wreath, and hung it on a nail on our front door. Meanwhile I sorted through the ornaments to determine which to put where. I found a large red satin bow with streamers and attached it to the wreath Jeff had just hung outside. In another box, I found a decoration for the dining room table—a small wreath with shiny red balls and tiny cones disbursed throughout. I secured a red candle in the center and then placed a glass chimney over the candle. On our living room coffee table and Florida room table, I arranged other candles in painted holders. I affixed our Hallmark-collection Christmas balls on the many drawer knobs of the hutch. "Should we get a Christmas tree?" I queried Jeff. "One like we had at the house?"

"No," he answered emphatically. "The apartment looks fine right now the way you have it decorated. We won't be having any company that I know of."

"That's right," I agreed, knowing no family members were coming. They all had plans of their own that would have included us had we accepted any of their invitations. This year, however, we decided not to travel such distances as North Carolina, Virginia, West Virginia, Kentucky, Michigan, and Washington where our combined seven children were spread throughout the United States like stars in the sky. Nor did we dare to favor one adult child over another. We'd just stay put. We didn't expect old neighbors or friends from the outside world either, and residents here wouldn't visit unless invited.

I completed the minutes of the Health Care Committee meeting and walked across the corridor to deliver them to chairman Stuart McKee. He wasn't home, but Ruth was there and insisted I come in and sit a bit. I liked her even though she appeared opinionated. Everyone has opinions but they usually aren't as vocal. I was glad she was our neighbor.

She pointed to a small tree sitting on an end table in their living room and said in her alto voice, "Our daughter brought us this tree. Isn't it ugly? I think it's ugly! I was going to buy this pretty tree that I saw in Macy's. But now I have this one. I can't offend my daughter. Don't you think it's ugly?" As usual, her expression was serious and rigid.

Impossible to joke with Ruth, but I enjoyed her, regardless, and I said, "No, I *like* that tree. The large red satin balls and deep green foliage. We don't have a tree. Just Christmas decorations."

She ignored my comment and said, "Don't you think the Christmas decorations in and around Sandycreek Terrace are outstanding? They're like this every year."

"Yes, they're beautiful! I've been staring at them, almost spell-bound. I like the icicle lights circling the gate house. And the lights around the gazebo and along the arched bridge. You can see the combined effect in full view when you drive through the gate and head toward the Club House."

"Have you noticed the lights strung around the Club House doorway? And along the walkway leading from the Palace to our apartments?

"And you say the decorations are like this every year, Ruth?"

When I rose to leave she said, "I'll see that Stuart gets your minutes."

We always met for dinner inside the front door of the Club House, Jeff riding in the facility car and I walking. This evening we stood there in the lobby and gazed at the transformation. I exclaimed, "Look Jeff. Look at all flowers along the hall in the planting areas around the library and toward the lounge and the dining room! Look at the multiple potted poinsettias inter-twinned with little white lights! They've replaced all the pumpkins that were there a month ago."

As we walked on, we saw more poinsettias in the planting areas across from the lounge as well as lighted sparkling reindeer standing guard. An eight-foot high tree made entirely of poinsettia plants divided the lounge from the dining room.

On top of the bar, a toy Santa smiled at us, and Amelia said, "Do you want to see Santa dance, Mrs. Metz?" She flipped a switch on Santa's side and *Jingle Bells* played while Santa swung his hips from side to side.

I walked into the library to borrow a large-print book and beheld a tall evergreen tree bedecked with white satin streamers reaching from the tree's angel-top down green pine boughs past red and white satin balls and white bows to the end of the branches.

Christmas dinner was open-seating held between one and four in the afternoon in the dining room. All residents were expected to be finished eating by five-thirty so dining room and kitchen staff could be home in time for their Christmas dinners. Jeff and I chose to go at three-thirty. I was still abandoning facility transportation, preferring to walk for the exercise and escape the wiles of lazy Liza. Both in red jackets, Jeff and I met in the lobby as usual and walked past the lounge into the dining room. After we selected a table where a server filled our water glasses, we rounded the buffet tables. Back at the first table, we helped ourselves to oysters on the half shell, shrimp, crab meat, and cheeses. After enjoying those appetizers, we went to another buffet table for turkey, dressing, mashed potatoes, gravy, cranberry sauce, and green bean casserole. Our entrées consumed, dessert beckoned from another table where Jeff chose pumpkin pie with whipped cream, and, ever the chocoholic, I decided on a piece of chocolate cake. All the while, a harpist played Christmas music at the entrance to the dining room. Back home and stuffed, Jeff and I reclined on the couch in the Florida room and watched TV.

That next evening, Resident Council Chairman Raymond Watson and his wife Victoria stopped in front of us in the lounge and introduced themselves, acknowledging we were fairly new residents and welcoming us aboard. "Victoria has poor vision," Raymond explained.

Even though I knew she was visually handicapped, her blindness was quite obvious to me. Her eyes were wide open, but they weren't focusing.

"Jeanie has trouble seeing, too," Jeff said. "I always tell people so they won't think she's ignoring them when they wave to her. She simply doesn't see them. And she doesn't recognize people she's met the next time she sees them."

"Oh is that right?" Victoria said. "Do you have macular degeneration?"

"I do have macular degeneration, but the dry type and not advanced. Just beginning. My problem is glaucoma which I've had since I was in my early forties."

Raymond said, "We go to seminars on vision diseases every chance we get. Trying to learn about the latest treatments. So far, nothing can be done for Victoria's problem."

As they walked away, I admired again Victoria's ability to walk ahead smartly and not faltering, like she had twenty-twenty vision in both eyes.

Now it was New Year's Eve. We dressed in our finery, Jeff in his black suit, red cummerbund, red printed vest, and red bow tie and I in my long black silk skirt and a golden-threaded top. We'd signed up for a table with couples we didn't know and went to the Palace at five, the designated time for the party to begin. A rectangular table at the entrance was filled with gold-colored paper crowns and silvery top hats. I placed a crown on my head, and Jeff plunked a top hat on his. When we walked into the large room we saw that a number of residents had come early, just as they had at the anniversary party. Apparently a common practice at all such affairs. After we found our assigned table, we greeted others already seated and sat in the last two empty seats. The table cloth was black with a gold-colored lace over-cover. Each place was bedecked with a toy horn, a fancy noise maker, and a champagne glass. A basket filled with red roses made a striking center-piece. On the stage, a curtain shimmered and glittered gold as bright lights played on it from above. Jeff noticed that a bar had been set up in an alcove to one side and made a b-line to it for my vodka martini since champagne made me ill. Servers were pouring the sparkling wine into all the glasses except mine turned upside down when Jeff returned with my martini and a Manhattan for himself. While a one-man band played our kind of music on the stage, we enjoyed shrimp salads followed by prime rib. The few couples on the dance floor were pros— waltzing, two-stepping, and doing the rumba. Conversation at our table consisted of the usual. "How long have you lived here? Do you like it here? Were you here for the last New Year's Eve party? Where did you live before you came here?" Even though many residents had met before and exchanged the same information, they'd forgotten what they'd heard before, so many residents and so much data to retain. With the arrival of dessert, an almost indescribable mound of chocolate over custard with nuts and whipped cream topping, conversation ceased again.

Dinner concluded, more champagne was poured, and an entertainer appeared on the stage. A comedian, he told jokes, juggled balls and tenpins, and sang funny songs. When he came down from the stage he walked directly back to Jeff and said, "How you doin' tonight, Mr. Churchill?"

Jeff and I laughed, but it was true. Jeff did resemble Winston Churchill, and he'd actually been mistaken for the Prime Minister once, he'd told me. Then the entertainer went around to other residents' tables. The music began again, and now many residents made their way to the dance floor. "Wanta try it?" Jeff asked me.

"Just don't whirl me around and let me go," I pleaded.

Residents started to leave the party at seven-thirty. We were home by eight and in bed by nine, never to see the New Year come in!

I saw our old Rotary friend Fanny Porter in the corridor the next day. Not having seen her at the affair last night, I said, "There were so many people at the party last night I didn't get a chance to talk to you."

"Oh we didn't go. Clyde and I like to dance and bring in the New Year. We go somewhere where we can do that. If you go here, the party's over by eight. What fun is that?"

I wondered how many other couples went off campus New Year's Eve, and I would have asked her but she was on down the corridor before I had my thinking cap on in time. When I got home I told Jeff, "I saw

Fanny, and she and Clyde went out on the town last night. Somewhere where they could dance and bring in the New Year at the right time. Not like we do if we party here. Do you think many other residents went off campus to celebrate?"

"No, I don't think anyone else from here has the energy to go anywhere else. Besides, not many can see to drive at night. But I'm not surprised Fanny and Clyde went out. She's full of pep, and she always liked to dance."

"You see well enough to drive at night, Jeff. You have excellent vision, and you're a good driver," I said.

"Would you have liked to go somewhere else instead of going to the party here? We could have. I didn't think to bring it up."

"No, I guess not. We don't belong to the club at Pine Gardens anymore. That's where we used to go. But the party last night wasn't our usual way to bring in the New Year. We didn't even watch the ball drop in Times Square on TV. I was there on New Year's Eve nineteen forty-five. In the big crowd in Times Square. In the Big Apple. It was so exciting! I had a wonderful time!"

"I'll bet you did," he chuckled while my mind went back to those months in New York City so long ago. I was taking a course in OR Technique and Management at the New York Hospital, part of Cornell Med Center. Back then in that metropolitan city, it was safe to walk the streets at all times of the day and night, and the city was filled with World War II soldiers, sailors, marines, and even merchant marines. I was young and single and having the time of my life! I smiled to myself. What an interesting life I'd had, and was still having even at my age, I might add. I was sharing my life with a wonderful husband whom I loved and who loved me and who showed it in many ways.

Eleven

Meetings

Most of the residents attended the Executive Director's meeting held each month in the Palace. An announcement of the meeting was always printed in the monthly *Periscope* and in the weekly newsletter. Residents attended because they didn't want to miss anything, and they attended if they remembered to go. Very few were disinterested. At one such meeting, Jeff and I first laid eyes on Dr. Tom Price. The Executive Director walked over to Dr. Price sitting in an electric scooter in front of the first row of seated residents and handed him a microphone before calling on him for his report. In a strong voice that commanded attention, Dr. Price told the residents he was a member of the Florida Life Care Residents Association known as FLiCRA and was Sandycreek Terrace's representative in Tallahassee. On his frequent trips to the state capital, he lobbied for CCRCs on legislative issues affecting them. He explained that currently the state was proposing a bill that would impose a hotel occupancy tax on residents of CCRCs. At that point, he asked all of us to contact our senators and representatives and encourage them to vote in favor of exempting CCRCs from such a tax.

Our neighbor Ruth Mc Kee was sitting next to us. She turned toward us, cupped her hand around her mouth, and informed us in a loud whisper, "Tom Price is a resident here but he's still a practicing physician. An important man in town. I'm not exactly sure when, but some years ago he enlisted a staff of volunteer physicians and nurses and started a health clinic for indigent women. Mostly pregnant. And children. Here in Jupiter."

I was interested in such a charitable person and practicing physician at his age and also remembered his letter of recommendation that I read when I reviewed the application for the Gold Seal Award for Park Place. So I was curious and whispered back to Ruth, "Why is he in a scooter?"

"His right leg's amputated above the knee."

"Is he a diabetic?" I asked, supposing he was.

"No. A circulatory problem," she whispered, her hand still cupped around her mouth. Then she sat upright in her chair and gave full attention to the Executive Director and his introduction to the subject of landscaping.

At the January Health Care Committee meeting, the third one I was attending and was now secretary and ready to take the minutes, I saw Dr. Tom Price again. He was advancing toward the conference room on his scooter. Finally I was to come face to face with the man who'd written the letter of recommendation I'd read before I wrote mine.

I watched his scooter stop a distance before it reached the conference room door. After he parked the scooter and dismounted, he walked into the room. I was amazed at his ability to ambulate some twenty feet with a prosthetic limb. All chairs at the long table were occupied by resident committee members and Park Place staff except the two between me and another resident. Dr. Price placed his hands, one on each chair arm, and eased himself into the chair beside me. Immediately in a pleasant voice soon to be most familiar to me, he explained to the group, "I'm here as the appointed representative of the Resident Council. You all probably know that one member of the Council is expected to attend each of the resident committee meetings every month."

Was I the only one who didn't know this? No matter. I watched Dr. Tom sit back in his chair and relax, and then I passed an attendance sheet around the table. It was returned to me containing the signatures of six resident committee members including Chairman Stuart and two staff, namely the Director of Nursing at Park Place and Amanda Murray, Manager of Independent Living Assistance. Dr. Price had signed as well. Although attendees glanced his way, expecting his comments, he contributed very little, not interrupting the progress of the meeting.

As I looked at the blank faces of the members and listened to a few of their questions to staff, I realized none, not even Chairman Stuart, understood what transpired in a long-term care facility such as Park Place.

One resident member said, "We all have Medicare. So if we get sick and have to go over to the nursing home here, to Park Place, Medicare will pay for our care."

"That's not quite true," the Director of Nurses said, saying no more and not explaining.

I couldn't just sit there; I had to speak up. The resident was due an explanation. I leaned forward in my chair and addressed her. "If you require skilled care as determined in writing by your physician and after you've been hospitalized for three successive nights, you will qualify for Medicare. But only for a limited number of days while an assessment of your needs is being determined. After that you will continue to qualify for Medicare only if you are improving or being rehabilitated, under a written plan of care, to the point of being able to be discharged. If you are not improving, your Medicare benefits will cease. Then you will be discharged. Or you can stay in the nursing home and pay according to the terms of your contract with Sandycreek Terrace." I glanced at the Director of Nurses, and she nodded.

"Well if I'm not improving, then Medicaid will pay," the resident said confidently.

I shook my head. "Not as long as your contract covers you."

"I don't understand."

"As long as a resident has an adequate source of money, Medicaid doesn't pay. Medicaid is for indigent people and people who have spent down their money in a nursing home and have only a specified amount left." I sat back in my chair, and Stuart, sitting across the table, gave me a look I interpreted to mean I'd said enough. I'd judged correctly because he immediately asked for a report from Amanda Murray.

At the end of the meeting as resident members and staff were leaving, Dr. Tom Price turned to me and said, "I'm glad to meet you, Mrs. Metz."

"I'm glad to meet you, too, Dr. Price," I quickly said. "And please call me Jean," I added with a smile

He put his hand on my arm and said, "Jean, you call me Tom." I would do that, I decided.

The Health Care Committee lacked its allotted ten members. To fill the vacancies, Chairman Stuart solicited residents. One stepping forth was Pam Butcher, my friend from Pine Gardens whose husband, Ben, had died of that massive cerebral vascular accident. I was happy to see her coming into the conference room for our second committee meeting of the new year, but sorry to see she was driving a motorized wheelchair! Had her polio advanced even further to the point of needing to purchase a scooter? She managed it adeptly, driving it up close to the table rather than deserting it for a chair. Not all makes of scooters were constructed to give drivers such an advantage.

Chairman Stuart McKee opened the meeting as soon as all members, the Resident Council's representative Dr. Price, Park Place's Director of Nurses, and Amanda Murray were seated. Tom Price reached behind him to the serving table, lifted up a platter of kitchen-baked cookies—chocolate chip, oatmeal raisin, and macadamia nut—placed it on the conference table, and gave it a shove toward the center.

Stuart first called on the Director of Nurses to give her report of Park Place's activity. As I looked across the conference table at her, I decided I might never get accustomed to nurses not dressing in white nurses' uniforms. I've come to agree nursing caps are archaic. Bobby pins used to gouge my scalp each time I fastened my cap to my hair. But I thought nurses looked unprofessional in those *scrubs* that looked like hospital patient gowns put on backwards.

At any rate, the Director of Nurses was wearing a tan skirt and long-sleeved tangerine sweater. In her Canadian vernacular, she gave the census and enumerated the number of Medicare, Private Pay, Life Care and Medicaid residents currently in Park Place and the number of admissions and discharges during the past thirty days. Then she announced, "State inspectors were here last week for our annual survey. The survey went very well, and we had only five deficiencies. Two were in dietary. Uncovered food was found in the refrigerator and a salt packet was found on a salt-free diet tray. Of the other three deficiencies, one was in activities and the other two had to do with nursing documentation. Nothing serious."

"No medication errors?" Tom Price wanted to know. "We had several during the last inspection because physician orders were misinterpreted, if I recall correctly."

"No med errors, Dr. Price," the Director of Nursing assured him. "Nothing having to do with direct patient care as far as nursing was concerned. Inspectors found two other deficiencies, but we showed them physician orders they had neglected to see. We're very happy about the survey outcome. We've sent in our plan of corrections."

As she passed over a copy of her report to be attached to my minutes, a general mumbling of pleased comments could be heard around the table. For my part, to have five deficiencies with only fifty-one residents in-house was not a record to be cheering. As a former nursing director of a nursing home with a census of two-hundred and forty-eight residents and of a state facility of one thousand beds, I considered even one deficiency too many for this small nursing home unit at Sandycreek Terrace. On the internet, I'd seen a statistical comparison of the number of staff employed in all Florida nursing homes, and the staffing at Park Place was above that required by state regulations, and it was greater than those of other Florida long-term face facilities. Why *any* deficiencies?

Next, Stuart called on Amanda Murray to give her report. This pretty middle-aged matronly woman was smartly dressed in a navy blue suit with white collar and cuffs and a silver-colored chain around her neck. She passed around copies of her report and then read it aloud. "Twenty independent living residents were given care in their apartments and cottages by our staff. Ten received lab service. Three received Medicare services from the agency. Blood pressure screening is scheduled for next Tuesday in the card room from one to two in the afternoon. Last month, one hundred and seventy residents received flu shots."

"You didn't run out of vaccine?" Stuart asked. His soft voice and relaxed position in his chair made me wonder if he was about to fall asleep or was as bored as he sounded and looked.

Amanda Murray smiled and chuckled. "No, we didn't run out, and we took care of every resident who signed up. I hope the vaccine will be more available next year. I hated to wait so long to immunize our residents. But we finally managed to acquire the amount we needed." (Jeff and I had received our flu vaccine at our physician's office, not waiting for the vaccine to arrive at Sandycreek Terrace.)

Stuart turned his head ever so slightly toward Tom Price, "Have you anything to add, Dr. Price?"

Tom shook his head. "No, I don't believe so," he said, his strong voice resonating.

I looked over at Stuart across the table. "May I ask a question?"

He smiled and nodded.

My eyes on the Director of Nurses, I asked, "When do you expect the surveyors to return for their follow-up inspection?"

"I should have mentioned that," she said, not appearing to be intimidated by my question or her negligence in addressing what I considered necessary information for committee members. They certainly needed to know that the annual inspection didn't end with the citing of deficiencies. They needed to know that something would be required to rectify the non-compliance of five regulations. "In two weeks," she continued, her unblinking eyes looking at me with interest. Of course she knew I'd been a state surveyor. Did she know I asked the question so committee members would be aware that another inspection would take place to check on compliance with the cited deficiencies? Members of this committee had a right to know this and to know if surveyors found the deficiencies corrected. I felt Dr. Tom knew why I asked because he looked at me and winked.

"If no one has anything else to add, the meeting is adjourned," Stuart announced in his sleepy voice. "The next meeting will be held the third Wednesday of next month."

The platter of cookies had sat untouched, everyone hesitating to be first to partake, I supposed. With the adjournment of the meeting, Pam reached over to the platter and removed the saran wrap cover. "I'm told these will get thrown out if we don't eat them," she said.

"That's right. So everyone should help himself," Tom Price advised.

At that point, a number of hands reached over the table to the cookies, mine included. I picked up some napkins from the serving table, gave one to Pam, and we wrapped several to take home—to avoid their being thrown out, of course. In fact, I helped myself to three, another for myself and two for Jeff.

I continued to have a problem learning names, names of employees as well as names of residents. Names seemed to go in one ear and out the other. Perhaps I just wasn't paying attention. Had nothing to do with hearing the names because I had acute hearing. Could it be my memory? Was I getting as bad as those residents bartender Amelia told us about? The ones who forgot to go to the scheduled memory class? No, I didn't think so. I just needed to concentrate, repeat the name three times to myself, or relate the name to someone I knew by that name.

As we sat in the lounge sipping our pre-dinner cocktails one evening, I said to Jeff, "Who is that woman standing by the piano?"

"The woman in the green dress? You know her. We've eaten with her and her husband," he said, studying me with his blue eyes.

"Well, I *don't* know her. I can see that her hair is gray. Most of the women have white hair, permed and kinky. They all look pretty much alike and dress alike. A number of them have the same matronly shape. Except the thin ones and the few obese ones. So who *is* she? She's thin."

"That's Judith Schreiber. I guess it's your eyes, Honey. You just can't see that far away." He fished in the dish of mixed nuts for a cashew then pushed the dish my way over the table.

"Judith Schreiber? That's right. She always wears dresses. I should have recognized her for that reason. From her dress. All of us females used to wear dresses before slacks became popular. She's out of the hospital? She was having kidney problems, I heard. Nephritis. I like her a lot. Remember when we went to their cottage for cocktails and those yummy homemade crabmeat squares? I was going to get the recipe from her, and I never did. You didn't care for her husband."

"Anti-U.S.," Jeff growled. "Why did he come here to live when he finds everything wrong? Has nothing good to say about our government." He grabbed the bowl and fished for another cashew and chewed it with deliberation.

Because Jeff gave thirty-three years of his life to the U.S. Navy, I understood his loyalty and intolerance of anyone's adverse comments about our country.

Yes, I had to admit some of the problem I had recognizing faces was my inability to see due to my optic nerve having been damaged by inadequate medication to control my intraocular pressure and misdiagnosis of my glaucoma when I was forty-two. A recent diagnosis of beginning age-related macular degeneration hadn't made me very happy but as yet hadn't adversely affected my vision. Otherwise I considered myself perfectly healthy except for slight hypothyroidism and a degree of osteoporosis, both being subjected to medication and neither slowing me down. Oh, I forgot to mention my pacemaker. My cardiologist required it be checked every two months, and it was always in ship-shape condition. Two sides and a corner of the pacemaker protruded beneath my skin and made a noticeable lump on the left side of my chest below my clavicle. But I wasn't planning on entering any beauty contest so it didn't matter. It wouldn't have been noticeable at all if I'd had more fat on my bones.

I looked over at Jeff sipping his drink and smiled thinking how extremely understanding he was about my poor vision. I could read headlines. He read articles of interest in newspapers and magazines to me, as well as reading my personal and business letters where the printing was small and/or faint. I've never known a person so patient and loving. Ours was a wonderful second marriage, a sharing one. How could I be so fortunate? But I feared I would outlive him. I tried not to think of that possibility although most wives outlived their husbands. Certainly a number of them lived at Sandycreek Terrace.

A couple of the times something triggered a reference to our ages Jeff had said, "We're going to live to be a hundred, maybe more. We're the world's oldest teenagers."

I had laughed at that. "It's our good genes. My mother lived to be ninety-four and yours also ninety some. But when we die I want us to die at the same time. In an airplane or car accident."

"That's what we'll do," he had promised me with a kiss.

My thoughts were interrupted by an approaching couple stopping at our little table.

"Mind if we join you?" loud words spewed forth from the tall, heavy-set stern-faced man in a brown vested suit. He was accompanied by a small smiling woman wearing a printed dress.

"No, no. Come right ahead. Sit down. Sit down. Join us," Jeff offered, looking up at the couple and motioning to the two empty chairs at our table.

"We're the Summners. I'm Greg and this is my wife, Shirley," the loud voice continued. "We're new here. Just came yesterday."

Jeff rose to half stance and said, "I'm Jeff Metz and this is Jean, my wife."

Smiling, Shirley sat down and arranged her dress, straightening the skirt over her knees while husband Greg eased himself into the other chair filling it from arm to arm. "How do you like it here?" the loud voice questioned.

After observing Greg Summners' paunchy jowls, my eyes dropped down to his protruding abdomen, and I knew I was staring at it and, in my mind, comparing it with Jeff's non-existent waist-line. I worried about Jeff's weight and feared he might reach Greg's extensive proportions some day. He needed to lose weight, but he loved to eat. "I like see food," he'd joke. "I see food. I eat food."

In a confident manner, Jeff was saying, "We like it here very much. It's a great place to live!"

"What was that you said?" Greg's loud voice caused others in the lounge to turn heads in our direction.

His wife said, "He said we'll like it here." Then in a lower voice, eyebrows raised, she continued as though needing reassurance, "You *do* like it here?"

I raised my voice, now cognizant of Greg's hearing deficit. "Yes indeed. I'm sure you will, too. Where did you live before you came here?" I asked, to make conversation, unaware the answer would trigger a confrontation.

"Originally lived in Pittsburgh," Greg boomed.

I perked up. "I'm a Pittsburgher," I proudly announced.

"We lived in Squirrel Hill. You know Squirrel Hill?" he asked me, leaning forward in his chair as best his weight would allow.

"I certainly do," I acknowledged, smiling at him.

"Lots of Jews live there. They're smart people. Made friends with many of them. Good friends. Wealthy people," he said, no reflection in his voice, but still decibels too loud.

"Yes," I agreed. "I knew people who lived there. Physicians. I worked for them at one time and liked them very much." I glanced at Shirley, patiently sitting with her hands folded in her lap and listening.

"I hear your son is governor of Pennsylvania." Greg was practically shouting.

"No, no," I said. Not my son. My nephew through marriage. My first husband's brother's son." I tried to keep my voice fairly low so as not to attract attention. I had a feeling residents near us in the lounge were listening to every word. I had to repeat in a much louder voice, however, in order to make Greg hear me. "How did you know I was related to the governor?" I was curious as I hadn't mentioned Tom and our relationship to many of the residents. And the Summners had just arrived.

"First people we met said people by the name of Metz had a son who was governor of Pennsylvania. Guess he gets his name in the Pittsburgh Press a lot."

I shook my head. "The Press has been out of business for years. The Post Gazette is the only newspaper in the city now."

"No, no," he contradicted. "The Post Gazette is the morning paper. The Pittsburgh Press is the evening paper. The *main* Pittsburgh paper."

"It used to be. But it hasn't existed for years. The Post Gazette is the only paper." I persisted but it was useless. This Greg knew or thought he knew everything about my city.

"You have your facts all wrong. The Press. That's the paper."

Thankfully, the Summners were approached by a hostess in the ubiquitous black-skirt-and-white-blouse uniform of dining room staff and were informed their table was ready. As the Summners rose to go to the dining room, Greg bellowed to the hostess, "Thank you very much. Thank you very much."

Jeff and I had been waiting for a window table and were now escorted to one a distance from Greg and Shirley. Nevertheless, we continued to hear, "Thank you very much. Thank you very much," every time a server set an item on the Summner's table.

TWELVE

FINAL

After dinner in the Club House, Jeff and I always parted at the reception desk, and Jeff walked out the front door to board Liza's transportation to ride home. I, in turn, happily walked around the corner to the double glass doors that opened automatically when anyone approached. Then I walked over a boardwalk past the front of the Palace, turned and went along the corridors protected overhead by the floors of the second-floor corridors. I passed the windows, blue doors, and yellow stucco-walls of resident apartments and glanced at the tiny courtyards in between. Each courtyard was filled with live palms—several low-growing sabal palms and one or two Chinese fan palms that reached up to and above the second floor apartments. In addition, all the courtyards contained little low-growing green plants and bright flowers. I liked the ones filled with white lilies. A number of in-the-ground lights cast their beams to the side and up the trunks of the palm trees. The lizards had gone to bed for the night, I supposed. During the day when I walked down the corridors one of those lizards would see or maybe hear my heavy foot approach and dart into the grass to hide, like a frightened child running to its mother's arms. Often I caught up with several single women slowly wheeling walkers and chatting together on their way home from dinner.

"Pardon me," I'd say, alerting them to my approaching presence. "May I pass you by? And did you have a nice dinner?"

"Oh hello there. Yes we did have a good dinner, thank you," was their response.

Many residents were single, more women than men, of course, and they seemed to enjoy their lives here. They made friends, paired up for meals, and went to activities together. If I were single, which I would never want to be, who among them would I want as a friend? I've looked at them and judged, unfairly perhaps, and then blocked out the thought of living without my man. I was thankful Jeff was in good health, except for his back pain. He needed to lose pounds, but, as I said, he loved to eat. Although he couldn't walk far, he could ride his two-wheeled bike without any pain, and this he did many mornings when I took my walk. He left the premises, rode across a main road into a retirement community, and sped along their five-mile-an-hour roads. I feared he would lose his balance, but, as I watched him, he appeared quite adept. What's to be will be.

Since the weekly newsletter contained menus for the current week, usually we'd plan on what to order in advance. Always five entrees were on the menu along with optional unseasoned chicken and catch of the day. Today after Jeff read the menu, we were having difficulty making a decision, which was often the case.

"What shall it be?" Jeff asked me as we sat at the kitchenette table eating the homemade vegetable beef soup he'd prepared for lunch. "The stuffed sole or the tenderloin tips?"

"I had fish last night. Guess I'll have the tenderloin tips tonight," I decided.

"I believe I will, too. They were good last time I had them," Jeff said, buttering his heated roll.

Residents who went to early dinner were leaving the dining room when we arrived that evening at six. We decided to ask several what they had to eat and if it was tasty. The first couple scowled and said, "We had tenderloin tips. They were tough as nails. Couldn't chew them! Don't recommend them."

We then asked the same question of the next couple walking toward us. "We had the tenderloin tips. Wonderful! Best they've ever been," they responded, smiling.

"They weren't tough?" we asked.

"Not at all. Melt in your mouth!" they said, still smiling.

So it all depended on your teeth or your point of view, and their responses left us without a clue. We decided to take the risk and order tenderloin tips.

The next evening, Donald Jordan was at the far end of the lounge looking pale and very thin. With him were wife Doris and their three sons all dressed in dark suits. At the piano, their minister daughter was just starting to play her father's favorite songs, and all were singing except for Doris who stood listening. Perhaps she had no singing voice. Everyone in the lounge stopped talking to listen. The family sang six songs, Donald's voice becoming ever weaker. Then they left, not staying for dinner.

One week later, we saw a single red rose and white baby-breath in a vase on the front desk. "Who?" we asked the receptionist.

"Mr. Jordan," she answered softly.

Then down the corridor across from the library on the small half-table usually decorated with a potted plant, we saw Donald's photo in a frame and beside it, also framed, the death notice and an announcement of a memorial service to be held in the Palace the next week.

We attended, of course, and were handed programs at the Palace door. On the front of the program Donald's photograph gave us a start. Such a likeness! The exact way he looked when we first met him! We took seats in two of the many set up in rows across the front third of the auditorium. In the far front on the left side, resident Sarah Grant was playing hymns on a piano. Apparently the lounge piano had been moved to the auditorium. The daughter, standing at the lectern, started the service with a Bible reading. In turn, each son rose, went to the lectern, and talked at length about memories of his father. Sarah played hymns, and attendees sang. The daughter recalled her memories of her father and then said a closing prayer.

Without our having noticed, the sons, relatives, and close friends had slipped to the back of the auditorium and now came forward, one by one, each carrying a red rose and placing it in a vase on the lectern. The bouquet thus formed was outstanding. Everyone was then invited to partake of the food already prepared in the kitchen, brought to the Palace, and arranged on long tables set up along the back wall of the room. On one side, another table, well stocked, served as a bar. Jeff and I chose one of the many tables positioned in the back two-thirds and along the sides of the room. We sat there enjoying drinks and snacks and watching the Jordan grandchildren at a nearby table as they giggled and gobbled up the food they'd loaded on their plates.

After dinner the next evening, Jeff and I paused to read the announcements posted on the bulletin board near the front desk. "See here, Jeanie" Jeff said to me. "That Sarah Grant's not only known for her piano playing. She's also Chairman of the Symposium. Here's her announcement as Chairman. At the next Symposium, she' going to introduce the speaker, a retired army general. He's a resident, and he's going to speak about his World War II experiences in the European theater. That's a subject of great interest to me. I'd like to attend. It's being held in the Palace on Friday at seven-thirty in the evening."

The next afternoon after lunch while I was clearing the kitchenette table, Jeff was reading the February edition of the *Periscope*. I'd found the monthly Sandycreek Terrace magazine in our facility mail box on my way back from my walk that morning. Jeff said, "This Sarah resident who plays the piano and chairs the Symposium also writes the Resident of the Month column in the *Periscope*. Did you know that?"

"Is that right? I'll have to read that column, or maybe you could read it to me. Does she write well?"

Since Jeff had been editor of a local weekly newspaper, a string reporter for three daily metropolitan newspapers, editor of his college newspaper, and was also very well read, he often critiqued articles in *U.S. News and World Report* and any other reading material at his disposal.

"Look here," he'd say to me. "This editor doesn't know how to spell. Used the verb lay instead of lie. Guess the subject's going to lay eggs. Here's another. A plural noun with a singular verb. Four of them is going."

His pet peeve was the use of the word America instead of the United States. "When will the news media learn to write and to say in news broadcasts *the United States*. How arrogant! South America is also America! We are *the United States*! Our nation is. We don't have a monopoly on the word *America*."

"Does anyone in South America care?" I'd asked.

"Of course they care!" he'd answered.

I always had Jeff critique the nursing articles I wrote before I sent them to the editor when given the nod to send them. Jeff's recommendations were invaluable.

At any rate, when I asked him about Sarah's writing he said, "She could do better. Rambles too much."

Gossip had it—yes, there was gossip here—that Sarah's husband died shortly after they moved into Sandycreek Terrace. She moved out of her apartment for a time and went to live with her daughter. Ever since she came back here to live, legend had it, she'd been very unhappy, grieving inwardly, and had buried herself in writing a book. Her career in social work gave her incentive and material to start writing her experiences. Any time we saw Sarah, she was always very serious, like she had the problems of the president on her shoulders. Never smiled. Would she smile at one of Jeff's jokes?

Serious Sarah saw me in the library one afternoon, approached me, and asked, "Do you know I write an article in the *Periscope* every month called Resident of the Month? I choose the resident and interview him or her and then write the article. With the resident's approval, of course."

I answered with a smile, hoping to get a smile in return, "Yes, Sarah. I'm aware of that. I enjoy your articles." I kept Jeff's opinion of her writing to myself.

She continued without smiling, "I'd like to interview you for the Resident of the Month article for the March issue of the *Periscope.*"

I was shocked and said, "Oh, Sarah, I hardly qualify to be written up in the *Periscope*. I've only been here three months!"

"Indeed you do qualify. More than most of the residents here. I want to interview your husband, too, but I'll wait a few months for that. I don't think it would be a good idea to introduce the two of you so close together."

I nodded, and she continued, "You've led a very interesting professional life. When would it be convenient for us to get together for me to interview you?"

I had an inspiration and said, "What I could do is give you a copy of my resume, and then we can go from there. How would that be?" I raised my eyebrows and waited for her answer.

"Wonderful," she said, in her businesslike manner.

I expected to be interviewed after she read my resume, but instead she wrote the article from the information in my resume. After she gave me the article to read, I gave it to Jeff to pass judgment and then added a few personal items such as number of children, grandchildren, great grandchildren, and a mention of my famous nephew, Governor Ridge of Pennsylvania. When Sarah learned about Tom, such a famous relative, she thought, she was quite impressed and insisted details about him be included. With that, off the article went to be printed in the March *Periscope.*

THIRTEEN
PERISCOPE

Jeff and I were sitting in the second row of seats in the Palace attending the February monthly Executive Director's meeting. I had a fairly good view of the Executive Director, a tall young pleasant-speaking man, always dressed in a business suit, white shirt, and tie, appropriate for his position. First he introduced the employee of the month, read excerpts from the article about the employee printed in the *Periscope*, presented her with a certificate, and shook her hand. All present clapped, and the obviously embarrassed woman covered her face with her certificate and hurriedly left the room.

He then introduced the resident of the month, following the same agenda as he had for the employee. The gaunt and spare former governor of Panama bowed his head, accepted the certificate, shook hands with the Executive Director, and stepped to the lectern. In a cracking voice he said, "I accept this certificate with gratitude and, after living here for six years, have to say Sandycreek Terrace is a fine establishment. I would not want to spend my latter years elsewhere." He bowed again, smiled at the audience, and walked hesitantly to his seat leaning on his cane. Enthusiastic clapping followed. After that, Marketing Director Virginia Friedman announced the number of sales for the past month and number and types of available units. Next, the administrator of Park Place, a recently hired young man, presented his report. He was replacing Mr. Valenzuela who had left to fill an executive position at the owners' company headquarters. In his report, he described the activity of the past month as to current number of Life Care, Medicare, Medicaid, and private pay residents, number of empty beds, expected number of admissions, and other pertinent facts about Park Place. Following that, the Manager of Independent Living Assistance, Amanda Murray, reported on her staff's activity for the past month. This included number of staff providing care, number of independent living residents receiving care, number of laboratory tests, and number of agency Medicare visits.

"Jeanie, do you understand what Amanda Murray means by Lab tests and agency Medicare visits that independent living residents like us receive?" Jeff asked me.

"Some of the residents are ordered lab work by their physicians. Maybe fasting. So if they're not able to get to a lab or prefer to have their blood drawn here early in the morning rather than go to a lab in town, Amanda arranges for a technician to draw their blood here. As for agency Medicare visits, if one of us residents is ordered physical therapy for strengthening and balancing exercises after hip replacement, say. Or is ordered nursing care to monitor a cardiac condition after by-pass surgery or apply sterile dressings to a wound, for example. That's after we're discharged from the hospital or from Park Place, and we're home. Amanda will arrange with her agency contact to send a physical therapist or registered nurse to our apartment."

"So Medicare pays for this physical therapist or registered nurse?" Jeff arched his eyebrows.

"For a limited time. Until a plateau is reached. An evaluation is done. Usually two or three weeks are the max. Then if a resident or a family wants more therapy or nursing care, that resident has to pay out of pocket."

"That sounds reasonable," Jeff said, turning his attention back to the meeting.

In khaki trousers, solid tan dress-shirt, tweed sport coat, and tie, Dr. Tom Price was handed the microphone by the Executive Director. As before, he sat up front in his motorized scooter. He gave a Florida Life Care Residents Association (FLiCRA) report and described his involvement with meetings in Tallahassee and other cities where he'd lobbied in the interest of all Florida CCRCs. Most of his concern today dealt with pending state legislative bills and financial issues. He presented his report in a clear concise articulate manner, readily heard by all the residents, even those with hearing impairments.

"Now there's a man who makes things happen," Jeff said looking over at me and continuing, "A professor of mine once said, 'There are people who make things happen, people who watch things happen, and people who wonder what happened.'"

Pensive, I said, "I never thought of it that way, but I guess it's true,"

Following Tom's report, the Executive Director addressed various resident concerns such as hurricane damage repair, plans for future landscaping, and food service improvement. He concluded by asking if any of the residents had questions.

A short painfully thin resident rose. Her aged voice rasped, "We just had a raise in our maintenance fee. It was less than I expected. But I'm concerned about next year. Will it be increased again? Many of us are on fixed incomes."

Via a microphone that he had just attached to his lapel, the Executive Director repeated the question for all to hear and then answered, "I expect the cost of living will go up. It goes up every year, and the owner has no way of stopping it." He smiled, and a few titters could be heard throughout the room. "We make adjustments with your fixed incomes in mind and increase minimally and only as necessary, I assure you." This started a barrage of questions Jeff and I listened to and considered picky and insignificant.

A month later at the March meeting in the Palace, there I was, standing nervous and self conscious beside the Executive Director at the lectern while he read excerpts from my article in the *Periscope* and presented me with a certificate. Everyone in the room clapped, as was expected of them, and, after thanking Sarah Grant for her article, I gratefully, probably not gracefully, found my seat and sank into it. Beside me Jeff patted my hand as though to say he was proud of me, I believe.

Wednesdays were Maid Marigold days, and this was Wednesday. We expected her to arrive around nine. So as soon as we woke up we said, "Up and at 'em. We have to strip the bed!" Jeff tore the pillow case and zippered cover from his feather-filled pillow. He pulled out the top and bottom sheets from under the mattress on his side of the bed. After I went through the same procedure on my side, I gathered bedclothes and other flat linens needing to be laundered and stuck them in the washer. Then I gaily said, "Have to clear the tables so Marigold can dust. I'll take care of the Florida room table cause most of the things there are mine. Of course I'll leave my beautiful flowers there. She can just move the vase to glass-wax the table top. Those red roses look perfect in the cut-glass vase that belonged to your grandmother. I'm so glad she gave it to you. And thanks again, Honey, for giving me roses for my birthday. They've opened up a little since Monday."

When the antique vase wasn't in use we kept it in the large étagère that had belonged to Jeff. The upper part was four-sectioned with glass doors and shelves filled with Lladro statues, ornate glass dishes, carved African animals, antique pitchers, and Japanese tea pots—treasures with deep meaning to either Jeff or to me. The tall cut-glass vase wasn't the only vase displayed, but it was the most beautiful. When it was in use I moved another object into its place to fill the space. Other pieces of furniture had belonged to Jeff, and many had belonged to me. Now, as I said, we considered them ours.

As usual, the dining room table was spread with stamps like a crazy quilt. "I'm going to leave the dining room table as it is," Jeff said. "I'm sure Marigold won't touch it if I leave it this way. She'll see it as a *do not touch* table."

"Fine," I said, knowing that, in the rare event the stamps had been stashed away for a few days rest, other items belonging to Jeff would appear on the table in their place. In that case, I'd tactfully inquire of Jeff, "How about these things on the dining room table? Do you want me to pile them on top of each other so Marigold can dust the cleared space?" I never discarded anything of his, not even an old grocery list even though I thought it was of no earthly value. It just might have a phone number jotted down on the back. We have this unspoken understanding—the owner of whatever it is decides when to trash whatever it is.

"No, I'll take care of them," Jeff would say and throw out what he didn't want and pile the rest on his desk in the den.

The other thing I undertook to do was pick up one or two pairs of Jeff's shoes (often stuffed with a pair of socks) from the dining room floor and place them on a dining room chair to give Marigold access to run her sweeper uninterrupted. When the washer completed its cycle I placed the clean laundry in the dryer. Marigold would remove it when she came, make our bed, and fold the remaining linens. Yes, I succumbed. I was now allowing Maid Marigold to make the bed, a task I had vowed was mine and mine alone. The first couple times, however, I made the bed *with* Marigold, just to make sure she knew how I liked it made. I wasn't so sure she wouldn't have made it my way without my lead. She'd been well taught. I imagine management expected residents to have at least two sets of bed linens, one in the closet for a maid to make the bed and a set on the bed that the maid would remove and place in the washer. My way was better, you see. Even though we had to strip the bed and put the dirty linens in the washer and transfer them clean into the dryer, I was afforded the luxury of not having to fold the linens! Any attempt to fold fitted sheets was a direct cause of hypertension, in my opinion.

A week seemed to fly by and it was Wednesday again. After getting the soiled laundry into the washer, clearing tables for Marigold to dust, and generally tidying the apartment, Jeff and I performed our routine twenty-minute stretching exercises. I didn't go for my usual daily walk nor did Jeff ride his bike. Time didn't allow on Marigold days. Instead, Jeff started preparing breakfast while I inserted my medicated eye drops. When I walked into the kitchen Jeff was placing two bowls of oatmeal on the kitchenette table. Already on the table were two glasses of orange juice, brown sugar, my tea, and his coffee. Then Jeff removed a pitcher of heated milk from the microwave and brought it to the table.

"Looks like we're having another good breakfast," I said, sitting down on my designated side of the table. Funny how, once chosen, a seat seems to be automatically and forever delegated or owned, as it were.

"After I get my morning kiss," Jeff said, leaning over and planting his lips on mine.

We had just finished eating when, on the stroke of nine, we heard Marigold's cleaning wagon clicking and clacking as it rolled up the corridor to our front door. Then the door bell rang, the door opened, and a cheery, "Good mornin'!" reached our ears.

"Good morning, Marigold," we both greeted her. "How are you this morning?" Jeff asked.

"I's fine. I's fine," she said, beaming and laughing as she brought in her black upright electric-sweeper, white string mop, and turquoise bucket of cleaning supplies from her cart. The first thing she did was gather up trash from our wastebaskets and our old papers piled near the door and throw them into a large canvas container propped upright on her cart.

"Your hair looks very nice this morning. Did *you* fix it?" I asked, studying the massive ringlets, black as first Fords, covering her head, each curl like a cork-screw.

"No, no," she laughed. "My daughter, my daughter. She fix," her Haitian English answered. She understood me only if I spoke slowly and used simple words and sign language, holding up my fingers to indicate numbers or to point.

To give her full range of the apartment, Jeff and I went into the den. Jeff read the morning newspaper while I tried to complete the crossword puzzle I'd started the day before.

Marigold took her equipment to the far end of the apartment, and, when I heard the dryer door scrape open I knew she was removing the linens, would make the bed first, clean the bedroom, and then the master bath. In time, we heard the buzz of the electric sweeper as it moved over the living and dining room carpet and approached the den. "I come in?" she asked with a broad smile, standing at the door to the den, sweeper in hand.

"Just the carpet inside the door and in front of the desk," I said, swinging my arm over the area I had in mind. I pointed to Jeff's desk covered three-deep with papers, pens, stapler, scissors, books, stamp dispenser, and ruler. "No dust," I instructed.

She laughed; her head bobbed up and down. "Yes, yes, I know," she said.

When she was finished she called out, "Good-bye!"

Both Jeff and I called back to her, "Good-bye, Marigold. Thank you for coming."

She did a fine job of cleaning, and I had the utmost trust in her. My jewelry box was always unlocked on my dresser top and my purse in sight on my filing cabinet. If Jeff and I planned to be away from the apartment when she was due to arrive, we'd leave the door unlocked and attach a note to the outside of the door advising her to enter.

One day I heard one of the residents say, "I won't have my maid come if I'm not going to be home."

Another time I heard, "I always lock up my jewelry when my maid comes."

Still another time a resident told me, "My maid never dusts, not even the tops of the furniture. I can tell, because I run my finger across the tops of my furniture, and my finger's powered with dust."

I smiled to myself, thankful our maid was trustworthy, conscientious, hard-working Marigold. Marigold cleans McKee's apartment after she cleans ours. One day Ruth told me Marigold was a single mother with two children, a daughter and a younger son who had learning disabilities. How sad! Amazing how she could be so cheerful all the time!

I'd noticed that Ruth had a knack of getting to know people and then making friends with them and learning all about them, an admirable trait that I didn't possess. I always felt fortunate to have Ruth as a neighbor because otherwise I wouldn't be as well informed.

One Sunday morning after returning from church, Jeff and I changed into every-day clothes and settled ourselves in the Florida room. Jeff intended to read the Sunday newspaper and I planned to read a nursing magazine with a magnifying glass. Outside, the sky was overcast and little light was coming through the windows and the glass door leading to the patio. Jeff flipped on the ceiling light, looked up, and stood there studying the light. "These lights aren't bright enough for you, are they? These," he said, pointing up to the combined fan and light fixture. "The ones in the den don't seem very bright lately either. Do you think they are?"

I looked up at the lights and said, "Not really. Even though there are four bulbs up there, they seem dim. Maybe we could replace them with higher wattage bulbs," I suggested.

The increasingly loud shrieking blasts of an emergency vehicle made us stop talking. We stood still and listened while the siren grew louder and then suddenly stopped. "They turned into Sandycreek Terrace," Jeff said.

"I guess so," I said, frowning. "The paramedics are instructed to turn off the sirens when they enter the gate, I understand."

"Yep. To ease residents' minds. But they hear it anyway."

"I know. It terrorizes me. I stop what I'm doing and listen to hear if the siren keeps shrieking. If it does, I know 911 has gone somewhere else. If it stops, I know it drove into Sandycreek Terrace and wonder, who is it this time? What resident's in trouble, and how much trouble? I even wonder it they're dead." I think all the residents hold their breaths because they've heard the siren and know if it ceases paramedics are on the grounds hurrying to one of the residents. It seems we hear these sirens almost every day any more," I ventured to say, sighing.

Jeff corrected, "Maybe every week. Well, back to the matter at hand." He looked up at the light fixture again. "You're right. Changing the light bulbs would help, would make a significant difference. I'm sure John or Matt will change the light bulbs. We just have to make out a work request. I'll go over to the front desk and do that. Possibly I can find out something about the 911 call."

John of John and Matt called the next day. On the phone he said to me, "We got your work request, Mrs. Metz. We always call before we come. Is this a convenient time for us to come?"

Now they stood in our Florida room, Matt leaning on the step ladder he'd brought, and both men looking up at the light and fan fixture. "Won't work," John said, shaking his head. "That type of fixture mandates no greater than sixty watt bulbs. And that's what's in there now."

"What're we going to do?" Jeff asked, looking at him with blue eyes wide open.

"I hate to tell you this, but you're gonna have to buy a different kind of fixture. That is, if you wanna spend the money," he added with a frown and a shrug.

"Hells' fire! Jeanie has to see! Guess we can get them at Home Depot?" Jeff queried both men with raised brows.

"That's the best place *we've* found," Matt offered.

"Just make sure you get the ones marked for hundred watt bulbs. And when you get them, give us a call. We'll come take these down and put up the new ones. In fact, we'll get the new ones out of your car and bring them in to the apartment. Just give us a call," John said.

When they were gone I remarked, "Aren't they the greatest pair? Who could ask for more?" I meant it.

"They are great, and that's what we pay for. That's why we're here. You understand that, don't you, Jeanie?" he said, wanting me to agree and giving me a hug.

In return, I squeezed him, felt his solid familiar body in my arms, and gave him a kiss, acknowledging this was a great service, and we had it because of *his* decision to be here.

"Might as well go shopping right now, don't you think?" Jeff announced, making up our minds just like that. Shortly, we were off to Home Depot to buy two new light-with-fan fixtures costing little more than the old ones, much to our amazement.

The next day, John and Matt were here again with stepladder and tools kibitzing as they had when taking away our glass table-top. Matt was saying to John standing on the stepladder under the fixture, "Ya gotta take that part off first. Who taught ya, anyway?"

John ignored Matt's question and said, "Hand me the screwdriver."

"Geez, ya have the screwdriver in yer belt. Can't ya keep track a yer tools? How about yer head? Can ya keep track a that?" And so on they joked until the jobs in both rooms were completed. They'd adeptly removed the old fixtures, affixing the new ones, stashing the old fixtures in the empty cartons, and carting them off.

When I answered the ringing phone one early afternoon it was Tom Price saying, "Jeanie, can you come to an Ethics Committee meeting in the conference room in an hour?"

In an hour? Short notice! However, I said I could. But, an Ethics Committee meeting? I had never heard of such a committee! No such committee was listed along with all the other committees that were printed in the *Periscope*, our monthly resident publication.

I made my way along the pale yellow walls of the corridor, past court yards, apartment windows and blue doors decked with wreaths of various kinds and into the Club House conference room located behind the reception desk. I was last to arrive and dropped into an empty chair at the conference table. I looked around and saw Tom first. As my eyes darted around observing other faces at the table, I recognized Park Place's Director of Nursing, and Amanda Murray. Four others, two men and two women, were unfamiliar. Almost immediately Tom said, "Before we discuss the ethical issue, I suggest we go around the table and introduce ourselves."

That's when I learned one of the men was Medical Director of Park Place, the other man a Chaplain. One woman was the nursing unit's substitute Social Service Director, and the other woman a Human Resources Director and HIPAA/Compliance Officer. As I listened to the conversations of several administrative staff, I learned the issue before the Ethics Committee today involved a resident in Park Place, formerly living in one of Sandycreek Terrace's independent living apartments with his wife. The resident was a cigarette smoker. Apparently residents were only permitted to smoke in a certain designated area frequented by staff. Supervision was required for careless smokers. This was a followed practice, not a written policy, I learned. It appeared the resident's wife, still living in an independent living apartment, was bringing her husband cigarettes and matches and leaving him to smoke unattended in his room whenever he wished. The wife was advised, nicely, to refrain from bringing in cigarettes or, if she did, to give them to the staff so the smoking could take place in the designated area. The wife refused. Continued requests by staff and refusal by the wife resulted in a confrontation between an irate vocal wife and the supervisor who threatened to prohibit the wife further visitation. To try to resolve this frustrating situation, this Ethics meeting was called today. Being the only non-staff person present, other than Tom who was also a practicing physician and well known for his importance to CCRCs as a member of FLiCRA, I wondered why I'd been invited to sit in on this dilemma. So I listened quietly to the explanations by the Director of Nursing, the substitute Social Service Director, and the Human Resources Director who appeared to be a company administrative employee. When all present turned and looked at me for some input, without hesitation because of my nursing home background, I guess, I immediately asked, "Is this resident a careless smoker? Do any hot ashes drop onto his clothes? Is there reason to be concerned about his smoking habits?"

I watched heads shake after each of my questions, and the Director of Nursing answered, "Not really. He's neat, never any ashes on his clothes.

He uses an ashtray. He doesn't smoke his cigarettes all the way down, and he puts them out carefully."

With this information and knowing all rooms were private, I was satisfied the resident smoker was not at risk nor was he a risk. I looked around at the concerned faces, visualized the regulations, and said. "The federal regulations in the section on Resident Rights state that residents have the right to engage in all activities as long as they do not harm themselves or others. He, therefore, has the right to smoke in his own room as long as you've determined he won't harm himself or others."

"Is that right?" the Human Resources Director said as though in disbelief.

So I continued, "You do need to have a written policy on smoking. And it should be read to all residents and family members on admission of any resident. The policy could state smoking under supervision only, if that's what you decide. That could include family or staff supervision. And in designated areas which could include the resident's room if the room is a private one. Of course a clause should be added to prohibit smoking where oxygen is in use."

That seemed to satisfy, or at least I guessed it did, since the meeting ended, and I was thanked for my input.

Fourteen

Activities

Jeff had made bacon, lettuce, and tomato sandwiches for lunch, and we'd made fast work of them and were munching on the chocolate chip cookies I'd *confiscated* from the Health Care Committee meeting yesterday. With Scottish judgment, I continued to bring home cookies from the meetings to prevent their being thrown out since committee members never emptied the platter sent to the conference room in advance of the meeting. Pam Butcher always joined me in this endeavor, both of us wrapping a few in paper napkins and carrying them home.

"I know you prefer oatmeal raisin, Jeff. But the kitchen sent chocolate chip and sugar cookies to the meeting. No oatmeal raisin," I said.

"That's the way it goes. These will do just fine. Didn't cost anything, did they?" was his frugal reply.

I laughed. "Always the miser," I said.

"I'm not a miser. We buy what we want and need. Reuderts and lollies."

It tickled me to hear those non-words Jeff injected into his conversation from time to time. He'd explained they were universal words meaning nothing, words he'd learned in the service from a junior grade.

"But it's not my nature to throw money away," he said and continued, reiterating the past experiences I'd heard before. "I've lived through the depression. My father went broke after he was a millionaire. I worked in a pickle factory to have money to get through college. I learned the worth of a dollar the hard way. I respect money. I don't want to be without it, so I won't spend it foolishly." His expression serious, he looked across the

113

table at me. "You laugh at me buying from Haband. Their clothes wear well, and they don't cost an arm and a leg."

"But they don't have style," I chided.

"Style, schmile. Who cares? They cover me."

I shrugged. Useless to argue, to get him to shop at nice local men's stores or department stores. And he refused to let *me* buy him clothes, much as I wanted to. I loved to shop for clothes, not for food. Jeff liked to shop for food, not for clothes. When his clothes came through the mail from Haband I watched him open the packages. Sometimes he'd pull out a pair of ordinary looking shoes. No style. Sometimes three flannelette shirts, exactly the same only different colors. Ordinary, farmer style.

All this isn't to say I didn't know the worth of a dollar or understand Jeff's point of view. I'd scrimped and saved when I was young. Put money out of every paycheck into a savings account, bought nothing for myself, and saved for a car. When I was married and raising three children the only purchase I made for myself one year was a tube of lipstick. Now that I had a little money, I spent it on good fashionable clothes. I mixed and matched the clothes in my closet, and residents, male and female, complimented me on my outfits. Perhaps my ego needed this.

When I married Jeff I quickly learned how he felt about money, his money and how he guarded it. How we would have managed finances as a married couple if I hadn't been financially independent, I have no idea because I liked to buy good fashionable clothes. Even though Jeff's assets far exceeded mine, since he knew about mine, he had said, in all seriousness, "I think it's only fair we set up a joint bank account with funds from both your and my social security checks to pay for household expenses. I'll handle my car expenses, and I suppose you will do the same with your Volvo."

"And I guess we'll file separately to the IRS, paying our own quarterly estimated taxes," I'd said, not posing a question but rather expecting an answer.

"Exactly," he'd said.

Although we had joint VISA cards, when the VISA bill arrived in the mail each month I quickly learned to write a personal check to cover the total cost of items I'd bought for myself or for gifts I'd bought for my relatives using the VISA card. Jeff, of course, did likewise for his purchases. As I've said, a year before we were married, Jeff purchased a long-term health care policy for me and continued to pay premiums each year, a gesture never ceasing to amaze me but for which I was truly grateful. He was also very generous and paid in full for trips we took to Rotary International conventions, several out of the country, trips for ship reunions, and for trips to see his children and friends.

I became accustomed to this way of handling finances and knew it was the sensible and fair way. But it seemed so different from sharing all income and expenses, as it had been from the beginning in my first marriage. Second marriages could be more wonderful than first marriages, but I could see how they could become quite entangled if spouses with individual incomes didn't agree to a system of handling disbursement of assets.

Still at the table, I changed the subject. "Who won the golf game yesterday? Did you read about the match in the paper?"

"Tiger Woods. No one came close. He's quite a golfer. Sure can hit that ball and knows where to aim it. Golf's fine for the pros. I like to watch. But I can't see amateurs getting out there and hitting a ball, trying to exceed their opponents. Billiards and pool are the same as golf, and playing them makes more sense"

"Amateur golfers try to improve their *own* game, lower their handicap, get some exercise, have some fun. As for billiards and pool, they don't hold a candle to golf!" I said emphatically. "People who play those games get no exercise, no fresh air. They don't get out on a course of nice green grass and walk around and swing their arms." In an opinionated but sensible way, I tried to explain this to Jeff who'd never played golf until he played with me nine years ago. I knew he'd never taken to the game, and we stopped playing when we got too tired to finish nine holes.

"What else was in the news today?" I asked Jeff.

"Not too much. A little about a new private school that's opening and the usual about the voucher system. What results is the bright kids are enrolled in better schools, and below average students remain in public schools where teachers are required to pass them even though they haven't learned enough to go on to the next grade." He heaved a sigh, frowned, and ran his hand over his bald head. "This No Kid Left Behind idea of George Bush's is nutty. We have to accept the fact that all kids aren't bright. Some are just average, some below average. The below average and slow learners shouldn't be expected to keep up, to take the same subjects. Some would do well in vocational schools." He looked at me and squinted. "All parents think their kids are geniuses. They push them ahead. Complain if a teacher doesn't give them good grades."

"I think one of the main problems is discipline," I said, tapping the table with my spoon. "Compared to many other countries, the U.S. is behind in education. Thirteenth from the top, I believe. Teachers can't teach because they have to spend precious time disciplining instead of teaching. College students aren't going into the teaching profession. That is, those who would make good teachers aren't."

Jeff cleared his throat and raised his voice. "Discipline shouldn't be a problem. There's nothing wrong with taking a pupil by the arm and telling her, 'Now, Nancy, you must behave.'" To demonstrate, he reached over and grasped my arm with his hand.

"Jeff," I emoted. "Teachers aren't allowed to touch students! They get fired if they do! The student tells his parents, the parents go to the principal or superintendent, and the teacher gets fired! It's not like when you were a principal. This is 2004!"

"That's what I hear but I don't believe it. A teacher should take a student by the arm and correct her or him."

I shrugged, gave up, and said, "We've been invited to the McKees for cocktails tonight before going over to dinner. You remember. It's on the calendar."

"I'd forgotten, but that's fine. Now if it's all the same to you, I think I'll go read my latest *U.S. News and World Report* and then take a little nap." Jeff pushed his chair back from the table causing it to scrape noisily on the tile floor. Mine scraped just as loudly when I rose to clear the table.

Easter being next week, as a house gift, I decided to take Ruth McKee a fancy plastic egg carton filled with eight decorated plastic eggs with ribbons attached for hanging. I'd received it from my daughter who lived in Kelso, Washington. Yes, I was re-gifting. Why not? I saw no harm in that, and I thought Ruth would like it.

Ellen and Harry Gorman were already at the McKees when we walked in. Another couple, Patricia and Horace James whom we'd seen several times in the lounge, were also there. In his usual outgoing way, Jeff quickly picked up on the conversation flowing among the three men. Not surprisingly, they were reminiscing about their experiences in the war. From the few sentences I heard Horace say, I gathered he'd been a Naval Academy graduate, had served in World War II for a short time, and then joined a family-owned manufacturing business. Apparently he'd retired a man of some wealth.

Jeff had learned during our previous visit at the McKees that Ellen's husband, Harry, was a successful building contractor, and, like Jeff, had served in the Navy in a destroyer, but in the Atlantic rather than the Pacific. In fact, he'd been in midshipman class the year after Jeff. We knew some time ago our host Stuart was with an army engineer corps in Alaska, sitting there the entire length of the war. Very few of the men living at Sandycreek Terrace have not served and been officers during World War II. It's our age, you see, we of the Greatest Generation.

As I talked with the women, Patricia James, no doubt a beautiful woman in her prime and still very attractive, impressed me as being like a prima donna who had never soiled her hands in a job of any kind. Probably graduated from college and got married like many of the women here. This wasn't to say she wasn't a refined and most pleasant woman for indeed she was. Ellen, as before, was also pleasant and enjoyable to talk with. Never smiling hostess Ruth didn't allow the female conversation to lag, bless her heart, nor had she ever any time I've been in her company. After about an hour, she looked at her watch and announced it was time for us to head for the Club House for dinner. We made our way to the dining room where conversation continued. Dinner concluded, I thanked Ruth for inviting us for indeed the evening had been enjoyable and quite a while since we'd eaten with other residents.

The weather was warming, and after exercising and before breakfast, I asked Jeff, "Shall we do our usual walk and bike ride or try the pool?"

Jeff cocked his head. "Well now, that's a thought. Why not go to the pool this morning? Let's do."

In our suits and cover-ups, I walked and Jeff rode his bike to the outdoor pool located just across from the exercise room. The sun had risen but the surrounding apartment buildings shaded the pool at this time in the morning. A blessing for me because of my eyes' sensitivity to the sun. In the pool, a male resident wearing a black swimmers' cap and protective goggles was swimming free-style around the circumference. A female resident, also wearing a swimmers' cap and goggles, was swimming laps on the far side where the water was deepest. Jeff climbed from his bike while I dragged a lawn chair close to the steps leading into the pool. I found a mountain of large terry-cloth towels stacked on a nearby bench, removed two, and placed them on the chair. We were ready to get into the water just as the two swimmers, unfamiliar to us, left the pool. Perhaps these experienced swimmers routinely swam at the same time every morning. We decided to arrive at the pool fifteen minutes later the next time, giving them more *wiggle room*, as Jeff liked to say. We would aim to be finished swimming before the aquasize class began and a group of female residents invaded the pool with their instructor, the Health and Wellness Coordinator. I'd seen them one morning in brimmed hats and dark glasses monopolizing the pool and performing their gyrations, like a Rockette comedy act.

As we stood there looking at the pool, we calculated its length to be about twenty yards, its width ten. The side closest to us was marked three feet, the opposite side four. A nice size for octogenarians. Jeff gallantly strode down the steps and made a noisy splash into the water while I slowly and gingerly put one foot on a watery step and then another, my right hand firmly gripping the warm shiny-chrome hand-rail leading down the steps to the bottom of the pool. I eased into the water to my waist and started to walk my way across the pool toward the deeper side, separating the shining, quivering water in front of me with my hands.

Jeff was ahead when I called to him, "Jeff, I don't believe the water's chlorinated. There's no odor."

"They probably use a different chemical, maybe bromine. One with no odor. Don't worry. It has to be safe," he assured me.

"The water feels nice and warm. Check the thermometer and see what it reads."

"Where *is* the thermometer?" he called back over the water.

"It should be tied with a cord to the top step of that ladder at the far end near you. That's where it was at Pine Gardens' pool."

"Eighty-eight degrees," he called back across the pool.

"Pretty nice," I said, and he nodded. "Perfect," I emphasized. "Maybe a little too warm. At least warmer than I'm accustomed to."

"They keep it that warm for old folks, not us," he laughed.

"Certainly not for us," I repeated, also laughing, and kept on walking continuing to push water away from me in walking breast stroke fashion until I was in the deepest water. Jeff was *walking* lengths. A Navy man not swimming? Maybe swimming wasn't a requirement to be in the Navy. I was beside him now and said, "I don't say I swim laps because I don't flip over at each end. I stop and then start again. And I alternate strokes. My favorite is back stroke cause it's relaxing, not strenuous." By now he was at the far end of the pool and didn't hear me. But it didn't matter.

After about six lengths of walking, Jeff climbed up the ladder out of the water, walked over to the hot tub a few feet away, and set the timer. "You should get out of the pool after a bit and come over here with me in this good hot water. Great for your back!"

"No thanks! I can't stand the heat of that tub. All that steam makes me sick!"

"It's not steamy, just nice and hot."

"Doesn't matter. I don't like it that hot," I called back. Then I swam to the end where a purple bougainvillea caught my eye straight ahead on the other side of the walk circling the pool. I turned and swam in the opposite direction to the end where I could just see the outside eating area of the Terrace with its tables and chairs and huge over-the-table umbrellas. I continued swimming just ten more lengths until I tired, this being my first swim in a long time.

When I climbed out I determined I'd buy a new suit. The suit I was wearing had a skirt panel in front, loose on one side, and rose like a sail in the water. I wanted a plain suit without a skirt. But all the bathing suits I'd seen in stores were bikinis or cut up so high at the thigh I'd be embarrassed to wear one. What were elderly women supposed to wear? After drying with one of the terry towels and handing one to Jeff having just walked over from the hot tub, I deposited my damp towel in the plastic receptacle on wheels marked for towels. Then I walked the short distance along the corridor past apartments with various decorations attached to blue louvered doors and past courtyards, admiring again their flowering plants and palm trees.

After we showered, Jeff righted his shoulders, clapped his hands, and said, "I feel great! Let's go again tomorrow only I'll shower over there in the men's locker room before I come home. How about poached eggs on raisin toast for breakfast? You're deserving. Are you hungry?" He studied my face with his blue eyes and that loving look on his face.

"I believe I *am* hungry, Honey. And poached eggs on raisin toast sound great!"

As usual, Jeff read the Palm Beach Post after breakfast and read out loud articles he deemed of interest to me. "Here's one of your pet peeves," he said, lowering his glasses from atop his head and straightening the pages in rustling fashion. "Fifty percent of the nation's population is overweight. Compared to statistics from other countries, our nation's far in excess. The once popular diet devised by Dr. Atkins has failed to curb the increase. And on and on. I know what you thought of *that* diet."

"Well of course. Pure nonsense! Eat mainly nothing but bacon and cheese? Ridiculous! And Dr. Atkins' weight is about three hundred pounds! Any sane person would steer clear of *that* diet. In yesterday's paper you told me an article was written about that old Terry Schiavo case again. Because of the right to life issue now being discussed. Her parents aren't going to give up, are they?"

"It doesn't look that way. They've appealed to the president. He'll not touch that with a ten-foot pole."

To date, Jeff and I hadn't taken advantage of any of the planned activities scheduled off the premises, or many in the facility for *that* matter. So far, we were too busy with our hobbies to get involved in activities. Nor had we started to go to exercise classes since routinely every morning before walking and biking and breakfast we completed a set of exercises our general practitioner had provided.

We both knew how to play bridge and enjoyed playing, but we hadn't done that either. A set number of residents played rubber bridge and duplicate bridge several afternoons and evenings each week in the card room. Several residents had asked us to play bridge. Barbara Donnelly was one. A tall thin ninety-year-old resident, she carried herself straight as a telephone pole and looked barely eighty. We'd passed her a few times since she lived several apartments down the corridor from us. One morning she stopped us in the corridor saying, "I'm Barbara Donnelly, and I know you're the Metzs. Do you play bridge?"

We acknowledged we did but hadn't played for some time.

"Can I interest you in a game? A group of us have two tables and play every Wednesday afternoon in one of our apartments, alternating weeks. When it's my turn can I call you to fill in? We usually have absentee players." She stood erect, eyes intent first on Jeff and then on me, waiting for an answer.

We looked at each other and shook our heads. "Gee, we're sorry, but we're too busy," we both said almost in unison.

"What are you busy doing?" she wanted to know.

Jeff said, "We write. Jeanie writes articles for nursing magazines, and I write editorials and letters. But mostly I work on my stamp collection."

"You have a computer and do this writing on a computer?" She acted amazed.

"Yes. We have a large screen desk-top because of Jean's poor vision," Jeff explained.

"My goodness! I suppose I should get a computer. I was a professor at Michigan State University, you know. Much responsibility and much experience. But I'm too busy with my bridge games to get involved with writing. Besides, I'm ninety, and I'd rather play bridge." She'd hesitated then said, "Well, now that we're here talking, do you have a minute to come and see my apartment? I've been wanting you to see it."

She led us down the corridor a short distance to her door, unlocked it, and ushered us in. The living room she showed us seemed larger than ours. Then in the kitchen she pointed to what appeared to be her pride and joy—a large window covered almost entirely with living vines, stems spreading horizontally, vertically, and diagonally with green leaves of varying shades intertwining. She stood back and explained, "I decided to

121

use plants as a window dressing instead of the usual blinds or curtains. What do you think of my idea?"

It was obvious she expected us to exclaim in ecstasy over her creation, but I was amazed at the effect, at the unruly growth not exactly pleasing to my eyes. I swallowed and managed, "It's certainly unusual and very creative."

She smiled, apparently pleased with my response.

When we got home Jeff said, "Why is it we're so busy we can't play a game of bridge once in awhile? But we *don't* have time, *do* we?"

"No, we don't seem to have time for bridge. We do lots of things that take up our time. I consider them important things. We go to Rotary meetings every Wednesday and to special functions Rotary plans and Past District Governor's meetings. We go to TROA, The Retired Officers Association meetings every month. I enjoy those dinner meetings at the Holiday Inn. The programs are interesting, and the members are fun to be with." I tried to enumerate more.

"Don't forget the Michigan Teachers Association meetings we attend each month. They're a little boring, but the members are nice, and I enjoy them. And church, of course." Jeff was adding to the list.

"I like to spend time in our apartment," I said in all seriousness. "Writing and listening to what you have written and making comments. Working crossword puzzles. Playing cribbage. Maybe we'll figure out a time to play bridge some day. And we could take advantage of some of the planned activities the Social Director arranges in town. The Mystery Trips, the Dine Arounds, the shopping trips, the concerts and plays. The Social Director even plans those seven-day cruises! I guess she goes along on all those trips, like a mother taking care of her children. Maybe a hen taking care of her chicks."

Jeff chuckled. "Yes, I imagine she does. What a job! Who wouldn't like that kind of a job? Getting paid for going on trips and to concerts and plays. Of course she has to make all the arrangements, and that's not always easy. Takes time. Yes, Jeanie, we'll have to start doing some of those things. But I'm like you. I'm busy doing things I like to do." He started to open the mail. "Here's another thing. We get so damn much junk mail! Takes time to go through all this!"

Fifteen

Acquaintances

It was Friday, April twenty-third, and I'd just completed the Sunday *Palm Beach Post* crossword puzzle. That is, I'd finished it to the best of my ability. Always three or four squares remained blank due to my lack of adequate vocabulary. Jeff would finish it in jig time. He had such profound command of the English language, and his vast amount of vocabulary astounded me. You have a dictionary in your brain in addition to encyclopedia information, I'd often told him. I wasn't well-read as he was, and my knowledge was limited, mainly to healthcare, whereas his knowledge covered many fields.

I abandoned the puzzle at the Florida room table and said, "I'm leaving this crossword puzzle here for your completion, Jeff. I've filled in as much as I can. You'll finish it in a flash. I envy you for the knowledge you have in that brain of yours."

"A veritable fountainhead of useless information. That's what I have," he said as I walked toward him.

I smiled at his description of his knowledge and paused to observe him at his hobby on my way toward the intended guest bedroom we'd made part den, part office, part computer room. He was sitting at the dining room table, his stamp collection spread out before him. Tongs held between his fingers, eye glasses perched high on his bald head, he was sorting stamps, separating them according to country and giving them their own area on the table. He handled them delicately, was very pleased with some for their value, but enjoyed them all. To me it was mind-boggling the number he had accumulated—those he worked with almost daily, those stored in closets here, and those in drawers in a rented storage locker in town. I glanced up at the hutch positioned on the wall opposite the dining room table and again admired the many colorful and beautiful designs on the bone-china cups and saucers my father had brought me from his fishing trips in Canada years ago. The hand-painted plates on the shelf below had belonged to my mother and father when they kept house and before they were divorced when I was fourteen. How long ago that was!

At the desk-top computer with its large screen bought especially for me because of my limited vision, I logged on and brought up AOL. Lo and behold, there was an incoming e-mail from the nursing magazine editor I'd sent a query of an article I titled, *How Different Are Nursing Homes in Costa Rica?* The editor liked the title! He wanted me to send the article for review!

Jeff and I had spent five weeks in Costa Rica the winter before we moved into Sandycreek Terrace. We'd used accumulated time-share-days for the most part and lived an unusual and interesting way of life there in that volcanic country the entire month of December and first week in January. In a rented car, we'd traveled miles over rocky roads with potholes big enough to swallow our car. Jeff had laughed when I said I wanted to tour a nursing home. But he'd humored me, and we'd driven to the address we'd found in the telephone book. I was shocked when I saw the building. It resembled a single family dwelling and turned out to have only thirteen beds and was privately owned and operated. No need to be larger, I soon learned, since most adult children in Costa Rica took care of elderly relatives in their own homes. For the same reason, it wasn't a mystery that six of its residents were citizens of either the United States or Canada. The proprietor found it necessary to advertise for out-of-the-country residents. The nursing home was so different from ours in the U.S. and the tour so revealing that I'd been inspired to write about it after I got home. I sensed it would make interesting reading for state-side nurses. Because of the time taken to obtain information from the proprietor's daughter, the only English-speaking staff person in the facility, the article had been long in the writing stage. I'd finally been ready to query an editor. The year before, I'd toured a 230-bed nursing home in Hawaii. I'd written an article about that fine facility and had it accepted and published by the same editor I just heard from today. My son Kirk always seemed interested in my writing and assured me, "As long as you keep writing and being published, Mother, you'll never become senile."

The next e-mail after the one from Editor Krisher was from my cousin, Mary Frances Gobin. She was attaching more information about our heritage project. A year ago, Kirk had suggested I comprise a genealogy of my maternal and paternal families. I'd thought about the idea for almost six months before I was motivated to jump into such a project. Needless to say, the request sent me on quite a search as I had little source for obtaining past history.

I decided to start with my father's family mainly because I'd heard three Kirk brothers had come over from Scotland to settle in the U. S. As a child, I'd met many of my grandfather's eleven siblings and their children. Through my childhood and teen years, I'd spent time with a second cousin, Mary Frances Gobin, whose grandfather and my grandfather were brothers. Fortunately I had her e-mail address, and I contacted her to see if she would be amenable to helping me with a genealogy. She was! From time to time and with long gaps in between we communicated about our heritage via e-mail. Although I'd lived a distance from Kirk relatives, Mary Francis had lived in close proximity to the brothers and sisters of our grandfathers and to their children. She kept supplying me with information, much more than was needed for a simple family tree. All was so interesting, however, that I decided to include everything she contributed. One bit of history she sent really amused me. According to her story, Uncle Mar, one of our grandfathers' brothers, was considered the favorite because he had shoe strings for his shoes while his siblings went without. Maybe I'd find something else interesting, for here on the computer was another saga to download.

A number of evenings when Jeff and I were in the lounge before dinner, empty chairs were always available at the table where Grace Terwilliker was sitting with her friend, Polly. Grace always motioned for us to sit with her. Although I'd never seen her standing, I figured she was short and dumpy the way she sat low in her chair gathered into it like a loaf of bread in a bread wrapper. She appeared to favor Jeff and told me I was fortunate to have him, that she missed her husband and hated to be single.

As we joined her and Polly at a table one evening, she asked Jeff, "How is your back?"

As before, Jeff said, "The same. No better. Can't expect it to be."

She shook her white-haired head and her large lips mouthed, "You won't listen to me. My back was worse than yours. All you have to do is have the same procedure I had. I'm pain free. Why won't you listen?" She stared at Jeff and shook her fist at him.

I interjected, "Grace, didn't you say that some time ago, you had a slow-release morphine drip implant for your back pain?"

"Yes, and it's very effective. What have you done about your back pain, Jeff?" she demanded.

Jeff repeated what he'd told her other times she'd asked. "I had surgery on my cervical vertebra, but this pain is in my lower back. And further back surgery isn't an option according to my neurology surgeon." I could tell Jeff was restraining himself, using patience as before.

Grace pinned Jeff with her eyes and said "I told you what to do, and you won't listen. Get what I have, and you won't have any more pain. Why don't you listen?"

Jeff continued to explain. "My back problem isn't the same as yours. I've done everything possible. Three injections of a steroid that only lasted a week each time and physical therapy."

Grace turned her head on its short neck and called over her shoulder, "Amelia, get me another drink."

"All right, Mrs. Terwilliker," Amelia answered from her station at the bar.

Polly had nodded in agreement with Jeff's comments and now critically eyed the two empty cocktail glasses in front of her friend. Although one evening Polly had claimed her memory wasn't very good, she did seem aware of her friend's attempt to once more try to prescribe a treatment for Jeff, and obviously she didn't approve of Grace's excessive drinking.

Another evening in the lounge before dinner, a male dining room employee was tending bar instead of Amelia. Even though all staff wore name pins as did this bartender, Jeff asked him his name before ordering our drinks. The tall blond I guessed to be in his twenties glanced at Jeff and answered, "Name's Chuck, Mr. Metz. What's yer pleasure tonight?"

"Mrs. Metz will have a vodka martini on the rocks with a twist and I'll have a bourbon Manhattan, extra sweet, on the rocks. Make it look like root beer."

Chuck set two short glasses on the bar, filled them with ice, uncapped bottles of vodka and bourbon and, with a bottle in each hand, simultaneously poured the liquors over the ice to within a half inch of the top of the glasses. Then he took the tops from the dry and sweet vermouth bottles and poured again simultaneously until the wine reached the tops of both glasses. As he took a pre-cut twist of lemon and rubbed it over the lip of my glass, he looked up at Jeff, "Cherry?"

"No, no. No garbage. No manna, no papa, no cumshaw."

Chuck gave Jeff a curious bewildered look. "Beg yer pardon?"

I didn't blame Chuck for his confused reaction. I'd heard Jeff use that phrase frequently and was accustomed to hearing it when he meant just plain *no*. It was something he'd learned in Japan after the war. A funny answer or saying. He explained, "I mean, no cherry, no orange peel, and no stirrer. Don't want to bruise the booze, Chuck."

"Right, sir," Chuck nodded.

"You a student?" Jeff asked him.

"Yes, sir. Go to FSU."

"What's your major at Florida State University?" I asked him, reaching for the drink he'd set on a cocktail napkin in front of me.

"Drama," he answered, placing the Manhattan on a napkin in front of Jeff.

"That's very interesting. A play could be written about life here in this community," I ventured to say as Jeff signed one of the cards from a stack on the bar. I was serious when I suggested such a play be written. I could picture the scenery, the characters, and the emergency vehicle entering the gate, sirens screaming.

"Yes, well maybe," was Chuck's dubious answer. Then, "I'm on the staff of a little local theater group here in town. I have a part in the play we're practicing now."

I was about to converse more with Chuck when I felt a pinch on my bottom. As I turned around to see the responsible party, I realized I'd never seen this person before. She was a small slightly plump female resident who gasped, "Oh I'm terribly sorry! I don't know what made me do that! I've never done anything like that before in my life!" she announced as her hand flew to her mouth and covered it. She looked at me with the most embarrassed expression. "You will forgive me, won't you?" she begged.

All of a sudden the scenario struck me immensely humorous, and I laughed out loud. "Of course, of course!" I said.

This broke the ice, and a broad smile spread over her pretty little face. "But I really don't know what got into me. I'm so sorry."

"Don't think anything more of it. It's forgotten. I'm Jeanie Metz."

"And I'm Kathy. Kathy Franklin. Come over and meet my husband," she said walking to a couch at the far end of the lounge. I followed her and Jeff followed me and we were introduced to Carl, a tall well-built man in a tan suit, green shirt, and striped tie. He immediately rose from the couch and his eyes twinkled when he smiled and said he was pleased to meet us.

"We aren't going to be very hungry for dinner," Kathy said as we all sat down around a rectangular glass-topped coffee-table. "We went to our favorite place this afternoon and made pigs of ourselves eating our favorite flavors of ice cream. Not one but several."

During our continuing conversation, I noticed husband Carl did little talking, much listening, and nodding in agreement while Kathy talked. This made me wonder, did Carl have a residual slowing of thought processes as a result of a previous cerebral vascular accident? Then because Kathy and Carl had registered for dinner before we had, they were called into the dining room first.

As with the Franklins, I was beginning to notice a definite dominate spouse in several other couples, one alert and leading, the other silent or saying little and following their spouse, both physically and mentally. It had been true of the Butchers, Ben and Pam, and was true of Patricia and Horace James lately, the wife being the dominate spouse in each case.

This realization made me think of Jeff and me. As far as I could discern, this wasn't happening to us. We were equally capable in all spheres. But the next morning, we did have a confrontation. At least I'll call it that. The mail in our lower mail box contained our maintenance bill for last month, the charge higher than usual because my cousins had visited for five days. Even though they'd paid for their guest room, a charge for their dinners was added. This caused no conflict. Jeff's grandson had been here a number of times and had eaten in the dining room. Jeff and I didn't keep track of these charges or refer to them in any way. We considered family members and friends ours, not his or hers. For some unknown reason, as we reviewed the bill, I suddenly remembered a clause in the contract we'd signed with Sandycreek Terrace before moving in. It specified that primary owners of living quarters paid a greater amount for maintenance than secondary parties. It didn't make sense to me, and I wondered why that was. So I said, "Jeff, you and I pay an equal amount into our joint checking account every month in order to pay the monthly maintenance bill."

He raised his eyes and looked from the bill to me with a curious expression. "That's right. What's on your mind?"

"I was just wondering why the contract specifies primary owners of living quarters pay an amount greater than second party residents. After all, we have unmarried couples sharing quarters and a pair of sisters living in one apartment. You'd think the maintenance fee would be the same for both." My eyes fastened on him as I waited for his reply.

"It is. Each resident is assessed an equal amount," he said in a confident and controlled manner.

I could visualize the words of the contract. I knew exactly how the contract read. I was able to do the same with the federal regulations for nursing home compliance. I knew exactly how they read. I knew I was right about the Sandycreek Terrace contract, and Jeff's contradiction irritated me. I raised my voice to emphasize, "Jeff, I know how it reads. The contract specifically quotes a lesser cost for the second resident."

"No, they're identical. And we agreed to pay the same. Has that become a problem for you?" Again his voice was calm as he sat looking over at me.

"It's no problem. No. That's not what I said. I said the contract...Well I could get the contract and read it to you." My eyes darted to the bookcase above the computer where a loose-leaf notebook held the contract. "Why don't you believe me?" I was positive I was right. Usually we agreed, shared the same ideas about religion, politics, how children should be raised, etc. Of course we had some differences of opinions such as private schools and spending money for clothes. And we kept our own opinions, always changing the subject amiably after discussions about such subjects. When the subjects involved medications, diseases, and healthcare issues, such as Medicare and Medicaid, Jeff asked me to explain, and he listened. In almost all other matters, he was more knowledgeable because of his excellent education, experiences, extensive reading, and mental capability to maintain information. In those matters, I always listened and accepted what he said as correct. Now he should accept what I was saying. I felt my temper rising, getting out of control, but I couldn't seem to help myself, and I said, "You won't believe me! Why won't you believe me? You never believe me!" I was angry and glaring at him. In my past life, my children obeyed me. Later, I'd been in charge whatever my position. Rarely did any one disagree with me, dare to contradict the boss. Of course Jeff had been in charge as a father, a Navy captain, and a high school principal. He'd been given the same respect.

"It's just that you're wrong about the contract," he said, keeping his eyes fastened upon me, his voice subdued.

I stood up and screamed, "I'm right!" My eyes felt like they were coming out of their sockets as I stood there looking straight into his face.

For a second silence prevailed and then, in a normal tone and eyes unblinking, he said, "I don't like being screamed at."

I stalked out of the room, feeling defeated, choking with tears, mad at myself for losing my cool, but still angry. He wouldn't admit he was wrong. Wouldn't offer to read the contract, the proof. But he'd been in control, hadn't raised his voice, had kept calm. And there was the rub. I'd lost control and I knew I'd want to apologize for screaming at him. I would, that is, after I calmed down sufficiently. When I did, we'd kiss and all would be forgotten. But I vowed to myself never to lose control again. After all, the subject of our dispute had been insignificant, not worth such radical emotion,

Sixteen

Travel

The end of May we started making plans to go north. Other residents were also talking about leaving for the summer and into the fall to avoid the inevitable hot humid weather arriving in dear old Florida every summer. The majority of the residents had originally lived in northern states, retired to Florida, and changed their official addresses, as did we. For some, a permanent move took time. They clung to familiar northern surroundings like a dog to his master. Called *snow birds*, they continued to own property up north, living six months there during warm months and spending six winter months in Florida where they either rented or owned residences and weren't subjected to freezing temperatures, snow, and ice. Very few residents at Sandycreek Terrace were native Floridians although many of the employees were born here.

A number of residents who didn't own property up north, still spent summer months at favorite northern haunts such as coastal areas of Maine, New Jersey seacoasts, and islands in northern Michigan—places they'd been frequenting for years. Some still fished, boated, and golfed when they *went on vacation*. In the lounge and dining room, I'd hear them mention the names of these wonderful places, not bragging, mind you, but with dreamy eyes and probably pleasant memories in their minds. The majority of the residents, however, had relinquished thoughts of leaving for any length of time, limited by disabilities and resigned to a sedentary life at Sandycreek Terrace.

As for Jeff and me, for seven years we'd been traveling to my favorite spot in Pennsylvania in a valley of farmlands surrounded by mountains. Not at all comparable to a resort or vacation vicinity, it was just a *down home country place.* As early as I was able to recognize my paternal grandparents and where and how they lived, this special spot had been deeply imbedded in my mind, a part of my life, and a haven to cherish. Born and raised in the city, I'd spent my summers, at a young age, with my grandparents, enjoyed the many-roomed farmhouse, played in the large front yard with the kittens, romped in the barn hay, fed the chickens, brought home the cows with Shep, the dog, and eventually dated the local farm boys.

When I was twenty-seven, my father bought a piece of property across the meadow from his parents' farm and had it deeded in his name and mine. On this purchase of three acres, a small one-hundred-and-thirty-five-year-old, two-story, four-room frame house stood, backed against a solid rock bank. The meadow in front bordered on two mountain streams, one coming from the tiny village two miles to the north, the other flowing down from the Sidling Hill Mountain. My father properly named the old house *The Shack,* for it truly was not much else. It had a pump in the front yard, an outhouse a short distance away, no electricity, and no heat. My father wasted no time having it supplied with running water, electricity, and two kerosene stoves. There, from time to time, he'd entertain fishing buddies also living in the city. More fish stories were told than fishes caught, I imagined. Before long, my father hired local farmers, self-taught in construction to build additions, the first being a bathroom. To accommodate the increasing number of people frequenting the Shack on weekends, the outhouse was kept in tact until a second bathroom was constructed. A knotty-pine paneled living room with a functional fireplace was second to be added. Then the kitchen was enlarged, and, on the second floor, a third bedroom and two clothes closets were added. A porch was enlarged and screened in. Lastly a large family room with two window walls and a stone corner fireplace completed the renovation.

Before my grandfather's death, he willed my father and me jointly an adjoining one hundred and forty five acres of which thirty were tillable and the remaining in woodland. An ancient unpainted barn adjoined the crop-land acreage.

The property jointly owned by my father and me with right of survival had been totally mine since my father's death in the seventies. I'd refurnished the Shack, enlarged the porch, installed a furnace in the basement, and had the frame exterior covered with vinyl siding. From four small rooms the Shack had expanded, like a blown up balloon, into seven rooms, two baths, and a screened-in porch.

I cherished this place in nowheresville and, as a single person since the early nineteen nineties, had been spending my summers there alone.

About mid-June 1997 when I picked up my mail at the village post office there was a letter from Jeff in Florida asking if he could visit. This was shortly after we'd been introduced in the spring by friends where we all lived in separate condominium apartments in Pine Gardens. I'd had just three dates with him before driving north. I reread the letter. How would I answer? If he came, what would he think of the Shack, so old, rooms added onto like topsy, no two walls even, steps creaking underfoot? Would he like this small Pennsylvania farming community? What would I do with him? For the nights, I would sleep him downstairs, I in my bedroom upstairs. But what about all day long? Then I had a revelation! Of course! Take him to visit Gettysburg, a trip of about fifty miles one way. After all, he was a military man and should be interested in that renowned Civil War battlefield.

He *was very* interested in going to Gettysburg, and amazingly, he liked the Shack and the surrounding countryside. He was captivated by the quaint nearby village of two-hundred-and-fifty people where everyone knew everyone else and everyone else's business. Located down the road two miles north of the Shack, the village of Wells Tannery boasted only two buildings, a post office and Presbyterian Church, aside from the villagers' houses. No grocery store, no pharmacy, no gas station.

Jeff immediately became acquainted with the female postmaster and her fill-in. They routinely held my mail until I collected it. I deemed it unwise to have a mailbox at the side of the state road near the lane leading to the Shack and no one living there all winter long. Besides, I had stamps to buy and enjoyed chit chatting with the postmaster and with village folk who would come in and sit conversing on a wooden bench waiting for the mail to be sorted. An authentic country post office, a dish of hard candy sat on the counter ledge and listed on a bulletin board were notices of house sales, tractor sales, auctions, and meetings in the Grange Hall five miles down a country road. A monthly calendar was tacked to the wall with a small U. S. flag on a stick stuck into the top. The room was barely big enough to take three steps in any direction.

Outgoing Jeff quickly made friends with nearby farmers and church parishioners, as well as Ron. Ron was my farmer, friend, and caretaker combined. Jeff was intrigued by his country drawl, limited speaking vocabulary, and farmer language, the likes of which he'd never heard. He was equally intrigued and amazed at Ron's intelligence, mechanical ability, fix-anything prowess, speed in completing crossword puzzles, knowledge of world events, and uncanny ability to master the stock market. I enjoyed Ron's frequent phrases of *and whatnot* and *you deserve an attagirl*.

This year by mid-June, we were packed and ready to leave Sandycreek Terrace for the Shack. Jeff had filled out the required form he'd picked up from the front desk supplying the establishment's *powers that be* with all the information they might need in our absence. This included our intended address, phone number, e-mail address, and next of kin. It also afforded us with a circle to check if we desired access to our apartment in our absence for temperature control, toilet flushing, and emergency purposes.

The evening before we planned to leave we met Betty Howe and Ralph Wilson in the lounge. "Are you planning to have dinner with anyone?" Betty asked in her demure little soft voice. After our negative response, she said, "Then let's join for dinner, shall we?"

"Of course," I said, without hesitation. "We'd love to. This will be our last dinner here for a number of months."

"Oh, you're leaving? Where are you going?" Betty asked. Her thin hand, lined with veins like blue strings under natural-colored nylon, grabbed at a printed scarf and rearranged it circling around the neck of her blue silk jacket.

When we explained our trip and described the Shack, she said, "That sounds lovely, doesn't it, Ralph? So many residents are leaving. Sandycreek Terrace will seem deserted. We're staying here. Aren't we, Ralph? Our age, you know."

Ralph nodded, smiled, and erupted into a prolonged coughing attack.

The next morning we started off to the Shack as usual in Jeff's Cadillac except we were leaving from Sandycreek Terrace, not from our single-family house in Pine Gardens. My twenty-three-year-old grandson had flown down from West Virginia and driven my Volvo to the Shack. We planned to leave the Volvo there to use next summer, flying up instead of driving all the way from Florida. Little did we know those plans would be thwarted.

I always marveled at Jeff's ability to drive around town in heavy traffic *and* on the open and not so open highways. I doubted many eighty-three-year-olds would attempt a trip of such length as ours was. Jeff was amazingly at ease behind a wheel. Maybe his quick reaction-time came from his flying experience during the Korean War and from his perfect distant vision sans cheaters. He wove in and out of traffic manipulating the car with the best of them, only one hand on the steering wheel most of the time. Often his right hand came over and squeezed my arm or held my hand, giving me a warm feeling and making me smile. I remembered again how, in describing us, he often told people, "We're the world's oldest teenagers!"

As we drove along I-95 from Sandycreek Terrace to Savannah, Georgia the first day, I made myself comfortable in the passenger seat and looked out onto the open highway. Beside me Jeff said, "Look there at all the ticky-tacky houses." He was pointing to identically structured houses built row after row along an acre of land. "And there's a stone orchard and there's another," he said, pointing out two graveyards but a mile apart. "You know," he continued, gesturing toward swamp trees, "Every time I drive through Georgia I think of General Sherman marching through this swampland driving out the Confederate soldiers."

We drove a number of miles on cruise control set at five miles beyond the speed limit as much as possible. Suddenly a red convertible flew by. Jeff's hand tightened on the wheel. "There's a young driver going like hell to get to hell," he remarked.

"Never a patrol car around when it should be," I said, reaching over and turning on the radio. Out blasted *I'm Gonna Hold You 'Til die*. I turned down the volume. "That's what I'm gonna do. Hold you 'til I die," I said, reaching over and patting Jeff's hand on the armrest between us.

135

"Sounds like a winner," Jeff said, taking his eyes off the road to look at me and wink.

We were driving slower now through a town, crossing over railroad tracks, then passing stately houses with tall white pillars, now a Dollar General, then a jogger, and now a sign advertising R D's Charbroiled Burgers. Out on the four-lane highway a truck darted across the road, missing us by inches. "Whee! Friend!" Jeff exclaimed in a not-too-friendly voice. "Tonnage rights. That's what he has. Tonnage rights."

Miles later, the rain started and persisted. I was mesmerized by the steady strum of the windshield wipers. The motion of the wheels rolling under us speeding us along rocked me like a cradle urging me to sleep.

The next day as we drove through North Carolina, Jeff said, "Look at that old tobacco shed in the middle of a plowed field over there. Must be a law forbidding tobacco sheds to be torn down." He leaned forward, looking at the odometer. "What do you know! We just rolled over one thousand miles!"

"Making good time, aren't we?" I said, looking over at him.

"Yes, we're moving right along. On target."

"Oh, I smell a skunk. Do you smell it, Jeff?" I asked holding my nose.

"You bet! Rather potent. Oops, I see a construction sign ahead. Construction all the way to Charlottesville. Better slow this wagon down." A car passed, slid in front of us, and put on its brakes. "Oh fella! That wasn't very kind of you!" Jeff exclaimed, obviously irritated but not swearing like some men would.

The highway, north and south bound, was divided by a stretch of land now, and we were driving along with juniper, cedar, and pine trees hemming us in on either side like a living tunnel. "Petersburg," Jeff said, reading a road-side sign. "Here's where soldiers fought a year-long battle during the Civil War. The Union army planned to dig a tunnel under the Confederates and plant a mine to blow them up, but their plan was too premature." Miles later on another sign he read, "Fort Union Military Academy," and then commented, "Virginia's big for military academies."

We were starting to see mountains in the distance, and then we were in the Shenandoah Valley, driving up and down those marvelous mountains of Virginia. "Look at that vista!" Jeff said, pointing at the landscape and waving an arm. I looked and beheld green hills and valleys and mountains as far as the eye could see. A beautiful vista, indeed!

Now on I-81, when a road sign advised us we were two miles from Staunton, Jeff said, "This is where they marched back and forth for four years until Sheridan knocked the snot out of the Confederates."

Just as I looked out the window and saw an advertisement for Grand Caverns on a billboard, a slow driver loomed ahead of us. Jeff said, "A fella just kinda campin' there. 'Keep moving, friend!'"

We passed a sign giving us the mileage to New Market and Winchester. Jeff said, "Both New Market and Winchester were Civil War sites. This valley was a breadbasket for the soldiers. Sheridan paid for the food he took from the natives, mainly Quakers. Then destroyed the food his army didn't eat before moving on so the Confederates had no food when they arrived. Sherman was his mentor in Atlanta and Savannah."

"Thanks for the adventure through history, Jeff. I appreciate it," I said.

"You're welcome. A sad war for the sake of preserving the Union. Let's try the radio again. Lighten things up," Jeff suggested, turning the knob on the dashboard. We hummed and tapped along with *King of the Road* and *Across the Alley from the Alamo*.

In Maryland, we veered onto I-70 and up into Pennsylvania and shining sun! Now turning off I-30 onto state road 915, Jeff steered the Caddy down our familiar five miles of steep winding mountainous road. I sat glued to my seat, hands gripped together, excitement flowing through me, and a grin transforming my face. I was back! I was back in Fulton County, in these Sidling Hill Mountains of Pennsylvania! I peered out the window, straining to see white dogwood blossoms. It was too late! They'd come and gone. Laurel, then, pale pink on low bushes. No. No laurel. Rhododendron, then. Yes! Yes, there it was on both sides of the road. Bushes large and flowers bright pink! Clusters of them! One bush after the other with a background of tall oak trees and shorter pines and saplings. Even the straggly underbrush was a feast to my eyes. "Look! Look at the rhododendron!" I exclaimed to Jeff, his eyes on the road, steering the car to accommodate the curves, foot on the brake to slow the acceleration as the road sharply descended five and ten percent grades like a plunging roller coaster track.

"I see them, I see them. They're a picture to behold!" he said changing gears to second. On the level at the bottom of the mountain, we turned in a lane, rumbled over a wooden bridge, and pulled up close to the Shack. Ron saw our car pass his house and immediately high-tailed it over.

"Have a good trip?" he wanted to know. "Hain't had much rain here. Gonna need it fer the corn crop an' the hay an' what not. Been mighty dry." Then he helped us unload our suitcases and the food we'd purchased en route. In the distance, we heard the sound of whirling mowers in farmers' fields, a constant sound from day break 'til sundown. I took a deep breath and inhaled fresh country air with aromas of hay and alfalfa.

From the room where we'd stored it for the winter, Ron took out the porch furniture, as I directed placement. "The redwood two-seater and matching straight and rocking chairs face the meadow, the small redwood tables in between. The old wooden rocker gets relegated to its space in the corner. Did you know my father bought it at his uncle's auction? I'll put the cushions on the seats." Then we went inside and brought out the long aluminum folding table and old folding chairs. My mother had given me the chairs and matching bridge table when I married in 1947. We placed the aluminum table and folding chairs facing the meadow and in position for eating. Lastly I covered the long table with a plaid plastic-coated tablecloth folded to fit.

"See you folks later," Ron said, leaving us to unpack our suitcases and put food supplies in the refrigerator and kitchen cabinets. Before we came, Ron had turned on the water since, in the fall, he'd drained the pipes and turned off the water source for the winter. He'd turned on the refrigerator and filled the ice cube trays, too. That evening we sat on the screened-in porch and relaxed with our cocktails. As we sipped our drinks and talked of plans for the morrow, we watched noisy squirrels climb up and down the thick trunk of the two-hundred-year-old Norway spruce near the corner of the porch. They jumped from its long branches over to adjacent branches of an ancient cedar, back down to the ground, and then scampered away.

Chirping birds outside our open bedroom windows wakened us at dawn the next morning. Downstairs we looked out the picture windows of the family room and there in the meadow were a doe and her twin fawns! "Shhh," Jeff cautioned as we stood motionless, quietly watching the doe standing erect looking and listening while her twin fawns nuzzled their noses into the wild-growing grass.

In the afternoon several days later, I heard the loud grinding of Ron's power mower in the meadow. I knew he would come in for a drink and stay for dinner after he finished his weekly mowing. So I called to Jeff, the forever chef, "Ron's here. Better put another potato in the pot."

His mowing completed, Ron walked onto the porch and into the Shack just as Jeff was mixing our drinks. He helped himself to his favorite brand of bourbon we always stocked in the dry sink for him.

Now out on the screened-in porch having our cocktails and looking out into the meadow, Ron said to us, "Took my neighbor to the hospital yesterday."

"The one you've been looking after?" I asked, turning my head to look into his green eyes in a tanned face.

"The one," he answered, his large hand reaching into the bowl of chips on the plaid-covered table. "Asked me to pay his light bill. Always pays cash. Never banks his money. Doesn't believe in banks."

"Not a very smart man," Jeff remarked.

Eyes crinkling, Ron laughed. "Depends on yer taste. I use two banks. One in McConnellsburg, nother in Waterfall. I go into his house this mornin' to git the money. He's got more money hid in that house than's in any bank."

"Really?" Amazed, I raised my eyebrows, remembering Ron's elderly neighbor who lived in an old trailer and never went anywhere, to my knowledge. I always thought he was poor, indigent actually.

Ron laughed again. "Yeah. Has it stuffed in cans an' jars an' whatnot. Musta pulled out a couple thousand dollars lookin' fer money to pay his light bill. Has it hid other places I hain't looked." Changing the subject, he said, "Bought some shares of Red Hat yesterday. Went up eight points today."

My ears perked up. "Do you hear that, Jeff?" I called into the kitchen where he'd gone to check on the potatoes boiling on the stove. "We need to buy Red Hat. It's red hot!"

"Maybe," Jeff said, bringing out the cribbage board and placing it on the plaid tablecloth. He looked at me. "Your deal. You won last night."

The three of us pulled chairs up to the table, and Ron looked on with interest as Jeff and I started to play. Except for the clicking of shuffled cards, the game proceeded uninterrupted except for occasional crafty cribbage comments and Ron's questions about the scoring. At the end of the game, Jeff having won and our glasses empty, we brought out the ham, mashed potatoes, and green beans. No fancy meals at the Shack. Just plain cookin.' But always dessert which is usually ice cream with a dab of chocolate sauce and cookies.

The next day as expected, Kasey, Jeff's grandson, came to visit from Holland, Michigan, driving his father's red sports car. We decided to take him to Gettysburg to see the battlefield. Before we went in to view the electric map, Ron's purchase of Red Hat ever on my mind, I found a telephone and called my stockbroker friend. "I'd like to buy shares of Red Hat," I told him.

"Purchase price sky-rocketed today. Are you sure you want to buy it at today's price? It may be due for a drop," he cautioned.

I didn't heed but instead responded with confidence, "Yes, I want to buy today. Buy 300 shares." My big mistake! The stock went up a little and then took a tumble. The next time I saw Ron I said, "Ron, Red Hat's not doing very well."

"Oh I don't have it no more. Sold it at an eight thousand dollar profit."

My heart sank. I should have listened to my trustworthy stockbroker.

It was just two summers ago that Jeff purchased a John Deere Gator from Tim Mosebey, a local farmer friend who was also a John Deere distributor. I'd asked Jeff what he planned to do with it, and he'd said, "I'm gonna drive it around your property. I'm interested in seeing just what all you have in your woodland. What's up the hill behind the Shack, for one thing."

I'd told him, "Years ago I planted a number of seedlings up there. Virginia pine and spruce. To keep down the undergrowth. My father used to plant potatoes up there. I haven't been up there lately. Go up and have a look," I'd said, pleased he was interested.

He'd come back down and confronted me. "That tract of land up there needs attention. Trees need trimming. Undergrowth needs cleared. I could make it a beautiful area."

"Be my guest," I'd said and smiled at him.

So almost every day now, weather permitting, Jeff got on his gator and drove it up a rather steep two-track trail to the top of a level area behind the Shack where he worked on his project of trimming and clearing.

Meanwhile, I was into a project of my own on the computer. The project had to do with Patsy Taylor, a former inspector of mine when I supervised licensing of assisted living facilities in Pennsylvania's Western Region. She was attending Penn State University, obtaining her master's degree in Health Administration. From time to time, she sent her term papers via e-mail for me to critique. The last one she'd sent, titled *Aging in Place*, struck me as being a possible continuing education course for publication in a nursing magazine. Since RNs must obtain twenty-four credit hours of continuing education over a two-year period to maintain their license, many nurses subscribed to nursing magazines and opted to take courses available in these magazines. I'd written and had published three continuing education courses in the past, so why not co-author this paper of Patsy's as a current course? I'd phoned her from Florida. "Patsy," I'd said. "I like your term paper, and I think it would make a good article for a continuing education course. How would you like to co-author it with me and submit it to a nursing magazine for consideration?"

"I'd love that!" she'd exclaimed. "How will we do that? What would we title it?"

"We'll use the same title as your paper. *Aging in Place*. I'll pick out certain sections of your article that we need to keep, delete some, and I'll add sections pertaining to nursing. I'll go ahead and do that and send you my version as an attachment to an e-mail." I could hear her squealing with excitement and smiled as I continued. "After you read it and send me your comments, we'll finalize it. I'll send a query now and let you know if the editor's interested. He knows me by now, and I'm pretty sure he'll want to review it. But we'd better not count our chickens before they're hatched."

"Great!' she'd almost shouted. "I'd give anything to be published!"

I received a positive answer from the continuing education program director. He'd been promoted to executive director, however, and instructed me to send the article to a continuing ed editor I'd never heard of, one in the state of California. We hadn't known it then, but that's when we'd met our waterloo.

Patsy and I had finalized the article to our satisfaction, communicating back and forth on our computers, and I'd sent it to the new editor. She'd come back to me with many comments and questions, the likes of which I'd never encountered before. We'd gone back to the drawing board, Patsy working on revisions in Pennsylvania, I in Florida. After much work, I'd sent our *perfect* article to this new editor. I was at the Shack when more questions were fired back from the editor. This was an irritating development, to say the least. Some of the questions applied to Patsy's part of the paper, some to mine. Patsy sent her answers to my Shack computer, and I combined them with my answers and e-mailed them to the never-satisfied editor a week ago.

This morning when Jeff went up on the hill in his gator, I went to the computer and clicked on *e-mail.* "Welcome! You've got mail," it said. I opened it and read, "Jean, I've sent your revised article to three reviewers. I'll contact you when I receive results from these reviewers. Thanks, M. J. Collins, Continuing Education Editor."

Frustrated, I e-mailed Patsy, gave her the news, told her we were in a holding pattern, and not to give up.

Seventeen

Summer

Every last Saturday in July, Homecoming was celebrated in Wells Tannery by villagers, nearby farmers, former residents, and interested and curious people from surrounding towns. Jeff and I looked forward to this event starting at eleven in the morning with a most unusual parade. Since police barricaded the road into the village at eleven, Jeff and I drove into the village before then and parked just off the road along a length of grassy lawn between two houses.

"Let's put our folding chairs in the shade of these trees," Jeff suggested to me getting them out of the trunk of the Caddy and opening them near people who were already sitting in shady spaces. In fact, both sides of the road going through the village were lined with parked cars and people of all ages, both sitting and standing. Porches of village houses were crowded with owners and their out-of-town relatives and friends, all expectant viewers.

Suddenly band music could be heard in the distance, and the crowd grew quiet. "I wonder if that's the Forbes Road High School band?" I said, straining to see the end of the road where the parade always started.

"Here come the fire trucks," Jeff said as four enormous fully-equipped shiny-red fire trucks and emergency vehicles approached and drove slowly by. Clearly printed in large letters on the sides of the vehicles were the names of the fire departments of nearby towns. Through their open windows flew pieces of wrapped candy thrown by the occupants to children standing by the side of the road, eyes wide open. Next came baton-twirling youngsters and a few toddlers guided by mothers. We smiled and clapped as they marched by clad in identical short skirts and skimpy tops, many out of step, batons swinging to the right and some to the left. Dropped batons were quickly retrieved by unabashed mothers as little feet continued to skip along. Behind them rode a modern tractor at a snail's pace, marching music blaring from a loud speaker atop its roof. Alas, not the high school band! Next rumbled a church float carrying parishioners dressed in old-fashioned clothing, holding hymnals, and pretending to sing.

"Look, Jeff," I said pointing to a farmer boy plodded along next pulling a calf by a rope down the middle of the road.

The parade continued with farm machinery, antique cars, and top-of-the-line car agency vehicles, all occupants throwing handfuls of candy out open windows. Again as candy flew through the air and scattered to the ground, children scurried around gathering as many pieces as their little hands would hold. Following them, various sizes of sleekly groomed horses with young riders pranced by. Then another float carrying a large cardboard replica of a church with a steeple and the words *Jesus Loves You* printed on the side. On-lookers clapped and waved as the parade moved slowly from one end of the village to the other and back again, a total distance of one and a half miles.

The parade concluded, the crowd started to disperse. We went back to our car and followed other cars down a partially paved road to the Park where the Homecoming celebration would continue throughout the day. As we left the Caddy the aroma of roasting chickens penetrated our nostrils. "Let's walk around and have a look," Jeff said, leading me by the hand around the park building where whole chickens sizzled on huge grills. They were being turned by a smiling perspiring farmer who, like a proud chef, was sprinkling oil on the birds and watching them change to a perfect bronze. We decided to eat and stood in line outside the door to the one-room park building. Along with the line, we moved inside and waited again. People were eating at two long tables, fans whirling overhead. With trays in hand, we helped ourselves to dishes of baked beans, applesauce, and canned fruit lined up on side tables. At the serving line, apron-clad women stood behind kitchen counters dishing out beef barbecues, whole chickens, and roast beef sandwiches.

"What are you having?" Jeff asked me.

"Chicken," I responded without thinking twice although the other two choices looked mighty tempting.

"I'll have chicken too, please," Jeff said to the woman holding an empty plate in one hand and waiting with questioning eyes for his order.

We continued on to a table containing an array of pies and cakes baked by local women. I picked up a piece of German chocolate cake with caramel icing while Jeff chose his favorite apple pie. After helping ourselves to beverages, we walked over to a small table manned by two more volunteers, each with a tin box of bills and coins. One scanned our laden trays and announced an amount. Jeff pulled the money out of his pocket and handed it over. Trays in hand, we walked to one of the long tables and sat down across from people I knew from years ago but had forgotten their names. We smiled, said, "Hello," and then gave full attention to our food, tackling the chicken like cave men.

Thankful for Wet Wipes and satiated, we went outside and were immediately confronted with a parked ice cream wagon. "How could anyone eat ice cream after all the food served in that building?" Jeff wanted to know.

"You'd be surprised. Many do. And the truck stays there all day. You'd be surprised how many people eat ice cream in addition to all the other food. Grape nut is the favorite," I said, thinking I just might have some myself after awhile.

"You don't say? I never heard of grape nut ice cream," Jeff said.

"You've never lived here," I responded and had to laugh.

The weather was pleasant and a few people were eating outside at picnic tables spaced in no special order on the grounds. A baseball game was in full swing, and children bobbed for apples or waded in the creek running along the edge of the property.

As I was watching people greet each other for the first time since last years' Homecoming, an elderly man grabbed me and said, "Jean! I haven't seen you in years! How've you been?"

Startled, I stared at him, and all of a sudden I recognized Mike Horton. I'd dated Mike when I was visiting my grandparents one long-ago summer. "Mike Horton! How are you?" I exclaimed, returning his embrace and feeling a bony body in my clutches.

I suddenly realized I'd heard that his wife had died several years ago. "I'm doin' okay. Goin' fer some ice cream now," he answered, and off he shuffled toward the ice cream wagon before I had an opportunity to introduce him to Jeff.

From mid-afternoon until late evening in a bandstand on the grounds, rotating groups of musicians played country music on banjos, guitars, auto harps, harmonicas, and accordions. We found a bench near the bandstand and sat down to listen. Many were sitting on other benches or on the grass, and children ran around laughing and playing tag. Ron came by and sat with us. With one of the musical groups, a female vocalist soloed in a soprano voice that shrilled on high notes like the misplayed strings of a violin. Each time she hit a high note, the three of us winced.

Although Homecoming was the high-light of summer for most people in the valley, Jeff and I also enjoyed family-style dinners served on Sundays in the fire halls of three nearby towns. Occasionally, farmer friends invited us to dinners. For special events to celebrate holidays and birthday, they invited us to cook-outs and picnics held outside on their sprawling lawns or in their huge barns in inclement weather. The food was always plentiful as extended families and guests never failed to bring something—a salad, a green bean casserole, chips and dip, baked beans, scalloped potatoes, a cake, or a pie. Our contribution was usually deviled eggs. One farmer's specialty was home made ice cream. To reciprocate, we invited a few special friends and served dinner in the Shack dining room or on the porch, sometimes grilling on the patio beyond the porch. We felt fortunate to have these farmers as friends. Always we went to our favorite restaurant, Ed's Steak House, the day we shopped for food thirty miles away in the historic town of Bedford.

What a different life from the one at Sandycreek Terrace! What a relief to see different faces, faces of all ages, faces of long-time friends, and no canes, walkers, or scooters. Therapeutic was the word. I breathed deeply and thanked God I had this retreat, this place where I belonged and had roots.

I knew Jeff enjoyed being here, too, but not in the same way I did. He'd probably be happy to get back to Sandycreek Terrace next month. But here he could and did dress as he pleased, for dinner as well. He wore baggy dungarees, red plaid cotton shirts, a Navy visor cap and carried several garden tools, like a typical farmer, the many days he drove up to the back woods in his beloved John Deere Gator. He told me, "I'm going to ride up and see how well my little evergreen trees are growing. The shoots I planted over the last six years."

He rode back down and announced, "Trees are doing fine! You should see them. I tried to pull up some underbrush and dig around, but all I did was whack off some dead branches. Just couldn't do any more! I don't have the strength I had last year. It's hell to get old!" He frowned, heaved a sigh, and parked his Navy cap on a knob of a ladder-back dining room chair.

One morning after coming back from the post office with our mail he announced, "Let's give a going-away party. Invite the neighborhood! Develop wild life. Throw a party!"

I ignored his attempt to be funny. "Have you lost your mind?" I asked. I stared at him in disbelief.

"No, no! I'm serious. Let's give a whopper. I'll buy a ham and a turkey. We'll make potato salad or buy some. Have baked beans, of course. Sliced tomatoes, pickles, olives, onions, buns. And a layer cake for dessert."

"What do you mean by invite the neighborhood?" Surely he meant our close farmer friends, about twelve, perhaps.

"The neighborhood," he repeated, a big grin on his face. "Post a notice in the post office, in the church. Invite any other friends you'd like to have."

I was aghast. "You must be kidding! In this little house? We don't have room!"

"Have plenty of room. The porch, the patio, the meadow. Open up the dining room table. Put in the two leaves. Put the food on it with the turkey and ham on boards to slice it as we go. And the other food. Spread it around the table. We'll book it as an Open House, and people will come and go. They won't all be here at the same time. Hell, Jeanie, this will be fun! Get that worried look off your face," he commanded me still looking shocked and disbelieving such an undertaking could take place. "We'll have a great time!" he assured me. "I'll do all the work. All you have to do is be hostess. Greet and talk to the guests."

No use to argue further; Jeff's mind was made up, and that was that!

We set the time for three in the afternoon. I even called friends who didn't live in the valley, as Jeff suggested. I called Dick Langdon and his bride in Hopewell. Dick's deceased wife had been my dear friend for years. And I called Dick and Doris Clark in Shellsburg. Doris was Director of RSVP, the Retired Senior Volunteers Program, at the local office headquartered in Bedford. I'd volunteered in that program for the past five years, and my most recent assignment was interviewing board members and writing their life stories (as much as they cared to have printed) for a column in the RSVP monthly newsletter. One such RSVP board member was Roxie. For my interview with her, we arranged to meet for lunch at a Bedford restaurant. She impressed me as a chic dresser and had a very natural-looking hairdo, one that I decided to imitate. I've shunned perms ever since. During lunch and the interview we'd had such fun that we decided to go shopping together afterward. One of the shops we chose was Elaine's Driftwood Gallery where I bought my first Vera Bradley hand bag because I admired the one Roxie carried.

In answer to my Open House invitation, she said, "I have houseguests."

"Bring them along," I said.

"All right. And I'll bring my male friend, too."

Jeff and I had no idea how many would come to our Open House, but Jeff had bought and prepared plenty of food, had cold beer on hand, and a variety of soft and *hard* drinks. Our good friend, Edith Mosebey, three farmhouses down the road, and without my request, had sent son Tim in advance with a number of much needed stack-chairs to arrange on the patio.

The first guests arrived at one-thirty not three! Apparently Ron's uncle and his girl friend didn't want to be late. We insisted they stay, and they did. Most of the others came at the advertised time with the exception of a few stragglers. Rosie not only brought her houseguests and male friend but also a neighbor who was most appreciative and even sent us a thank-you note, the only one we received. After coming into the dining room and filling their plates, almost all our guests went out to the patio to eat. They sat on the chairs, the half wall on one side of the patio, and the steps leading to the porch.

148

I don't believe our thirty guests, mostly farmers, knew the meaning of the words *Open House*, however, for they stayed until dusk, all of them except the postmaster and her husband, that is. So much for Jeff's *they won't all come at the same time and they'll come and go*. But we were happy they stayed, had good appetites, and seemed to enjoy themselves. Now the clean up! And bless him, dear Ron stayed and worked like a Trojan until the Shack looked like no party had ever been held. Jeff had had his bash, and I was not the worse for it. In fact, I *had* enjoyed it and, for the most part, had just played the role of hostess.

September arrived, and Jeff and I discussed our trip to Arlington, Virginia to attend his ship reunion that was always held annually at some special venue in the U.S. Every year since we'd been married, we'd joined Jeff's ship mates who served on the USS Case Destroyer in the Pacific during World War II. At the conclusion of this year's reunion, we planned to drive directly back to Florida.

News on TV alerted us to a small hurricane brewing in the Caribbean Islands. *Frances*, newscasters were calling it. We listened throughout the day and learned she was increasing in velocity and moving north. The next day, Frances was upgraded from a category three to a category four, was passing west of Cuba and continuing due north. We listened again in the evening and were apprised her course had changed, the eye increasing in size and expected to hit the southwest coast of Florida. As erratic as she seemed to be, we feared for our CCRC and surrounding area. In the morning, the TV newscaster was saying Frances was now heading for Miami and then up the east coast of Florida! Yes, we did have cause to fear for Sandycreek Terrace.

"That means Jupiter! I wonder if Sandycreek Terrace is prepared?" Jeff exclaimed, eye brows knitted, a worried look on his face.

I said, "At the last executive meeting we attended the man in charge of security talked to us residents about preparedness. We were strongly advised to stock up on drinking water, canned foods, and flashlights. Hurricane shutters would be attached to all windows, he said. The Club House has an emergency generator in the event power is lost. Park Place has one, too. I remember how seriously he cautioned about hurricanes."

"That's right, he did" Jeff said. "He also said Sandycreek Terrace has arrangements with other CCRCs and resorts up north near Orlando and down south near Miami to take in our residents if they have to be evacuated. I hope that's not necessary."

I frowned. "Moving ninety and hundred-year-old people isn't wise in any case, health-wise especially. And we have several hundred-year-old women and ninety-year-old men and women. Would be quite a job to move residents in Park Place." I continued to frown, thinking of such an undertaking. I'd never witnessed a hurricane or been anywhere a hurricane was predicted. I did remember the tornado in little Boston, a town near Pittsburgh. At least I remembered the results. The night that catastrophe had occurred I was on the operating room staff of a nearby hospitals. The entire O.R. staff was called out to care for the wounded arriving in ambulances and by the car-load. We worked all that night and the next day, non-stop.

Jeff started up the steps to the second floor. "I'm gonna get into the web. See if I can get any details about our area down there."

Also concerned, I started up after him and into the guest bedroom where, three years ago, we'd assigned one wall to a desk equipped with a computer, monitor, and printer.

Jeff had activated the computer and logged on when I walked into the room. Excited, he said, "Look here! I've found a web site talking about Jupiter. Now it's talking about Sandycreek Terrace! They've evacuated all the residents!"

"They must be expecting the worst! If the buildings are damaged, it might be a while before residents can be moved back," I reasoned out loud. "What about us? How will we know? How will we know if we should go back?" I was getting more and more concerned.

The next day on the same web site, the company that owned Sandycreek Terrace and other CCRCs throughout the country gave viewers a telephone number for relatives to use to inquire about the status of evacuated residents. We called but got no information about the condition of our Jupiter complex. Attempts the next few days brought only information saying the residents were safe in their temporary homes.

Three days before we were to leave for Arlington, repercussion from Frances was felt as far north as Pennsylvania and beyond. Not as a hurricane, but as torrential rains and high winds. At the Shack, since the meadow between the house and the streams had frequently flooded, we knew what to expect, we thought. Jeff moved his Cadillac and my Volvo to higher elevation where we'd always moved cars before when the streams overflowed and filled the meadow.

Rain that started in the morning continued all day and was still pelting down when we went to bed at nine that night. The meadow was flooded, but we had expected that. Jeff got up two hours later, traipsed down the stairs in his bare feet and jamies. When I heard the door to the porch open I knew he was going outside. I went to the window above the porch and saw that he'd turned on the flood light. Tree branches blocked my view, and I couldn't see anything so I waited. Then I heard the porch door bang closed and the old wooden steps to the second floor creak under Jeff's bare feet.

"I think we're going to be all right," he said to me. "That flood light has a powerful beam. When I flicked it on I could see the cars clearly. The tires are sitting in water, even on the higher ground where we moved the cars. But the water's not up to the hubcaps of either car. The water's muddy, and the whole place out there is like a lake. The water's still covering and obscuring the meadow, of course. The dusk-to-dawn light showed me that. I could even see the bridge and part of the lane leading to the main road. Everything's under some water but not much, I don't think. I doubt that the state road going north to the village and south to route US 30 is under water. Rain seems to be letting up. We're going to be all right," Jeff assured me again and climbed gently back into bed.

In the morning, we were up before seven and dressed. The rain had stopped. Jeff went out to the cars and came back. I looked at his blank expression and waited. What news did he have? "You need to come out and have a look," he said to me in an unusually somber voice.

I didn't know what to expect as we both went out onto the porch, the patio, and down onto the soggy ground. Ahead of me, Jeff opened the front door of the Cadillac. Water pooled on the floor! The front seats were in horizontal positions! In mud, we walked around to the Volvo. That's when I saw the trunk lids of both cars standing ajar. The Volvo's sunroof was wide open! Its front seats reclined above a floor of muddy water! In shock, I stood there, saying nothing. I glanced toward the lane and saw one edge of the wooden bridge jutting unevenly out of muddy water, the remainder invisible! The lane was covered as well! Dejected, dazed, we walked back into the house.

Suddenly I remembered my father recalling a time when the creek flooded the meadow up to the house, the water rising seventeen inches in the cellar. What about now? I hurried into the kitchen and opened the door leading to the cellar. The water was right there! Up to the top step! Another eight inches and into the kitchen!

I flipped the light switch. No light! I walked to the sink and lifted the spigot handle. No water! "Jeff," I called to him in alarm. "We don't have electricity! We don't have water!" I went into the dining room and picked up the phone. Ah, a dial tone. "We have phone service! I'm going to call Ron. Tell him we have no water," I told Jeff.

"Yeah, well," Ron said. "Been up all night. Man and his truck got stuck in front a my house. Heared 'im screamin' an' struck out t' see. There he were, standin' on the roof a 'is truck sayin' he don't swim. Had t' wade out an' git 'im down. Brung 'im in t' the house an' give 'im dry clothes an' whatnot."

"You mean 915's flooded? I had no idea conditions were *that* bad!"

"Yeah. Road's supposed t' be closed all the way t' the top of the mountain but this bird, he don't pay no attention. Thought he could git through with 'is truck. Ya hain't got no water? I'll be over soon's I ken git through. May be a while."

I thanked him and reiterated his big news to Jeff.

At four that afternoon, things looked a little brighter. The electricity had come back on, and we saw bare-footed Ron wading across the lane and over the heaved-up bridge. His jeans were rolled up to his knees, and he was carrying a gallon bottle of water. Apparently the water had receded to the point where he had just now been able to come. We walked out onto the patio to greet him,

He stopped at our cars and gave one glance. "Totaled," he announced, shaking his head. "Mother boards flooded. Have ya called yer insurance company?"

That hadn't occurred to us. Back in the house, Jeff picked up the phone and dialed. A voice answered after his explanation of our plight. "Can't get over there for several days. We're flooded, too," Jeff was told.

"I'll help ya unload the cars," Ron offered.

Of course. That *was* the next thing to do. In preparation for our trip back to Florida, the Caddy had been partially packed with items now thoroughly mud-soaked. My dear Volvo, meant to stay at the Shack for our convenience next summer, was history. The end to that idea! And to the car I'd driven for years and dearly loved. Oh well, I knew I shouldn't be driving any more with my impaired vision. But I could have driven around the valley on country roads safely, couldn't I? Its demise saved me from making the decision as to whether to eventually sell it or give it to one of my grandchildren. But which one? Daniel or Elizabeth? Sometimes things have a way of working out on their own.

With Ron's help, we unloaded the cars of all contents. Jeff spread out the mud-soaked world atlas on the porch table although I couldn't imagine it would ever be legible enough to read if it did dry, what with all that mud. I removed the slightly damp woolen stadium blanket from its sturdy zippered plastic bag and hung it on the patio railing. Ron carried in items to be washed and dried and handed them to me standing at the kitchen sink. A number of items went into the trash.

"Jeff," I wailed, remembering we'd invited seven of our farmer friends for dinner. "We can't have our dinner party tonight. I'll call everyone and explain. They can't get here anyway. They can't drive over the bridge, heaved up as it is. Maybe they can't even get in the lane."

I opened the door to the cellar. The water had receded, but the cellar floor was covered with mud, the dehumidifier ruined, of course. Ron, bless his pea-pickin' heart, went down and cleaned up the entire mess after I gave him his requested rags, bucket of water, and soap.

Jeff stopped sorting glove compartment items. "We're in a fine kettle of fish. We have no car to drive to Arlington to the Case Reunion and back to Florida! I'll call my friend, Bill, at the Chevy dealership."

"It's Sunday, Honey. Will they be open?" I ventured to ask.

"Maybe not," Jeff said and wasn't surprised to receive no answer when he dialed the dealership in Bedford where he'd bought his Cadillac from salesman Bill several years ago. "Maybe they have a web site. Just a thought. " He went upstairs to the computer and came back down. "Got the web site. No used Cadillacs, only new ones. Two used Chevys, however. Never buy a brand new car. It depreciates the day you drive it onto the road."

That was Jeff's philosophy. I'd heard it before. More than once.

Early the next morning, I lay in bed and listened to the noise of Ron's tools putting the bridge back in place. As soon as Jeff reasoned the Chevy dealership would be open, he called and explained his dilemma to salesman Bill. When he hung up he turned to me and said, "Bill's on his way to the Shack. Says he has two relatively new Chevys he wants me to see."

"You mean he'll drive the thirty miles to the Shack to take you back thirty miles to the dealership and then bring you thirty miles back to the Shack?"

"That's what he said. But of course if I buy a car, I'll be driving it back here by myself." Jeff grinned, looking like a kid about to get a new toy.

The two men had been gone less than an hour when the phone rang. On the other end of the line, Jeff said, "I've examined the two Chevys. They're the ones listed on the web that I brought up yesterday. I judge either one would suit our purpose. One is four years old with sixty thousand miles. The other's two years old with twenty-five thousand miles. It's an Impala, Chevy's best but also much more expensive. What do you think?"

I had to give him an answer even though I was fairly sure he'd already come to a decision. That's been my experience in matters of this kind, but I appreciated being asked my opinion. And I imagined if I had a strong opinion differing from his, he would honor it and act accordingly. This time I said, "Honey, you'll be the driver of that car. You should get the one you think is best. Does either one have a warranty?" I asked.

"The newer one. And I think that's the one we should get. What do you think?"

"I agree," I said without hesitating.

"It might be some time before I get back, Honey. Papers to sign and all that. I'll be driving it home. See you soon as I can."

When I heard a car rattle over the wooden bridge I hurried out to see the purchase. "Well, it isn't a Cadillac, but I like the silver color," I said looking at the Impala sitting near the totaled Caddy and Volvo. "How do you like it? How does it drive?" I wanted to know.

"It will do just fine. I like the way she handles," Jeff assured me, patting the silver hood with the palm of his hand. "After I'd signed all the papers and written a check, I had to wait while they put on my Pearl Harbor Survivor plate."

"Of course," I said, knowing how much that license plate meant to him and remembering the times people had stopped and looked at it and then thanked him along with a nod or a shake of the hand.

The morning of the day we planned to drive the short distance to Arlington, we were still waiting for the insurance adjustor who had been contacted three days before and had promised a next day arrival. In not too pleasant a mood, Jeff called the agency. I waited to hear the outcome. Would we be able to leave today? Tomorrow? Would we make the reunion at all?

Jeff put the receiver in its cradle and turned to me. "'You're on his schedule,' that's what I was told."

"On his schedule for today?" I asked, knitting my eyebrows, skeptical.

"That's what the woman said, but she didn't know exactly when. Wasn't sure."

So we went ahead as though we were leaving in an hour. We had breakfast; Jeff packed a lunch to eat en route; I stripped the bed, put the bed linens and used towels in a plastic bag to take back to Florida to wash. Yesterday we'd brought in the porch furniture and stacked it in a room. The grill was now covered, off the patio, and on the porch. Packed suitcases were downstairs ready to be taken to the car. The refrigerator had been emptied except for items left for Ron to take for his own use. We were ready to go!

Three hours later, the adjustor's car rattled over the bridge and stopped. We hurried out to meet him. He climbed out of his car with a clip board and pen in hand. First he glanced over at the meadow, water still standing in low areas, and then he looked at our sad cars. "Had quite a flood, didn't you?" he commented in a friendly way. After he opened the car doors, checked the odometers, the floors, and the back interiors, he made numerous notes on the forms on his clipboard.

We stood watching and waiting for a verdict. I was holding an invoice containing a record and the cost of the new air conditioner I'd had installed in the Volvo at a dealership in Greencastle last week. "Will this invoice influence the appraisal," I asked, handing it to him.

He studied it and nodded. "Yes, it will. I'll attach it to my report. I can't give you a date for tow trucks to arrive. They're a busy crew. Lots of flooding. You don't have to be here when they come."

No sooner had he left than we hastily packed the car. But before we locked the door of the Shack to head for Arlington and eventually Florida in our silver bullet, we checked the web site. Residents had been returned to Sandycreek Terrace. It was safe for us to go back.

Jeff's shipmates were happy to see him. For the next four days, the old World War II sailors who had been together on a destroyer and were survivors of Pearl Harbor celebrated along with their wives and several adult children. First off, all gathered in the hospitality room of the previously arranged-for hotel for drinks and snacks and reminiscing.

The first full day, our group toured the new World War II Memorial. Next, we attended the Color Guard Ceremony at the Navy Memorial in Washington, D.C. where the ship's crew placed a wreath on a memorial. While there, we were invited to tour the Navy Memorial Museum and to gather in the auditorium to see the movie, *At Sea*. The movie completed, Jeff, being the only surviving officer of the Case, was requested to come onto the stage to say a few words. He was then presented a plaque commemorating the 1935 launching of the USS Case.

After hugs and goodbyes, Jeff and I parted from the group and began our long drive to Jupiter and Sandycreek Terrace.

Eighteen

Autumn

We were back! As we drove through the gate at the entrance to Sandycreek Terrace, Jeff looked around at the buildings and landscaping and said, "My, it's good to be back."

Didn't I just know that's what he would say! His exclamation was one of relief, almost joy. Maybe it was in response to being off the highway, free from the hassle of driving in traffic. But it was more than that, I felt sure. He really *was* glad to be back in our CCRC. I, on the other hand, couldn't say I was glad to be back. I didn't feel that way. I'd *been home*, enjoying my roots, old familiar surroundings and friends.

Now here we were cloistered again. Was that a good word? Maybe unfair. We certainly weren't in confinement; we could leave any time we chose. And we would, of course. But we were back to living with all elderly people. Of course, *we* were elderly, but we didn't feel elderly, never admitted it, at any rate. Weren't we the world's oldest teenagers, as Jeff frequently said? Several parishioners of the village Presbyterian Church were elderly, but here we were *all* elderly. We were back again with the abundant canes, walkers, scooters, limpers, humped backs, and arthritic postures and where a resident died every month or was admitted to Park Place. Where sirens blared until they entered the gate and made residents hold their breaths and wonder what resident needed emergency help. People died off campus, too, but I didn't know them, maybe one or two, not the majority as I did here living closely together. I knew I should be happy in this lovely place. I *did* enjoy my life with Jeff, our companionship, our sharing, our expressions of love.

I was pleased with the service we received, meals prepared and served

157

to us every evening with cocktails in advance. We enjoyed excellent food, whatever we desired from a lavish two-sided menu. I looked forward to Marigold's once weekly apartment cleaning and our bed made with clean linens without my lifting a finger, like living the life of Mrs. Heinz. Don't misunderstand. I liked the pleasant friendly residents and the courteous staff. I had to admit my ego was inflated at the Health Care Committee meetings when I had an opportunity to contribute information about long-term care that enlightened other members. The lovely library had large-print books I could borrow for an extended length of time or just sit in there on a comfortable couch and browse through books in front of a gas-burning fireplace in cool weather.

In our apartment filled with familiar furnishings, Jeff and I conversed on interesting subjects. He'd read me articles of interest, point out grammatical errors in newspapers and magazine articles, tell me jokes, and reminisce about past experiences of his boyhood, college days, and even about funny events that happened in the midst of a tragic war. How he survived as a high school principal was also interesting to hear. Best of all, we enjoyed each other. So why shouldn't I be glad to be back in Sandycreek Terrace the same as he? Perhaps more time was needed for me to adjust, to feel at home. After all, we moved here just eleven months ago, and we've been away for four.

Our Chevy was beyond the gate now, and Jeff drove slowly to our building so we could observe the damage wrought by hurricane Frances. "Look," Jeff exclaimed. "The carports are leveled! Look at all those trees! Down on the ground. Tiles off some of the roofs. Going to take some time to make repairs."

Our building appeared to be intact, no tiles off the roof. We parked and barely had time to unload our luggage before going to dinner. The receptionist at the front desk seemed glad to see us back. She opened a notebook and checked us in. This reminded me of my nursing school days. We checked out of the nurses' residence when we went out on a date, and the house mother checked us back in when we returned.

In the lounge the first people we met were Betty Howe and Ralph Wilson. Betty, the sweet little ninety-year-old lady, looked just the same, and Ralph, the hearing impaired resident who gave Jeff his address when asked his name, stood there smiling as usual. The two unmarried residents were a constant couple, it seemed.

Betty greeted us with a welcoming smile. "When did you get back?" she wanted to know.

"Just today. An hour ago," we said, smiling back at her.

"You probably haven't had time to catch your breath. We're not eating with anyone. Would you like to join us?" Betty asked us.

"Love to," Jeff replied, and I quickly agreed, thinking that here they were, the welcoming committee, just as they'd been the farewell couple before we left.

Together at a four-top table in the dining room, Jeff and I described the events of our summer and the loss of our two cars. Betty and Ralph listened intently, and Betty, with a look of disbelief on her sweet little face, voiced amazement at the tragic conclusion. "You mean Frances affected you that far up north?" She clutched at the scarf around her neck, and I recalled why she wore it. It was to hide her pocked skin, riddled from numerous squamous cell removal surgeries.

Ralph's southern voice slurred, "What did you say the hurricane did?" When Jeff repeated the story of the catastrophe Ralph shook his head and muttered, "You mean total destruction of both your cars?"

"That's right. Had to buy a car to get back here," Jeff said.

"Oh my! What a pity! What a shame!" As usual, Betty's interest and concern appeared genuine and heart felt.

As we ate, we listened to *their* tale of hurricane Frances and the evacuation of residents from Sandycreek Terrace. "I was fortunate to be able to go to a friend's home in a safe area, and Ralph's son took him to his house a distance away," Betty said, patting Ralph's arm.

I was barely able to interpret Ralph's southern drawl when he said, "Many residents were evacuated. Moved to different places."

"We heard about the plight of those evacuated residents," Betty said, leaning forward, fork in mid-air. "Ralph and I were very fortunate. Residents who were evacuated came back very displeased. They said they were fed, but the food was mediocre. They all had to sleep in one large room on cots. Some had difficulty getting up from those low cots. You know how that would be. Some have trouble getting out of chairs let alone getting up from such a distance near the floor. In the middle of the night when they had to go to the bathroom, they had trouble seeing. No night-lights or lights of any kind, you see. And one bathroom had to suffice for a number of people."

Between clearing his throat many times and coughing, Ralph managed to say, "The ones I spoke to say they'll never agree to be evacuated again. They'll stay here and face the consequences."

Although Ralph had lived in many northern and western cities, he clung to that southern speech of his, like a baby clung to its teething ring. For some reason, this irritated me because of my need to continually ask him to repeat. Why couldn't he stop trying to be southern and speak plain English like the rest of us? We've eaten with Ralph and Betty a few times before, and each time I've tried diligently to be patient and understand him, but I've failed utterly, regardless of my acute hearing and resolve.

These characteristics about Ralph didn't seem to bother Jeff, and I had to admit Ralph was a pleasant, very nice man, and he was kind to Betty and seemed fond of her. He'd been a civil engineer in his other life, and he and Betty had been friends before their spouses had died. They had their own living quarters, but I suspected they spent much time together. At least we saw them at parties and other events together, and always they ate dinner together. Betty made no bones about her age. Told everyone she was ninety. Ralph was probably close to that age but never said as much. Even though he used a cane, both he and Betty had excellent postures and walked at a good pace without noticeable difficulty.

Our server, an unusually tall female, was new to us. We complained about the open door to our left leading to the veranda and causing a cool breeze to enter chilling us and our main courses as well. She closed the door, noted that we'd finished our main courses, and asked, "What would you like for dessert? We have peach pie, bread pudding, and our usual selection of ice creams and sundaes."

"Do you still have that purple haze ice cream you had last night?" Betty asked.

"I'll go and check," she said, leaving for the kitchen and towering over other servers as she passed them.

When we got back to our apartment after dinner Jeff said, "Guess I'd better take my bike out of the living room and park it outside our front door again. And I'd better get back in the habit of riding it every morning while you take your walk." Because we had a recessed entry to our apartment, security had permitted us to park it outside. We felt it best, however, to bring it inside during our lengthy absence.

Lately I had to admit I was depending on Jeff more and more because of my poor vision. I'd drop an earring on the bedroom floor and couldn't find it; the hands on my watch were unclear much of the time. He'd come to my rescue by finding my jewelry and telling me the time. I was using my sense of touch more, feeling my ear lobe to locate the hole to insert my ear ring, feeling for the hole in my sandal strap to insert the buckle, feeling the crumbs on my place mat but not seeing them.

As for Jeff, his back pain was worsening. I realized this when he brought forth a cane out of hiding, started walking with it right there in the dining room, and commented, "I'm going to start using this when I walk outside. Did I ever show you this cane? Friend of mine who worked in a furniture factory made it for me."

He wiggled the cane in front of me. I took it from him to examine. The entire length was carved like a totem pole with faces of kings and queens. The handle was a likeness of a head of a duck. "How unusual!" I had to say, observing it more closely. "Quite a piece of work! Art, actually."

"*Is* nice, isn't it?" he said, grinning. The way he walked around the apartment testing the cane, a bandana hanging half-way out of his rear pants pocket, made me grin, too.

The next evening, Sarah Grant, the resident who wrote articles for publication in the *Periscope*, the monthly magazine, cornered Jeff after dinner. "I want to interview you for Resident of the Month," she said, long face serious, like a judge during a murder trial. "The article will appear in next month's *Periscope*."

Shortly after she interviewed Jeff but hadn't completed the article because she wanted Jeff to review it first, she fell on the boardwalk between the entrance to the Palace and the Club House. She fractured her right radius and sustained multiple bruises and abrasions of her face. I offered to type the revised article for submission to the editor of the *Periscope*.

Not wanting to appear in public until she recovered substantially from her banged-up condition, she invited Jeff and me to her apartment to review a revision of the final draft. I was truly impressed with her apartment! She'd crocheted or needle-pointed scatter-rugs, covers for decorative pillows, and intricate patterns she'd framed and hung on the walls. She'd even woven a room-sized rug for her sitting room. All were works of art. All masterpieces. Most impressive was a throw-rug woven in a design to match the wall paper in the guest bathroom. A piano, small organ, and many pieces of fine furniture over-filled the rooms.

As we left, I realized I now knew much about Sarah I hadn't known before. Aside from her ability to write and play the piano, I'd learned about her talent to design and produce works of art and now I knew she played the organ as well as all kinds of music by ear on the piano. I'd also learned she was writing a book about foster care.

As a social worker, she had placed children and elderly people in foster homes and assisted living facilities, and she knew, first hand, about the abuses that occurred in these homes and the difficulties of finding safe environments and caring caregivers. Currently she kept abreast of the status of these foster homes and assisted living facilities. She even communicated with several of her placements. For some time, she'd been in charge of the Symposium, providing the speaker for the monthly evening event held in the Palace. Quite a remarkable woman!

One change we noticed in resident status on our return was that of Grace Terwilliker, the woman who'd insisted Jeff subscribe to the same back treatment she had. She was limited to two drinks before dinner. As we joined her and her friend Polly at a table in the lounge one evening, she again insisted Jeff should have a morphine implant to control his back pain.

She asked again, "How is your back, Jeff?"

When Jeff said it was no better and he didn't expect it to be because further back surgery was not an option, Grace said, "I told you what to do, and you won't listen. Get what I have, and you won't have any more pain. Why don't you listen?"

Jeff tried to explain again saying, "My back problem isn't the same as yours. I've done everything possible. Three injections of a steroid two different times only lasted a week each time. And physical therapy had no appreciable effect."

"Didn't that help at all?" she asked.

"No."

"That's why you need what I had done. Why don't you listen?" she persisted.

I leaned forward and said, "Don't you have to have the pump replaced with morphine routinely?"

"Well, yes. But that's nothing." She waved away the thought with a flick of her ponderous palm.

"I wouldn't want to go through that," Jeff said.

With a disgusted look, Grace said, "Oh you don't want to get better," and picked up her drink.

Polly, sitting beside her, rolled her eyes as if to say it's no use talking to her.

"You're impossible!" Grace said to Jeff. Then seeing her glass was empty, she turned to Amelia at the bar and called over to her, "Fill my glass, Amelia."

Amelia said, "I can't do that, Mrs. Terwilliker. You've had two drinks."

"Oh!" Grace uttered in an exasperated manner. She jerked her head and settled back in her chair, eyes downcast.

Polly nodded as if approving Amelia's answer to her friend while Grace sat quietly wrapped in her chair. Would she be able to walk if she ever did get up?

Jeff and I became aware of a resident we'd never seen before. She had a pleasant face and didn't appear very elderly. Each evening she came into the dining room gripping two large bags at her sides, one in each hand, and wearing a full-length raincoat always draped over her shoulders. The bags weren't purses; they were larger, similar to tote bags made of sturdy canvas-like material. Nor was it hardly ever raining. How account for her raincoat? Residents were calling her The Bag Lady. Usually an elderly man trailed behind her, accompanying her to dinner. We were told he wasn't a resident of Sandycreek Terrace but that he lived in a nearby residential community and was The Bag Lady's guest. After dinner, bags in hand, raincoat over her shoulders, her male friend following, she traveled from one dining room table to another seeking a couple to play bridge. At times, she'd get a positive response, and the couple would join her and her friend in the card room.

One evening we agreed to play bridge when she approached our table. In the card room, she removed the cover from a table, retrieved playing cards from their stored spot, and invited us to sit down. She dealt the cards and proceeded to instruct us in the art of the game. We already knew how to play although we hadn't played since we came to Sandycreek Terrace. The bidding began, and again she started to teach. We informed her that her *kind tutoring* wasn't necessary. Her instructions continued, however, while her guest remained silent. At the end of a rubber, Jeff and I had racked up an overwhelming score, and, as we left the card room, we said to each other, "Never again!"

NINETEEN
PARK PLACE

The phone rang at noon on Thursday, October seventh, the day before Jeff's eighty-fourth birthday. On the other end of the line, Jeff's grandson Kasey said, "If it's okay with you guys, I'm going to drive up tomorrow. I wanna wish Grandpa a happy birthday. I have to come back to school Sunday, so I won't be staying long."

Both Jeff and I had picked up phones at the same time, and we both told him to come ahead, we'd be happy to see him. Ten minutes later, the phone rang again. I answered and heard, "Hi, Grandma. It's Daniel." What a coincidence! Two grandsons calling so close together!

"Why Daniel! How nice to hear your voice. How are you?"

"I have a few days off. Would it be all right if I came to visit?"

"Oh course!" I said, excited at the prospect. "When can you come?"

"I can get a flight Saturday. Arrives at the West Palm airport at eleven in the morning, if that meets with your approval."

"Yes of course. We'll meet you at the airport. At baggage claim. How long can you stay?"

"I can get a flight back to Louisville Tuesday. But I just have a carry-on, so I don't need to go to baggage claim. I'm flying Southwest Airlines, and I can meet you at the curb outside. I'll watch for you to drive up."

"Great!" I said. "We'll call ahead and make sure the plane's on time. Jeff's grandson Kasey will be here Saturday and Sunday. You met him at the Shack one summer. Give you someone to hang-out with. What's your flight number?"

After I hung up, I called to Jeff, "Guess what! That was Daniel on the phone! He's coming this weekend, too. This is grandson weekend! And your birthday! I don't think Daniel knows it's your birthday, and I didn't tell him."

"That's great!" Jeff said and chuckled. "We can show them off."

"Right! We can sleep one in the living room and one in the Florida room. Probably Dan in the living room because that couch is longer. You had it in your condominium apartment. I remember how I thought you should have had it facing side-ways." I laughed thinking how strongly I felt about the way it was positioned, not voicing my opinion at the time, of course. "Kasey's much shorter than Daniel. The couch that used to be in my den should be suitable for Kasey." I looked at Jeff for his approval and received a nod.

The sleeping arrangements worked out just fine, and the entire weekend was fun. Kasey, a seasoned visitor by now, took Dan over to the Club House to see the exercise room and have a work-out on the stationary bicycles, treadmills, and the balancing, weight lifting, and stretching equipment. We went to the dining room for dinner Saturday evening, and, before dinner, Jeff and I proudly introduced our grandsons to our resident friends who greeted them with smiles and handshakes in the lounge. Sunday after we shared a large cheese, mushroom, and pepperoni pizza for lunch, Kasey drove off to his university, and I showed Dan the croquet court, swimming pool, library, card room, and art room. Then Dan and I played cribbage with the end score in his favor. He won again when he played opposite Jeff. Unfortunately I had an ophthalmology appointment the nest day in Palm Beach Gardens at Bascom Palmer Eye Institute, always a prolonged visit. Daniel opted to stay in the apartment where he found reading material to occupy his time. His first visit ended all too soon.

Mr. and Mrs. Harry Scott were among newcomers to Sandycreek Terrace since we'd been away for the summer. We met this couple in the lounge one evening before dinner and learned Harry was a retired attorney and Bonnie a former legal secretary. Bonnie was a large dark-haired woman, very alert but quite incapacitated and needing continuous oxygen supplied by a small oxygen tank she carried with her in a canvas bag. When Harry heard me tell Bonnie I had been a registered nurse, he informed me he had had three years in medical school before changing his major. His medical background had been invaluable in his legal practice, he said.

We were in their company again the evening Irene Trenton invited us to her apartment for cocktails before dinner. I'd met Irene in the library the day I was seeking large print books. As a Library Committee member, Irene was devoting two hours of her time to the library this day. All committee members volunteered two hours twice a week and put returned books away, cataloged newly donated books, and assisted residents in their search for particular books and information. I'd told Irene, "I'm not interested in mystery books or those written by Danielle Steel. My preference is Anne Tyler or authors whose plots are meaningful and characters unusual and interesting." She'd helped me find a book to my liking. As we'd talked I learned she was a retired high school teacher and a very enjoyable conversationalist.

The evening we were invited to Irene's apartment, Jeff used his totem pole cane as we walked over to the Inlet Building in the rain. We rode the elevator to the third floor and walked the carpeted hallway to Irene's apartment. We'd been to this building before when we'd visited Pam and Ben Butcher when Ben was still living. Again we realized how much this building was like a hotel whereas our Sentinel Building was like a motel with outside corridors and no common areas.

When we walked into Irene's well-appointed living room there sat Dr. Tom Price dressed in a tweed jacket, his slacks hiding his prosthetic right leg. Harry and Bonnie Scott arrived directly behind Jeff and me, and Irene invited the four of us to choose any seat in the living room. I saw now that Bonnie had a sallow complexion and very poor posture. She chose to sit in a straight chair, her oxygen tank in its canvas bag by her side. Harry sat down on a couch beside her. He combed his fingers through his sandy white hair, and his large blue eyes in his fine-featured face protruded as though indicative of hyperthyroidism, I thought.

"I can make any drink you choose," Irene sang out from her kitchen. As guests gave her orders it was apparent her liquor cabinet was stocked with a variety to please everyone's taste. Without being asked, Tom was served Amber Bock beer and no glass. How did Irene know what he drank and how he liked it served? And did I detect a fondness in his voice when he thanked her for his beer?

Conversation flowed freely while we drank and munched on appetizers. Since Harry had graduated from Dickinson University, a law school in Carlisle, and so had my nephew Tom Ridge, and since I was familiar with that part of the state, Pennsylvania seeped into the conversation. Irene's home state was Michigan. As usual, sparked by mention of Michigan, Jeff talked of his beloved Holland, joking that it was on the civilized side of the state opposed to Detroit where crime abounded. All present had been to Holland, Michigan during tulip time and exclaimed about the beautiful flowers and Dutch dancers in their wooden shoes. Bonnie contributed much until she suddenly sat back in her chair and was quiet, apparently needing to rest. During the conversation, Irene spoke lovingly about her deceased first husband, a physician in practice with Tom Price. We learned she had come to Sandycreek Terrace with her second husband who had died three years ago.

The next day on my way to the mailbox, I saw our neighbor Ruth McKee sweeping leaves deposited on the walk in front of her apartment by the night's storm. She stopped sweeping and said, "I saw you last night in the dining room with Dr. Tom Price and Irene Trenton. Who was the other couple?"

I told her so she'd be able to add to her wealth of information. Again it seemed to me that her role at Sandycreek Terrace was gathering and imparting information.

"Did you know," she said, "that Tom's wife, Elizabeth, is a resident in Park Place? She's crippled by a recurrence of polio?"

I didn't know, of course. So at the close of the next Health Care Committee meeting, I had an opportunity to ask Tom about his wife's health. "Elizabeth's in Park Place. Our nursing home. You can go and visit her. She'd like that very much," he informed me and added, "But go in the afternoon. Her caregiver's busy with her in the morning. She might appear to be sleeping. Don't let that stop you. Just knock on the door and walk in."

One afternoon shortly thereafter, I walked over to Park Place, passing the wreathed apartment doors, the palm trees and flowers in the courtyards of our Sentinel Building, on past the Palace, into to the Club House and past the front desk, dining room, and beauty salon. All along the halls of the Club House colorful, striking, framed paintings hung like a wallpaper design. They were large and small, the efforts of talented residents. When I crossed the covered latticed-walled walkway, I admired again the little pink and white impatiens blooming on either side of the walkway. Doors opened automatically when I pressed a red button. And there I was, back in a nursing home! Not as a director of nursing or as a surveyor, but as a visitor. I couldn't explain the haunting feeling that suddenly overcame me. The environment was familiar yet the staff looked at me as though I were a stranger. I wanted to say, "Don't you know who I am?" From force of habit, I inhaled more deeply than necessary and detected a faint odor of urine common in all nursing homes, more so during times of linen changes but also on a permanent basis in most.

After saying hello to the secretary manning the circular center-station, I inquired as to the location of Mrs. Price's room. Given directions, I walked down the second of four wings past rooms occupied by one or two residents and on to Elizabeth's private room. She did, as Tom had said, appear to be sleeping. But when I knocked on the open door, her eyes fluttered and opened and, in a barely audible voice, she told me to come in. Her motionless body was positioned in a recliner placed between a window and her bed. I walked in, passed the bed, and stood near her, observing the little face topped with curly white hair. Her chin almost touched her chest. I introduced myself, and her thin lips opened a tiny bit forcing out a half smile while little beady eyes peered out at me. "Tom said you might come," I heard her say. "I'm glad you did. Have a seat. The chair over there or the bed."

The chair near the window on the other side of the bed would have been inconvenient for conversing considering her head was turned toward the bed. Therefore I chose to sit on the side of the bed, easing between a walker stationed at the foot of her recliner and foot of her bed. A small table to her right held a telephone, a magnifying glass, and a hand towel.

I started a conversation by telling her, "Jeff, my husband, and I moved into Sandycreek Terrace just about a year ago. We'd lived in Pine Gardens before we moved here. We had a large single-family house, but it was getting too much for Jeff to keep up. To pick the oranges and grapefruit from the trees in the backyard, you see. And climb up a ladder to change a light bulb or fix a ceiling fan."

She was attentive and her eyes focusing on me but her head remained motionless. Except for her frail hands and arms moving occasionally over her lap, she was immobile. Paralyzed, I realized. Her responding words came slowly, and I leaned closer to hear.

"You have children?" she asked me.

"Three," I answered, holding up three fingers. "A boy and two girls."

"I have three, too. Two girls and a boy. He's the youngest."

Although difficult to hear, the response encouraged me to continue. "My son's the oldest. That's what I hoped for because I always wanted an older brother. I have no siblings," I explained.

The conversation went on from there as we talked about where we'd lived, where our children lived, and where we'd traveled. She and Tom had traveled extensively, I learned. When I glanced at the large clock on the wall across the room I saw I'd stayed a half hour. Long enough, no doubt, as her voice was becoming weaker and more difficult to hear. "I'd best be going, Elizabeth." I said to her.

Her eyes focused on me again, and her thin lips moved. "Thank you for coming. Come back."

"The pleasure was all mine, Elizabeth. And I'll be back next week," I promised her and left. I knew at that moment I was committed to make every effort to visit weekly.

Jeff and I were becoming acquainted with an interesting and prominent couple who lived in one of the cottages and always seemed to arrive in the lounge before dinner at the same time we did. The couple's name was Ferris. They'd been residents for six years. Paul Ferris had been a colonel in the U.S. Marine Corps during World War II and was very well liked by the residents because of his charming and especially friendly personality.

One evening in the lounge, he and Jeff started a conversation about their days in World War II, and one experience led to another. As Jeff has this uncanny ability to do, he managed to have Paul expound on his extremely interesting life history. The story was that as a lad of eighteen, a third generation German American, Paul, along with other youths of German decent, had been offered a free university education in Germany by the Nazi government. Paul grabbed that educational opportunity. When World War II started quite naturally he was expected to join the Nazi army. Terrified, but able to speak fluent German and English, he somehow miraculously escaped from Germany to Austria where an acquaintance provided him transportation to Switzerland and from there to Genoa, Italy. He was then able to be evacuated on a U. S. ship to the United States. After he joined the U. S. Marine Corps, he rose from private to colonel.

Under what circumstances Paul met Penny and married her we were not privileged to know, at least not yet. At any rate, they were exact opposites in personality. He was unassuming and quiet, and she was highly opinionated and self-aggrandizing because of their influential contacts. To hear wife Penny talk, she and Paul knew every important person in every renowned place in the States and abroad. When we mentioned a place we had frequented she had been there in the most elite section and knew prominent people who resided there. Perhaps her constant attempts to impress people replaced some lack of security she'd experienced in her past life. Served as her support system, so to speak. Paul appeared to ignore such claims to fame and tolerated her braggadocios conversations.

Unfortunately, Paul was now suffering from congestive heart failure. His cardiac problem required frequent admissions to Park Place for a stay of several days after which he'd be discharged to their cottage. I found myself feeling sorry for Penny. When Paul was in the Health Center I had an opportunity to talk to Penny alone. I realized she was very concerned about Paul, and I developed a fondness for her.

The same admissions and discharges to and from Park Place were true of Bonnie Scott because of her chronic obstructive pulmonary disease. Before long, however, Bonnie was admitted permanently to the nursing home unit where husband Harry visited her daily.

One afternoon as I was going to the library to return a large-print novel, *Back When We Were Grownups*, by Anne Tyler, I was about to pass Harry Scott standing at the entrance to the Palace. I stopped and asked, "How's Bonnie, Harry?"

A frown clouded his handsome face. "She's not doing well at all. She's not getting the care she should. The care I expected her to get in Park Place."

"I'm surprised to hear that. I thought our nursing center had a great reputation," I said.

"So did I," he said, shaking his curly-haired head. "They let her fall."

"Oh no!"

"Yes. And she's been deteriorating ever since."

"I'm so sorry to hear that, Harry." Now *I* was frowning. Was he confiding in me because we had something in common, I an RN and he in med. school and changing majors after three years? Or was he complaining to more residents than just to me? Regardless, that encounter gave me a certain relationship with him that I hadn't experienced before.

TWENTY

NEIGHBORS

I'd folded and returned clean clothes to bureau and dresser drawers and was on my way to our den to check incoming e-mails when I passed Jeff hunched over the dining room table. Head bent, his eyes closely scrutinized a stamp gripped on its very edge with tongs he held in a slightly trembling right hand. Not Parkinson's. The symptom was unilateral unsteadiness seemingly worsening and for which he had medication but rarely took because of prostate side effects. I smiled at him, admiring his patience and diligence and interest in this hobby of his. In the den, I sat down at the computer in my pumped-up chair, pulled out the shelf holding the key board, and clicked *start*. I was eager to find out if editor Krisher had responded to my yesterday's query about an article I titled, *Why Bingo?* I brought up e-mail, clicked *read*, and scanned the in-coming mail. There it was! Third on the list. A response! He liked the title and subject matter and would like to review it. "Yippee!" I cried out loud. I was experiencing the thrill I always got when an editor sent a positive response to a query. I went to *my documents*, brought up the article, read it over, and made a few changes (substituting *that* for *which*, deleting a *the*, and correcting a typo). I attached it to a brief thank you message and sent it on its way. Unfortunately, this article was not destined to appear in the nursing magazine, being replaced by another considered more appropriate at the time, apparently. I can't expect all my articles to be accepted and published, can I?

Most people, except for nurses interested in long-term care, would find my articles boring. But geriatrics, my specialty for years, was a subject I could write about with some degree of knowledge. The number of years

I'd been in that field startled me when, the other day going through my wallet, I found two out-dated frayed cards proclaiming I was an RNC, the C standing for Certified. How proud I'd been of that first certificate! At the time, I was one of only one hundred and forty-three nurses in the entire country certified in geriatric nursing by the American Nurses Association. (Back then and even today, geriatrics is not considered an exciting field of practice by the nursing profession. Few RNs seek that specialty.)

Certificates were valid for seven years, and after fourteen years I hadn't attempted to be certified a third time. The first time, I had to pass a lengthy written examination and produce verification of my years of geriatric experience and hours of continuing education in gerontology.

When I applied the second time I qualified because I'd written and had published that book on how to choose between a nursing home and board and care home, the latter now generically referred to as assisted living facility. The book was quite a chore. I wrote it on a Brothers typewriter with the aid of white-out before the days of computers. Books by first-time unknown writers usually end up in publisher's slush-piles. In my case, fortune was on my side. The publisher I queried had just placed her mother in a nursing home, and to her the subject was most appealing. The only problem was that I'd written the book intending it be an expose' of the long-term care industry. The care residents were receiving in nursing homes was poor and even worse in assisted living facilities. The parts of my book speaking to these ills were chopped. In essence, I was required to turn the book into a nice little story about elderly people living in these two types of facilities and, in so doing, provide a comparison.

I wanted to be published, so, with regret, I made the revision. My book was published and had positive reviews by news media, but it didn't sell. As it stood, the topic was of little interest to the public, apparently. Who wanted to read about debilitated old folks and where they should live? Good thing I didn't depend on my writing for my livelihood! But, would the book have found a market had it been an expose'?

I was most proud of my recent article currently published in *Geriatric Nursing*, an upscale nursing magazine. When the three promised editions of the magazine finally arrived at our door yesterday Jeff looked at a copy and said, "So this is the special magazine containing your article?" He leafed through the pages, found my article, and looked up at me. "Looks good! Very impressive! Why do you favor this magazine? Why's it mean more to be published in this magazine?"

"Because it doesn't contain advertisements by hospitals recruiting nurses, or agencies appealing for travel nurses, or manufacturers touting their braces, wheelchairs, and whirlpool tubs. It's professional. With this published article, I'll be provided author recognition on a web site."

"Is that right? I'm proud of you, Jeanie. Always proud of you. How many bucks do they pay you for this masterpiece?"

"Don't try to be funny, Jeff. No legal tender, unfortunately. At least I'm keeping my brain active and getting a little ego-builder as well. Kirk tells me, 'As long as you write as you've been doing, you'll never be one of those little old confused ladies.'"

"What your son says is true. But you wouldn't be regardless," Jeff said, grinning at me.

"I prefer to write rather than volunteer as a pink lady at a hospital, read mystery novels, or watch television, even if writing becomes nerve wracking at times. I figure I'm being productive, sharing my nursing experiences with other nurses even though reimbursement is but a pittance considering the time I spend. The thrill of being published is my remuneration."

"I enjoy writing, too. I wish I had more time to write. I spend too much time with these stamps. It's a great hobby, and I've done it for years, but it's very time-consuming. Some day I'll sell my stamp collection and get down to writing," Jeff said.

I doubted he was serious, would ever give up his hobby, but I said, "You write so well, Jeff. Much better than I. You've had all that experience writing in your college publications and editorials for those syndicated newspapers. You have such a wonderful command of the English language."

I was back on the computer the next day rereading the e-mail reply from editor Krisher when my thoughts were interrupted by Jeff calling me from the dining room. "How about going out for the mail, Jeanie, or are you too busy?"

"No, no, not busy," I said, getting up from the computer and grabbing the mail box key from its designated spot on the bronze spoon holder on the wall near the door. In our house, the spoon holder had been a wall decoration, but here, serving as a key ring, it had a practical purpose. I visualized the spot in our former dining room where the unusual bronze spoon holder had hung next to the hutch displaying my bone china cups and saucers. The dining room had been separated from the spacious living room by a couch, and beyond through three sliding glass doors could be seen the lengthy lanai with its tables and chairs, TV, and whirlpool tub. What fun we'd had in that secluded tub many evenings before dinner! Even had our cocktails there. A shame we had to leave it.

Mailbox key in hand, I let the door swing closed behind me and stepped out onto the pavement. As usual when I walked along the corridor, I first passed Ruth and Stuart's apartment on the left, the Gathers apartment on the right, and the guest room, also on the right. These guest rooms, of which there were six in the entire complex, were as nice or nicer than most motel rooms. They were attractively decorated and were furnished with a king-size bed, dresser, full-length mirror, ceiling fan, TV, phone, full-sized bath, and closet. My cousin and her husband had stayed in one when they came to visit last March. Continental breakfasts were included in the eighty-dollar-per-night room.

The last apartment I had to pass before coming to the mail boxes was on the left and was occupied by a single female resident who received twenty-four-hour care. We'd never seen the resident, only the care givers who walked a fluffy white-haired dog out on the premises and brought in bagged meals to the apartment. One-a-day contracted meals were available for residents unable to go to the dining room for meals and to residents preferring to eat these meals in their living quarters. Meals with requested items were required to be ordered by phone one hour in advance of pick up. Dining room staff placed these meals in large brown paper bags, and residents or care givers retrieved them from a designated station near the dining room. A nominal fee was billed for delivery by a kitchen employee. Jeff and I hadn't *ordered-in* as yet, preferring to go to the dining room to eat.

When I came to the mail boxes located on the wall across from the perpetually sprouting Grecian fountain, I encountered our neighbor Ruth McKee. She was wearing dark sunglasses on her rarely-smiling chiseled face. To my surprise, she'd changed her former hairstyle. Her milk-white hair was no longer perfectly straight, parted in the middle, bangs cut straight across her forehead like Cleopatra's, and the rest cut mid-neck and straight around like the bottom of a lampshade. That style had always amused me the way her hair rose up and settled back down when she walked. Now her hair was parted on one side and swept to the other side in an attractive way, and it was longer and a bit tapered at the ends.

"I just got home from the hospital. Spent the entire day there!" Ruth announced in her direct theatrical manner. "Stuart's there!" Then she stared at me through her sunglasses, holding me where I stood, her hands thrust out in front of her, palms open wide in a helpless gesture.

"Oh Ruth!" I exclaimed with real concern about Stuart and asked, "What happened? Nothing too serious, I hope."

"God yes! He fell in the bathroom! I don't know if he blacked out or what. But he fell and broke his shoulder bone. I've been there all day long!" Her strained voice continued commanding my attention. "The surgeon worked on him for a long time. Bones splintered, I think. Arm's in a big sling that goes around his shoulder and arm to his wrist. He's in so much pain!"

"Did they operate? I mean, is there an incision?"

"No, no incision, thank God!"

"A closed reduction, then. And keeping the fractured scapula in alignment, fixated with the sling." I was thinking aloud.

"I guess so. You know more about those things than I do."

"I'm so sorry, Ruth. Is there anything we can do? Anything at all?"

"Oh, I don't know. I'm just so upset! I don't know how long they'll keep him. God knows, I hate to be alone. I've never been alone. Have you noticed anything unusual about him lately?"

She gave me no time to answer before saying, "Lately I think he's been a little confused." The firmness of her voice and stoic expression were ever more pronounced.

"No, Ruth, I haven't noticed anything like that," I was able to say.

"I'd better go call my daughter," she said and left.

I inserted our key in our upper mailbox in line with many other mail boxes, all identified with apartment numbers, and reached in and pulled out pieces of mail. Most were addressed to Jeff. He received much more mail than I because he contributed to military and other organizations, supported political aspirants, and subscribed to multiple magazines. Usually some of the mail was addressed to both of us. In our lower box, also one of many marked with apartment numbers and where security distributed inter-facility mail, I found the new Sandycreek Terrace Weekly Newsletter. The cover was colored green this week. Last week's cover was yellow, the week before, pink. At a glance I saw daily activities listed on the cover as well as drawings of pumpkins and information about the upcoming Halloween Party.

I took the mail back to the apartment and sat down at the kitchenette table with a magnifying glass to read the contents of the Weekly Newsletter while Jeff joined me and started sorting the remaining mail.

He patted his shirt pocket and said, "My glasses. I can't find my glasses. I've looked everywhere. Have you seen them?"

"I can't say I have," I said, noticing that the case in his pocket was empty. "Are you sure you've looked everywhere?" I went on a search. In the den I peered at the papers on his desk and lifted a large manila envelope. Then I looked among the stamps on the dining room table, glanced at the magazine-littered coffee table in the living room, and went to the Florida room to check the table there. Finally I went to the guest bathroom used by Jeff. There under a section of the morning newspaper were the missing glasses.

"Here they are, Jeff!" I said, bringing them to him. I picked up the Weekly Newsletter again, and inside on the back of the front cover I read a summary of the Saturday night in-house movie, *Ladies in Lavender*. Its length was one hundred and four minutes, shown at four-thirty in the afternoon and repeated at seven. Jeff and I had been going at four-thirty. The same handful of residents attended at that time, and we'd been eating dinner after the movie with two of the attending couples. The Crackerjack movie was showing Wednesday afternoon and was a four-star movie. We'd yet to attend where crackerjack and beverages were provided on a help-yourself-table. The monthly shopping trip was scheduled for Palm Beach Gardens Mall. My preference was a small shopping center close by that had a few small clothing stores and salesgirls who helped me read sizes and prices and advised me on colors and what best suited me.

On the next page was the announcement of the monthly Birthday Luncheon for all residents having birthdays in October. And there was the Golf outing the Social Director arranged for golfing residents to play *Best Ball* for nine holes at nearby Johnathan's Landing golf course. Even though I tired on the eighth hole the last few times I played golf, maybe I *could* manage *Best Ball* for nine holes. I'd think about it. The Mystery Ride write-up was next. "Honey," I interrupted Jeff. "We should sign up for the Mystery Ride some time. And the Dine Around. We wouldn't have to drive. Just register and take the facility bus. The Social Director always arranges for residents to go to a nice restaurant in town once a month. I guess she goes too. I've heard McCarthy's is a favorite. But the one this month is at Bistro Tuscan Grill in Palm Beach Gardens. Italian cuisine and delicious desserts, it says."

I kept on reading and saw visits to the Flagler Museum listed one day and to the Kravis Center for *My Fair Lady* in West Palm another. "Jeff, are you listening? I think this upcoming Island Princess Cruise going over to the Jupiter Lighthouse and to view the houses of celebrities Bert Reynolds and the late Perry Como and on up the Indian River would be interesting. Don't you? The cruise, luncheon included, costs thirty-seven sixty a person. That might be too expensive. What do you think?"

"That does sound interesting. We'll think about it," he answered.

"I think you'd be interested in this Men's Football Huddle next week, Jeff."

"Yes, I heard Harry Gorman talking about it. I intend to sign up. They serve hotdogs and sauerkraut and baked beans."

I didn't bother reading the Croquet notes and Bridge and Scrabble scores because we hadn't gotten involved. Some day bridge, perhaps. We always paid particular attention to the section called Resident Update listing residents who'd been admitted to Park Place and to the local hospital and those who'd returned from either place to their independent living quarters. As usual, one entire page was devoted to *Healthful Wisdom* written by the Health and Wellness Coordinator. Always listed was the weekly schedule for Aquasize, Strength and Conditioning, Balance Training, Sit and be Fit, Chair Yoga and Stretching, and Tai Chi.

"Jeff," I interrupted again. "Here's a special paragraph signed by the physical therapist of Park Place. He's offering to evaluate independent living residents for their balance ability."

Another entire page was provided by Dr. Tom Price and contained information about Florida Life Care Residents Association (FLiCRA) whose mission was to monitor state and federal pending legislative bills and laws and regulations effecting CCRCs. Last and perhaps most important for Jeff and me was the full-page weekly menu. We dwelled at length on this page each day to determine what of the wonderful foods we'd order for dinner that night.

"How should we dress for the Halloween party?" I queried Jeff as I finished reading the Weekly Newsletter and then waited for him to disengage himself from the latest *U. S. News and World Report.*

"I haven't given that any thought. When is it?" he asked me, laying the magazine on his knees.

"October 31ˢᵗ. Even though my blue jeans are at the Shack, I thought I'd dress as a cowgirl. I have a cowboy hat, checkered red and black vest, and a red bandanna for my neck."

The bandanna had been given to me by my supervisor at my retirement party. I still remembered that stormy wintry evening of the party given by my little group of inspectors at the home of one of my staff. Although they'd all chipped in to buy me a mahogany jewelry box and a round silver monogrammed pin, my beloved boss had given me this red bandana I still had. He wanted me to have something belonging to him.

I loved them all, those people I'd worked with for six years in the Pittsburgh State Office Building. Under the Department of Public Welfare, we were responsible for inspecting and licensing, in twenty-four counties of Western Region, an incredible number of personal care homes, generically known as assisted living facilities. Mandated to be licensed for the first time, many proprietors refused to apply for licenses. They didn't want inspectors invading their premises and snooping around. We had to search them out. Some day I'd write about those six years and the weird situations we encountered.

Jeff was saying, "I guess I could go as a cowboy. I have blue jeans and a red and yellow checkered shirt and a straw hat. Would that do?" His blue eyes looked up at me for an answer.

"That old frayed falling-apart straw hat with a hole in the crown?" I looked at him in dismay. Surely he wasn't serious about wearing *that* hat.

"Guess that wonderful hat wouldn't do. Is that what you're implying?" He gave me a grin and a wink.

"Yep," I said, smiling back at him. I loved it when he winked at me. Then I changed the subject and opened the Newsletter to the article submitted by the physical therapist. "I'm thinking of taking advantage of this offer by the physical therapist. I know my balance is poor. I'd like to see what he has to say." I got up and attempted to walk straight ahead heel to toe without hanging onto furniture, but it was useless. I simply couldn't and knew I should be able to.

"Good idea," Jeff said. "I'll go with you and have him evaluate me, too."

I got on the phone and called the therapy department for an appointment. The next day, both Jeff and I went over to the P. T. Department located in Park Place. Physical therapist Bob took Jeff first, had him stand arms outstretched in front and hold that position for three minutes. Then he had Jeff stand feet apart, raise his arms over his head, and turn his head from side to side. Last, Jeff was instructed to walk straight ahead placing one foot directly in front of the other, heel touching toe.

"Your balance seems fine," Bob said to Jeff. He looked at me, gave me a big smile, and said, "You're next."

I went through the same drill. But I couldn't stand perfectly still for three minutes. My body swayed this way and that. When I tried to walk as Bob directed I faltered and couldn't keep my balance. I knew I'd flunked.

"You, Mrs. Metz, have a high degree of imbalance. You could certainly be helped by therapy sessions. Would you like to try them?"

"Indeed I would," I answered with an emphatic nod.

Bob informed me, "Medicare will pay for eight sessions if your physician signs a form I will give you. I'll also give you my written evaluation for your physician to read. Wait here, and I'll have it for you in a few seconds."

Two days later, we were off to Dr. Gray's office, obtaining his signature on the document. "Now we're going to drive to a costume shop," Jeff said, turning the car around and heading toward a small mall on Federal Highway. Inside, Jeff tried on cowboy hats, found one to fit, and continued to shop.

"What are you looking for now?" I asked, most curious. Then I saw him with a toy gun in his hand. "You're going to buy *that?*" I asked in disbelief.

"Sure am," he laughed. "Who ever heard of a cowboy without a gun?"

I had to admit he had a point.

I started my balancing sessions by pumping a stationary bike for ten minutes, five pounds of weights attached to each foot. On the parallel bars, I walked and lifted my feet over obstacles, first one direction and then the reverse. Occasionally I glanced at other residents in sessions with physical, occupational, and speech therapists. We were all in one large room containing a full-sized bed frame with a foam rubber mattress, stationary bicycles, parallel bars, rubber balls of various sizes, cones, a high chair for occupational therapy, scale, and closet for supplies. Bob's small office was attached to the P. T. room. "How many post-op patients do you see?" I asked Bob one day.

"Four right now. One hip and two knee replacements and one back surgery. Mostly it's rehabilitation from strokes and for severe arthritis."

"You keep pretty busy, don't you? Are the other staff that I see working with you full-time employees?" I asked.

"The S. T. and O. T. are part time," he answered.

Half-way through my sessions, Paul Ferris was wheeled in and seated on a stationary bike. I thought about his experience in Nazi Germany as a student, how he escaped being in Hitler's army. He didn't notice me right away, but when he did I said, "Hi Paul. How you making out?"

He smiled, "Could be better. But they're treating me pretty good. Can't complain."

Bob said to me, "We work with him every day. He needs a lot of rehabilitation. But he's a strong-willed man. He tries hard."

One day, Bob directed Paul and me to throw a medium-sized ball back and forth between us. Paul caught the ball every other time. I missed twice. I wondered if he'd remember me and the fun we had during our P. T. sessions when he was once again discharged to his cottage and saw me in the lounge before dinner.

After I'd had six of my eight treatments, Bob had me walk in and out around various colored cones placed in measured distances. My final day, he gave me a paper explaining exercises he wanted me to perform at home to maintain the balance I'd acquired in his sessions with me.

Stuart McKee was home from the hospital receiving physical therapy in his apartment. When he went to dinner, his jacket was positioned on his back over his shoulders. The unimpaired arm was in a sleeve, and the affected arm, still in a sling, peeked out from the front edge of his jacket while the other sleeve dangled loosely at his side. As always, wife Ruth walked with determination, preceding her husband.

October 31st in our cowboy and cowgirl costumes, Jeff and I attended the Halloween party and sat at a table with eight other residents, some we knew, others we met that evening. Tablecloths were orange colored and napkins were black. In the centers of the tables stood small scarecrows surrounded by miniature corn shocks. Some residents had gone to great lengths to appear in unusual and creative costumes. Ruth and Stuart were dressed in jewel-bedecked outfits, elaborate sparkling crowns on their heads. Stuart's flowing cape hid his sling. Three single women were dressed as three blind mice. Raymond Watson, Chairman of the Resident Council, was dressed in top hat and tails while his wife Victoria was dazzling in satin and pearls and a mink boa around her neck. From the unfaltering stately way she always carried herself, one would never know she was almost totally blind. At a distance near the dance floor, Sarah Grant, pianist, writer of the *Resident of the Month* column in the *Periscope*, and chairman of the Symposium, was sitting at a table for eight and beside her was Harry Scott. I thought of Harry's poor wife, a permanent resident in Park Place, and realized this wasn't the first time I'd seen Sarah and Harry together. I imagined that others, female residents that is, had at least raised their eyebrows.

TWENTY-ONE
EYES

One morning the next month, Tom Price called and wanted to meet us for lunch in the Terrace, the small informal dining room. "No doubt he wants you to do something. Something having to do with your Health Care Committee," Jeff said to me as I put the receiver back in its cradle and apprised him of Tom's request.

"I'm wondering if he's going to ask me to serve as a permanent member of the Ethics Committee," I said, thinking back to that one meeting I'd attended.

"We'll go and find out. I'm glad we're going to the Terrace. I can wear what I have on. Don't need to change clothes or wear a sport coat," Jeff said.

By now I'd most certainly become accustomed to his disinterest in clothes. Comfort was foremost. He'd grab whatever his hands touched first and don a pink striped shirt and plaid trousers or a black sport coat and navy polo shirt. Ungodly combinations! I'd promptly ask him to change if I saw him so regaled before we were at the door leaving to go to dinner.

"Now Jeff, we have to be dressed in something decent," I said, looking at his red shorts and orange jersey. But I was totally wrong about Tom's reason for wanting to have lunch with us.

We walked over to the Terrace, Jeff using his cane, and we joined Tom already out of his scooter and seated at a four-top table. After a few pleasantries and giving our lunch order to server Emily, Tom asked Jeff a few questions about his years as a high school principal. Our orders arrived, and after eating a bite of his Cobb salad, Tom looked at Jeff and said in his courteous yet compelling manner, "Jeff, the HMS Committee, that is the Housekeeping, Maintenance, and Security Committee, needs a substantial resident member. I'd like you to serve on that committee. With your career experiences, you'd be a natural. A valuable addition to the committee."

Jeff stopped his fork mid-way to his mouth and frowned. "I planned not to get involved in committee work, Tom. I find it an honor that you asked me, but I came to Sandycreek Terrace to relax, take it easy, pursue a hobby or two." He shook his head, ate the bite on his fork, and took a drink of water from his stemmed water glass. He gave a little chuckle. "You better find someone else. Someone better qualified."

Tom put his hand on Jeff's arm and fastened his eyes on him. "Now look. Let's be serious. Let me put it this way, Jeff. I'm the chairman of this committee until January. Ray Watson, president of the Resident Council, agrees with me that you should serve on this committee. You think about it. Come to the next meeting, and just sit and observe."

When we got home Jeff sat down on a dining room chair, took off his shoes and socks, and said to me, "You know, Jeanie, I really don't want to serve on any committee. I've had my fill of committees. I just want to do what I want to do. Period."

"Tom told you to think about it. That's all," I advised, looking at his serious expression and into his blue eyes.

Three days later, Jeff and I were eating a breakfast of poached eggs on raisin toast he'd prepared using his electric egg poacher and our new fancy toaster from Crate and Barrel. He looked up at me from his plate and said, "You know, maybe I could spend one day a month going to that HMS Committee meeting."

"You could," I said. "After all, these little resident committee meetings aren't anything like the meetings you had to deal with when you were high school principal. You might enjoy it." I ate another forkful of my poached egg on toast.

"I'll go to the meeting and see what it's like. I don't have to become a member. Just see what it's all about." Jeff took a swallow of his coffee. "How long does your Health Care Committee meeting last?"

"An hour at the most. That's all the longer any of the committee meetings are supposed to last."

When Jeff came home from the scheduled HMS Committee meeting the next Monday morning I met him inside the door. "What happened at the meeting?" I asked, eager to hear.

He laid stapled pages on the dining room table and confronted me with, "I went and sat in the back of the room, preparing to be an observer. Then Tom told me to come up to the table, and he introduced me as a new member of the committee. A new member, mind you. So I'm a member. I had no choice!"

I giggled. "That's interesting. Then what?" I said, still wanting to hear more.

"The meeting began. The representative from the Housekeeping Department gave a report, then the representative from Maintenance, and then Security. All employees of Sandycreek Terrace, of course. Lots of discussion about picky things like where pets are walked, who walks them, who picks up droppings. And the trash rooms and how residents are throwing the wrong things in the wrong receptacles. A crooked stop sign that should be straightened. Things like that." He jerked his head and raised his eyebrows. "Rhuderts and lolliies. Not too bad. Sort of interesting. Guess I can stand to go once a month." A little grin flashed over his full face.

I nodded and smiled back. "Sure you can," I said, voicing utmost confidence. "For the good of the cause, of course." We both laughed.

The next day we were sitting in our ophthalmologist's examining room, I in the patient chair, Jeff in a chair against the far wall, waiting for Dr. Davenport. Eventually from another examining room, in he strode. The familiar, tall, thin man with reddish hair wore a long white lab coat and a welcoming smile on his handsome boyish face. After sitting down at his desk and glancing at my medical record open in front of him, he stood up, had me remove my glasses, and instilled anesthetizing eye drops. Then he rolled his stool over toward me, sat down, moved the black ophthalmology machine alias split lamp, in front of me, and said, "Let's have a look."

After my years of familiarity with this machine and others like it, I didn't need him to tell me where to place my chin and forehead. As I looked straight ahead, he shone a white light directly into my right eye and then into my left. Next came the blue light for the tonometry test to determine the intraocular pressure in both eyes. Fearful, I waited for the verdict. Were today's pressure readings acceptable with my history of glaucoma? The intraocular pressure needed to be in the low teens so as not to cause further optic nerve damage. How many times in the past forty years had I waited for this verdict? Too many to count! My vision, my ability to continue to keep seeing depended on the count, a low count.

Dr. Davenport rolled his chair back away from the machine. "Twenty eight in the right, twenty two in the left," he said. No expression.

"Not good," I said, heaving a serious sigh.

"Not good," he repeated.

"So now what?" I asked, looking hard at my kind ophthalmologist whom I'd been seeing religiously every two months, sometimes every two weeks, for seven years. "I need to see a glaucoma specialist, don't I?" I was convinced I had no choice.

"Yes, you do," he agreed, eyes focused on mine. "We're at that point. You're on maximum drugs, both topical and oral, and they aren't holding down the pressures."

"Years ago I had a trabeculectomy performed on my right eye at Bascom Palmer Eye Institute in Miami," I told him. "I understand that procedure is only good for a certain number of years. Maybe I need another trabeculectomy?" I was both suggesting and asking.

"Yes. I'll refer you to Dr. Greenfield. He's the glaucoma specialist at Bascom Palmer now. They have offices in Palm Beach Gardens where you can see him first. Much closer than Miami. I'll make the call. They'll get in touch with you for an appointment."

He managed a smile; we shook hands; and Jeff and I left the office.

On the way home, Jeff removed his right hand from the steering wheel, reached over, and squeezed my hand. "I'm sorry," he said, somber faced.

I appreciated his empathy, his sincerity, and his understanding. A wonderful man. How fortunate I was! "It's just part of my life," I said. "I've been battling this disease for years. If it hadn't been for Dr. Jocson at the Eye Institute at the University of Pittsburgh Medical Center, I wouldn't have the vision I have today. I'm thankful for that. And thank goodness we're close to Bascom Palmer Eye Institute! It's rated number one in the nation for eye care." I looked over at him and said, "You remember, don't you Jeff, when we started to get serious? I confided in you. I told you about my serious eye problem and that some day I might be blind. I needed you to know."

"No problem," he said softly and patted my arm.

We drove a few more miles, Jeff steering the Chevy into the faster moving lane in the escalating traffic. I continued to be amazed and impressed at his ability to stay relaxed and keep his cool. If a driver cut directly into the lane in front of us, he'd say, "Thank, you, friend!" instead of swearing like some drivers I've known. If the car in front of him didn't move when the light turned green, he'd say, "Do you plan to sit there all day?" instead of honking his horn. He was not a slow driver. In fact, he drove fast and cut in and out of lanes to avoid being held up by slow moving traffic. But he did it safely. Nor did he think twice before making a U-turn (a *uie*, as he called it) to avoid driving farther than necessary. He'd try to out-smart traffic lights, slowing down if the light ahead was red, mandating it to turn green, or speeding up before a distant green light turned red. As yet, his distant vision didn't require him to wear eye glasses. I relaxed when he drove.

Now I said, "A trabeculectomy isn't so bad, Jeff. At least the one I had eleven years ago wasn't. Of course, I'm older now."

I wanted Jeff to say, "You don't look any older," which he usually said at times like this. He didn't. Instead he said, "Yes, you are older, sweetie." Then he asked, "If Dr. Greenfield says you have to have that procedure, will you have to stay overnight in the hospital?"

"No, I didn't before. I had to report early in the morning and was discharged late afternoon of the same day. But because I had to be there so early in the morning, I had to stay in a hotel in Miami overnight so I could be at the hospital for early check-in. It's a long drive down to Miami from Jupiter."

"I understand," Jeff said. "We'll wait and see what Dr. Greenfield has to say. O. K.?"

"Yes," I said, smiling back and settling into my seat.

One week later, we were in Dr. Greenfield's examining room after waiting for almost two hours in the waiting room where Jeff read his *U S News & World Report* and I watched people wait their turn and come and go.

Medium height, medium build, young, pleasant-faced Dr. Greenfield walked into the examining room wearing a white lab coat over his dark slacks, white shirt, and tie. He shook my hand and then Jeff's hand, sat down at his desk, and leafed through my two-inch thick chart. It was filled with medical information covering forty years of eye treatments. A nurse took my glasses and instilled anesthetizing eye drops in both eyes. Without a word, Dr. Greenfield rolled his chair over in front of me and positioned the ophthalmology machine. Without being instructed, I placed my chin and forehead where they belonged. Dr. Greenfield looked into my eyes with a white light and then zeroed in with a blue beam and performed the tonometry test for intraocular pressure readings even though a technician had read the pressure shortly after we arrived. I was glad he did. His reading would be more accurate, I knew. He rolled back to his desk and penned notes in my medical record. Now he looked me squarely in the eyes and announced, "I'm scheduling you for a right eye shunt implant in five days. November 24th."

Surprised, I looked at him quizzically and said, "Not a trabeculectomy?"

He smiled. "No. You've had a trabeculectomy in that eye. A shunt is needed now. We insert a tiny tube to drain the fluid."

"All right," I answered, convinced. He was the boss, the specialist. Not to question. I looked across the room to Jeff. He seemed to be studying me and gave me a worried smile.

The nurse handed me my glasses and said, "I'll take you to the coordinator up the hall. She'll provide you with all the information about your procedure. Information about your admission. And answer questions you might have."

Jeff and I followed her up the hall. In a small office, the coordinator rose behind her desk, introduced herself, and offered us seats. The information she provided resembled the memory I had of my trabeculectomy adventure at Bascom Palmer Eye Institute years ago. I helped myself to one of her professional name cards from a holder on the tiny table at my elbow and learned she, too, was an RN. At my request, because I wanted to know about this shunt procedure, she handed me a pamphlet explaining glaucoma and its treatments. "The surgery is called a Baerveldt implant," she informed me. Then she gave us the name of a hotel where Bascom Palmer patients were charged a reduced rate. She also gave us maps of the Miami area around the hospital.

On the way home, I suddenly remembered our standing invitation for Thanksgiving dinner at Chick and Betty Hahn's, our friends of long standing still living in Pine Gardens, our old *stamping grounds*. "We'll have to phone the Hahn's and tell them we can't make Thanksgiving dinner. I'll hardly be able to go anywhere two days after surgery," I said, watching cars fly by us on I-95 while we passed slower moving vehicles.

After Jeff veered over into the far left lane after first allowing a red convertible to whiz past on the left, he said, "You're right. We'll have to cancel. But there'll be other Thanksgivings. You might feel like going over to the dining room and eating turkey. Or we could bag it and eat in. We'll wait and see how you feel."

The evening prior to surgery, Jeff and I had a nice dinner in the dining room of the Miami Marriott Hotel and then retired for the night. The alarm set for four-thirty the next morning, we rose, dressed, and, without breakfast since I was ordered nothing by mouth after midnight, we left the hotel to be at the hospital by six. Even though Jeff had studied the map, many streets were one-way and very confusing being named with numbers, all either east or west. In pitch-darkness, we drove a block or two and then Jeff had to get out of the car to read the street names under a street light. This traveling through Miami's deserted streets continued for almost an hour until we found the Bascom Palmer Eye Institute parking lot.

The surgery was a success, I was told as, semi-conscious, I was helped from the O. R. table onto a carrier. Taken back to the six-patient room, I was monitored for vital signs by a nurse until fully recovered.

TWENTY-TWO
POST-OP

The next day I reported to Dr. Greenfield's office in Palm Beach Gardens. A technician removed my eye patch and cleansed around the eye. I was then seen by Dr. Greenfield who, after examining my eye, pronounced the condition of the eye to be good and gave me written post-operative orders for medication and care of the operative eye.

That evening I felt something wet on my right cheek. I reached up, touched my cheek, and gazed at my finger in horror. Blood! Frightened, panicky, I called, "Jeff, I'm bleeding! My right eye is bleeding!"

He hurried to me standing in the Florida room and examined my eye. "Pretty bloody. What do you want me to do?" he asked.

"Call! There's an emergency number. On the information they gave me." I pointed to the papers on the table.

Jeff grabbed the phone and dialed. After he gave a message, he replaced the receiver and turned to me. "The answering voice said she'd give the message to the doctor right away."

We waited one-half hour, one hour, two hours! Hell," Jeff said. "This is far from *right away*!"

We waited and waited, I nervous, dreading the worst. Would I have to go back to the O. R.? Would I lose the sight in my right eye, my better eye? Jeff was worried too; I could tell. We tried to put in the time talking of other things, and finally, five hours later, the phone rang! Jeff grabbed it, and I could hear a female voice say she was the on-call ophthalmologist. As explicitly as he could, Jeff explained the problem. Then he turned to me. "She wants to know if the eye is still bleeding."

I shook my head. "No," Jeff answered.

He listened again and then asked me, "Are you having any pain in that eye, she wants to know?"

I shook my head.

"No, no pain," Jeff told her. After listening again, he said, "She wants you to come to the office first thing in the morning. She says she'll be there and see you right away."

When we arrived in the morning we were relieved to learn Dr. Greenfield was there. I preferred to be seen by him, of course, and said so to the clerk at the desk. She honored my request. After Dr. Greenfield examined my eye he said, "Everything appears to be all right. Probably a tiny capillary ruptured. Nothing to be alarmed about. Just keep the appointment we made yesterday."

"What a relief!" I said and watched him give me a little smile before he left the examining room to attend another patient.

Day after day, I medicated my eye with anti-inflammatory eye drops, wore an eye shield over my eye at night, tried not to cough, sneeze, stoop, lift anything heavy, or exercise—all in accordance with the written instructions.

I avoided getting my right eye wet by wearing my eye shield when I showered. Since I couldn't risk performing my twice weekly shampooing, I took advantage of the services of our hair salon and of beautician Ethel who, until now, had only trimmed my hair every six weeks. For the shampoo, I wore my eye shield and cautioned Ethel not to let water or shampoo get near my eye.

"I'll be very careful," she said. "I won't rub your head or move it, just gently massage. Was the operation painful? Does your eye hurt now?" she wanted to know

"No, it doesn't hurt at all. Of course I was given a local anesthetic and a sedative before surgery. It didn't hurt after surgery," I told her as she worked the shampoo into my scalp and through my hair.

"My younger son's scheduled for a cornea transplant as soon as a donated one becomes available," she told me.

During the weeks of my twice-weekly visits to the beauty salon Ethel and I carried on a number of conversations as beauticians and their customers were apt to do. We talked about our families, her sons and an expected grandchild, my adult children and where they lived. We talked about vacations we'd taken, ones we'd particularly enjoyed. She seemed very interested in the nursing article I was co-authoring with Patsy Taylor. Each time I came she asked, "Have you heard from the editor? Has she accepted your article yet?"

The last time she asked I had to answer, "Not the way it's presently written. We had to revise it again. The editor's sending it to more reviewers."

"I think that's terrible! As many articles as you've written and had printed without any hassle. Why does she have to be so picky?"

"That's the writing racket," I told her. "Sometimes it's frustrating. An author has to be patient."

"I don't have that kind of patience," she said.

I finally was able to wash my own hair and went to Ethel for trims only.

Week after week I kept appointments with Dr. Greenfield, but the Baerveldt implant didn't kick in. The intraocular pressure was elevated more than ever, and I was again prescribed medicated eye drop to try to control the pressure. Dr. Greenfield didn't explain why the surgery was dubbed a success but ineffective for the expected and desired result. I must have been one of the few patients who didn't respond. Lucky me!

An unexpected call from my daughter, Mary Ann in West Virginia, brought a smile to my face. For a few days, she and husband Steve could get away from the office where Steve practiced internal medicine and where Mary Ann was office manager. Would it suit us to have them visit?

"Of course! We'd love to have you!" I exploded. "We'll reserve one of the guest rooms. At least we'll try to. They're very popular."

"No, no, don't bother. We'll get accommodations in town. We get special rates at the Sheridan and others."

Why would she do that, I wondered, and then suddenly remembered their smoking habit. No, they wouldn't be able to smoke in guest rooms here. Mary Ann had cut down but hadn't quit. Would she ever? Why did health professionals still smoke? I'd smoked socially years ago, and my first husband had been an addicted smoker. Perhaps we were to blame for my daughter's habit. "You're flying, of course?" I asked.

"Yes. We've checked flights and can get one arriving in West Palm Monday at ten in the morning. We'll rent a car."

"How long will you stay?" I asked, getting more and more excited.

"We can't stay long, Mum. A return flight non-stop to BWI leaves Wednesday late afternoon. We plan to take that."

"I'll be happy for whatever amount of time you can stay."

They were impressed with our apartment as they inspected from room to room. "It's bigger than I thought it would be," Mary Ann said. "You have a view of a pond and fountain out your bedroom window. How nice!" Now in the bathroom pointing at three pictures on the wall she said, "I'm going to steal those pictures. I've been looking for pictures like that for over a year, and I can't find any."

"Sorry. You can't have those," I laughingly told her. "The wall would look empty without them. When we go shopping we'll see if we can find some in the store where I bought these."

In the Florida room, Mary Ann stopped in front of the painting of the Shack. "Where did you get this? I never saw this before!" she exclaimed.

"Kirk and Sally gave it to me for my birthday last year. A friend of Sally's is an artist. She gave him several photos of the Shack, and he painted this using the photos."

"I like it!" she said. "I really like it!"

"You can't have that either," I said, laughing again. "When I die you can have it. That is if Kirk and Sally don't want it."

"They probably will," she lamented.

"Come on, we'll take you and Steve on a tour of the facility."

That evening in the lounge before dinner, we introduced and showed them off to various residents. Ruth and Stuart McKee shook their hands. "It's nice to meet you. Where are you from?" Ruth asked, eyes burrowing in on them from her serious face.

"We're from West Virginia. Martinsburg," Steve said.

"Then you're not from Pittsburgh? Your mother told me she was from Pittsburgh."

"We were originally from Pittsburgh. But then Steve moved his practice to Martinsburg," Mary Ann explained.

"Oh, your husband's a physician?" Ruth turned and looked at Steve with added interest.

Mary Ann smiled and said, "Yes."

"How was the weather up there when you left?" Stuart wanted to know.

While Steve was telling Stuart that the weather was rainy and cold, Ruth quizzed Mary Ann, "Do you have children?"

Mary Ann answered, "Two," and then turned to meet ninety-year-old Betty Howe and southern muttering Ralph Wilson.

"How very nice to meet you," Betty said in her soft spoken voice, extending a bony hand to Mary Ann and Steve. "You know, we residents always enjoy meeting young people."

Ralph reached out his hand to Steve and Mary Ann and smiled broadly.

"How long are you staying?" Ruth asked. When she heard they were only staying two days she said, "You must come back soon and often. I'm sure your parents miss you."

Doris Jordan and Sarah Grant walked up to meet our guests and asked if the young people belonged to Jeff or to me. "This is my daughter, Mary Ann. But Jeff considers her his daughter, too," I told them. "And her husband Stephen."

After several more introductions and greetings, we went into dinner.

A competitive swimmer in her teens and lifeguard in her twenties, Mary Ann swam multiple laps in the pool the next morning while Steve worked-out in the exercise room with a stationary bike, the treadmill, and weights. That afternoon, we all went to my favorite shopping mall, and Mary Ann and I cruised various shops and made small purchases. I determined what I'd buy her for Christmas when she admired, at great length, the nutcrackers in the Christmas section of a unique gift shop I favored. Unfortunately we couldn't find pictures like the ones she threatened to steal from our bathroom. While we girls shopped, the fellas sat outside on a bench, Steve enjoying cigarettes, Jeff with his once-a-week cigar.

Back in our apartment I gave Mary Ann two table scarves crocheted by her great-grandmother. They were two of four I'd come across during our move and that I'd been saving for her. The other two I was keeping for my son whenever or if ever he and Sally visited. Mary Ann spied a fluted milk-white vase trimmed with purple pansies in the étagère and said, "I've always loved that vase. Will that to me, Mum,"

I opened the glass doors and removed it from the glass shelf where it sat next to an antique cranberry-colored glass pitcher and matching bowl my mother had given me. "Here," I said. "You can have it right now." Might as well, I reasoned.

I'd heard Jeff say he intended to give some of his long-time treasures to his children and grandchildren as presents for important occasions. He'd said, "I'm going to gift them while I'm living, to prevent squabbles after I die."

"You seem to be unsteady when you walk, Mum. You're not walking deliberately as I remember," Mary Ann said after watching me walk around the apartment. "I think you should remove these runners in the living room and dining room. They're pretty, but they could cause you to fall. Throw rugs are hazardous!"

I remembered citing nursing homes for having throw rugs that could cause residents to fall and fracture hips. "Maybe we should remove them," I remarked. "I went to P.T. for balance training some time ago, and I still practice those exercises here in the apartment. But I know my balance is poor."

I understood my daughter's concern. Should we remove the runners? Make out a work request to have John and Matt in maintenance come and take them away? We liked them, the way they enhanced the apartment and preserved the wall-to-wall carpet. They'd been even nicer in the larger space in our house. Jeff and I would have to talk about living without them before we made out a work request.

Twenty-Three
Incidents

As Jeff and I passed the front desk on our way into the dining room one evening, there on the counter was the ubiquitous single red rose and white baby breath in a bud vase. "Who this time?" we asked the receptionist. She answered in a soft voice, but we didn't recognize the name of the deceased resident. It helped not to know the resident, but it was still an unpleasant reminder this was God's waiting room. How much time did Jeff and I have to be in this world and were we making the most of it?

In the dining room that evening, our server was Richard, a favorite of all the residents. Somehow he managed to talk and joke in a friendly manner without stepping out of the role of employee by being aggressive or interrupting residents' conversations. His lively personality captivated residents. This extremely tall, thin, dark-haired, young man approached our table, his white-sleeved long arms in constant motion.

"What can I get for you tonight, Mr. and Mrs. Metz?" he asked, bowing and arching his eyebrows. "Our special tonight is succulent leg of lamb, mouth-watering and cooked to perfection and served with delicious green mint jelly. Two mint jellies, if you like. I've had nothing but raving reviews from those I've already served." He nodded as though to accentuate his approval of the special and displayed open palms in a gracious manner.

"I might just have that, Richard," Jeff said and then asked, "What's your last name, Richard?"

"My last name is Sericelli," Mr. Metz." Then he reached across the table and picked up a rating card found on all tables for residents to rate their dining room experience. He printed his name on the back of the card and handed it to Jeff.

"And what nationality is that name?" Jeff asked, always interested in heritage.

"Name's Italian and German, Mr. Metz. Italian and German."

"Interesting," Jeff said. "And are you in school, Richard?"

"Yes, sir, Mr. Metz. I attend Indian River Community College. Plan to be a chef." He placed his hands above his head to form the shape of a chef's hat.

"You come from a large family?" Jeff pursued.

"Not large. Just a younger brother and sister. Now I'm off to put in your order. Want you to have the lamb before it's gone."

Not far from out table along with their husbands sat two women I genuinely liked. One was Kathy Franklin, the resident who had pinched me on my bottom. The other was Patricia James, the resident I'd decided had graduated from college and either came from a family with money or married a wealthy man and had never needed to work a day in her life. The two women were similar in their polished manners, were quiet speaking, friendly, and polite. They resembled each other in looks, too, although Kathy had a round face and was shorter than Patricia. More unusual, both had husbands who were similar. Each man was tall, of approximately the same weight, fair completed, extremely polite, and both apparently were post-cerebral vascular accident survivors with definite memory debility. I was favorably impressed with their abilities to appear to follow conversations with nods and smiles. They were both aware of their gentlemen roles as they pulled out chairs for their wives and then went to the bar for drinks for them.

Jeff and I had had dinner with each couple. When we had dinner with Patricia and Horace James, Patricia had invited another couple and, at the table in the dining room, had placed hand-printed name cards to identify our seating arrangement. So like her, so accustomed to hosting and fine dining.

At the ophthalmology office, Dr. Greenfield finally gave me the green light to go swimming again. My right eye had healed from shunt surgery, but the intraocular pressure was still uncontrolled, even though I was continuing to instill two medicated eye drops twice a day as prescribed. The intraocular pressure in my left eye was also abnormally high. I was very worried about it, as well as my right eye. Surely optic nerve damage was occurring. Why wasn't Dr. Greenfield going ahead with the trabeculectomy on my left eye? At my next appointment, I asked him, "What about my left eye?"

"Can't do anything with the left until the right eye is controlled. When it's controlled, we'll perform a trabeculectomy on your left eye."

So he still had hopes my right eye would respond to the shunt surgery, the Baerveldt implant? But why wasn't it responding? Would it ever respond? I wasn't really dwelling on my vision situation because I kept busy with other things. I knew I was very lucky in many other ways, and I wasn't blind, after all.

Paul Ferris, the Marine major who'd escaped from Germany when a college student just before being recruited in Hitler's army, was back in Park Place. I remembered how he and I had *played ball together* when I went to P.T. for my balancing exercises. Wife Penny, skinny like a willow reed, walked around the lounge before dinner like a lost child. One evening, she wandered up to us and proclaimed with conviction, "He's not going to come back home this time. I know he's not getting out." We tried to console her, but she wandered off to approach other residents with her thoughts.

Usually every morning on rising, Jeff and I habitually performed our routine exercises as we had since shortly after we were married. We performed this ritual in separate rooms unless we were away and in a motel room or in a guest's bedroom. Exercising was one of the many things we shared. Our six years of marriage had been most rewarding, proving our complete compatibility including sexual enjoyment. Some mornings, lying in bed, I'd suddenly feel fingers massaging my back, traveling down, lingering and circling over my lower spine. By now, I recognized this prelude to another ultimate orchestration. Even though we were both age seventy eight on our wedding day, I considered being sexually active a natural consequence of marriage, a bonus, actually. I understood many older couples, some even younger than we, didn't engage in this heavenly activity any longer and even had separate bedrooms. What a shame! In Jeff's and my book, no age limit existed.

On rainy mornings after exercising, I went over to Bay Building to take my walks. Connected to our Sentinel Building with a walkway, it had many more corridors and thus provided more walking area. The first few times I walked there I got lost in its maze of corridors. I finally pinpointed landmarks such as benches, a lily pond, mailboxes, and an elevator. Where I had turned right initially, I learned to turn left when retrieving my steps. I learned other tricks, too. I'd breathe deeply and walk more slowly when waifs of frying bacon, toast, and brewed coffee escaped from certain apartments. I'd increase my pace and hold my nose where cigarette fumes permeated the air. Occasionally the aroma of perfume floated into my nostrils and lingered. It reminded me of the times later in the morning when I'd pass maids' carts in the corridor and smell their aromatic cleaning products. The maids always doused themselves with an enormous amount of perfume, it seemed, for when I passed them grouped together talking the mixture of their various perfumes was like passing a cosmetic counter in the old Woolworth's five and ten cent store. Our maid, Marigold, was an exception. I never smelled perfume on her when she came to clean our apartment.

TWENTY-FOUR
CHAIRMAN

December 7, 2004. Time to send Christmas cards. Jeff and I sat down at our desktop computer, brought up a colorful holiday border design, and started to compose a Christmas letter. "Let's not make it a long letter narrating every single thing we've done all year long, like those boring kinds we receive from some of our friends," I said, wrinkling my nose.

"Right," Jeff agreed. "They start out with the weather and continue with paragraph after paragraph describing trips they've taken, illnesses they've endured, and extended family festivities."

"We do have to start with *Merry Christmas and a Happy New Year.* Then we could say, *For us it has been a very good year, And now that the holidays soon will be here...*" I offered.

"Sounds like a poem," Jeff said. "Why don't we make it a poem?" He cocked his head toward me.

"Why not? What's the next line?"

"*We want you to know we are thinking of you. And though we have troubles...*"

"*They are but a few,*" I added. "*We're another year older...*"

Jeff said, "*And deeper in debt, And we haven't arrived at the graveyard yet.*"

I laughed. "Oh Jeff, we can't say that in a Christmas greeting!"

"Why not? Make people laugh. You laughed. Greeting. We have to get that word in. How about, *This is our chance to send you a greeting, Although 't would be better to do it by meeting. We'll do it this way, 'Fore our thoughts go a-fleeting.*" He leaned back in his chair, his hands off the keys.

"Those last lines don't rhyme. How about this? *We'll do it this way, Before our thoughts go astray?*"

"Better," Jeff said, changing the last line. "Not exactly worthy of

202

Wadsworth, but good for amateurs. Let's print it off! How many copies do we need? A hundred? That should do it. We'll run them off on our new printer and then print address labels."

Before I married Jeff, my Christmas card list totaled about thirty. Jeff sent greetings to all living military buddies and wives of those who'd died. He sent them to old friends, immediate family, close relatives, administrators of his college, several retired teachers, and even his first wife's matron of honor. He included my name as well as his. They all sent in return. Thus our long list.

A notice from management was sticking in our door the next morning. It was a reminder to all residents that they were expected to contribute to an employees' Christmas fund. A suggested amount was one thousand dollars per couple. Contributions were to be placed in an identified box located at the receptionist desk. Money would be divided and dispersed equally among employees according to years of service. Residents were also reminded employees received no tips or other benefits from residents throughout the year.

Jeff made out our check and dropped it through the slot in the box on our way to dinner one evening. He also left our Christmas letters at the front desk to be mailed. On the dining room our server was Bud, according to a name pin on his white shirt. He was new, and when he was filling our water glasses we told him to bring us crackers with our salads instead of rolls. "We like our rolls to come with our entrée' so they're warm. If you bring them now, they'll be cold when you bring our main course," Jeff explained.

"I understand, Mr. Metz," he said, politely.

"And Bud," Jeff said. "We'll both want the petite filet, and we'll want them char broiled. Pittsburgh. Do you understand we don't want them cooked very long?"

"Yes sir. I do understand exactly what you mean, Mr. Metz. I've worked in other restaurants, and I know what you mean." Short, slight of build, dark haired, he had a pleasant voice and a nice smile.

"Have you seen the sautéed vegetables? Are they cooked to a mush or are they crisp?" Jeff asked.

"They are crisp. I'm sure you'll like them, Mr. Metz," Bud said, confidently. "I'll bring your salads now and the crackers." Then he stopped and pointed to the floor and said, "Oh there, on the floor. Something's shining. I believe it's a watch. Is it yours, Mrs. Metz? Here, I'll pick it up."

I looked at the watch Bud was holding and said, "No, Bud. It doesn't belong to me. But thank you. You might want to take it to the front desk. The receptionist handles lost and found items," I advised.

As Bud left our table, Jeff said, "Now there's a good server. Not like some who don't know anything about the food or how it's prepared."

When Bud returned with our salads we noticed he was limping. "You're limping. Did you hurt yourself, Bud?" Jeff asked.

"No, I didn't, Mr. Metz. "I have a deformed knee. From birth. Thank you for asking."

The next day, Jeff and I decided to hang our Christmas wreath on the wall outside our door and decorate the apartment as last year. While fastening a red-and-gold-colored satin bow and red ribbon onto the wreath, I noticed how stiff my fingers had become. In fact, the middle finger of my left hand hesitated and clicked before it opened. Arthritis, I surmised. The bow and ribbon I attached to the wreath had formerly secured a large box containing my last year's Christmas present from my daughter, Mary Ann. She always went to much expense with her Christmas present wrappings. That extravagant trait couldn't be attributed to my genes, believe me. I still saved ribbons and wrapping paper from presents I received, providing they were in reusable condition. Apparently Jeff had done the same and stored them in our former garage, because when his daughter Susan was helping us move and working in the garage, I remembered how she threw out many wrappings she deemed despicable. My frugality started long ago. With my first job, I saved every penny possible to buy a car. When dating, I had two dresses to my name, one I'd made myself.

After attaching the bow and ribbon from my daughter's present to our Christmas wreath, I cut the continuous red ribbon in half to make two streamers coming down from the bow. Decorated that way, the wreath looked just fine. In fact it looked very attractive, I concluded.

Jeff announced his return from his December Housekeeping, Maintenance, and Security Committee meeting with a definite closure of our apartment door. "How was the meeting?" I quickly asked, all ears.

In a not too soft voice, he said, "You want to know what happened? I'll tell you what happened. What I more or less expected to happen. I'm chairman for next year."

"You are? Good!" I grinned at him and waited to hear the details, the whole story.

"As you know, Tom Price is chairman. He opened the meeting. After the heads of the three facility departments gave their reports and committee members voiced their concerns and had their questions answered, Tom said, 'It's time to appoint a new chairman for next year.' Then before anyone could say anything, a committee member said, 'I nominate Jeff Metz to serve as chairman for two thousand five.'

"'Any more nominations?' Tom asked. There were none. So yours truly is chairman. Railroaded!" He laughed sardonically.

I smiled. "That's great! You'll make a great chairman."

"Well, it might be kinda fun, as long as it doesn't interfere too much with writing my autobiography that I'd like to start writing. We'll see," he said and sat down and took off his shoes and socks.

The morning of the third Monday in January Jeff, now chairman of the Housekeeping, Maintenance, and Security Committee, went to the meeting held in the Club House card room. To get prepared for today's meeting, he'd sent out an agenda to all members the week before. He'd also asked for and received reports from the facility's department heads. Another step he'd taken was to purchase a tape recorder to activate at the meeting. He planned to play it at home after the meeting when writing the minutes. That was my Jeff, always thinking ahead, always organized, always prepared.

Before he purchased the tape recorder, I'd said, "You don't have to write the minutes, Jeff. You can appoint a secretary to do that. Our Health Care Committee has a secretary, as you know. I am it!" But he'd said *he'd* rather write the minutes. Needed to get them written just right was what he meant. That's just the way he was, and I'd learned that was just the way he was.

I'd noticed he was kind of wound-up in preparation for this first meeting as chairman, and I could hardly wait for him to return.

"Well, how did it go?" I asked, scarcely allowing him time to enter the apartment.

"Fine! It went just fine, I believe. But I want to tell you, I could hardly believe what happened! Last month, I told everyone to have a joke or funny story to tell before I started the meeting this month. So this morning I asked who wanted to tell a joke. Clarence stood up and said *he* did. He proceeded to take off his shirt! Bareness personified! Then he shouted, 'Look at my arm, God damn it! I fell and got hurt because the God damn drainage system doesn't work.' He pointed to his arm. 'Management's to blame, and they're gonna have a lawsuit on their hands! Water comes down on the walkway and doesn't drain off. I have to walk there! Nothing's done about it. I pay good money here not to have this happen to my arm, damn it!'

"He's yelling over my head, and then all of a sudden, also behind me, the Executive Director's yelling. I hadn't seen him come in. He's threatening Clarence with a raised fist. Then Clarence raises *his* fist. I thought the two were going to go at it. I'm sitting there, and the two of them are shouting at each other over my head. Then Clarence says, 'I'm resigning from this committee,' and he stalks out of the room with the Executive Director following him."

"Wow!" I said. "Then what did you do?"

"I guess we all took a deep breath. I started the meeting. Didn't ask for any more jokes or stories, let me tell you. We'd all had enough. I'll save the jokes for next month. Old business was all about pets. The dogs and cats. Someone complained again that residents with pets aren't picking up droppings when they walk their pets. Their dogs. One member said, 'Mrs. Petrovich never carries a scoop and never has a plastic bag with her when she walks her dog.' Others agreed this lady walks her dog and never picks up droppings. Others cited many places they've seen these droppings. Then a woman complained about feral cats."

Jeff had eased himself into a dining room chair, and I sat down too, grinning and waiting to hear more.

Jeff continued, "Then the man in charge of maintenance spoke up and

206

said, 'About those feral cats. One year we got rid of all those feral cats, and then we got rats. Rats by the dozens around the back door of the kitchen. Had to get rid of them somehow. So we brought back the feral cats.'

"Then one of the women. Women out-number men on the committee, naturally. Just as they do here at Sandycreek Terrace. One of the women complained about raccoons and thought they were responsible for some of the droppings. Someone blamed bob-cats she'd seen."

"My heavens!" I said, changing position in my chair and clasping my hands together.

"Listen," Jeff said, raising a pointed finger. "I want you to hear this. The new man in charge of security leaned over my shoulder and asked if he could say something. 'Of course,' I said. He said, 'Ain't any of them things! I tell ya, ain't any a them things. It's them toads what does it!' I thought that was priceless! Stopped all those ladies' wagging tongues."

I laughed along with Jeff, but he wasn't finished.

"Then Irene Trenton complained about the trash rooms. They seem to be a continual bone of contention with her. Trash put in wrong containers, trash on the floor, big cardboard boxes not being broken down to fit into receptacles. The new committee member said light bulbs aren't being replaced in outdoor lamps along the corridors. And a resident in Inlet Building wants the canopies, the umbrellas over the outdoor tables on the Terrace patio changed. She'd like blue. She'd complained about this at our last meeting. She hates the colorless ones that are there now. On and on."

"Well they are rather drab," I offered.

Jeff continued, "I asked for everyone to give their names as they start to talk. For the purpose of the minutes. When I listen to the tape recorder I won't recognize voices and won't know who said what. Unless they first say their names."

"Good idea," I said. Then I laughed. "That was quite a meeting!"

"It was. For next month, I asked committee members to write out their complaints and ideas and submit them to me in advance of the meeting. Oh yes, I forgot to tell you the Executive Director cornered me after the meeting. He wanted to tell me that Clarence has been a problem resident. He's easily irritated and explodes at the least provocation, the least inconvenience he encounters. He's had a number of meetings with Clarence. Gets him settled down. Clarence apologizes, and then before too long, he's raising the roof again about something."

The next day at the desk-top computer with Jeff at the lap-top he had started to use and that was placed on a small table to my right, I found it difficult to work on my nursing article. Impossible to concentrate when HMS committee members' voices were darting into my ears from the recorder at my right, blocking out my thoughts! Besides, their comments were far more interesting than dwelling on my dry serious subject. So I stopped typing. As I listened to the recorder, I felt like I was actually attending the meeting. If I'd been there, I'd have laughed out loud at some of the members' comical comments. I heard Jeff's voice reminding speakers to state their names before commenting, for inclusion in the minutes. When the meeting seemed to get out of hand I'd hear Jeff's voice again, bringing the meeting to order by one of his tactical jargons. Jeff played his recorder for a few minutes, turned it off, placed his fingers on the key-board of the lap-top, typed, and then turned on the recorder again.

As I continued to walk to the Club House, to the mail box, and to the car, it seemed to me as if more and more residents were using canes and walkers and were ambulating with hesitant baby-steps and bent over shoulders. Even Jeff was complaining more of pain when he walked, and he was using his cane more frequently. He actually had two canes. One was plain and a bit too long for his height and rarely used. The other was the totem pole cane made of mahogany by a friend who had worked in a furniture factory. People who noticed that cane, and many did, asked to see it and studied it closely.

Jeff had typed his name and address on a label and affixed it to the duck's neck. All residents were requested to attach their names to all ambulatory aids for identification purposes. Not infrequently, canes were forgotten and left in the lounge, in the dining room, library, and other common areas. Occasionally a resident took off with another resident's walker or scooter. For some reason, seeing Jeff using a cane didn't adversely affect me. Perhaps this was because he didn't use it in the house or for short distances and also because it was a work of art and admired by so many of the residents.

Penny Ferris was correct. Her husband, Paul, my buddy for workouts in P.T., did not return to independent living from Park Place. One evening on our way to the lounge and then the dining room, a red rose and white baby breath appeared in a bud vase on the front desk counter. Again, as always when we saw the red rose in a bud vase, we stopped and asked the receptionist. "Paul Ferris," she told us.

That same evening in the lounge as we sipped on our drinks and waited to be approached by a hostess and led to our dining room table, a woman we'd not seen before ambled into the lounge, hesitated, and looked around. The dining room's Assistant Manager, seeing the woman who now appeared bewildered, approached her and said, "May I help you?"

"I'm to meet my friends here, and I don't see them," the worried woman wailed.

When the Assistant Manager asked for the friends' names the trembling voice told her. Apparently the Assistant Manager recognized the names and inquired, "Might you have the wrong night?"

"No, no. Tonight is the night. I've looked and looked, but I don't see them." She cast her eyes down at her wrist watch.

The Assistant Manager continued to advise her saying, "The residents you mentioned are registered for tomorrow night in our reservation book. Would you like to be seated in the dining room?"

"No, I'll wait for my friends," the resident said and started to walk about the lounge, still bewildered.

Jeff and I glanced at each other with identical thoughts. *Another confused resident.*

TWENTY-FIVE
LEO

One morning when I awoke and went into the master bathroom I noticed the night lights had burned out. A series of tiny lights, they were strung about two inches from the floor along and under the full length of the cabinets, sink, and long counter-top. They allowed just enough light to enter our bedroom to enable us to see to make necessary bathroom trips during the night. If I went into the bathroom after five in the morning, a little red light would be flashing above the emergency pull cord. Immediately I'd press my finger on the button under the light, and the light would disappear. A corresponding light in security headquarters would also be extinguished. This was part of the security system. Residents were instructed to turn off the red light on arising every morning. If a corresponding light in security headquarters was still flashing after eleven in the morning, security would phone or come to the apartment to see if anything was wrong.

At any rate, with the night lights now burned out, we completed a work request form. That very afternoon, John of John and Matt was at our door. As this was the first time these night lights needed replacement, I asked John, "Do these lights burn out frequently?"

"All the time," he said. "We're always replacing them. They weren't exceptionally good buys in the first place."

"These bathrooms are quite large," I commented.

"Yes, they're intentionally large to allow for maneuverability of ambulatory aids," he explained. "The grab-bars and adjustable seat in the shower stall are also features to accommodate residents. So is the large-sized tub."

Jeff came into the bathroom while we were talking. "While you're here, John, would you mind moving our TV in the Florida room just a bit to the right and then back against the wall?"

"Sure thing. Be glad to do that," John said, and he gave the TV a mighty shove before he left.

"This gives us a little more room to walk between the TV in the Florida room and that end table in the living room."

"Yes it does," I agreed. "And isn't that John a nice guy? I admit, Jeff, it is great to have this service." He nodded and winked, letting me know I was acknowledging a good reason for us to be living here.

In the library one afternoon, I saw Irene Trenton sitting on a couch in front of the fireplace leafing through a large picture book titled *China*. I sat down in a chair opposite her and she glanced over at me. "How have you been?" I asked her.

"Much back pain. I'm trying to find a good book to read to take my mind off this pain. How about you?"

"I'm getting arthritic," I said. "The fingers of both my hands are getting stiffer. Worse in the morning when I wake up. The middle finger of my left hand hesitates and clicks before it fully opens. I exercise my hands, opening and closing them until they function fairly well."

"I'm upset that Vioxx was taken off the market. I loved that medication!," Irene said with a clap of her hands.

"I used that med, too. It worked for me. I wonder how many studies were conducted before it was determined or proven to be harmful and taken off the market. When I took Vioxx I had no arthritic symptoms and could even walk with more ease."

"My G P prescribed Celebrex to replace Vioxx, but it wasn't effective."

I nodded and said, "I was prescribed Celebrex, too, and then Mobek, but neither was user-friendly and actually made my mobility worse. I rue the day I was no longer able to purchase Vioxx."

"Do you go to the exercise classes?" Irene wanted to know. "I go to both Strength and Tai Chi. I find them beneficial."

"No, I don't go, but maybe I should. I exercise at home every morning."

As I walked back to the apartment and passed several residents walking slowly using canes, I was thankful I was fairly physically fit, not bent over a walker or driving a scooter. Yes, Jeff and I should continue with our exercise programs every morning, and I should continue my walks and Jeff his bike rides.

March 15, 2005 and I was now eighty-five years old! I looked admiringly at the bouquet of twelve large long-stemmed red roses and said, "Jeff, these roses are more beautiful than they were yesterday." When he'd left the apartment yesterday he'd told me he was going shopping for food. But he'd returned sans food and with these beautiful red roses for my birthday.

"They've opened up some from their buds yesterday. I'm glad you like them," Jeff said, smiling at me and giving me a special birthday kiss.

I'd followed the instructions clamped to the cellophane wrapping the roses and cut inches off the stems, removed leaves below the intended water-line, and mixed the preservative powder in the water that I'd poured into the tall, antique, cut-glass vase. Once again I'd taken the vase out of the étagère and placed another object in its space. The flower arrangement looked perfect where I'd placed it in the center of the Florida room table. And I'd be able to smell the rose aroma since I often sat at that table.

"It's time to open your presents," Jeff said, carrying the boxes that had come in mail deliveries during the week and placing them on the table by the roses. "If they were my presents, I'd have opened each one as it arrived. You tell me it's customary for your family to wait. I think that's a bunch of bunk!"

"No it is not! And yes we do wait. For the day itself. The exact day of the birthday. At Christmas it's the same. Not one day before does one open one's presents!"

"Kirk and Sally will no doubt bring you a present when they come. Too bad your son couldn't get here for the actual day. And Sally, too, of course. We have a guest room reserved for them, don't we?" Jeff asked.

"Yes,, the room's reserved. I was able to get one in our building. The one three doors down the corridor. They're coming as soon as they could.

Kirk had to be in New York City this week to present that new educational program. I'm just sorry they can't stay longer. The first time they've been here and a short weekend at that."

"We'll make the most of it," Jeff said, looking into my eyes and blinking.

And we did make the most of it. We met them at West Palm airport and started the apartment tour the minute we opened the door. "I like your kitchen," Sally said, standing in the middle of the room and looking around. "Nice and compact. Everything's handy. And your lace curtains. They're pretty, make for privacy, and leave in plenty of light."

"Furniture fits nicely in the living and dining rooms," Kirk said, observing our arrangement.

"There's the painting of the Shack!" Sally exclaimed, standing in the Florida room now and looking at the painting she and Kirk had given me. "Looks great there! The perfect spot! You see it when you sit at the table and pass it every time you walk into the bedroom."

"I like your patio," Kirk said, looking out the glass door and windows at the end of the room.

"How about this bedroom? Really big! Nicely decorated, too. Kirk, look out the window at the pond. Very nice!" Sally exclaimed.

"Let me show you the clothes closet," Jeff said, leading them over to the walk-in closet. "Observe. Two long walls. Racks up and down, filled with Jeanie's clothes!" He gestured toward the two walls holding my clothes. "I'm allotted this one rack on this one short wall." Jeff's hand swept the third *long* wall. "Wouldn't you call that discrimination?" He chuckled.

"Wait. Just wait 'til we show you the den," I said to my son and daughter-in-law. "All Jeff's jackets and sport coats are in the wall-long closet in the den. He has ample space for his clothes!" The two visitors laughed.

"Wow! What a bathroom!" Kirk said as we walked into the master bath with its large tub, shower stall, and sink lining one wall, a full-sized mirror above. "What's that cord hanging down on the wall over there?"

"That's the emergency cord. We're to pull it to alert staff if we need help." I explained. "We haven't had to use it and hope we never do."

"What would happen if you pulled it?" Kirk asked, knitting his brows.

"A security staff member comes. Then a nurse from the health center. And then they evaluate and decide whether to call 911," Jeff said.

We showed the guest bathroom next and lastly the jam-packed den. "I like all these chairs in here. Room for everyone to sit. Whose pictures are these?" Kirk asked, pointing to the photos hanging on the wall above Jeff's desk

"They're of my son and three daughters, two of my grandsons, and one's of Jeanie and me. Over here above the closet are my World War II medals in that frame and photos of the destroyers in which I served," Jeff said, motioning to the lengthy impressive array.

After the tour, I brought out the crocheted pieces similar to those I'd given Mary Ann. "Your great grandmother, mother of your maternal grandmother, crocheted these," I said, handing them to Kirk. He examined them, studying the stitches and handling them gently and lovingly. Then he passed them to Sally.

"We'll put them under glass in a frame," she said.

"That would be a great idea! I never thought of doing that. But then Sally, you would. You're the artist. All those stained glass designs you make." I looked back at the crocheted pieces and said, "I remember watching my grandmother crochet and knit with her stiff crooked fingers. They were crippled from arthritis," I said. "I gave your sister similar pieces when she visited. Mary Ann, that is. You kids should have them."

We left early for dinner so we could escort Kirk and Sally on a tour around the premises. They showed interest in everything—the exercise room, swimming pool, card room, library, art room, assistance in living office, and tiny one-room bank employing a cashier three hours a day on week-days. In the lounge residents greeted and welcomed them as residents always do when introduced to the younger generation.

"This is your first time here?" Sarah Grant asked. "You should come more often. Your parents are a fine addition to Sandycreek Terrace."

"You come from a good state," Ralph Wilson said in his southern drawl when Sally told him they lived in North Carolina.

Stuart and Ruth McKee made their way over and immediately Ruth said to Sally, "Do you belong to Jeff or Jean? You resemble Jean." Sober-faced, she was staring at Sally.

Sally smiled and said, "Thank you for the compliment but no, my husband is her son."

"Oh," Ruth said, frowning. Ever the one to seek information, she continued, "Do you have children?"

"I have two grown sons," Sally told her.

Ruth was about to ask more questions when Stuart, who had been standing by quietly waiting for his wife, guided her into the dining room.

The next morning we took Kirk and Sally to the Terrace for breakfast where we introduced them to our favorite Terrace server, Emily. Emily never walked but ran around from table to table making certain all residents had exactly what they ordered. "With all this food, we won't need lunch," Kirk said, raising a forkful of cheese omelet to his mouth.

"This is such a nice little restaurant," Sally said, pouring cream into her coffee. "Informal. Not large and lavish like the dining room decor, although that was lovely and the food was delicious. My petite filet was perfect! Just the way I like it cooked."

The next weekend, Kasey, Jeff's grandson, was visiting again from his medical university in Davie. "It's okay for me to come this often, isn't it?" he asked, appearing in shorts, bare top, and carrying a duffel bag he quickly deposited on the living room floor. He stood there flexing his arm and chest muscles made massive from years of competitive wrestling. I couldn't help peering at muscles that looked like broad ropes rippling under his tanned skin.

"You bet it's O. K. for you to come any time you can!" Jeff said. "Listen up! When we hear from you kids we old folks brighten up and come alive!"

We did enjoy his visits. He talked about his required medical courses, his younger brother's achievements in college wrestling, and his first and only girlfriend whom he intended to marry. In fact, this visit he described the engagement ring he planned to have made—a pink sapphire surrounded by tiny diamonds in a white-gold setting. He took advantage of the exercise room where, while he worked-out on the many machines, he was getting to know some of the male residents. He became particularly friendly with Dr. Tom Price and Leo Badalatto, a former Steeler football player. Amazingly, Leo had been Kasey's idol for years.

It was truly notable how residents, old as we all were, showed an interest in anyone younger, especially two or more generations younger. Babies in guests' arms were oohed and aahed over, and old eyes followed pre-school-aged grandchildren as they trotted and skipped through the dining room, their little high-pitched voices shrilling and bringing smiles to wrinkled faces. When Kasey, so enamored of Leo, asked him for his autograph one evening in the lounge Leo acted both pleased and embarrassed.

We found Leo to be a most friendly guy, big and tall, and who, incidentally, had moved into Sandycreek Terrace with Roberta Pilgrim, a woman we knew. I'd known Roberta for just a few years; Jeff had known her for quite some time. I met her when I attended The Retired Officers Association (TROA) meetings with Jeff, and she attended the meetings with her husband, also a retired military officer. Upon her husband's death, she continued to attend TROA meetings, just as Fanny Porter had attended Rotary meetings after her husband's death. Through communication with mutual friends, Jeff and I learned Roberta had a male friend. The male friend turned out to be Leo Badalatto, and indeed, when he moved into our CCRC, Roberta moved in with him, sharing an apartment. Many evenings in the lounge they joined us for cocktails and then for dinner. A beautiful woman, a meticulously coiffed blond with not a hair out of place, she always dressed in magnificent clothes.

One evening, Roberta invited us for cocktails in their Inlet apartment. She especially wanted us to see the change she'd made in their living quarters. She said, "I despised the fact that when we sat in the living room we could see right into the kitchen! Now who wants a view of the kitchen when you're sitting in the living room? Especially when you're entertaining guests. So I hired an interior decorator to create an arrangement to hide the kitchen."

As she showed us the creation, we were looking at elaborate greenery in an enormous Grecian gold-edged container atop the kitchen counter. It definitely obscured the kitchen when we took seats in the living room. Leo mixed drinks in the *hidden* kitchen, and Roberta served them, slinking slowly across the carpet dressed like a fairy tale princess in an ankle-length lime-green satin gown embroidered with golden threads and crystal-like beads.

As we sat talking and sipping drinks, Roberta began to present an unusual behavior. While others were talking, she hummed softly. I listened but couldn't decipher a tune. She interrupted the current conversation by saying, "My husband, Clifford, was a wonderful man. *You* knew him, Jeff. Wasn't he wonderful? I miss him. I miss him." Her voice quivered.

Jeff agreed her husband had been a wonderful man, and then again she directed her conversation to Jeff and me saying, "Leo looks at every woman here. He doesn't care about me."

Concerned and uncomfortable, I looked over at Leo, but he was sitting quietly, acting as though he hadn't heard her. How could Roberta say such things when Leo had just allowed her to decorate the apartment to her liking and probably at his expense? In our presence at least, he'd shown her every attention a woman could possibly want.

Subsequent evenings when we sat with them in the lounge before dinner, Roberta hummed a non-tune and accused Leo of staring at other female residents. Always she talked about her house in Massachusetts which she said she still owned and yearned to return to.

When we next saw Leo he was alone. "Where's Roberta?" we asked.

As he stood tall and erect, long arms dangling at his sides, he looked down at us and said, "She left. Moved out." Although his expression was still rather bland as it had been the times Roberta had accused him of infidelity, this time it also portrayed a strange mixture of bewilderment and lack of concern.

When we got back to our apartment that evening I said to Jeff, "What do you make of Roberta? She's been acting strangely, humming like that and accusing Leo of infidelity. Then she moves out after being here only three months. Don't you think she's psychotic?"

Jeff scratched his bald head. "She appears that way to me. At least mentally unstable. Yes. She's foolish to move out of Sandycreek Terrace. She needs to be in a place like this. That was obvious."

"Poor Leo. I thought he was very nice to her. He didn't seem too dejected, did you think?"

"Well, he's a big man. Had lots of experiences in this world. He'll be all right. Besides, it's none of our concern." Jeff gave me a pat on the arm and that loving look.

Shortly after Roberta's departure, into Sandycreek Terrace moved petite, young-looking, smart dresser Muriel Lowrey. Leo was the one who introduced this new resident to me one evening in the lounge. When she said she was from Michigan I assured her Jeff and she would have much in common and much to talk about. "Oh is that right?" she said with a degree of uncertainty. I introduced Jeff when he came over to us with our drinks. Although I opened the subject of Michigan, after Jeff and Muriel exchanged just a few sentences about the state, the topic was dropped like a hot coal. The next evening and other evenings after that, Leo and Muriel were together in the lounge and then ate dinner together. Neither one seemed to be interested in anyone else or anything else, for that matter.

A week before Easter, a notice of a hymn sing was posted on the bulletin board across from the front desk. It advised that Sarah Grant would be playing the piano and Gloria Semple, a resident and woman we knew from our church, would be leading the singing. All residents and friends were urged to attend and join in the singing. On my way to the library one day after I read the notice, I met Sarah leaving the library. She stopped me. "Jean, you're planning to come to the hymn sing on Thursday at four o'clock, aren't you?" Since I hesitated, she appeared worried and said, "You must come! I'm playing the piano. Do come and bring Jeffrey."

She always called Jeff Jeffrey and was the only person who didn't call him Jeff. I had to smile at that and told her we'd try to make the hymn-sing.

We did go as did a number of residents. In fact, quite a group gathered in the lounge and sat in chairs and sofas close to the piano. Perhaps Sarah had begged many to attend as she had urged us. Song sheets were distributed, but Sarah played without music as usual. Gloria stood next to the piano song sheet in hand, belted out the songs, and led the attendees. All tried their best to perform in some fashion. My limited vision didn't permit me to read the printed sheets, but I found I didn't need them. I actually remembered the tunes and the words from my past years of singing these familiar hymns in the many churches I attended. As I sat next to Jeff and could hear him sing, I realized again, as I did the mornings we attended church services, that he had a very nice tenor singing-voice. After forty-five-minutes of old voices singing bass, tenor, alto, and soprano, early diners went into the dining room while others stood around conversing and eventually went home to return for dinner at a later hour.

The application for the JCAHO Gold Seal Award had been mailed months ago but the award had not yet been granted to Park Place. Dressed to attend a Rotary noon meeting with Jeff in Jupiter in one hour, I received a phone call from the new administrator requesting me to come to Park Place as soon as possible. I walked over immediately. In a hallway of one of the wings, I was introduced to a JCAHO representative. He'd come to tour, talk to the staff, and apparently meet the people who'd written the two letters attesting to the merits of the facility. After a short conversation with him as I was leaving, in walked Dr. Tom Price, author of the other testimonial letter.

The award was granted shortly after the JCAHO representative's visit. To celebrate the award-winning occasion, the powers that be held an open-house in Park Place. They invited health professionals of the community such as physicians, dentists, social workers, pharmacists, hospital administrators, and owners of long-term care facilities. Tom Price and I were the only residents invited. I felt it only fitting to take Jeff with me. And I did. A large white cloth covered the central nursing station and on it an elaborate spread of food was arranged in tiers. In the center of the display was an identical ice carving of the award. The magnificent arrangement transformed a simple nursing station into a show place like an hors d'oeuvres table at a country club banquet. On side tables, coffee in urns and chocolate desserts enhanced and completed the sensational scene. I mingled with guests, playing a hostess role, or at least that's what I thought I was doing.

Twenty-Six
A Trip

The second weekend in May during Kasey's next visit he asked about my great grandchildren. "Grandma Jean, how many do you have?" he wanted to know.

I smiled to myself, thinking of their cute little faces in the photos my younger daughter Kathleen sent recently, the ones I'd affixed with magnets to the refrigerator door. "Four. Three girls and a boy," I told him. "And I've only seen the oldest. A girl. That was when she was two and I went to visit my daughter for the Christmas holidays." I remembered sitting spread eagle on the carpeted floor in Kathleen's living room and rolling a tennis ball along the floor to a curly-headed tot, she also spread eagle on the floor some feet away. I could still hear the peals of laughter emulating from Alex as we rolled the ball back and forth aiming it into the vees formed by our legs. "They live in Kelso, Washington," I continued. "My daughter and her husband and Jamie, my granddaughter, her husband, and the four children. Alex was two then and now she's eight. The youngest is three."

"You should go and visit them before they get any older," Kasey wisely advised.

I wasn't sure if Kasey's prompting was responsible for our making plans to go all the way to the state of Washington, but decide to go we did. Indeed, I was rather taken aback when Jeff jumped on Kasey's bandwagon and said, "We should be able to get a time-share for at least a week near Kelso, Washington. I'll get out the Atlas and the RCI book listing time-share resorts and look for ones close to Kelso. Then I'll make the call."

I was delighted, to say the least, and hadn't given any thought to where we'd stay and for how long. But here was Jeff already thinking ahead and making decisions and plans. That had always been my role in my other life. I'd been the instigator and planner. It had taken me some time to get accustomed to having my role be taken over by Jeff, to step back and let him take this responsibility. Second marriages require adjustments, I'd learned. I was now satisfied to have him do the planning. I'd also learned it was better to wait for him to initiate an action, such as the purchase of a television set, acceptance of an invitation to attend a brokerage presentation luncheon, plans to travel to a Rotary international convention. I might inquire a time or two about the possibility of such an action after he'd mentioned it, but then say no more and wait until the idea had firmed in his mind. Always before following through with a decision, however, Jeff would say, "If it meets with your approval." I liked that consideration, and I've never had a reason to disapprove, but if I had I wouldn't hesitate to voice my opinion.

Wives need to gain clues and insights about husbands. And a second husband may be very different from the first in a number of ways. I found Jeff to be quicker to understand my thoughts, more outwardly affectionate, more of a conversationalist, more of a sharing companion, and more fun.

I guess I showed my excitement about plans to travel to Washington because Jeff looked at me and gave me a grin that spread under his twinkling blue eyes. Again I realized how fortunate I was to have him as a mate. After all, the trip was being planned to see *my* family, not *his*. Maybe it was because the suggestion had come from his grandson. But no, I rather thought it was because he truly felt it was time for me to be seeing these children, and, of course, he also loved children. And we were actually going to Washington!

Jeff went to his desk and spread the map and RCI Travel book open in front of him. I sat in another chair close by listening eagerly as he dialed RCI and talked to an agent. He inquired about one resort after another, ones on the coast west of Kelso and on a lake north of Kelso. They were all reserved, no vacancies! Jeff didn't give up, and the conversations continued. Finally I heard Jeff say, "We'll take it. Yes, for eight days and nights. A Visa charge." After reading off the VISA number and expiration date and rattling off our phone number, he returned the receiver to its base. "Had to make a reservation for a time-share in the foot-hills of Mt. Hood in Oregon, the closest available to Kelso. The place sounds good but much larger than we need. Accommodates six people. It's eighty miles from Kelso, but that doesn't matter. We were going to rent a car anyway. We'll drive around and see the scenery. This should be fun!"

"Sounds great!" I exclaimed. "But why couldn't you get something closer to Kelso?"

"Vacation time must have already started in the northwest. I've never been to Oregon. Mt. Hood's supposed to be beautiful. We'll have a good time," he assured me.

It just so happened at this particular time that the two older great granddaughters were scheduled to dance in an upcoming recital, I was informed by my daughter delighted to learn we were planning a visit. So this was definitely the time to go! Our plane reservations would land us in Portland the morning of the day of the recital. That night, we'd stay in a motel near Kelso, spend most of the next day at my daughter's house, and then on to our time-share that evening.

I wanted to buy gifts to give to the kiddos and remembered a train set a resident had just bought when she visited the Flagler Museum. She'd set the tiny train set on the lounge bar for residents to watch and enjoy. Electrically activated, the train traveled around on a track inserted in a scenic eighteen-by-eighteen-inch heavy cardboard. For carrying and storage, the board folded in half to fit into a box along with the train and electrical apparatus. "Jeff," I said after he made our plane reservations. "We have to go to the Flagler Museum."

"Why is that?" he asked, staring at me and forcing his eyes wide open as he often did when expecting an explanation.

"Remember that train set that resident brought into the lounge and set up on the bar? When a button is pressed on the board the train travels all over the board on tracks. It would be a perfect gift for Jake! She bought it at the Flagler Museum Gift Shop. Maybe they'd have something there for the girls, too."

"I'm sure they would. When do you want to go?"

We arrived at the Museum before the gates opened at ten the next morning. After a wait of five minutes, we were allowed in the gift shop without paying to tour the Museum since we told the supervisor we had only come for gifts, the train set in particular. In the shop, darkened because of a power shortage and with only daylight filtering through one casement window, I bought two train sets at Jeff's insistence. "The little boy needs two, not one set," he said.

I also found necklaces for the three girls and ear rings for my daughter and granddaughter.

We flew into the Portland airport since it was closer to Kelso than the Seattle airport. I'd been excited from the start of the trip, but at the Portland airport my spirits soared. Who would meet us? My daughter, Kathleen, of course. But I was certain we'd have to wait to see the kiddos until we got to Kelso. We headed toward baggage claim to a carousel where Jeff retrieved our two medium-sized suitcases. Here at our prearranged meeting place I looked around for Kathleen. She was nowhere in sight! Then a tall young stranger came toward us smiling and greeted me with a big hug. I assumed she was a friend of my daughter's and said to her, "This is my husband, Jeff."

Suddenly I spied Kathleen approaching and holding the hands of a little boy and smaller girl. Beside them walked two taller girls and behind all five of them trailed a tall thin young man. The group stopped in front of us—four little pairs of eyes staring up at Jeff and me! The eyes continued to look at this old lady as I hugged Kathleen. And all I could say was, "Oh, my goodness!" Then I bent down and gave each child a hug, or tried to. The littlest one had to be Tessa. She didn't respond, just stood there like a poster picture. Jake shied away, clinging onto his grandmother and hiding his face on her legs. The next oldest, Courtney Jane for sure, let me hug her, and Alex, the oldest, put her arms around me. Then she smiled sweetly and handed me a gift-wrapped box I suspected contained candy. Almost instantly, I realized Kathleen's friend was actually my granddaughter Jamie standing there still smiling at me. I grabbed her and exclaimed, "Oh Honey, you're Jamie. I didn't know you!"

She was laughing and saying, "I know you didn't know me. Have I changed?"

The inflection in her voice made me know she wanted me to think she'd changed, had improved in her looks. Six years ago when I'd last seen her she was heavier. Not that she was actually slim now, but I certainly wouldn't tell her that. So I said, "Yes, you have changed. You seem taller and slimmer. You have a beautiful smile."

"My hair's different, isn't it? Longer?" She waited for my reaction.

"And a little lighter in color, I believe," I said, studying the massive tresses for a moment. But I was being pulled, my hand grabbed by a little hand that began to gyrate and swing both of our arms to and fro in perpetual rhythm.

All at once everyone was in motion as someone started the family parade. Four children tried to go four different directions until they were curtailed by adults and lead into a single line, more or less. Jake broke away from his grandmother and darted forward. He caught up with Jeff, put his little hand in Jeff's large one, and hung on tightly, taking two skipping steps to Jeff's one long stride. I had but one charge, or rather Courtney Jane had one charge since she'd never released my hand after first grabbing it and forging ahead dragging me along with her. Through crowds of travelers and vast expanses of airport walkways our little group proceeded. Finally we arrived at a car rental desk

where Jeff went through the process of getting our rental car.

It being time for lunch, three cars headed for a pre-determined restaurant. Here another circus ensued with nine different orders, decisions changing in mid stream and baffling the poor waitress standing there patiently. While waiting for delivery of food orders, restless children banged flatware on the table and quickly sent a knife and fork spinning to the floor. They played footsies under the table and changed positions on the bench circling a table meant for eight now occupied by nine. Before dessert arrived, I opened the package Alex had given me in the airport. It was indeed a box of candy—my favorite Russell Stover chocolates—and I passed it around the table. "One piece per person is allowed," I stated firmly, and amazingly all obeyed. Dessert was a disaster. Large sundaes ordered by the already sated children became toys that were stirred round and around by long-handled noisy spoons resulting in spillage on the table and multiple sticky fingers. That accomplished, three vehicles left the parking lot.

The children rode home with their parents while Jeff and I followed Kathleen's car to her house. Since Kathleen's husband, a river boat Captain, was working on the Columbia River this weekend, Jeff and I had Kathleen to ourselves but not for long for shortly four children came scampering into the house.

"We brought our dancing costumes!" Alex and Courtney Jane's shrieking voices announced.

Immediately they proceeded to don their tutus and twirl around the living room. Alex, taller and thinner in a black and white net outfit, was poised and graceful whereas Courtney Jane giggled in her all red costume with a tilting headpiece that went flying when she finally lost her balance and fell. Grandpa Jeff clicked the camera many times. Then while Kathleen was preparing dinner, Jeff and I distributed our gifts.

All was going along swimmingly until I decided to act like a teenager. We'd eaten dinner, the two girls had stood patiently in their costumes while their mother applied makeup, and one of the vehicles had just taken off to the theater with the children and their father. Jeff and I were to ride in the SUV with Jamie and Kathleen. I saw I needed to negotiate a high step to get into the back seat of the large vehicle, but I was agile. No problem! I would demonstrate. I lifted my right leg, planted my right foot solidly on the carpeted SUV floor. Too quickly I brought up my left leg to follow suit. I felt my shin touch something hard. No matter, just pull your leg up into the back seat, I said to myself. I did, but I could feel it scraping and scraping as I pulled. Better take a look, I decided as I sat down on the seat. I rolled up the left leg of my slacks and peered at my shin. Bleeding!

Beside me on the seat, Jamie reached into a box at her side and brought out a dressing. She placed it on my wound and secured it with adhesive tape. "Does it hurt, Grandma?" she asked.

"No," I answered, and it didn't. "How on earth did you happen to have a bandage so handy?" I asked.

"We keep a first aid kit in the car all the time. You have to when you have kids, you know," she laughed as she explained. "Do you think you can go to the recital?"

"Of course! I wouldn't miss it! I'll be fine," I assured her.

In the theater, my left leg propped on Jeff's knee, the wound was silently continuing to bleed. Jeff and I craned our necks and focused intently on two girls, ages six and eight, twirling on their toes in their tutus along with many other dancers on stage. The performance ended, clapping erupted, and Jeff, Jamie, and I made our escape through the crowd and drove back to Kathleen's house.

In the bathroom, Jamie proceeded to play nurse again. "It's still bleeding, Grandma. You need another bandage," she said to me. Hunkered down in front of me as I sat on the edge of the tub, she removed the bloody dressing and scrutinized the wound. "You need sutures, Grandma," she informed me.

"I do? Are you sure? Can't you just close it with adhesive tape? Use the tape like steri-strips." I didn't want to spoil the party by going off to the hospital.

"No, I can't do that. I know what you mean, but the cut's too long, and it's still bleeding a lot."

The serious tone of her voice was unmistakable. I had to trust her judgment. She could see the laceration better than I. "Then we better go to the emergency department. Where is the hospital, Jamie?"

"It's in Longview, just a couple miles from here," she explained as she applied another dressing and rose from her hunched-over position.

After I explained the situation to Jeff, he and Jamie and I boarded our rental car, and Jamie drove us to the hospital. At ten in the evening the emergency department was indeed active. Jamie found a wheelchair near the entrance and wheeled me to a window manned by an employee. I handed her my Medicare and Tricare cards, waited for her to make copies, and returned them to my wallet. An attendant arrived and wheeled me into an examining room. Shortly after I'd climbed onto the examining table, a physician walked into the room. He removed the dressing, peered at the wound, then peered at me and asked, "How did this happen?"

"I thought I was twenty-one and jumped into an SUV. But I didn't quite make it and scraped my leg trying to board." My career having been nursing for many years, I always tried to be friendly with physicians.

"What did you scraped it on?" he wanted to know.

226

"I believe it was metal." I did think it was.

"We'll give you a tetanus injection. Now let's see what we can do about this laceration. Have to stop the bleeding first before I can suture it." H applied pressure and then clotting material and left to attend another emergency.

Jamie was standing near the head of the examining table holding my hand when she spotted a pillow on a nearby stand. "Would you like a pillow, Grandma?" she asked and, retrieving it, placed it under my head.

"Thank you, Jamie. Examining tables are notoriously pillowless."

Back in the room, the physician examined the still bleeding laceration. "Here, young lady," he said to Jamie. "Keep pressure on this site." He handed her a bulky dressing, and she did as he instructed.

Minutes passed, the clock kept ticking, and poor Jamie kept applying pressure. Finally I said to Jeff sitting in a chair on the other side of the room, "Jamie's going to pass out if she has to stand here much longer. Please go out in the hall and see if you can locate the doctor, Jeff."

Jeff came back with the physician who removed the dressings and said, "I'll try suturing, but I doubt they'll hold. Your skin's very thin down here."

For what seemed like hours, he painstakingly worked on my leg until he'd closed the laceration with thirteen interrupted nylon sutures. Then he applied steri-strips the length of the wound and then a dressing. Jamie sat in a chair at the head of the table and watched the entire procedure with apparent interest, and the thought occurred to me that this granddaughter of mine would make an excellent nurse.

At twelve-fifty in the morning and after my tetanus injection, we were free to leave. To my amazement when we walked through the waiting room on the way out, there sat Kathleen and Alex. An anxious smile on her face, Kathleen stood up and said, "The hotel where we made your reservations for the night is the Montecello here in Longview. Your room is right across the alleyway in a new addition to the hotel. We can easily walk there. I've been over and told them to hold your room."

"Thank you, Honey," I uttered weakly and, leaning on Jeff's arm, I hobbled across the alley to the hotel.

Now all five of us were in the hotel room, and I immediately sank onto the bed. Alex walked over to me and handed me several flowers. "Oh thank you, Honey," I said while Kathleen explained, "Those flowers are from the bouquet she was given at the end of the recital."

Then I realized Alex had been sitting in a hospital waiting room for almost three hours waiting for her great grandmother to be taken care of and holding flowers to give to her. What a dear child!

Finally alone in the room, Jeff and I went to sleep only to wake some hours later, the sun streaming in the window. "How's the leg?" Jeff asked. "Able to walk over to the dining room for some breakfast? I'm famished!"

"I'm in no pain. I'm sure I can walk just fine. Let's get some food," I was quick to say.

Jeff and I walked into the high-ceilinged lobby of The Montecello Hotel and admired the elaborate antiques and solid old mahogany furniture of the well-preserved hotel as we continued on oak floors to the dining room. The large room was divided into several small sections, and an attendant invited us to sit wherever we desired. Not wanting to walk far, we chose a table in the first section and sat down.

At a table to our left, an elderly woman sat reading a newspaper and eating scrambled eggs and bacon. She put down her paper, looked over at us, and said, "You're new in town, aren't you? I'm Jean Marx. This is my home. I rent an apartment on the second floor of this hotel. They have good food here." Then she looked at my leg. "What's wrong with your leg? I see it's bandaged." She smiled broadly and kept looking at my leg.

I attempted to explain what had happened.

"Oh my dear. What a shame! I hope they took good care of you at the hospital. Did they?" she quizzed, raising her eyebrows.

"Indeed they did. I had an excellent physician in the E. R. He did a fine job suturing my laceration."

Jeff leaned forward and added, "We can't say enough for him. He worked very hard and long."

"I'm going to church with a friend but I have time to go up to my apartment first. Here. Take my newspaper. I'm finished with it," she said, thrusting it on Jeff who gladly accepted.

In no time at all, she returned with a cane in hand. "Here, take this," she said, handing me the cane. "I have another one just like it upstairs. I don't need two. Now I must go out to meet my friend." With that she left the dining room.

At my daughter's house, I propped myself on the sofa, legs elevated. Jeff busied himself taking photos of Alex and Courtney Jane holding their recital bouquets and posing in their ballet costumes, having worn them to their grandmother's house again. Then Jeff took several photos of Jake playing with his new train set. He took Tessa out onto the patio and photographed her as she stood smiling up at him, bangs across her forehead and down into her eyes.

Not to be outdone by her older sister, Courtney Jane pulled out two flowers from her recital bouquet and brought them over to me on the sofa. I smiled, smelled the blossoms, and thanked her profusely. I had to be content to stay propped there and watch the activities, listen to little voices, squeals of laughter, and a squabble or two, and store the scene in my memory bank. After everyone gathered around the dining room table, I finally got up and joined them to enjoy a spaghetti and meat ball meal prepared by Kathleen. Then Jeff and I bade farewell and drove off to our time-share at the foot of Mt. Hood.

The surrounding grounds of the rustic wooden guest buildings were lush with thick dark-green plants and various colored flowers. We entered our building from a long planked porch and found it to be as large, well furnished, and equipped as advertised. The following day, Kathleen and Jamie came and stayed two days with us in the spacious cabin, sleeping in the two upstairs bedrooms. After they left, Jeff and I toured the foothills of Mt. Hood by car, absorbing the beauty of the landscape, the mountains, valleys, and streams. Days later, we were in the Portland airport again, I thankful for Jean's cane. Never before had I had a cane in my hand for my very own use.

Now in the air sitting in the window seat beside me, Jeff said, "We should be home by five-thirty."

"In time for dinner at Sandycreek Terrace," I ventured to say.

Jeff agreed, but we were dead wrong. When we landed at the Houston airport after five airborne hours another plane was parked at our intended arrival gate. Apparently it had no plans to move in the near future for our plane sat on the runway like a side-tracked train. We got more anxious as

DOROTHY BERTSCH

the minutes ticked by. Jeff kept looking at his watch and saying, "We're not going to make our connecting flight at this rate."

I felt a flood of heat rising to my neck when I glanced at my watch. It was fifteen minutes before our plane to West Palm was scheduled to leave! We'd have to taxi to that gate this minute in order to make our flight! This very minute! And Houston airport was huge! Our scheduled departure gate was in a different concourse entirely. Once we got off this plane, we'd need speedy transportation. Was that even a remote possibility?

"We're starting to move,"Jeff said, excitedly. "The other plane's moving away from our gate. Do you have all your belongings so we can exit quickly?"

"Yes," I answered, clutching my purse and portion of newspaper with a half-completed crossword puzzle.

We were off the plane! We hailed transportation! We sped to the gate and got off near the desk! But we were too late. The plane, the attendant said, had departed. My heart sank.

"Nice kettle of fish," Jeff remarked greatly irritated. "When is the next plane to West Palm?" he asked the attendant.

"Tomorrow morning, sir," she informed him.

"Damn!" Jeff said. "Now what are we supposed to do?"

"They'll put us up in a hotel. They always do," I offered.

"Maybe. And we checked our luggage. We have nothing for staying overnight. Not even a tooth brush."

That was true. We preferred not to be burdened with luggage on the plane, lifting it up and putting it in an over-head compartment. "We can ask for a kit containing essentials. I've done that before. We should ask for a voucher for a meal, too." I looked at Jeff and realized how upset he was, his jaw tight, and his face a faint shade of red. If we were younger this might have been a lark. But shoot, we weren't young any more. We'd counted on being home for dinner.

After pursuing our needs for what seemed an unreasonable length of time, walking from one area to another, waiting each time and tired, we were finally provided with an emergency kit, meal voucher, and hotel room accommodations. The next day after an uneventful flight, we were back in our most welcome apartment, vowing never to fly again.

I voiced the thoughts I'd had in the airport. "The layover might have been a bit of a lark had we been some years younger, Jeff,"

"Hum," he mumbled and then groaned, "It's hell to get old."

TWENTY-SEVEN
HOSPITALIZATIONS

Time to visit Elizabeth Price in Park Place. I'd been fairly faithful with my weekly visits, but the trip west had delayed my seeing her for about three weeks. Today, as usual, she appeared to be sleeping. A soft knock on her door brought instant eye contact. I walked in and sat on the side of her bed as usual in order to be close enough to carry on a conversation. She looked at me and said, "You got your hair cut."

"Yes I did," I answered, surprised at her keen observation. "I got it trimmed Friday. It needed it after we got back from our trip. How have you been, Elizabeth?"

"Nothing changes," she said in a whisper. A little louder she asked, "How was your trip?"

As she sat there in her recliner, wearing a pink pants suit and white socks, her body inert, I told her about our trip to see my four great grandchildren. A little smile spread across her face as I described the older two in their tutus, Jacob playing with the train set, and Tessa with bangs in her eyes. I didn't tell her about my accident, my lacerated leg, but I did relate the incident of the missed plane connection and our overnight stay in Houston. When I finished that story she said, "Oh that was a shame."

We sat quietly for a few minutes before she pointed to a photo on her bedside stand. "My grandson was here to visit me. My daughter Kristine's son. He plays a tuba in the band at school."

Even though Elizabeth couldn't show much enthusiasm, I knew she was extremely proud of her grandson, and I exclaimed over the photo of the young boy holding a shinny tuba almost as big as he was.

Then she noticed the bandage on my arm and asked, "Did you have blood drawn today?"

I could hardly hear her, but she was looking at my arm, and I realized she was asking about the lumpy dressing. "Yes, I was at the lab this morning and had blood drawn for my yearly physical. The dressing's so big because I bled quite a bit after we left the lab. I'm on a blood thinning medication, and I started to bleed at the restaurant. We went right to a restaurant because the lab work was fasting and we hadn't eaten breakfast. When I started to bleed I asked the waitress for another napkin and some ice. Poor girl saw all the blood and ran and got me not one napkin but a bundle of them and ice. I applied them and held my arm up in the air." I demonstrated by raising my arm. "Then the manager brought me a bunch of gauze and a roll of adhesive tape. And that's what you see." I pointed to the lump of gauze on my arm.

"Did you have breakfast?" Elizabeth wanted to know.

"Yes, we finally had breakfast, and the bleeding finally stopped." I could see she was getting tired. I glanced at the large clock on the wall and saw I'd over-stayed my usual half hour. "I'd better run along. I'm due to go to the Health Care Committee meeting. I'll be back next week," I said and gave her hand a pat before I left.

I'd no sooner entered the conference room to attend the meeting and seated myself when Tom Price walked in with both his wrists splinted. Now what? When he'd arranged himself in a chair next to mine, lifting his prosthetic leg and placing it in position, I asked him, " Why the splints? Carpel tunnel?"

"No. Just getting weak and need to strengthen them."

I nodded, feeling sorry. Somehow it didn't seem fair he should have these physical problems. "I just came from visiting with Elizabeth," I told him.

"I'm going over to see her as soon as the meeting's over," he said.

A new resident by the name of Lottie Yurasik moved into Sandycreek Terrace in our absence. She was about my size and full of pep, vim, and vigor, as we used to say. Before too long, we saw her in the company of Alan Armstrong, a single, tall, handsome man and resident for approximately eight months. They appeared to enjoy each other's company as they ate together in the Terrace, attended social events together, and sat in the lounge together waiting to be seated for dinner.

In the Terrace one morning as I passed the table where Lottie was seated, she stopped me. "I like that top you're wearing. I really like it a lot. In fact," she added, "I'm going to steal it for my wardrobe." Several other times she saw me she remarked, "You have pretty clothes."

I noticed Jeff got a twinkle in his eyes when someone compliments me on an outfit I was wearing. His wardrobe was ample, but he had no fashion sense, how to combine colors or fabrics. I stopped him from wearing a dark brown sport coat with black trousers, a striped shirt with plaid slacks. Things like that.

I must admit clothes were my down-fall. In my early twenties and on through the years I was raising three children, I made my own clothes. I liked to sew, and making them saved me money. Now that I couldn't see to sew and had enough money, within limits that is, any piece of clothing striking my fancy in my favorite stores was subject to my indulgence or at least my consideration. I figured wearing the latest styles kept one looking younger. And I aimed to do just that. Keep looking as young as possible.

I wasn't the only woman at Sandycreek Terrace who aimed to look stylish. Most of the female residents dressed nicely and modernly, but a few were ahead of the pack. Take Betty Howe, for instance, the resident who coupled with Ralph Wilson, the hearing impaired, devotedly southern-speaking resident. Betty, now ninety-one, put fine fabrics on her slim figure, making her appear strikingly fashionable. A few of her particularly elegant clothes she'd purchased in China some years ago, she told me. Then there was Patricia James, the resident I judged to have come from wealth and who probably hadn't needed to work a day after she graduated from college. She had eye-catching pants suits of expensive-looking fabrics in pastel colors that enhanced her feminine features. Penny Ferris was another, a widow now that my P.T. friend Paul had died. She slowly slinked around the lounge before dinner wearing pants suits and skirt suits in smashing colors and attractive designs I found myself envying. These women had slight figures, providing the ability to buy petite sizes that fit to a T. Maintaining a slim figure required watching intake, omitting fats, cutting down on cholesterol, and choosing nourishing foods, a regimen I was quite sure these women followed.

Studies on nutrition had proven older people stayed healthier if they ate less. I intended to practice sensible measures for the rest of my life. From the looks of a few of the residents, they apparently didn't plan to do that, especially when tempted by our menu offering such desserts as pecan pie, double chocolate cake, hot fudge sundaes, and an occasionally-offered cherries jubilee. I'd heard female residents say they gained ten pounds the first month they were here.

After our trip west, Jeff and I went back to Dr. Greenfield, my glaucoma specialist, for my scheduled appointment. I was in his examining chair, and he'd shone the white light and then the blue light in both my eyes. Now he wheeled his chair back from the slit-lamp machine and said, "Your intraocular pressure in your right eye is within normal range for you."

"It is? I said, hardly able to believe what I was hearing. So the shunt had finally kicked in! Amazing!

"You need to continue administering the same local intraocular pressure-controlling meds, however. And you may now have the trabeculectomy in your left eye. I'll schedule you for surgery two weeks from today."

I nodded and smiled, pleased that my left eye would finally get the attention it needed.

"I see by your chart you're on plavix. Ten days before surgery, you must discontinue taking your plavix," he said.

I nodded, aware plavix was a blood-thinning med, and bleeding during surgery was a no-no. After surgery, I would resume plavix. As before for the shunt procedure, the nurse instructed me to go up the hall to obtain pre-op instructions.

At home that evening, I phoned Mary Ann, my West Virginia daughter. During the day, she still managed her husband's internal medicine office and taught ballet to five-year-olds on Saturdays and late afternoons several days a week. Her brother would sometimes say to me, "Mary Ann knows everything. Just ask her." And then he'd laugh.

I'd laugh, too. But I did this tongue in cheek because, even though she gave that impression, she truly did seem knowledgeable about many subjects, especially those connected with health. And indeed, I loved her dearly. In fact, Kirk had often said she was the most intelligent in our family and should have gone into medicine instead of vocational rehab. Now on the phone, I told her the news about my approaching surgery.

"Mother," she started, "Do you know the reason that shunt finally kicked in?"

"No," I answered. Of course I didn't know why the shunt suddenly decided to function. Apparently Dr. Greenfield didn't know, or at least he didn't tell me. I assumed he and I both considered the expected result required more time to materialize, in my case.

"It's because you took that trip out west," Mary Ann announced with conviction.

"What could that possibly have to do with it?" I asked, disbelieving her statement entirely.

"The ride in the airplane. The pressurized atmosphere. Definitely caused the shunt to function."

I doubted the validity of that reasoning. But after I hung up, I told Jeff what she'd said, and to my surprise he responded, "I believe that could be true."

All of a sudden Jeff was about to sell his stamp collection. At least to me the decision was sudden because I'd seen the amount of time he'd spent with his hobby and the fondness with which he'd handled those stamps. The project had filled many of his waking hours. Apparently, however, he'd been considering selling his collection for some time. When I voiced my wonderment and confusion about the subject he said, "I want to start on my autobiography. And I don't have time for both. Besides, these stamp albums are getting too heavy for me to handle. They get heavier all the time. Guess I'm not as strong as I used to be. I'll keep some of them. My U. S. collection. Sell my foreign stamps. All except the Swedish ones. I'm fond of those."

My shock at his announcement dissipated when I thought about the weight of the albums and the vast number in his storage locker in town. He frequently drove there, picked up a few albums, and brought them home. "How will you go about selling them," I asked. "Put an ad in a newspaper?"

"No. *Stamp News* advertises all the time. I've seen a couple ads I plan to contact."

Of course that would be a source. Those *Stamp News* magazines arrived faithfully in the mail every week. They landed, for lack of a better place, in the guest bathroom Jeff used, and they cluttered up the counter top next to the sink. He might read a page or two, rarely more, but never threw them out. I finally considered *them* to be collectors' items, just like the stamps. When we were expecting visitors, I gathered them up and placed them in the magazine rack sitting on the floor by the tub.

The second contact Jeff made was interested and arranged to come across the state to see the collection. He arrived with another man, looked over the albums here at the apartment, said he'd stay overnight in town, and meet Jeff at the storage locker the next morning. He wanted to see the bulk of the collection.

After the men left Jeff said, "I know what I'd like for the entire collection. He should meet my terms."

When Jeff returned alone from the locker the next day he said to me, "Didn't get the price I wanted, but I went ahead anyway. Glad it's done. Now I don't need to keep the storage locker. But I do have some furniture there. A table and a couple folding chairs and a lamp I'll have to bring home. Also an album of U. S. stamps."

I nodded. "Too bad you didn't get the amount you expected." I felt sorry for him, knowing he had much invested in his hobby, not only in money but in time.

"If you're willing, I'd like to go tomorrow and clear out the storage locker and give back my key to the manager. Won't need that any more. One less key to have around. I can use your help in the locker." Jeff looked at me with his blue eyes opened widely, his forehead wrinkled. I recognized that familiar, questioning, fixed gaze waiting for my answer.

"Of course I'll go," I said, giving him a big smile.

The next day in the storage locker, even thought the entire building was supposed to be air-conditioned, I began to feel hot sitting there on one of the two folding chairs. Jeff was sitting on the other at a little table looking through an album. He seemed to be taking a long time for this project, a long time to clear out the locker. Now he was searching through drawers, deciding what to keep and what to heave into an empty cardboard box on the floor. I couldn't feel any air-conditioning. The little room was getting warmer every minute. This folding chair was uncomfortable. In fact, *I* was uncomfortable. I moved from side to side, straightened up, bent forward, and generally changed to every position conceivable. Nothing helped. The bare overhead light bulb, even though of low wattage, seemed to throw off heat. I also felt slightly nauseated. I needed air! I needed something! "I'm sick!" I told Jeff.

"I'll soon be finished," he said, continuing to sort, deeply engrossed in his project.

I tried to tell him how I felt, but my faint words didn't make sense. So I got up and started to leave the locker room. Out in the hall I grabbed onto the wall to steady myself.

"Wait, wait," Jeff said, suddenly aware I had left the room. Behind me now he said, "Don't go down that hall. There's a stairwell right across here. It leads to the first floor near the outside door. I'll be down in a minute, after I lock up."

Somehow I weaved down the steps and at the bottom I looked for a place to sit down. All I could see was a factory pallet not much higher than the floor, so I dropped down onto it. As I sat there, I suddenly remembered that I hadn't taken my plavix for five days in preparation for the trabeculectomy. A man came along and offered to let me sit in his car parked outside the door. I tried to talk but could only shake my head and keep sitting there. Before long, the manager approached me, apparently sent by the man who'd offered me a seat in his car. "Is Jeff coming down?" he asked, looking at me with concern.

I nodded, and with that Jeff appeared. He and the manager helped me out to our car. In the car I noticed my lips were numb, and I had difficulty raising my right arm. "Jeff," I managed to say, attempting to turn toward him. "I'm sick," I finally said and tried to say more but still couldn't pronounce words that made sense.

"I'll get you right home. Or should I take you to the hospital?" He looked over at me and started the car.

I managed to nod my head.

"Home? Shall we go home?" He waited for my answer.

I shook my head.

"To the hospital, then?" He eyed me with a worried look.

I nodded and held my head that was beginning to ache. I knew I was having a TIA, a trans-ischemic attack. I'd had such a mini stroke about ten years ago when I was spending the summer at the Shack. Actually, I'd gone on a bus trip with a senior citizen group from Bedford, a delightful historic town of Revolutionary War days located some thirty miles west of the Shack. I'd decided to take the bus trip because I was getting a bit bored with my solitary life at the Shack. After driving my Volvo to the travel agency in Bedford I'd boarded the bus and sat beside a friendly talkative woman. On the way back from our destination and viewing of changing autumn leaves, we stopped at a restaurant. During the meal, I attempted to answer a question posed by the person beside me. After several unsuccessful attempts to make words come out as intended, I resigned myself to eating the remainder of my meal in silence. Back in the Volvo, my lips numb, my head a little fuzzy, and the fourth finger of my right hand refusing to bend, I almost drove into the emergency department of the Bedford County Hospital. Bull headed, I guess, I drove right on past. Now at the Shack, I phoned my daughter in West Virginia. "Take two aspirins," Mary Ann commanded. "Two three-hundred-twenty-five milligram tablets. I'll be there in the morning to take you to my cardiologist."

So that's how I knew I was facing another TIA. Fortunately the storage lockers were about a mile from a hospital. At the emergency department door Jeff found a wheelchair and wheeled me in. An attendant at a nearby desk asked me questions I was unable to answer other than by sign language—waving my hands, shrugging my shoulders, and shaking and nodding my head. She returned my Medicare and Tricare cards to Jeff and told him to take me on back to an examining room. By the time I was helped onto an examining table I had regained my ability to speak almost normally, but I still felt groggy. After continuous blood pressure monitoring, venous injections to draw blood samples, an IV heparin lock inserted in my left arm, a continuous intravenous of normal saline in my right, and an examination by the E D physician, I was admitted.

My room was a private one, and, being an RN and now feeling fully recovered, I had lively conversations with staff and was given rather special attention, or so I thought. Funny how nurses who become patients feel at home in hospitals, free to joke and be friendly with staff. Even though hospital policy usually prohibited patients from possessing medications in their rooms, I asked Jeff to bring in my meds when he returned for an evening visit. As it turned out, I was permitted to administer my own eye drops and even the blood pressure medication since the hospital pharmacy didn't stock that exact brand of hypertension med.

First thing in the morning I was visited by a tall dark-haired pleasant young physician who was taking calls for my general practitioner. Since the cause of my TIA was the discontinuation of plavix in preparation for my trabeculectomy, I wanted to be certain this young doctor had ordered or would order plavix on the physician order sheet in my chart. So I said, "Have you ordered plavix for me?"

He looked at me, a little frown shadowing his handsome face. "I've ordered aggrenox instead. You're to take it twice a day. That medication will be better for you. Have you ever been seen by a neurologist?" he wanted to know.

I tried to remember; then it came to me. "Once up in West Virginia," I said finally, thinking back to my first TIA.

"If you're not familiar with a neurologist here, I'll order a consult with Dr. Perry."

I thanked him, and he left as abruptly as he'd arrived.

The next morning, the sun was streaming in the window directly opposite the head of my bed. No matter how I moved in the bed, the sun shone directly in my eyes. Out of the corner of a blinded eye I suddenly realized someone was entering my room. I supposed it to be a member of the housekeeping department or a certified nursing assistant and said rather loudly, "Please close the drape at that window. I'm being blinded!"

The small figure in a sport shirt and trousers rushed over to the window, closed the drape, and sat down in a corner chair close to my bed. My eyes, only partially recovered from the sun's brightness, now focused on this new arrival. Suddenly I was aware the person was my GP. I guess I should have known, the way he'd darted into the room and closed the drape. His quick movements were just like those he made in and around his office, always making me smile at his display of energy. "Oh, doctor!" I exclaimed, horrified that I had ordered my superior in the medical profession to *stoop* to close the drape. "I didn't realize it was you. I'm very sorry."

"No need to apologize. You needed the blind closed. I closed it. Now what are you doing here?"

"I guess I had a TIA," I said, unhappily, not wanting to acknowledge my plight.

"What were your symptoms?" he wanted to know.

I told him and asked, "How am I ever going to have my eye surgery if I get a TIA when I discontinue my blood thinning med? I need that eye surgery to preserve the little vision I presently have in my left eye!"

"You should be able to have the surgery. You're on aggrenox now. You'll only have to discontinue aggrenox five days in advance of the surgery. Not ten as with plavix."

"Oh, great!" I said and heaved a sign of relief.

"I see by your record my associate ordered you to be seen by a neurologist. Dr. Perry. He's a very qualified neurologist. You'll like him. He won't be in to see you until late afternoon. After his office hours." With that explanation, he, too, left as quickly as he'd come.

I *did* like Dr. Perry. After quizzing me at length, he gave me a thorough physical examination, told me he was ordering aspirin 81 milligrams to be taken daily in the morning along with aggrenox, and said he'd be back tomorrow.

"You'll discharge me tomorrow, won't you?" I asked, raising up on my elbows and giving him a pleading smile.

"The day after tomorrow," he said firmly and left.

Jeff was visiting me twice a day. Each time I could hear him coming down the hall, the thump of his cane on the tiled floor. This evening I heard him approaching again. After a loving kiss, he sat down in a chair near my bed. "I can't go home tomorrow," I informed him, looking as dejected as I felt, I'm sure.

"And why is that? I thought for sure you'd be home tomorrow, as well as you seem to be getting along. Are you feeling worse?" he asked, laying the crossword puzzle section of the newspaper on the over-the-bed table.

"No, I'm fine. But Dr. Perry, this neurologist that's been assigned to my case, says I can't leave until the next day." I fiddled with the bed sheet, pleating and straightening the top hem.

"Guess we just have to be patient. How's the food here?"

"I must say the food here is amazingly good. The hospital dietary department is trying a new system. They provide patients menus and a number to call to order meals at a time patients want them delivered, within reason, that is. Dietary also maintains physicians' dietary orders on all patients. Orders such as low salt and ADA diabetic diets. I ordered a chocolate cookie for dessert for lunch today, and dietary said no, I couldn't have one."

"Is that right? Why not?"

"Well, Jeff, you know I'm not supposed to have caffeine because I have glaucoma. Chocolate contains caffeine. I suppose the doctor ordered no caffeine. Or maybe that's standard procedure here. When dietary sees a diagnosis of glaucoma maybe they just automatically don't serve coffee, tea, cola, chocolate, and so forth. I'm not sure. But that's what happened to me and my ordering a chocolate cookie."

"Shoot! You eat chocolate cookies and chocolate candy at home."

I knew he was saying this in a defensive, not accusatory manner. "I know. I cheat a little." I said. "But I watch how much I eat. I really do. I actually deprive myself."

"Sure, sure. But I'd say that's probably correct, knowing how much you love chocolate candy." He laughed, and so did I.

After a stay of four days, I was discharged. I called Bascom Palmer Eye Institute to cancel my eye surgery. "I had a TIA as a result of not taking my plavix for five days," I explained. "But I've been ordered a new med. Aggrenox. I'll only have to discontinue it for five days before surgery. Can we set up another date for the trabeculectomy in my left eye?" After a short wait, I was advised the surgery had been rescheduled for the tenth of August.

I placed the receiver back in its cradle and sat there in the Florida room contemplating. Then I called out, "Jeff!" He was in the den typing on the computer, probably working on his autobiography. With our date book in hand, I went to the den where he'd stopped typing and was turned around to see what I wanted. "I called Bascom Palmer. To cancel the surgery. And I explained about the TIA. They've rescheduled the trabeculectomy for August tenth." I stood waiting for his reaction.

"Well," he said pensively, scratching his head. "That takes care of any plans we had to go up north. To go, as we usually do, to Pennsylvania to the Shack for any of the summer months. Too bad, kid, but I guess we'll just stay put. Stay here for the duration. It won't be that bad. In fact, it's very nice here in the summer. I've stayed here many summers and enjoyed it." He gave me a big smile and a wink.

I breathed a deep heavy sigh. "I've never stayed here in the summer. It gets so hot and humid. I hate the humidity. I can't breathe!"

His eyes fastened on mine. "Now look, Sweetie," he said. "Our apartment's air-conditioned. The Club's air-conditioned. So is the car. You only have to be outside to go from one air-conditioned place to another. You'll be fine."

I nodded, not too convincingly I'm sure, and resigned myself to a long, hot, humid summer. After all, my eyes were the important thing right now. Any time I wanted to I could look at the framed picture of the Shack hanging on the Florida room wall, the painting Kirk and Sally had an artist paint for me for Christmas.

Twenty-Eight
More

Exactly one week later Jeff was driving me to the cardiology office for a pacemaker check. On the way, he stopped at Office Depot to buy ink cartridges for our desk-top printer. While I was sitting in the car waiting, I began to get pains in my chest, just under my sternum, and also some shortness of breath. When I complained to Jeff, now back in the car, he wanted to go immediately to the hospital. "No. Just take me to the cardiology office," I insisted. They'd take care of me there, I figured. And in a way, they did.

An office nurse guided me into an examining room, took my blood pressure, squirted two puffs of nitroglycerin into my mouth, and called 911. In short order, in tromped the paramedic boys with their equipment. They took my pressure again and informed me they were taking me to the hospital. "No. No. I'm going home," I informed them. "I'm O. K., and I'm going home where I belong." I was trying to be friendly and humorous at the same time, but I was also very serious. After all, I'd just been in the hospital and didn't want to go back.

Jeff commanded my attention. "Now Jeanie," he said, looking very worried. "You are going to go to the hospital." He was giving me an order I couldn't fight.

With that, the boys brought in their stretcher waiting outside the examining room door. I was propelled onto it, strapped, wheeled out of the office, and lifted up into the back of the emergency vehicle sitting with its engine running. I continued to kid with the paramedics as we drove off, and they wound a blood pressure cuff around my left upper arm, stuck a cannula into my nostrils to administer oxygen, took my pulse, and documented on a form secured to a clip board. Their monitoring continued throughout the ride, the screaming siren barely audible to me.

Now I was in a hospital E D examining room again going through the same routines I remembered from a week ago. Jeff, poor thing, was there watching and waiting. I got the needle sticks again, one to draw blood for lab samples, another for the IV heparin lock to remain in a vein in my wrist at its jointure with my thumb. That one hurt like sixty. But it was there in case I needed an instant infusion, which of course I wouldn't. But who was I to tell them that? We waited for the physician on call. Finally, in he came. I recognized him. He was Dr. Dudley, a previous physician of mine with whom I'd parted in preference to my current G P. Would he remember me? If so, how would he react? Angry because I'd left his practice for another?

I needn't have worried. He did remember me, but he was quite friendly and examined me with care. He admitted me, however. I even had the nerve to say, when he was leaving, "Could you arrange to have me admitted to a private room?"

He turned, looked at me, and said, "Oh that's right. Many of the rooms here are semi-private. I'll see what I can do."

Whether it was he or my nurse friend Mary Lou who arranged for a nice private room with a view of the Inlet, I'll never know. It just so happened after Dr. Dudley left, into my E D examining room walked Mary Lou in full nurses' uniform and heavier than I'd ever seen her. I knew her from Rotary since her husband was a Rotarian, and she attended social events with him. I also knew she was an RN. Even so, I was surprised to see her. I was even more surprised when she told me she was the supervisor that day.

"Of the entire hospital?" I asked, impressed.

"Yes, for this twelve hour shift," she responded, standing erect with a clip board on her arm and smiling at me. "Is there anything I can do for you? Do you want anything after you're admitted?"

"Would it be possible for me to have a private room?" I asked this gingerly because I doubted the possibility either she or Dr. Dudley could arrange this. Surely all the private rooms were filled.

"I'll see to it, Jean," she said and left with, "Have a good rest."

Jeff had been sitting there listening. He looked at his watch and said, "Looks like you're going to be well taken care of, Honey. If you don't mind, I'm going to run along. Go home and get something to eat. I'll be back tomorrow." He came over to the carrier and gave me a good-bye kiss.

I hated to see him leave. I hated myself for getting sick, for being a worry to him, and for causing him to travel back and forth to the hospital to visit me each day I was *confined.* I knew he'd visit faithfully out of loyalty and love, and then he'd come again to take me home when I was discharged.

Later that evening, my cardiologist entered my private room. I admired his tall stately well-proportioned figure, his fine-featured handsome middle-aged face. He sat down leisurely in the chair at the foot of my bed, my medical record on his knee. Our dialogue began by his saying, "I'm going to order an angiogram, a cardiac catheterization. We need to know if there's a blockage or narrowing in your coronary arteries." He stopped when I raised my hand.

"How long will all this take?" I asked, leaning forward in bed. This was Friday and too late to expect any procedures be performed today or scheduled until after the weekend.

He tapped his pen on the cover of my medical record. "The cath lab isn't open Saturdays or Sundays, so I'll schedule this for Monday. They'll come in and prep you early in the morning. I'll have the results the same day." He opened my chart, scribbled orders, rose out of his chair, shook my hand, ever smiling, and left the room.

My West Virginia daughter phoned, and I told her the doctor ordered a cardiac cath and I had to lie here in this room until Monday for the procedure to be performed.

"Are you familiar with cardiac catheterizations?" she wanted to know.

"No, of course not. I haven't a clue. I haven't worked in a hospital for a thousand years." I waited for this daughter of mine to tell me about the procedure.

"I'll tell you about it," she started. "I had one a few years ago. You won't mind it. It's a relatively simple procedure. You'll get a flushed feeling when they inject the dye into a vein in your groin, but that's all

246

you'll feel. After the procedure you'll have a five pound weight on the injection site, and you'll have to keep perfectly still. Your legs, that is, for six hours afterward. You'll be fine. I'll call you back tomorrow."

The next morning I heard Jeff coming down the hall. Or rather, I heard his cane clonking on the tile floor, loudly because it needed a new rubber tip. The clonking progressed until his familiar figure filled the doorframe.

"How you doing, Honey?" he asked, coming in and planting a kiss on my lips. Then he handed me the crossword puzzle section of the Palm Beach Post and a pen I'd requested when he phoned about a half hour ago.

I told Jeff about my conversation with Mary Ann last evening and that son Kirk also phoned last night and again a bit ago. Then my breakfast arrived and I offered Jeff a muffin and several pieces of fruit which he gladly took. Probably hadn't had much breakfast at home.

On Monday the team from the cath lab arrived in my room at five-thirty in the morning. They shaved me, gave me a sedative, and wheeled me away. I remembered nothing until I was back in my room being helped into bed. The unit nurse took my vitals, flushed the I. V. heparin lock, and offered me a drink of water. The leads were back, stuck to various locations on my chest, like stamps on an envelope. I counted eight of them, each with wires leading to the weighty monitor in the pocket of my patient gown. They'd be sending wire, not wireless, messages to the nurses' station down the hall. This one-pound monitor, this black box in the pocket of my gown, weighed me down like an anchor every time I got out of bed to go to the bathroom or to sit in a chair to eat a meal. My hate-affair with black boxes began last week when I was hospitalized for the TIA and was saddled with one then. Trapped, as it were.

In the afternoon the cardiologist rapped gently on my door and entered. In a well-tailored light-gray suit, he sat as before in a chair at the foot of my bed, my medical record in hand.

"The results of the cardiac catheterization are very promising," he said, and a smile spread over his handsome middle-aged face. "I'd expected to find a blockage because of how you presented in my office. But your body's taken care of it for you."

"Then I can go home today?" I asked, hopeful, my eyes pleading.

He cleared his throat, gave a little cough, and said, "You seem to be doing very well. Yes, you can go home. But not until three this afternoon."

I was delighted! I phoned Jeff and gave him the good news. He was there at two. We watched the clock. At three I pressed the call bell. The nurse assigned to me this shift came to my room. "Yes?" she said, approaching my bed.

"Didn't the doctor write an order for my discharge?" I asked her, looking at my watch.

"Yes he did," she said. "But this is change of shift. After I give report, the on-coming nurse assigned to you will work up your discharge."

I thanked her, eagerly took the hated black box out of my gown pocket, and pealed off the leads sticking to my bod. No need to wait for the nurse to do that! I was chomping at the bit to leave. No need for the nurse to spend time preping my body to leave. All she'd have to do was the paper work. I placed the entire contraption of wires and black box on the over-bed table. Good riddance! I opened the night stand beside my bed and pulled out my clothes. Now fully dressed and ready to leave, I sat on the side of the bed dangling my feet while Jeff and I made conversation. An hour went by. I activated the call bell. A nurse I hadn't seen before entered my room. "I'm working on your discharge," she said.

"It's not like in the old days," I ventured to say to her, really wanting to know why it was taking so long to be discharged.

"No, it isn't," she acknowledged and went on to explain. "There's much paper work. I'll be through pretty soon." She left.

We waited another hour. "I'm going to see if I can find her," I said to Jeff and went out into the hall and walked to the nurses' station. The assigned nurse was sitting at a computer. I stood there, waiting. Finally she looked up at me. "I'm just about finished with your discharge," she said gruffly, obviously irritated and sounding like a disgusted parent talking to a disobedient child.

Not wanting to delay her further, I said nothing, turned around, and walked back to my room. "She's just about finished," I told Jeff.

"Are you sure?" he said with a smirk.

"So she says. Can we believe her?" I felt like being sarcastic. I heaved a sigh, and sat back down on the bed. Upsetting as the delay was, I could do nothing about it.

A head nurse came into the room and reached for the black box on the over-bed table. "You still here?" she said jokingly.

"Obviously," I said, not too pleasantly. "It's taking forever to be discharged."

"She's new. Need this for another patient," she explained, jiggling the black box she'd picked up.

So that was it. The nurse was new, unfamiliar with the form and probably with the computer as well.

One-half hour later, the novice nurse came into my room with a sheet of paper. "These are your discharge instructions," she announced and then read what was typed on the form—everything I already knew.

Jeff stopped the car at the pharmacy, picked up the prescribed nitroglycerin, and we were home at six. Over cocktails I said to Jeff, "It's no wonder there's a nursing shortage. All that paper work! It reduces nurses' time to care for patients. Darn shame! Nurses don't choose the profession to do all that paper work! No wonder many are seeking non-nursing positions in the work force."

I cringed in our apartment every time I heard a siren. Jeff and I always said, "I wonder who it is this time?" After my experience in the emergency vehicle, I could relate to another resident in a similar situation. I'd stop what I was doing and listen to hear if the screaming blasts were silenced at the guard gate as was required when the emergency vehicle entered the grounds of Sandycreek Terrace. Continuing blasts would disturb and frighten the residents who would wonder and fret over what resident was in trouble, so it was thought. Even with that precaution, residents, unless they were greatly hearing impaired, could hear the sirens before they approached the gate. If the screams lessened and then faded completely, residents would breathe easily, knowing the paramedics had driven on further to another emergency site. If the sirens suddenly ceased, residents would know a desperate resident had pulled the white bell-shaped knob dangling from a length of cord fastened to the wall in one of the rooms.

Pam Butcher had pulled the knob dangling from a cord on their living room wall to get help for Ben. Someone from security had responded first and then called Park Place for nursing staff assistance. Again I shivered, imagining myself pulling a cord if something similar happened to Jeff.

TWENTY-NINE

SCOOTER

It was July, 2005. Jeff, and finally I, were resigned to staying in Sandycreek Terrace all summer long rather than going up north, my eye surgery scheduled just a month away. Besides, my recent habit of visiting hospitals caused us to fear being thirty miles from a qualified hospital and not a very large one at that, as was the case when living at the Shack. So it was continuous life in Sandycreek Terrace. I thought about the Shack. Nobody there all summer. Didn't they say a house, if it sat unoccupied, deteriorated? Maybe similar to people deteriorating if they sat unoccupied. I'd never thought of that similarity before, but now I did. The Shack sitting unoccupied and all those people sitting unoccupied and deteriorating in the nursing homes I'd seen in my nursing career days as surveyor and director of nursing. Here in independent living quarters at Sandycreek Terrace, a CCRC, such was not the case. Because so many activities were scheduled, residents were hard-pressed to get involved in all of them.

A number of residents had gone north now, and the dining room was less crowded. The bag lady was still here, walking with a bag swinging at each side and the ubiquitous khaki raincoat draped over her shoulders, like an actress playing some bizarre role. How did she stand the weight and warmth of that coat in this humid eighty-nine degree weather? She was alone now. We understood her male friend was sick. One evening after she ate dinner and was leaving the dining room, she stopped at the table where Clarence was eating alone. Clarence, the resident who'd made a belligerent spectacle of himself at Jeff's committee meeting, acknowledged her presence. We were sitting at a nearby table and heard her say, "Clarence, are you free to be my boyfriend?" Apparently his answer was a negative one since she didn't tarry long.

Jeff had started his autobiography and was planning to write it in four volumes covering four periods of his life. The first volume would contain recollections and memories of his life in Holland, Michigan, from childhood up through the age of twenty. He planned to title it *My Paradise, My Father's Hell.* The second would detail his Navy and war years and be titled *Every Day is Navy Day.* A third would describe his second career as a teacher, high school principle, entrepreneur, and family man. The title for that volume would be *It's Not School I Hate, It's the Principle.* The fourth, covering his years in retirement including yours truly, was still lacking a title.

As Jeff was spending much time at the computer writing his first volume, he brought up the internet from time to time. One time an ad for an upscale scooter grabbed his attention. He phoned the New Jersey number appearing on the screen. "I'm just calling to get information about the scooter you're advertising on the internet," Jeff explained. When he hung up he turned to me and said, "A voice said a representative from the company would get back to me. I gave our number."

In about two hours the phone rang. Jeff answered and listened for a few minutes. Then I heard him say, "No, no. I'm just after some information that I'm sure you can provide on the phone. I'm a busy man and don't have time to spend with a salesman."

I watched Jeff while he held the phone to his ear, listening again. Then he answered, "Well all right, if you say the presentation will take only twenty minutes. I have time for that. Yes, that day will suit me."

"So you gave in, and someone's coming to talk to you about a scooter?" I said with a grin when Jeff put the receiver back in its cradle.

"Yes, I relented. Lenny Swartz, a company representative from Mobility Incorporated, is coming Thursday to talk to me about his product. Show me his product," Jeff informed me. "He said he understood I was interested in their product and he'd like to come and give me all the information. He was very polite. Said he understood I was a busy man and he'd only take twenty minutes of my time. Insisted he'd take only twenty minutes of my time. Not too pushy. Persistent, though. Wanted to know what day of the week would be convenient for him to come. We settled on Thursday."

"Are you seriously considering buying one of those scooters?" I asked. Was Jeff falling for a line of bologna? A very unlikely action for my miser mister!

"Just want to hear his pitch. Don't have any intention of buying one," he told me, lowering his eye glasses from atop his smooth head and going back to his magazine reading.

Thursday morning at eleven a knock on the door interrupted our typing. Jeff was at the lap-top composing the first chapter of his autobiography and I at the large-screen desk-top revising an article for a nursing magazine. We both jumped up and went to the door. There stood Lenny Schwartz. But only for a minute for he was inside, handing me a box of gingerbread from Publix. "I come bearing gifts," he announced. A tall well-proportioned man with a long face, Lenny then shook our hands and introduced himself. He emphasized he'd like to sit down with both of us. I saw no need for me to be included as Jeff was the interested party, and I started to leave the room.

"Oh please don't leave, Mrs. Metz. I want you to see my slide presentation, too. Only take a few minutes."

The three of us sat down at the glass-topped table in the Florida room where Lenny set up his slide projector. It reminded me of the X-ray view-box used in the O. R. years ago. "This will take less than twenty minutes," he assured us.

"Are you sure, Mr. Schwartz?" I said, hoping to get back to my article before I lost my train of thought.

"Absolutely. Less than twenty minutes," he promised. "And please call me Lenny."

He smiled as he talked and pointed to various features on the lighted screen as one picture flashed to another. The clock kept on running past twenty minutes, and I was getting restless. Finally I asked, "How much more is there to see?"

"Just a little more. Just a little more." But once the *little more* was completed, Lenny immediately produced a catalogue from his briefcase and tactfully introduced us to pictures of various models of scooters called Rascals. While we looked at these, he read descriptions and contracts. Then he asked Jeff questions about his needs, his ability and inability to walk, and his back pain. Jeff appeared mildly interested, and the more he portrayed interest and the more questions he asked, the more Lenny went into detail. Then I found myself asking questions. Surely this would be a nice means of transportation for Jeff. I looked at my watch. Two hours had passed. At this point, Jeff and Lenny got down to serious business—prices. One model seemed to be a favorite with Jeff. "How much for this baby?" he asked Lenny.

"Beauty, isn't she? Starting price is about ten K. Can't find any scooter like it on the market anywhere close to that price."

"My God!" Jeff exclaimed. "You think I'm Bill Gates or Richard Mellon? I don't want to buy the company. I don't have that kind of money."

"Well now, Mr. Metz. I said that was the starting price. We do have methods of lessening the cost. We offer a lower price if paid in three equal payments starting within thirty days after signing the contract. Reduces the cost by ten percent." Lenny arched his eyebrows and looked at Jeff, obviously for his reaction.

"What about paying in two equal payments?" Jeff wanted to know.

"Twenty percent less. This is a mighty fine scooter. You'd be the envy of all your friends."

Jeff shook his head. "I don't need it that badly. What would it cost if I start the first of two payments with the delivery of the scooter?"

"Let me make a phone call," said Lenny. "May I use your phone?"

I handed him the phone sitting on the small table next to me. He made his call. "George," he said. "I have a customer here that's interested in model six-hundred-fifty-two." He listened then said, "He lives in Sandycreek Terrace." He listened again. "Yes, in Palm Beach County, Florida." He waited and listened. "Yes. Yes. No problem. All right." He handed me the receiver and turned to Jeff. "I can offer you a price close to six thousand. I can have one here in two days. And you want red? Red's a knock-out!"

Jeff nodded. "Yes, I'm partial to red. On trial. You said I'd be given a week's trial period."

"Right. You try it out. If you don't like it, we'll take it back."

I looked at my watch again. It was two o'clock! Twenty minutes had turned into three hours!

"Tell you what," Lenny said. "I happen to have a demonstrator out in my van. Only been driven several times. No reason you can't have that for less money. But it's blue. Dark blue. Very pretty shade of blue."

That didn't seem to phase Jeff although I thought it would. He'd always had red cars. Red Cadillac's. Even had a tan Cadillac he had painted red. Maybe color didn't matter when it came to scooters and price. At any rate, he didn't flinch when he heard the color blue.

"Does it have all the special features?" Jeff wanted to know.

"Certainly does. Head lights, horn, backup lights, clock, seat raises, the works. I'll go out and get it. Won't take me but a minute to get it."

He left and was back with a carton, scooter enclosed. A big strong man, Lenny brought the large box into the dining room, uncrated the scooter, and put it together. I suddenly realized this scooter had never been driven. It was brand new! We stood back and admired the shinny dark blue Rascal ready for Jeff to test drive. He sat down on the leather-covered seat while Lenny pointed out the location of forward and backward drive, speed settings, lights, horn, lever to elevate the seat, and clock. Then he demonstrated arm rests and handle bar mobility.

Outside into the corridor the two men went with the Rascal, I following. "How fast does this vehicle go?" Jeff quizzed.

"Five miles an hour," Lenny answered.

"Five miles an hour. Is that right?" Jeff mused, hesitated, and then sat on the seat. He put his hands on the handle bars and pressed a black lever. Instantly he was propelled forward down the corridor!

"Whoa!" Lenny called out, hurrying after him, his jacket flapping in the breeze. "Don't press that lever all the way! Slack up! Ease up! Press it slowly."

Jeff removed his thumb from the lever and the Rascal stopped. He tried again.

"That's the way," Lenny said, encouragingly. "Now press the lever the other way, and you'll back up."

Jeff backed up a little and then went forward again, up the corridor to the intersection where a perpendicular walkway advanced to the parking lot. Here he turned the Rascal around and returned, blowing the horn and grinning broadly. "I just might learn to like this," he said, getting off.

We all went inside to the Florida room table where Lenny brought out forms, explained terms of the contract, and pointed to a line for Jeff's signature. Jeff went for his check book and wrote a check for half the total amount which, with the second check of an equal amount, would be less than half the initial cost quoted. He handed the check to Lenny, and Lenny gathered up the packing and was gone. My watch told me it was four o'clock. I grabbed the ginger bread. I was famished!

THIRTY

MEDICATIONS

Since Jeff was now self-propelled on his scooter, he no longer needed the services of lazy Liza to drive him to the Club House for dinner. He drove the Rascal, always passing me at a high speed of three or four miles an hour and scaring ambulatory residents walking slowly with or without the assistance of canes or walkers. Sometimes he beeped the horn to alert residents of his approach. Before long these residents became accustomed to Jeff's capers on his way to dinner and, upon seeing me finally advancing, would say, "He's winning," or "You'll never catch up," or "Why don't you ride with him?"

I'd answer them by saying, "I'm in no hurry," or "I value my life too much to ride with him."

Since the trabeculectomy to be performed in my left eye was scheduled for August the ninth at Bascom Palmer Eye Institute in Miami, I began the discontinuation of my Aggrenox and aspirin five days in advance, as prescribed. The fourth day, not having taken those meds for that number of days, I was in the Florida room, working a crossword puzzle when I suddenly felt strange, unable to work the puzzle, and my vision blurred. The pen I was using refused to remain steady between my fingers. I laid it down, moved over to the nearby couch, and lay down. Another TIA, I realized immediately. I called out to Jeff working at the lap-top in the den. He came immediately.

"What's wrong, Jeanie?" he asked, seeing me lying on the couch. He felt my head. I made sounds that weren't words. "Oh God," he uttered and hurried to the pull cord in the bathroom.

When he went to answer a knock at the door a man from security had already entered. On his cell phone, the man called Park Place and then walked into the bathroom to deactivate the alarm. Jeff stood by, looking down at me, concern covering his face. Two staff from Park Place, one carrying a blood pressure cuff, came into the apartment. "How do you feel?" one asked.

I couldn't answer.

She took my pulse. "How do you feel?" she asked again.

Annoyed, I stared at her. Why didn't she take my pressure, call 911? Finally she did take my pressure.

The man from security looked at her and asked, "Should we call the paramedics?"

"I guess," she responded, apparently uncertain.

I needed to tell Jeff where my Medicare and Tricare cards were so I could hand them over when I got to the hospital emergency department. I needed to tell him they were in our bedroom in my pink purse on my filing cabinet. I made a noise and Jeff looked at me, eyes questioning. I tried to tell him my cards were in our bedroom in my pink purse, but all I could do was point to our bedroom and say, "Pink. Pink."

He finally understood, followed the direction of my pointing finger, and brought out my pink purse just as 911 arrived. The paramedics loaded me onto their carrier and toted me out to the emergency vehicle sitting, motor running, at the entrance to our building. Again I was riding to the hospital with three paramedic boys dutifully performing their tasks.

I knew the E. D. routine well. Needle in a left arm vein to draw samples for lab testing, IV heparin lock in a vein in my left wrist, an intravenous of normal saline in a vein in my right arm, cannula in my nostrils to administer oxygen, and continuous blood pressure monitoring. A human guinea pig I was again. I had to go to the bathroom, but everyone had left to attend other emergencies. Finally Jeff arrived, walked into the examining room, and explained, "I had a hard time finding you. There are so many rooms in this emergency department. And they're all filled."

I was able to talk now, and I smiled. "I know. I've watched paramedics bring in one carrier after another." Desperate now, I said, "Jeff, will you please see if you can find someone to come and help me to the bathroom?"

"Sure," he said and left. Soon he was back with a male attendant.

"I need to go to the bathroom," I told him.

"You're not allowed to walk," he said.

"Then will you please get me a bedside commode?"

"I can't do that. You're not allowed off the table. I'll bring you a bedpan."

"I can't use a bedpan. I'm not successful using one of those things!" I informed him emphatically.

"It's the best I can do," he told me in a matter of fact manner.

I was truly desperate now. "All right," I agreed. But he'd be sorry.

We waited for the E. D. physician to come to examine me and decide my fate. Poor Jeff, there he sat, waiting patiently. Finally it was my turn with the physician. Would I be discharged or admitted?

"Your pressure hasn't stabilized, and some of your blood work is abnormal. I'm going to admit you," the female physician informed me. She looked at her watch. "Have you had anything to eat since you came in?"

"No," I said, thinking it must be dinner time by now.

"I'll order you a box lunch. You can eat here in this unit. It will be a while before a room is ready."

"All right, thank you," I said and then looked over at Jeff. "You might as well go home, Honey. You can probably make it in time for dinner in the dining room."

After he left my box lunch arrived. I ate the ham sandwich and chips and was finally admitted. My room, miraculously, was a private one, even without my request.

Again leads were stuck to my bod, and the intravenous and oxygen discontinued. The head nurse wheeled in a computer and recorded my medical history, asking question after question. For an hour and a half she moved her fingers over the keyboard like a stenographer. Unbelievable! Was this medical advancement? Was it even nursing? When I worked in a hospital attending physicians covered much of this information in short order, writing with pens on their history and physical forms in medical records. Of course this was far more inclusive and contained facts and information to be available for what was now called *outcome oriented* and *evidence-based practice*. Physicians still had to document their data.

DOROTHY BERTSCH

When *dear* Dr, Perry arrived the next afternoon, trying to be funny, I said to him, "It is I again."

"I see," he said, unsmiling, standing beside the bed looking down at me. "What symptoms did you present this time?"

He was so young, younger than my son. Nice-looking, too. About five feet ten. I told him what happened.

"Are you sure it wasn't stress? You're about to have eye surgery, aren't you?"

I looked at him hard, serious-like. "I don't believe in stress, Dr. Perry," I told him. "It's a much over-used word these days. And I'm accustomed to eye surgery. It doesn't *stress* me. I stopped the Aggrenox for four days. And the aspirin also. As you ordered. That's what caused the problem." I waited for his reaction.

He sighed then said, "Yes, I guess you're right. Do as I say. Grab my hands as tightly as you can. Now try to force my hands away from you. Now try to bring them toward you. Close your eyes and touch your nose with the index finger of your right hand. Now with your left index finger. Good." Satisfied that I'd successfully passed his neurological examination, he sat down to write in my chart.

"How am I going to be able to have the trabeculectomy if I can't take a blood thinning med without having a TIA?" I asked him, greatly concerned. I didn't want to lose the little vision I still had in my left eye. That would happen unless the intraocular pressure could be controlled. Optic nerve damage would occur.

He stopped writing and looked over at me. "What's more important? Your vision or not having a stroke?"

"Not having a stroke," I quickly answered. I did have vision in my right eye. A stroke was the last thing I wanted. In nursing homes I'd seen the results of many strokes. Female residents with paralyzed arms, unable to feed themselves. Male residents with inert legs in geriatric chairs, unable to walk. Residents laughing at nothing, crying out for no reason, sitting staring at the floor. All in la-la land as a friend of mine customarily called people with brain damage. Never, never did I want a stroke!

I was discharged and went home. The next day, Dr. Perry phoned. "How *are* you, he wanted to know?"

"I'm fine. But I'm still concerned about not being able to have eye surgery. I'll lose the sight in my left eye," I told him.

He reminded me again of the choice between blindness in one eye and a stroke. Then he said, "There *is* a medication you could take safely. Lovenox. But it's administered subcutaneously twice a day for five consecutive days. You wouldn't want to come into the office twice a day even if our nurses did administer daily subcu meds to our patients, which they don't. Do you have a nurse friend who would administer the medication subcutaneously twice a day for five days?"

"I'm a nurse. I can administer it to myself," I assured him.

"One more problem," he said. "It's expensive. Prohibitively expensive."

"How expensive?" I asked. To preserve my vision, money was worth spending, wasn't it?.

"One thousand dollars an injection."

My brain worked the math. Ten thousand for a total of ten injections! "I'll have to think about that," I told him.

After I placed the receiver on the stand, I turned to Jeff who was in the kitchen making a pot of home-made chicken vegetable soup. I told him about my conversation with Dr. Perry.

Without a moment's hesitation, he said, "We have Tricare. Maybe the cost would be less getting the drug through Tricare. Get the prescription, and we'll take it to Walgreen's. This time, we won't use their mail order pharmacy. Takes too long. We've used our Tricare card at Walgreen's other times, and they've honored it."

At Walgreen's Pharmacy, Jeff handed the prescription to an employee behind the counter. "Before you fill that, let me know how much it will cost," Jeff said.

"I'll have to check it in our book," the employee informed us. She came back to us at the counter. "That will be nine dollars," she said. "But we don't have it in stock. We'll have it for you Thursday after three o'clock."

My back teeth about fell out. I was amazed beyond belief! The difference in cost! We walked out of Walgreen's, I grinning, Jeff saying to me, "Aren't you glad you married a military man? We military men finally received the drug benefit government legislatives have had for years."

Back home I called the nurse coordinator at Bascom Palmer Eye Institute to reschedule my trabeculectomy. I told her about my TIA and the subcu med. She called back and said, "You're trabeculectomy is scheduled for August twenty-fourth. Not sooner because of your TIA. Start the subcutaneous medication five days before surgery."

I did just that, using the pre-filled syringes of sixty milligrams of Lovenox and injecting the med into various sites in my abdomen twice a day for five days, five days prior to surgery. Each time, Jeff sat in a chair next to me, ready to help. He removed paper sleeves covering the sterile syringes, carefully handed me the syringes, watched while I inserted needles and injected the med, and took back used syringes to discard.

We drove to Miami the day before surgery, stayed the night in the hotel catering to Bascom Palmer patients, and drove over to the hospital before dawn the next day. En route to the hospital and with map in hand, poor Jeff had to stop and get out of the car a number of times to read street signs up close in order to find our way. No fun driving in unfamiliar downtown Miami with its one-way streets in pitch darkness! I felt sorry for him but thankful to have this determined patient man of mine. All I could do was sit quietly in the front seat and clasp my hands, trying to concentrate on a prayer.

THIRTY-ONE
ADJUSTMENT

The surgery was successful! No more swimming for awhile, back to Ethel for hair shampooing and chit chatting, and frequent trips to the ophthalmology surgeon to check intraocular pressure and healing. By the end of September recovery was complete and the intraocular pressure within normal range for me without the use of medicated eye drops. I still needed to continue anti-inflammatory eye drops twice a day, however. Even though I had no residual effects from the TIAs, the possibility of another scared me silly. What if I should sustain a stroke the next time? A full-blown real live stroke! I could be paralyzed and not able to speak or swallow. I knew all about those strokes. For years, hadn't I observed and been responsible for the care of elderly nursing home residents incapacitated by strokes? Those with paralysis of the left leg and arm and confused, or with paralyzed right arm and leg, mentally alert but unable to talk sensibly. How very sad! What if that happened to me? My mind kept dwelling on this possibility. I wouldn't be able to manage all the financial responsibilities of the Shack property. That was a given. Who then? Who would do it? My son, Kirk, of course. He should, and I knew he would if he knew all the ins and outs. He'd need to know about the taxes and other obligations and peoples' names and their telephone numbers. Thelma Souders, the tax collector. Tom Newman, the cable television man. New Enterprise Electric Company, another example.

Several years ago, after I'd reached eighty and after my daughters agreed, I'd deeded the property to Kirk with the understanding that, upon my death, he'd make sure the property stayed in the family and was handed down to grandchildren. I could depend on him. But I intended to live there any time I so chose. That, too, was understood. Nor had I given over the responsibility of the management of the property. Of performing *that* task, I was quite capable, physically and mentally. But what if? What if a stroke should suddenly stop that capability? It's time. Time to give that responsibility to Kirk. I must apprise him of every single detail. He needed to know about the account at the bank seven miles down the road from the Shack. He needed to know what oil company filled the two fifty-gallon tanks in the basement. He needed to know Tom Newman allowed me to pay for just the months I was at the Shack instead of paying a yearly fee. He needed to know the arrangement I had with Ron Black who paid a rental fee for the use of thirty acres of cropland and I paid him a monthly fee for being caretaker when I wasn't there. He also submitted a bill for the work he did at the Shack, work such as mowing the meadow, repairing plumbing, and odd jobs popping up from time to time. I needed to tell Kirk about the taxes due twice a year, one school, the other township, and the arrangement I had with the electric company during winter months. These were not minor matters!

I went to the phone and dialed Kirk in North Carolina. Would he be surprised at my decision and my request for him to take over this responsibility? No, I didn't think so. A caring son, he'd called me daily when I was hospitalized and had been calling me at home every Sunday for years.

He answered the phone, and I started right into the subject. "Kirk, I've decided it's time for you to take over the Shack property responsibility. You know, if I should have a major stroke, I couldn't manage the affairs at the Shack. How do you feel about handling that responsibility?"

"Be glad to do that, Jean," he answered quickly and willingly. He hadn't called me *Mother* for a number of years. At some time after he married Sally, he'd started calling me Jean. Perhaps because Sally, her mother still very much alive, called me Jean from the time she first met me. At any rate, I've gotten accustomed to his calling me by that name. It would seem odd today to hear him call me Mother.

Delighted to hear his quick response, I continued, "I need to apprise you of a number of things. I'll call you after I have all the documents gathered. And I'll go over everything with you and mail the papers to you along with the Shack check book. I rather hate to give up this responsibility. Stop taking care of everything. It's helped me keep mentally alert."

He snorted a half laugh. "You don't have to worry about keeping alert mentally, Jean. All that writing you do will keep you alert," he assured me. That off my mind, I assembled the documents and followed through with the arrangement.

Snow-bird residents were beginning to come back to Sandycreek Terrace. Surprisingly, I wasn't envious of their summers up north. I couldn't explain it. Why didn't I feel deprived, nostalgic thinking about former summers spent at the Shack? Why wasn't I the least bit angry at having to stay here at this CCRC all year long? Of course this was common sense telling me after all my recent health misfortune Sandycreek Terrace was the best place for me. At least it was this summer. And living with Jeff was fun. From almost every room, I could hear each sound he made. And he did make noises; he was not a quiet man. I knew when he was in the kitchen making soup or biscuits for strawberry shortcake. Drawers opened and banged closed. The refrigerator door slammed shut. He whistled or hummed. Or uttered obscenities when something dropped on the floor. "Jesus!" he'd say when the handle of the waffle iron came off in his hand. In the den, I at the computer, he at his desk, I smiled when I heard him talking out loud to his checkbook. "What the hell?" I'd hear him say when he couldn't reconcile his bank statement with figures in his checkbook. No matter what I said, I always received a response, often a laugh. He always laughed when something he read struck his funny bone. And he always chuckled at my meant-to-be-clever remarks, even if my attempts were poor ones. At times he whistled a favorite tune, one I recognized. Yes, I truly enjoyed Jeff as my house mate. Thank goodness I had a buddy!

That evening we sat sipping drinks with Betty Howe and Ralph Wilson in the lounge before dinner. Betty worked her bony wrinkled hands together and frowned as she started to talk. "I sold my car today, and it made me sad. I feel as though I've given up my independence. I'm ninety-one years old, you know. Of course I shouldn't be driving any more."

"I understand how you feel, Betty. *I* don't drive any more. I don't see well enough to drive. I'm a road-rage hazard," I said and laughed.

"Ralph will drive me when I want to go somewhere, but I hate to impose." She looked over at him, patted his knee with her skeleton fingers, and smiled at him. He made no comment, couldn't hear her, of course, deaf as he was.

"You can take the facility car," I suggested.

"Oh yes, I can, and I will. But it's an adjustment I'll have to make. I'm afraid I'll be losing more than my independence by not having my car to drive. I'll lose ability otherwise. To keep alert, for instance."

Jeff looked at her and said, "You'll be joining the rest of us. Jeanie and I each have half a wit. Between us we have a whole wit." He chuckled, and I smiled, listening again to one of his favorite sayings. At least Jeff's witty remark made Betty smile, too.

With that, a hostess called them into dinner. They'd arrived in advance of us, and we would be called next.

So far, Jeff and I hadn't taken the facility car or bus. We had no need as Jeff drove anywhere we needed and wanted to go. He was still an excellent driver, could drive as well or better than anyone on the road. For the most part, he was still a patient driver and continued to say, "Thanks, pal," when a driver cut in front of him and then slowed down. He still made quick lane changes along with the best and stayed in the fast lane most of the time. I continued to marvel at his ability to drive with one hand, his right hand reaching over to my left forearm and squeezing or holding my hand for several minutes, longer sometimes.

Another evening in the lounge and having been residents for almost two year now, we introduced ourselves to a newly-arrived couple. "I'm Dorcas Sexton," the female of the couple quickly responded. "And this is Don, my husband. His vision is very poor. He won't know you when he sees you the next time. He has macular degeneration. He has *very* poor vision," she emphasized with flashing black eyes.

Jeff hastened to say, "Jeanie can't see either. She's practically blind."

"Do you have macular degeneration, too?" Dorcas wanted to know, peering at my eyes.

"No," I said. "My problem is glaucoma. I do have age-related macular degeneration. But it's in the early stage and the dry kind. So far it hasn't affected my vision."

"She's had glaucoma for over forty years," Jeff interjected. "She can't see you unless she's on top of you. I like to explain this to people so they won't think she's ignoring them when she doesn't speak to them." Jeff was directing his words to Don as well as Dorcas.

The tall thin man wearing a light tan-colored suit and green and blue striped tie leaned forward, apparently hearing as well as visually impaired. "Repeat your names for me, please," he said.

"Where did you live before you came here?" Dorcas asked. When we told her Pine Gardens she immediately said, "Why I know people there. Do you know Bea Burton? She's a lovely lady."

"Yes, we know Bea," Jeff responded.

I chimed in, "We've known her for some time, but I've known Nick for the better part of my life. They're a couple." I imagined she knew Nick as he and Bea had been living together in Pine Gardens for six years although not married.

Dorcas made no reference to Nick but said, "I'm going to invite Bea to come for dinner some evening. Since you know her, would you like to join us when I arrange it?"

"We certainly would! Just let us know," I told her. "We'll look forward to it," I added.

On Thursday, October sixth, Jeff's grandson, Kasey, phoned. We were expecting him for the weekend, driving up from his medical school at Nova University in Davey, a two-hour drive. His visit had become a monthly routine. He said he was coming this weekend because it was his grandfather's birthday on Saturday.

"Grandma Jean." His young familiar voice came clearly into my ear. "I can't make it on a Friday as I usually do because I have to coach a wrestling match tomorrow evening. So I'll be there Saturday."

"That's fine. You won't miss the exact day of Jeff's birthday."

"Right. I'm bringing three presents." He laughed.

"Three presents? You had said you were bringing *a* present, so I thought you were bringing only one. Are the presents big?" I asked in fun.

"Yes, they're big." He laughed again.

"You better put the top down to have room for them," I suggested. "Will you be here in time for lunch?"

"I'll put the top down. I'm *pretty* sure I'll be there in time for lunch."

"Your grandfather's at the store, but I'll tell him you called. We'll see you Saturday. And you drive safely."

"I will," he promised and hung up.

The next day, the mail brought Jeff a birthday card and a book from Kasey's mother, Mart, who recently moved to Greenville, North Carolina. No greeting from Jeff's son in Virginia or from his other two daughters, one in Kentucky, the other also in Greenville. I thought this strange, especially since this birthday was Jeff's eighty-fifth, a special year!

At noon on Saturday, Jeff started to make lunch for the three of us. At twelve-thirty, he said, "Wonder what's keeping Kasey? He should be here. Hope he hasn't had an accident."

"It's only twelve-thirty," I said. "He probably had school work to attend to. Maybe something having to do with the wrestling match last night."

At one Jeff said, "I think we should go ahead and eat. Kasey can eat when he comes."

"All right." I knew Jeff wanted food eaten when he had it prepared. That's the way he was.

We were starting to sit down when a knock came to the door. The door flew open without our help, and in bounded first Mary Jo, Jeff's youngest daughter, then Mel, her friend, followed by Mart, and lastly, Kasey, all yelling, "Happy Birthday!" Two large helium balloons bobbed about in the air. Armloads of boxes got in the way of hugs and kisses, and laughter resonated through the room.

"What a surprise!" Jeff exclaimed, obviously overcome. His mind always on food, he said, "I'll make you something to eat if I can find enough."

"No, no, we brought food," Mary Jo cried out. "Stopped on the way and bought some."

Into the kitchen the girls took their purchases. I watched them open box after bag—ham, cheese, chips, pickles, tomatoes, potato salad, and a loaf each of rye, wheat, and Italian bread. Before long, chattering away and taking sandwich orders, the girls had lunch made for everyone. We all crowded around the dining room table and dug in.

Mary Jo started the conversation, chewing on a bite of her sandwich. "We got up at five-thirty this morning to drive to the airport to catch our plane."

"It was late," Mel cut in.

Mart said, "They came so early to pick me up I didn't get a chance to brush my teeth." She laughed and turned to Kasey, "You remember how I always made you brush your teeth as soon as you got out of bed, son?"

"Yeah," he said. "Now I wait until after breakfast. Everyone should brush their teeth after they eat."

Jeff looked at Kasey. "Everyone should brush *his* teeth."

Kasey looked back at his grandfather with a quizzical frown. "What did I say? Oh yeah. You're correcting my English. Okay. Everyone should brush *his* teeth. Is that better?"

We all laughed, knowing Jeff's habit of correcting grammar. Then he said, "I get so irritated when I read the newspaper or a magazine and find incorrect usage of words or wrong tenses. I've threatened to write to the editor. In fact, I have written several times. And the word *America* infuriates me. Why can't they write the United States? We're not America. We're the United States. Brazil, Columbia, Canada, they're all America. How arrogant can we be? Even the president uses the word America. Why can't he say the United States? We, the people of the United States. Doesn't he remember the Preamble to the Constitution?"

"Now, Dad, you're making too much of this," Mary Jo said.

"No, I am not! You kids should bear that in mind."

Kasey changed the subject. "I had to wait for these three at the Palm Beach airport. That's why we were late getting here."

"Yes," Mel said. "The plane was late getting in. Kasey picked us up at the airport. I'd never been to the Palm Beach airport. Kind of a nice little airport."

Mary Jo turned to Kasey, "I hear you and Candy are history. Is that right?"

"Yeah, we broke up. It's her mother's fault. Made her go to college at home. Wouldn't pay her tuition if she came to Florida and enrolled in a college here. To be with me. We had it all planned. Now that we've been away from each other and she's been under her mother's influence, she's having second thoughts about marrying a med. student in the Navy program."

"Maybe it's just as well, Kasey," Mel offered. "She's a lot younger than you, isn't she? Maybe too immature for you."

Kasey shrugged his muscular shoulders, his wrestling shoulders. "Maybe. But she was the kind of a girl I wanted. Sweet and innocent."

"Golly," I said. "You had the ring picked out, didn't you? Planned to give it to her for Christmas, didn't you?"

"Yeah. You're right, I did. Say, are there any young girls around here? I'm looking."

Everyone laughed. "Young girls in this old folks' home? You expect to find a girl in with all these elderly people, Kasey?" his mother asked.

"We have some pretty young hostesses in the dining room. Some young servers, too," I said, trying to be helpful. "This morning on my walk, I passed a young jogger. Probably visiting a grandparent here. But she would have been too tall for you, Kasey."

He gave me a sad smile.

I said, "By the way, Kasey. How did the wrestling match go last night? The one you were coaching?"

"Oh I wasn't coaching any wrestling match. I just made that up. My excuse for not coming yesterday. I had to wait until today in order to pick up the presents at the West Palm airport." He laughed, and so did I and everyone else.

"I have a present for you, Dad," Mary Jo said, suddenly leaving the table and grabbing a package from the couch.

"Your coming here is present enough for me," Jeff said, smiling at the group. He tore open the wrapping and opened a box containing swimming trunks.

Kasey eyed the trunks, brows knitted. "They don't look big enough."

"Oh, they're fine," Jeff said, putting them back in the box.

They looked small to me, too, and I was sure they wouldn't fit Jeff.

"Here's something else, Dad." Mary Jo handed him two Cuban cigars.

"Ah, now you're talking!" Jeff said, grinning and turning one around in his fingers and reading the Cuban name on the wrap-around band. Then he raised the cigar to his nose and inhaled deeply.

I couldn't stop from frowning. I didn't approve of Jeff's love of cigars, his habit of smoking one once a week when he read the Sunday newspaper out on the patio or enjoyed one at the inlet beach after he went shopping for groceries. But he didn't inhale, so I supposed I should tolerate this indulgence.

The group went out to pool-side, Jeff putting one of his new cigars in his pocket and leading the group to show off his new method of mobility—his new toy, the Rascal. Because of bright sun that tortured my eyes I didn't go along to the pool but stayed home and cleaned up the lunch mess.

We all went over to the Club House for dinner, and Jeff proudly performed introductions to our resident friends in the lounge. "This is my daughter, Mary Jo, a cardiologist in Greenville, North Carolina. And this is her friend, Mel, an anesthesiologist there. And this is my other daughter, Mart. And you all know her son, Kasey, my grandson, a med student at Nova."

Kasey, a frequent visitor, shook hands and talked to his doctor friend, Tom Price, and Harry Scott, the attorney who'd been in med school and then switched majors. Kasey had met both men before and spent time with them in the exercise room.

Mary Jo had called Sandycreek Terrace in advance from Greenville, talked to the chef, and arranged for a cake to be served at dinner. At the end of our meal, the cake arrived lighted with many candles. We all, including residents at nearby tables and staff, sang happy birthday to my smiling Jeff. That night, Kasey stayed in our apartment, sleeping on the large living room couch, as usual, while the girls went to their reserved motel room at the Holiday Inn in town. They returned in the morning for good-byes, and then all left, Kasey driving to the airport in West Palm. How quiet our apartment seemed after they were gone!

THIRTY-TWO
WILMA

It was Tuesday, October eighteenth, when we first heard the name Wilma. She was big! A category five! And headed for the Caribbean Islands. We'd invited Jim and Jane Horner to our apartment for cocktails before dinner that evening, and we four had touched briefly on the subject of hurricanes before the conversation turned to life in Sandycreek Terrace. Jim and Jane were recent residents we'd met in the lounge a week ago. I'd instantly taken a liking to this couple and wanted to know them better. Jim was a retired physician with a former practice in Connecticut. Outgoing and a good conversationalist with a ready smile, he had sparse brown hair, was short in stature and thin. Jane was his same height, but her body frame was larger. She combed her white hair back from her face and secured it with a clip at the nape of her neck. Although she was quiet and reserved tonight, I had the impression she would be quite friendly once we became better acquainted.

The next two days, the eye of the hurricane lingered over Cozumel and Cancun, playing havoc and causing much destruction. We turned on the weather channel and watched off and on throughout the day. Wherever we ran into residents, they were talking about Wilma. She was taking her time to move and weakened to a category four according to weather experts who also told us she seemed directed toward the Florida Keys and then northwest toward Naples.

"The West Coast, Jeff. Not our coast," I commented on hearing that announcement from the commentator.

"Could change direction any time. We can't be complacent. I've been around hurricanes."

So Jeff had been around hurricanes, knew about them. I never had. "I never have," I said. "I can't imagine what they're like. If this Wilma heads toward the East Coast, toward Jupiter, I suppose residents will be evacuated from Sandycreek Terrace like they were when Frances hit. Many of the residents are saying they won't leave. They'd rather stay here and suffer the consequences rather than go to the place they were sent before, they say. When Frances hit here."

The weather channel was reporting that evacuation processes had begun in the Keys. The commentator was uncertain of Wilma's direction but not of her intensity and extensive coverage. The Florida Keys were still predicted to be her next target, but whether she would then head west or east was undeterminable. Now a category three, she was still treacherous and moving slowly north.

Here at Sandycreek Terrace on Saturday, I looked out onto our patio from the glass door of the Florida room and saw an employee tying our outdoor furniture to the patio railing and placing our four little tables upside down near the railing. I opened the glass door and questioned, "You're really expecting the hurricane to come here?"

"Yes, mam," he answered without hesitating.

I hadn't been concerned, didn't think she would come east. Perhaps I should change my mind. I went to tell Jeff what was happening on the patio. He went to the Florida room immediately and stepped out onto the patio. For only a second he watched the employee securing the outdoor furniture and then told him, "I'll take the tea wagon and lamp into the apartment."

"Thanks a lot. That'll help me," the employee acknowledged, still diligently pulling another cord through the railing and around the arm of a chair.

On Sunday at two-thirty in the afternoon, we received a hand-carried bulletin at our apartment door. It read, *All residents are requested to attend a meeting in the Palace at 4:00 p.m. today.*

At four o'clock the majority of the residents shuffled into the Palace, some walking independently, some with decided limps, others with the aid of canes or pushing and leaning on walkers or driving scooters. Jeff had driven his Rascal; I had walked. The way he drove his scooter—like he was in a kiddy-car race—amused rather than adversely affecting me like all the other scooters seemed to do.

Anxious babbling voices suddenly silenced when the Executive Director strode to the front of the room and stood at the lectern. The tall young man, always immaculate in suit and tie, appeared serious, not favoring the audience with his usual smiling countenance. Apparently aware that all present were hurricane conscious and thus needed no introduction to the reason for the impromptu meeting, the Executive Director fingered his microphone and started his message in a steady, calm, loud voice, loud for the benefit of the hearing impaired. "Can everyone hear me?" Yeses vibrated throughout the room, and he continued, "All entrances to all buildings are being secured, and hurricane shutters are being fastened to all windows and glass doors. The exception is the Sentinel Building. That building is the newest, and windows and glass doors were built with tempered glass and thus are considered to be safe without shutters. To enter the Club House you must use the front entrance." He paused. The room was quiet. He continued. "Everyone should have bottled water, canned food, and flash lights on hand. Candles are not permitted to be used. In case of evacuation, which we hope will not be necessary..." He coughed, looked around. "We have arrangements with two facilities to take our residents and care for them as long as necessary. One is a resort in the northern part of the state. It is presently vacant, for the most part, as vacationers have not yet arrived. The other is a facility south of here. We have an emergency generator operational for the kitchen, dining room, and most of the other rooms in the Club House. We will be able to continue serving meals. Are there any questions?"

A resident in a back row raised her hand. Her voice was barely audible as she said, "What about Park Place, our Healthcare Center? If evacuation is necessary, will those residents be evacuated?"

"Yes, they will be. Along with all staff willing to go. If there are no more questions, this meeting is adjourned."

Many of the residents remained in their seats, talking together. The female resident sitting next to me was pulling a sweater closer around her shoulders and then crumbling a tissue in her hands. She said, "I simply won't go if they say we're going to be evacuated. When we were evacuated last year it was awful. We had to sleep on mattresses on the floor. I had a terrible time getting up from that mattress. And there was only one bathroom for all of us. You weren't here, were you?"

"No. We'd gone up north. To Pennsylvania. But we lost two cars up there."

"How was that? The hurricane didn't go that far north, did it?" she asked, as though disbelieving me.

"We had floods as a result of Frances. And our house is near two creeks that flooded due to all the rain." Then I looked at her and asked, "How would you manage if you didn't evacuate? Aren't you required to evacuate?"

"They can't force anyone to leave. I wouldn't have electricity, of course. But I've stored food and drinking water."

As I was walking to dinner that evening, I met a much older couple who lived in Bay Building. "How do you like living in a cave, dark like a coal mine?" they asked me.

So, shutters were already attached to windows and glass doors in some of the buildings. Plain to see no time was being lost. "Oh, we're not living in a cave," I said. "We don't have shutters. We're in an apartment that doesn't need shutters. We're in Sentinel Building," I said, trying not to express my delight about not living in a cave. We were fortunate!

Monday morning, October twenty-fourth, we woke up to dark skies and a strong wind. After breakfast, we sat in our Florida room where, through the wall-length of windows and glass door, we could watch for the approaching hurricane being described by the television commentator. As time went on, the sky grew darker, the wind increased, and the rain began. We continued to stay in the Florida room with the TV and radio giving us news. Wilma was now over the Keys, then over Naples moving twenty miles an hour. Suddenly the TV stopped functioning, but the radio continued talking. Jeff rounded up a number of candles and three candle holders, ignoring the Executive Director's *no candles* ruling. He placed them on the Florida room table along with two flashlights, one he'd purchased a few days ago. He'd also bought a grill and a bag of charcoal plus a frozen pizza and other food supplies. Under the kitchen sink, we had five one-gallon plastic bottles filled with tap water.

We continued to sit and look out through the glass door and windows and watch the brewing storm. Suddenly the wind picked up considerably! It blew the fronds of palm trees planted between Bay Building and ours. It blew and blew! Now it was whipping the branches in a leftward direction! The limbs were bending, bending, almost touching the ground! I was frightened! Would the trees be uprooted? Their trunks were dreadfully skinny. Bang! An empty plastic flower-pot blew onto the patio, hit the half-wall, rolled over the concrete floor, and wedged itself against our white ornate flower-crock. The rain continued to pelt down and blow against the glass door and windows.

I looked over at Jeff, my forehead furrowed, my eyes questioning our safety. "You scared?" he asked me. "You needn't be. We're secure. Relax and enjoy the show."

At eleven, the radio stopped talking. The lights of the chandelier over the table went out. We'd lost power!

"Are you frightened?" Jeff asked again, eyeing me across the table.

I breathed deeply. "No," I assured him, looking into his steady blue eyes and shaking my head. "As long as I'm with you. It's exciting, isn't it? It's exciting watching a hurricane. But I wish we hadn't lost power."

"*I* think it's exciting. And we'll be fine. I just checked the faucet. We still have running water, and we have bottled water and food. And we have flashlights and candles." He pointed to the supply on the table.

As we ate a little lunch in the kitchenette, the wind constantly rattled the front door and drove a dribble of rain under the sill and onto the floor. The phone rang! We both jumped! I got up to answer. "This is the receptionist at the front desk. A brown bag with your dinner is being delivered to your door this afternoon. Did the dining room call you?" To my negative reply, she said, "You better call them," and hung up.

Concerned, I phoned the dining room only to receive a recorded message informing me I'd called the dining room. Not much help! I'd wait for them to return my call. They didn't.

Mid afternoon the sky brightened, the rain stopped, and the sun came out! "The eye of the hurricane is passing over us right now," Jeff informed me, chuckling. All was quiet, sunny, and pleasant. Like a normal Florida day.

"Is that the end of the hurricane?" I asked Jeff, showing my ignorance.

"No, no! We're midway through. More show to come. Just wait!" He grinned at me.

I tried to smile back, thankful I was sharing this scary event with a knowledgeable confident person. And sure enough, in twenty minutes the sun disappeared, the sky darkened, and the wind picked up. It blew harder than ever! But it blew in the opposite direction. The palm branches were now leaning the other way, to the right! Again they were blowing and bending almost to the ground!

"We're now seeing the fullest effects of the hurricane," Jeff informed me, excitement in his voice, his blue eyes twinkling.

Again, I feared some of the smaller trees would surely uproot, perhaps even the tallest palms as the wind whipped them harder than ever. I voiced my fears, "If a tree is uprooted, it could blow over here and come crashing down onto our patio, even through the windows and glass door!"

"No, no that won't happen. Those trees won't be uprooted just because their branches are blowing," Jeff assured me.

They did hold firm, and I needn't have worried. Windy as it was, the rain didn't return. By five that evening, the wind settled down considerably. Our bagged dinners arrived with a hand-written note stating breakfast would be served in the dining room the next morning from nine until ten-thirty.

At six, Jeff poured our usual cocktails and lighted the candles, and there we sat sipping our drinks in romantic fashion at the Florida room table. Then Jeff served our dinners consisting of ham slices, tossed salad, veggies, and cake. After dinner, we played our usual cribbage game by the *unusual* light of candles. "Your turn to deal I believe. It's always your turn," Jeff said, handing me the deck of cards.

"It is *not* always my deal. Only when I've won the last game. You deal first more often than I because you win more often than I," I told him in our usual cribbage manner.

"Certainly seems like you deal every single hand," he bantered back.

"You'll probably skunk me tonight. Ruin my reputation as a first class cribbage player. What is the score anyway?" I asked.

"Let me take a look." He referred to the long-running score sheet. "The score's zero. You won last night."

"So you were ahead before and for many games before that, and I finally whittled you down. Now we start from scratch."

The next morning, all was calm. I wore a sweater and felt invigorated by the fifty degree weather as I walked over to the dining room while Jeff drove the Rascal. Numerous residents were milling around several buffet tables. I watched bright-eyed Dorcas Sexton propelling Don by the arm as he staggered blindly alongside one of the tables. He really had very poor vision, I now realized. Must be almost blind, I thought. I headed for a small rectangular table where the Dining Room Supervisor, of all people, was making made-to-order omelets. I couldn't suppress a laugh when I saw this tall, heavy-set man, usually in suit and tie, now wearing a tall stiff white baker's hat atop his thick black hair and a large white apron around his wide belly. There he stood behind the table shaking a skillet containing chopped onions and green peppers, his white baker's hat jiggling on his head. Two other skillets occupied similar burners, all in a row. A large pitcher of grease and two large pitchers of beaten eggs stood to one side while on the other side of the burners stood large bowls of chopped tomatoes, peppers, onions, mushrooms, shredded cheese, and bacon bits. The Supervisor, alias chef, was displaying his culinary art and cooking expertise by putting on quite a show. After he took orders from residents, three at a time, he placed ingredients into skillets, and shook the skillets briskly over the burners. At the exact right moment, he lifted each skillet in turn from a burner and gave it a quick upward thrust. The omelet left the pan, flew up into the air, and turned over. As it descended, he caught the omelet in the pan and returned it to the burner for final cooking. Then he flipped it onto the paper plate held by a watching waiting resident. When it was my turn, I held out my paper plate and received my made-to-order omelet.

The foregoing was such a delight to watch that I thought, oh how I wish I had a camera! I'd bring one tomorrow morning, I promised myself. Jeff followed me carrying his omelet, and we took a gander at the other buffet tables offering cooked cereal, fried potatoes, cubed fresh fruit, French toast, Danish pastry, orange juice, coffee, and tea. We helped ourselves to a few items and found a seat at one of the tables. My omelet was simply delicious, the best I'd ever tasted, bar none! What's so bad about a hurricane?

When we got home from breakfast and I opened the door to our apartment there sat Kasey straight ahead of me on a dining room chair grinning from ear to ear. He said, "Drove up from school to get away from Wilma. Much worse there. No power or water. Hope it's okay to stay until Sunday. Even then, power isn't guaranteed to be restored."

"Look who's here, Jeff," I said as he came in the door after getting off his scooter. "He's staying until Sunday. He drove up from Nova University. Says Wilma is much worse there."

"Great! Glad to have you!" Jeff exclaimed, giving his grandson a big bear hug.

"I brought a steak," Kasey said. "Knew it would spoil in my refrigerator without power."

"Good!" Jeff said. "I bought a grill and charcoal. You can grill it out on the patio when we go to dinner tonight. Residents are being served two meals a day. We're choosing breakfast and dinner."

So when Jeff and I went to dinner Kasey cooked his steak out on the patio. But as we sat at the table in the dining room, I felt guilty. Here we were eating in the dining room and Kasey was eating alone at the apartment. Forehead furrowed, I looked across the table at Jeff and said, "It doesn't seem right, does it? Leaving Kasey to eat alone? But I'm quite sure, under these circumstances, residents aren't permitted to bring guests to dinner without a way to pay for them. What do you think, Jeff?"

"I don't know what to think. But I've been feeling the same way as you. Guilty. He'll be all right, though. He's a big boy. Twenty-five years old."

I heaved a sigh, glad Jeff was of the same opinion. After we ate dinner, however, I asked the Food Service Manager if we might bring a house guest to meals. He hesitated but a second and then said, "Yes, yes you can."

That evening, another notice was delivered to our door. It read: *All residents will be entitled to two meals a day served as buffets in the Club dining room through Friday. No guests, absolutely no guests will be served.* That put Kasey at the mercy of the food we had on hand, which really was ample.

Another notice arrived informing us staff would be rounding to all apartments and cottages starting at ten in the morning to help residents clear their refrigerators of all food stored in refrigerators and freezers. The notice reminded us power had been off and would likely not be restored for some time and food spoilage was inevitable. Our refrigerator, including freezer, was loaded!

"Hell's fire!" Jeff exclaimed, his eyes flashing. "No way do we want the contents of *our* refrigerator destroyed. We've been very careful not to open the doors of the refrigerator or freezer, and we still have ice cubes in the freezer. Besides that, I planned to take Kasey and go for ice at a local store. Now I'll wait to go until after staff have come and gone."

Would we be able to fend off employees determined to empty our refrigerator? How would we do that? And why was Jeff waiting until after the employees came before going for ice? The store would be bombarded with customers wanting to buy ice.

I had my answer when Jeff said, "I don't want to leave you alone to plead our case for keeping our food. Kasey and I will wait until they've gone before leaving to go for ice."

He then proceeded to move to the kitchen counter all items in the frig except a bottle of milk and a carton of eggs. Food in the freezer was left as it was.

When two employees arrived mid-afternoon, the male member shouted when he saw the refrigerator doors closed. "Open the doors! The doors must be kept open!" He immediately opened the refrigerator door. When he looked inside and saw the bottle of milk and carton of eggs he exclaimed, "Oh, these have to go! Didn't you read the notice that was distributed?"

As he made a move to remove the milk and eggs, Jeff calmly but firmly said, "We're keeping them."

"Oh no," the employee said and opened the freezer door. Inside were our many precious frozen packages of food. "Oh my!" he uttered.

"We're keeping everything," Jeff said with authority as Kasey and I looked on.

The staff member, suddenly realizing, I suppose, Jeff's intention to stand his ground, braced his shoulders and spoke with authority. "Then you'll have to sign this paper." Anger apparent, he handed Jeff a form which Jeff quickly signed. At this point, the two staff members left to attack the next apartment.

Jeff and Kasey left to buy ice to preserve our food. I was glad Jeff hadn't left me to face the *Mafia* alone. I couldn't possibly have demonstrated the same military authority Jeff used so effectively.

Jeff and I continued to eat two buffet meals in the dining room. Unfortunately, however, when I took my camera to the next breakfast to photograph the Supervisor, alias chef, in his omelet-making get-up, he was no longer making omelets. Just my luck! On Saturday, regular dining room hours and service resumed, and Kasey was able to accompany us to the dining room for dinner.

Wilma caused Sandycreek Terrace some destruction but not enough to require evacuation of residents. All carports were downed, shingles blown off roofs, and landscaping damaged beyond recovery. Repair was non-existent at first what with insurance claims delayed and repair crews in great demand throughout the state's affected areas. Hospitals and clinics had priority. As Jeff and I drove out on the roads to physician and dental appointments and shopping centers, we passed houses and buildings covered with blue tarp. I also noticed something else, something that raised my spirits, and I exclaimed, "Look, Jeff! There's a power and light truck from New Jersey. And there's one all the way from Ohio. Now isn't that wonderful! To have other states respond and help with our emergency?"

Weeks later, repairs began at Sandycreek Terrace, first the roofs and then the carports. Even so the work was slow as workers waited for supplies, still delayed by shipments to priorities. "It'll take months for landscaping refurbishing," Jeff commented.

Thirty-Three
Disney

At Sandycreek Terrace, repair of the destruction caused by Wilma was not about to dampen plans for Halloween celebrations. Residents were invited to a parade to be presented in the lounge by employees the day before the residents' scheduled Halloween party in the Palace. Jeff and I went at the appointed time and found seats among many other residents already in prime positions for viewing. Janet, the Social Director, was emcee. She started the performance by welcoming everyone to the show. The parade began as the first costumed employee appeared from the back of the dining room and walked to the edge of the lounge where Janet was standing. In her condescending, school teacher voice, she twittered, "Ladies and gentlemen, here comes Mr. Frog." Her attention turned to the costumed character, and she instructed, "Bow to the people, Mr. Frog."

Dressed like a frog, the employee came forward waving his arms and kicking his feet as he jumped along through the lounge past seated staring residents. He stopped to bow to one curious resident and then another, waved his arms and kicked his way past more viewers, and then disappeared into the hall while residents tried to guess who he or she could be. Janet laughed and shook her head and said, "No, no. None of you has guessed correctly."

Next from the back of the dining room in sauntered a tall individual dressed like a jail bird in black-and-white striped shirt and pants, black hair hanging down around his face, and a black mustache straggling over his upper lip. "This suspicious character wishes to remain anonymous, ladies and gentlemen," Janet announced. All of us laughed with her as the jailbird passed pieces of miniature Snickers bars to admiring residents, attempted to shake hands, and then departed, following the frog.

A resident sitting near me giggled and said, "That's Richard. See how tall he is? I'll bet any money that's Richard, our favorite server."

"And here comes Miss Muffet. Everybody clap for Miss Muffet," commanded Janet. The dainty miss, eating fake curds and whey, paused and curtsied as she followed the jailbird. We had no idea who in the world this miss might be but suspected she, too, was a dining room server.

"Dr. Jekyl. You all know Dr. Jekyl," Janet insisted as though talking to her students. Dr. Jekyl loomed into the room, his hands, fashioned to look like claws, pretending to grab and scare female residents who shrieked and drew back in a pretense of horror as he passed.

"Meet Mr. Skeleton," Janet's voice quivered as the next participant came into view, eyes peering out of a skull towering and bobbing above a black robe painted with white skeletal bones from the neck down to the toes. "More scary than Dr. Jekyl, wouldn't everyone agree?"

"That's the Executive Director," a resident shouted, and Mr. Skeleton handed her two Miniature Milky Ways.

All heads turned back to Janet who was holding her sides with laughter and saying, "Ladies and Gentlemen, I now present our five-hundred-pound fat-lady from the circus." Into the lounge floated a person whose clothes were obviously stuffed with pillows and balloons making her so obese she had to turn sideways and still could scarcely fit between the rows of seated residents. She, too, distributed candy bars before she bounced, waddled, and floated out of the lounge.

"Who was that?" the clapping residents wanted to know.

Janet kept them guessing and finally said, "You really want to know? You can't guess who that was? I'll tell you. But don't you dare tell her I told you. I promised not to tell. It was Amanda Murray, our Manager of Independent Living Assistance."

Amanda Murray? The residents were shocked, and I among them. To think that grotesquely fat character was beloved Amanda Murray. How spirited of her!

The parade concluded, prizes were awarded by a foursome of judges, their decisions based on loudness and length of resident applause. As only hourly-rated, not salaried employees were entitled to prizes, poor Amanda Murray, in all her regalia, had to settle for the fun she afforded the residents, and also the fun she afforded herself, I was sure.

The very next week, we were in Disney World. Why were we there in that throng, that sea of humanity, that cross-section of people from all over the world? We'd planned it that way. Not originally, that is. And not at *that* vacation spot. First of all, we owned a time-share entitling us to one week a year at resorts specified in the contract. In a weak moment, we'd bought this time-share when we'd stayed at the Coco Beach Resort six years ago. We hadn't taken advantage of the time-share, hadn't gone to a resort last year or this year. Now, in November, we had two weeks entitlement available. The second reason for our excursion and exact week to be away from Sandycreek Terrace had been determined by the housekeeping department. Our apartment had been scheduled for its routine yearly cleaning and carpet shampooing taking two days plus carpet drying time. We needed to move our bodies out to let workers move in.

For this exodus, we decided to drive to the west coast of Florida and stay in a resort on that coast for the week. While there, we planned to visit Jeff's friends, Bill and Ginnie Jesick who lived in Naples. Bill had been best man at our wedding. We also planned to visit my deceased cousin's husband age 92, spry, quite alert, and sporting a girlfriend, no less. Both lived in a trailer park in Englewood, north of Naples.

On making inquiries, Jeff was told no resort was available in that particular area of the west coast. We were disappointed, but Jeff shrugged and said, "How about going to Key West?" I liked that idea, but again no resort was available.

"Shoot, let's try Kissimmee, Mickey Mouse land," Jeff suggested.

"Really?" I said, surprised at *that* choice, a child's playground. "What would we do there?" I wanted to know.

"Holy smokes! What anyone does there. Take in the attractions. Eat hot dogs. Go on the rides. Go on the adventures."

I looked at Jeff's animated face. "At our age, Jeff?" I thought it impractical. Jeff with his cane, not able to walk far. I, forbidden much sun exposure. Then I remembered my first trip when my first husband and I had taken our children there long ago. I'd especially enjoyed Epcot.

Jeff was saying, "We're the world's oldest teenagers! Have you forgotten?"

"No, I haven't forgotten. All right. Let's go," I finally agreed, knowing Jeff and his made-up mind. "Doesn't this remind you of the difficult time we had getting a time-share near Kelso, Washington? We probably won't be able to get one in Kissimmee, either. "

"Maybe. Maybe not. But we're not giving up yet." Jeff placed the call, and the response was positive! We had a reservation at a resort. We were going to Disney World!

After a leisurely drive to Kissimmee, we found the resort named Vacation Village at Parkway without too much difficulty other than driving past it twice and having to turn around twice to eventually find the elusive entrance. Jeff parked in front of the Resort Check-In Building and went in to register and get keys to our apartment. In the car, I waited and waited and waited. Finally I went in to determine what was causing the delay. Surely something was wrong. I found Jeff standing at a counter across from an agent. Multiple forms were spread out on the counter top, and the agent was pen-pointing to items on one of the forms and explaining activity options. It seemed we were entitled to a complimentary breakfast or lunch on Sunday, followed by a brief presentation. We were to decide between breakfast and lunch, plus a preferred time, and call him after we'd reached a decision.

"I'm Mike. There are two Mikes working here. I'm Mike M and M. When you call don't ask for Mike. Ask for M and M. That's me." Now he was looking at me as well as Jeff and continuing to explain printing on an orange-colored form. "Here," he said, pointing with his pen and circling two items, "You can choose to have a free night at Arabian Nights or fifty dollars in cash." He moved his pen to the right side of the form and drew lines in front of several items. "For sixty-nine dollars, you can have a day at Epcot which is a one-hundred-and-sixty-dollar value. Or you can have one of these other tickets for this amount," he said, continuing to mark lines with his pen. "You take this and think it over." Then he handed us a small white complimentary meal reminder-card on which was written his phone number. "There's a deposit of twenty dollars for the breakfast. It's refundable."

Jeff shelled out a twenty-dollar bill.

"Don't forget to call me in an hour," he said, smiling, gathering forms he'd shown Jeff before my arrival, and handing them to Jeff. We thanked him and went out to our car.

Our quarters on the third floor of the seven-story condominium building consisted of two separate apartments, each with a separate private entrance and key. We chose apartment A and walked through it viewing the living room, dining room, bedroom with king-size bed, fully equipped kitchen, bath with shower stall, and whirlpool tub situated between the bathroom and bedroom. Then we walked out the living room's sliding-glass door onto a large balcony furnished with a table and four chairs. We reentered the apartment through another sliding-glass door leading into the bedroom.

A fifty-six-inch TV in the living room faced a couch that opened to make a king-sized bed. A smaller TV in the bedroom sat on top of a four-drawer dresser facing the bed. In the bathroom we found multiple washcloths, hand and bath towels, beach towels, and bath mats. "Look at this," I said, opening a plastic bag on the kitchen counter. I pulled out a roll of paper towels, small box of Tide, packet of dishwasher soap, soap-filled scrubber, two rolls of toilet paper, packets of liquid soap for baby care, sink cleaner, and large and small plastic bags. One couldn't ask for another necessity! Then I remembered to push down the lever in the freezer compartment so we'd have ice cubes for our drinks before dinner.

The phone rang. It was M and M. "Have you decided on your preference for breakfast or lunch?"

Since we'd made our decision on the way up to the apartment Jeff said, "We choose breakfast at nine Sunday morning."

"O. K. that's fine. Be at Building One at nine. You'll find a garage on the ground floor of the building if you want to drive," he informed Jeff. Our apartment was in Condominium Number Four.

The next day, Saturday, we oriented ourselves to the resort, walking around the grounds and viewing two large pools for adults, two children's pools, and a small spa. At the spa a male guest noticed the Pearl Harbor cap Jeff was wearing to protect his bald head from the sun, and he interrogated Jeff at length about that fateful World War II day.

Sunday morning we drove to the designated building, parked in the garage, and walked up a full flight of stairs to the second level of the building. Here we were immediately greeted by a woman who took our breakfast reservation card and told us to have a seat. Almost instantly a tall, well-built man, perhaps in his early fifties, came toward us, introduced himself as Dennis, and offered to take us to the Radisson Hotel breakfast in his car. I managed to double myself in half to climb into the back of his small two-door car and sit down with my knees under my chin. In place of a non-existent air conditioner, warm breezes coming through the open windows made it possible to breathe.

The large Radisson dining room was abuzz with numerous chattering people. Dennis led us to a table for three where a waiter quickly appeared, took our drink orders, and said he'd bring each of us orange juice as well. We'd expected to be eating with a group of people, not alone with one host. Why was he with us? What about the brief presentation? Wouldn't we be joining a group of people to listen to the presentation by a presenter explaining the surrounding area and places we'd be interested in seeing, such as Epcot? We were expecting a program similar to that given at other time-share resorts where we'd stayed.

Dennis was announcing that breakfast was a buffet. Since we opted to have made-to-order omelets, we were required to stand in a long line, order in turn, receive our omelets, and then pick up other desired foods we passed on our way back to our table. When finished eating Dennis suggested we leave a couple dollars as tip. Wasn't Dennis the host? Shouldn't he have left the tip?

Back in Dennis's car I sat crunched on the back seat as Dennis drove across the highway to Celebration. He explained that Celebration was an incorporated town started by Walt Disney who had originally planned to have this residential community be a part of Epcot. As we rode along wide streets, Dennis pointed out large beautiful houses, one more breath-taking, more interesting than the last, architecture varied and modeled after houses reminiscent of those in New England, Virginia, New Mexico, and New Orleans. Delighted, I was viewing large houses with tall pillars, wrap-around porches, balconies, dormers, widow's watch-towers, and next, black iron grating on windows and doors of Spanish architecture. Some houses were white frame, some red or white brick, others adobe stucco, a few painted pink. In my second life, I had decided I would be an architect, so I feasted my eyes on these marvelous mansions. Beyond the houses we passed a large school, then a hospital, a fire station, a shopping area with restaurants, and finally a golf course and club house. When Dennis drove out onto the highway I vowed to visit again, but at a more leisurely pace, this unique incorporated town named Celebration. It was a truly beautiful town.

As we drove along, Dennis asked us about our Coco Beach time-share and expounded on the virtues of time-shares at Vacation Village. "Here we have nine condominiums now erected, and plans for twenty more. The acreage it covers is unbelievable. And do you realize its close proximity to Disney World? Orlando is the most visited vacation place in the U. S. You can't have a better location to own a time-share."

By now we'd tumbled to the realization that Dennis was a time-share sales agent. He had no intention of telling us about places we'd like to visit, tourist attractions we shouldn't miss. This was certainly not like the presentations we'd experienced at other time-share resorts. We were being presented a sales pitch. Jeff said, "Look here. We're not interested in buying another time-share. We want to sell the one we have."

"I understand," Dennis said. "I'm not a hard sell. I'm just telling you about *this* time-share. It has benefits others don't have." Then he proceeded to talk about the point system available at this resort, how limitless it was for reservations, how time could be exchanged for points that could be used to take cruises, air flights, and much more. "Perhaps your time-share contract can be converted to a point system," he said.

"We'd be interested in that," Jeff responded.

"I'll find out for you," Dennis said, indicating an interest on our behalf.

We were back in the garage and parked. Notebooks in hand, Dennis led us up the stairs and into a large room with multiple small tables where, at each one, a sales agent was talking to individual couples seated and listening. The scene was exactly the same we'd experienced when we'd bought our Coco Beach time-share. Dennis seated us at one of the tables and opened one of his books. "Let me explain a few things," he began and then posed the following questions. "Where was the last place you used your time-share? How long did you stay? Where do you like to go best? Would you go back? Do you fly? How many times a year do you travel?"

After we answered I folded my hands and bluntly asked, "Are you trying to sell us a time-share?"

"Yes," he answered.

"We only want to know about the point system you mentioned," Jeff said. "Does our time-share qualify?"

With no hesitation, Dennis said, "It doesn't, but it would if you added it to points from the resort here."

"You mean, we'd have to buy a time-share here for that to happen?" Jeff asked.

"Let me tell you how that would apply," he said and then took his pen and tablet and started to add up figures.

Jeff and I looked at each other and shook our heads. "You don't seem to understand," Jeff said. "We don't intend to buy another time-share."

Dennis rose. "I think I can help you. Just sit here a minute. I'll be right back."

He returned with a small, dark-haired, younger man who sat down at our table, listened to Dennis explain our situation, and then started *his* sales pitch.

"No," Jeff said, irritated and stopping him abruptly. "What is it about the word *no* that you don't understand? Don't take any more of our time. We're not buying a time-share!"

I piped up, "We want to sell *you* a time share."

He apparently got the message because he left us to Dennis who asked us to go into another room for a minute. There he handed us over to a woman at still another table in a smaller room full of tables with people seated and talking. This woman asked us to have a seat to answer a few questions taking twenty seconds.

I said, "If this is only going to take twenty seconds, I'll stand."

She said, "Fine. Do you have a watch to time me?" I showed her my watch.

She started by asking us if Dennis had treated us well. We said he had.

Then she started to ask us the same questions Dennis had asked us. I interrupted, "Your twenty seconds and more are up!"

"Just a few more," she said.

Jeff, now extremely irritated and also standing, said, "We're not answering any more questions. We're leaving!"

As he turned to go, she said, "Wait. I need to give you a form for you to receive your refund for the deposit you paid for breakfast. You need to fill out this other form in order for you to get your free gift. I'll write down the address of the place where you get these." This took more time while Jeff and I became more and more exasperated.

With forms in hand, we went to find Dennis who had told us he'd show us the way out. We looked for him in the large room where we'd been seated with him. He was nowhere to be seen. A young woman came by, and I asked her where Dennis was. She didn't seem to hear me or understand the name Dennis. So, completely out of control by now, I shouted, "Where is Dennis?"

She glared at me, turned to a man coming toward us, and said to him, "This woman is shouting at me."

I thought the man was going to reprimand me or take me to jail, but at that point, Dennis arrived. It appeared he hadn't planned to see any more of us. "I have another tour," he said not too pleasantly. None the less, aware we were angry he said he'd escort us out. We went down the steps to the garage where he led us directly to his car. Thinking he would take us to *our* car in this immense parking arena, we climbed in. He tore out of the garage and was driving so fast we'd almost gotten to our condominium building when we informed him our car was back in the garage.

"Your car is in the garage? You drove? I thought you walked." Now he *was* truly upset, but he spun his car around and drove us back to the garage and to our car. Jeff thanked him and told him he'd treated us well and, to appease him, explained that what had been so disturbing had been the time consumed and the treatment we received after his presentation.

We expected to pick up the deposit refund at the desk at Vacation Village where we'd paid the deposit for our breakfast. Not so! We had to drive to another building to receive the twenty-dollar deposit and our free gift. Inside this building we were directed to a desk where the woman behind the desk said, "You don't get the twenty-dollar deposit in cash. It's deducted from the cost of your free gift. You get a Park admittance of your choice for a price less than it would cost otherwise. What is your choice?"

"Sea World," we told her, having decided in advance.

"That Park admittance is sixty dollars," she announced. Then she stood there and waited while Jeff doled out forty dollars to get tickets for admission to Sea World, our *free gift*.

Back at the apartment, we sat in the living room trying to calm down. The advertised *brief* presentation and breakfast had taken three and one-half hours! We'd fallen for the complimentary breakfast gimmick. Should have eaten breakfast in our apartment and not wasted an entire morning. We'd be smarter the next time, if there *was* a next time. We vowed we'd never be confronted with such a marketing masterpiece again!.

Monday we followed signs to Epcot and waited in line to pay nine dollars to get into a parking lot some distance from the entrance. With the help of his cane, Jeff made it to the area marked WHEELCHAIRS. That was after we passed through the gate where we'd forked over our tickets prepaid to the tune of three hundred and seventy five dollars purchased at the condo office window. For fifty dollars each, we rented scooters. "These will entitle you to go to a special entrance at each Adventure. Not have to wait in line with people standing and waiting to get in," the agent told us.

Jeff had retained some memory of other times he'd been to Disney World and with people passing us right and left said to me, "I'll lead the way, and you try to ride beside me or keep close behind."

This wasn't easy. The park seemed to be seething with humanity. Not another soul in the entire park was over sixty-five, and only several were even that old. It seemed that ninety nine percent were children, babes in arms, and parents in their twenties, thirties, and forties. The other factor of note was the size of the attendees. Scarcely able to ambulate, to force one fatty thigh forward against the other, a notable number in the four hundred pound category waddled slowly from one attraction to another to look but certainly not fit into the seats of boating Adventures. Those in the three hundred pound category were numerous, their lardy buttocks in fantastic individualized motions as they walked slowly along. At least one-half of the population weighed two hundred pounds, give or take a few. Saddest of all were the plump children of the heavy-weight parents, children who were already numbered among the obese, the sixty percent over-weight in the U.S.A. And not all, by a long shot, were speaking the language with which we were familiar.

As I drove my scooter alongside Jeff's, I said, "Have you ever seen so many obese people all in one place?"

"No. It's scary and disgusting. Imagine trying to win a war with soldiers weighing three hundred pounds?"

He would think of that aspect. All those years he'd spent in the service. "My concern is for the children of those parents. Don't the parents have any common sense? Is food that addictive? The more you eat, the more you crave, I guess."

"You have that right," Jeff acknowledged. "Let's try that Attraction. The one straight ahead. Take a nice indoor boat ride."

As the scooter agent had said, we were waved to a gate leading us to the side of a boat wavering in water. We climbed in and were whisked ahead, jolted and bumped along to view fish and creatures of the deep blue sea. Next we parked our scooters, remembering to pocket the keys, and entered a space-ship where we stood against a wall in a designated spot. In seconds we were lifted off the ground, transported into space, and whirled around and around! I held on for dear life as this vehicle continued to whirl us around and around almost touching celestial bodies. Then, as quickly as we had been propelled up into the sky, we were abruptly dashed back to earth. The flight having ended, I climbed back into my scooter in a dazed state. Needless to say, I did not particularly enjoy *that* ride. In fact, it scared me shitless, to coin a phrase.

"How about a hot dog?" Jeff suggested.

We drove our scooters toward a stand, barely missing collisions with children dashing in front of us. Every time I slammed on the brakes of my scooter, I feared I'd sustained a whip lash. At the stand, Jeff forked over a ten dollar bill for a foot-long dog which we divided after adding mustard and chopped onions. I must say it was mighty tasty and a pleasant respite from the scary rides.

Our next Adventure was a ride in General Motors Crazy Cars. I climbed in first, and we sat down on a long wooden seat, hard like a concrete slab. "Hold on to the bar in front of you and press your back against the seat back. That way you won't get thrown around," Jeff instructed me as we were propelled forward with a jerk. Immediately we were whizzed at high speed with centrifugal force that smashed us down in the seat again and again and again! Would it never stop? I screamed and screamed with each mighty jolt, certain every bone in my osteoporosis body would break.

"Lean back! Lean back and brace yourself!" Jeff called over to me.

I tried. Believe me I tried. But my body kept sliding on the seat, and I kept on screaming. Miraculously, when the ride ended and I stood up, I was actually able to walk naturally without feeling any pain or broken bones.

After several more Adventures, we drove our scooters toward an ice cream stand visible in the distance. Again we narrowly escaped running into children and adults who seemed not to hear or heed our scooter horns. Would I be sued if I hit a child and caused fatal injury? Or even minor injury? The thought scared me silly. We finally maneuvered our way to the stand where we purchased five dollar Crispy Bars on sticks, hard chocolate coating on vanilla ice cream. I can still savor mine today, it tasted so delicious.

Another day at Epcot and then a day at Sea World where we totally enjoyed Earth, viewing planting methods of the future: tomatoes growing on trees, green beans thriving on trellises, onions as big as volley balls. We enjoyed that trip through the gardens to such an extent that, when the ride ended we asked if we might stay seated and ride through again. We were afforded that pleasure by a smiling attendant who appreciated our interest.

"Before we go home, I'd like to go back to Celebration," I told Jeff. "I'd like to buy Kirk his birthday present at that pro shop. He plays so much golf I always like to gift him something golf-related, and I know that pro shop will have just the right thing. Something he's not seen anywhere else."

"Good idea! I'd like to drive through the little city again," Jeff said.

Packed and ready to leave, we headed for Celebration. Through her streets we drove slowly, eyeing the lovely homes, all occupied, Dennis had said. "Look at those tall pillars! Look at those second floor balconies! Look at the roof, at the widow's watch!" I exclaimed, pointing at one and then another picturesque abode but favoring the spacious early American replicas.

In the pro shop the saleswoman who was also the buyer for the shop showed me exactly what I wanted—something different, a gray-colored polyester suede zippered jacket with a darker colored back yoke to wear in cool weather. I also chose a shiny metal divot-repairer inscribed with the Club's logo.

Now we were at the entrance to Sandycreek Terrace saying, "We're back!" Jeff activated the electronic mechanism attached to our car's sun-visor, and we drove into our gated community. We'd been gone a week which, in itself, wasn't unusual for residents. Any time during the year, many went away for a week or longer to visit families or take cruises.

But we, this particular week, had gone to Walt Disney's spectacular imaginary world, of all places! Were we out of our minds? Not the choice vacation spot for eighty-five-year-olds. Did Walt Disney ever envision octogenarians playing in his Mickey Mouse playground? I wish I could tell him we'd risked our necks but managed quite well, even had fun, and were still alive to tell the tale of our adventure. I'd tell him his playground gave us the opportunity to be around young people and away from canes, walkers, wheelchairs, and people walking bent over and limping. Yes, we had *our* physical health problems, would inevitably have more in the future, but we'd had a fun week away.

As we stepped into our apartment, we were reminded the housekeeping crew had visited in our absence. The carpet was spotless, all furniture polished, kitchen appliances washed clean, and walls free of black marks caused by Rascal-maneuvering which sometimes occurred when Jeff took it in and out of its parking place in the apartment. This parking in the apartment was undesirable but necessary because leaving scooters outside unattended was against establishment rules and considered a fire hazard.

The windows had been washed inside and out, and the patio hosed as well as all the patio furniture. Four times a year, the patio had a thorough hosing. If we were home, we could see and hear the water's loud splashing on the patio floor as it gushed from a hose being held at a distance by a maintenance employee.

We were back in time to attend the Forum presentation in the Palace. Most of the residents knew Sarah Grant as writer of the Employee of the Month column for the *Periscope* and for her piano talent, occasionally playing old and new popular songs, hymns, and classical renditions by ear on the lounge piano at cocktail time. They also knew her as Chairman of the monthly Forum, always arranging for interesting speakers. Tonight *she* was the speaker. Her topic was *Can Foster Children be Saved?* The topic was also the title of a book she'd just completed. As tonight's speaker, she told about her experiences as a social worker placing orphan children and those with incompetent parents (with histories of drug and alcohol abuse) under the care of foster parents. She described sad and funny incidents occurring in foster homes. "I write to five teenagers who've been placed in foster homes and who've lived in various foster homes for ten years. Every month I go and visit three of them. Their survival tactics are truly amazing," she told the audience. Because she wanted residents to buy her book, she tried to spike interest by saying her book contained many details and also her impressions of what was right and what was wrong with the social service system today.

At the conclusion of her talk, she announced, "I'll be at the back of the room to sign my book for anyone interested in buying it."

Two days after the forum presentation, Sarah was leaving to go to four northeastern states, including New York and Connecticut, where she was scheduled for speaking engagements followed by book-signings. She wasn't returning until after Christmas.

What's next with enterprising Sarah, I wondered? Will her literary ability entice Harry Scott? Did he receive an e-mail message giving him her address up north? We did. The one we received indicating it was sent in case we wanted to send her a Christmas card. Surely she'd want to hear from Harry.

Thirty-Four

Happenings

Since we'd been away in Kissimmee and hadn't eaten at Sandycreek Terrace for a week, we were each entitled to seven make-up meals, one meal per day as our contract stated. To eat these meals before the end of the month, we could eat breakfast or lunch in the Terrace or lunch in the dining room. Both the relaxed atmosphere in the Terrace and the permitted informal attire were appealing, and we chose the Terrace to eat five breakfasts and two lunches each. One of the mornings we ate breakfast there a familiar male resident who was a retired engineer and his son who lived in a nearby neighborhood were also eating breakfast. Since the two men spoke rather loudly, the room was small, and no other diners were present their conversation carried to our table. Our ears pricked up when their topics proved to be interesting, and we sat there eavesdropping.

At first they seemed concerned about the education of U. S students versus foreign students with visas studying in the U. S. The son was saying, "Dad, my daughter, the medical student at Boston University, told me the majority of medical students are Asian."

The resident said," The Asian graduates from Ohio State University, my alma mater, are all competent engineers. Foreign students are better qualified and therefore are hired for high tech jobs in the United States."

The son agreed. "They're qualified to be atomic scientists. Regardless of visas, foreign students don't return home but stay on in the U. S. working in high tech jobs."

"Take education on the lower level in the U. S. Elementary and high school levels," the resident said. "I have a good opinion of private schools. Their policies requiring uniforms and not accepting under-qualified kids."

"I agree with that," I said to Jeff. "Uniforms create a dress code so students, or rather parents, aren't vying to out-dress, out-fashion other parents' children. Financially deprived students admitted on scholarships don't feel inferior or conspicuous as they would if they wore out-dated hand-me-downs. They all look the same and are nicely clothed."

The son was voicing grave concern. "Dad, what should be done about exceptional students? And what becomes of the U. S. should rock star prevail?"

We weren't able to hear the resident's answer because server Emily came to our table to take our orders. The next topic of conversation at the father and son's table was one we talked about frequently. The son said, "The media is influencing the public more than ever. The great amount of information given the public and also the tremendous amount of misinformation, as well."

Next we heard the father stating, "Much aircraft is being built with exotic material but with limited durability."

Emily returned to our table to refill Jeff's coffee cup. She was an amazing server who remembered residents' likes and dislikes after just the initial contact, and she always bustled about the room like a person trying to catch a train. She and Olga, a female cook, were usually the two employees manning the Terrace. Olga's eggs benedict and cheese omelet were unexcelled, like a dish prepared for the President. If Emily was required to fulfill another assignment, such as taking doughnuts and coffee to the card room for Travelogue viewing, Olga would pinch-hit in Emily's brief absence. In clement weather we ate on the patio, and Emily served us as cheerfully and efficiently as she did indoors. We had only one minor complaint, another reason for our eating on the patio as frequently as weather permitted. Emily, overheated by her weight and pace and complaining of hot flashes, turned the six overhead fans on high as soon as she arrived for duty. This chilled us and the hot food as well when we ate indoors. We and other diners finally learned to bring sweaters and request fans be turned off.

Sunday was a busy morning in the Terrace as some residents arranged to meet there and eat a leisurely breakfast together. Pam Butcher was one of the residents who met with a group of women Sunday mornings, and we were glad she'd found friends to enjoy. We noticed she frequently joined several of these residents in the dining room for dinner. Other residents habitually arrived directly from church services. Because of the Terrace's Sunday popularity, lounge bartender Chuck was often reassigned to assist Emily. Poor Emily rolled her eyes and heaved deep sighs at the sight of Chuck and his slow shuffling movements. As if still asleep, he gradually wended his way among his assigned tables. She, on the other hand, hurried around overseeing the entire room, even observing missing items on Chuck's assigned tables and providing them.

On my way to the beauty shop one morning, I passed the bag lady in the lobby near the front desk. As usual she was carrying two bags at her sides, one in each hand, and shouldering a raincoat. I stopped and asked, "How are you this morning?"

"I'm upset!" she said. "This isn't a very good morning for me. They sent me a girl who can't drive, and I have to stay inside all day!"

It was then I noticed a small woman in a white uniform standing a few feet away. "I'm sorry about that," I said and walked away, not knowing what else to say. As always on my way to the beauty salon I passed the library, lounge, and cloakroom adjacent to the dining room before turning right into the beauty salon.

"Just take a seat in my chair. I'll be with you in a minute," beautician Ethel told me as I walked into her shop. "You want a dry-cut again?" she asked.

"Yes," I answered, and then as she viewed my hair like a sculptor about to mold clay I asked her, "Do you happen to know the resident everyone calls the bag lady? I just passed her. She was complaining that she'd have to stay home today because they sent her an aide who can't drive. Do you know that resident?"

"I surely do," Ethel said, circling a towel around my neck and then covering me with a blue plastic cape she secured at the back of my neck. "She's been in here twice for a hair styling."

"I wasn't aware she has to have a caregiver," I continued.

"Yes, some days she gets quite confused. She had an accident with her car, and now she's not allowed to drive. A caregiver drives her car for her."

"But she can play bridge and play it well. My husband and I played with her and her male friend one evening," I said, finding it difficult to believe the bag lady was so confused as to need a caregiver. I looked in the mirror and saw Ethel pick up hair clips and a pair of scissors from the shelf over the sink.

"She does play bridge. You're right," Ethel agreed. "And isn't it amazing how confused people can do some things very well? Her male friend is just as confused as she is. He applied to live here but he wasn't accepted."

I could hear and feel scissors snipping at a layer of hair on the back of my head as I said, "My cousin who has Alzheimer's Disease plays bridge and works the New York Times crossword puzzles, amazingly. I always wonder whatever does the bag lady carry in those bags of hers? One day Jeff, my husband, asked her, and she said, "'Everything I'll ever need.'"

"That's right," Ethel said, continuing to snip away. Then she stopped cutting, looked at my reflection in the mirror, and said, "I hear her house burned to the ground and she lost everything."

"Is that right?" I was beginning to feel sorry for the bag lady.

Ethel dropped chunks of my hair on the floor and continued, "Since then she carries *everything* with her. She's prepared for anything that happens. When she was ready to pay me she opened one of her bags and took out a large roll of twenties. I could see *more* rolls in her bag. She must have had thousands of dollars in there and check books and multiple other items."

"My heavens!" I tried to visualize the scene. "She probably carries her passport as well, I offered, watching more clumps of sandy gray hair fall onto the blue plastic cape and slide down to the floor.

"Oh, undoubtedly," Ethel agreed, laughing.

"I guess the raincoat's necessary in case of rain, I said, glancing at my shorn locks in the mirror. Ethel started to cut my bangs and I closed my eyes. Once again I realized hair dressers are well informed because of all they learn from their clients. She took a towel from a drawer and brushed away pieces of hair that had landed on my face and were tickling my nose. "Would you please trim my eyebrows, Ethel? They grow so long so fast, and they curl. I inherited them from my father." Ethel laughed. Then she eyed her completed cut, plugged in her hair blower, and waved it over my entire head to remove all the loose hairs.

After she removed the blue plastic cover, I pushed myself out of the beauty chair and rose to my feet. Across the room a resident peered out at me from under a dryer and said, "Your hair looks very nice from the back. *Very* nice."

I thanked her and wondered what she thought it looked like from the front. I didn't inquire. I really didn't care what it looked like from the back, but I did care what it looked like from the front. I didn't recognize this resident because of her wrapped head under the dryer and because of my poor vision. If I'd known her, I might have asked her about the front. I thanked Ethel and left the shop knowing her fee plus tip would appear on our next month's bill from the business office. Now I was eager to tell Jeff what I'd learned about the bag lady.

At the conclusion of today's Executive Director's meeting, a female resident rose and voiced a concern about pets walking freely in common areas and relieving themselves. The Executive Director responded, "No pet is permitted in common buildings, and *all* pets must be walked on leashes when not inside living quarters. No exceptions!"

That very next day a memorial service was being held in the Palace for attorney Harry Scott's wife. She'd died in Park Place after being admitted there a little over a month ago. A large number of residents were in attendance at the service sitting in folding chairs set up to form two rows with an aisle in between. As Jeff and I walked in to take our seats, we noticed tables set with napkins and flatware lined up along the sides and back of the room as well as a partially-set long buffet table, all indicating refreshments would be available after the service.

Family members of the deceased were seated on folding chairs near the front of the room on one side of the aisle. I nudged Jeff seated beside me when I spied, there in plain sight would you believe, a white fluffy-haired dog wagging its tail and walking freely among family members of the deceased close to the aisle. "How about no pets in common areas?" I whispered to Jeff. He smiled and nodded. "That's the way it goes," he whispered back his favorite saying and then said, "If you can't laugh at a few things around here, you'll cry."

The service began, and a small child belonging to a family member lost her cookies and was carried out of the room. The white fluffy-haired unleashed dog continued to wag its tail, sniff, and walk between family members' feet. So much for the Executive Director's promise that no pets were allowed in the facility's common buildings, and all pets must be walked on leashes!

Until now we'd never signed up for any of the off-campus events such as shopping trips, mystery rides, and dine-arounds, planned by Janet, the Social Director, and accessed via the facility bus. But this week I decided to go to the luncheon at Miss Laura's Tea House, advertised in the Weekly Newsletter. When I mentioned the event to Jeff he said, "No, I don't want to go. Sounds like a female festival. You go ahead. That should be fun for you."

"We'll be going in the new bus. It's maiden voyage," I told him.

This newly purchased bus had been the topic of much discussion and investigation before the final purchasing decision. Dr. Tom Price had been the catalyst who'd recommended a new bus to management, the old one breaking down from time to time. Tom wanted a bus equipped to carry residents' scooters thus enabling those never before able to take the bus to benefit.

We'd had a phone call from Tom one day. "Jeff," his familiar legislative voice plummeted over the wire. "I'd like you to come to the front of the Club House in your scooter as soon as you can make it."

Jeff left immediately, knowing not to delay in complying with any request made by our important man on campus. When Jeff returned he told me, "Management's about to buy a new bus. I guess the present one's old and in need of too much repair. Probably the original bus at the conception of Sandycreek Terrace. At any rate the one being considered for purchase was in front of the Club House when I got there. Tom wanted to see how scooters would fit into it and how many would fit."

"Oh, so they're going to replace our bus with one that's scooter accessible?" I asked.

"That's the plan. Pam Butcher was there with her scooter. I suppose Tom summoned her like he summoned me. With Tom's scooter that made three scooters available for trial."

"So did they put all three on the bus and did they all fit?"

"They did. And now the residents who depend on scooters will be able to go to Publix and Walgreens to shop and to entertainment spots on the bus with other residents. But I'll never put mine on there. Not as long as I can drive our car and manage with a cane after we drive to where we're going."

The bus had passed its examination, and now I was about to ride in it to Miss Laura's Tea House. I mounted the new bus in front of the Club House entrance at the assigned time, settled back in a comfortable seat, and fastened my seat-belt, ready to go. My first ride in the facility's multi-resident transportation old or new! Ten female residents were seated on the bus when I boarded. A newly hired black female named Althea, large and strong-appearing, was at the wheel smiling and proud to be the first driver of the new vehicle.

Janet, the Social Director, arrived at the bus door, still ajar, and boarded. Young, her skirt above her knees, and her hair swept up and held in place with a rhinestone clip, she looked like a kewpie doll. "Ladies," she announced getting our attention with her high-pitched condescending voice, "We're waiting for one more resident who signed up to partake of this lovely luncheon. She'll be along shortly." With that she left the bus and went back into the Club House. Shortly she emerged with the tardy woman.

"Is everyone ready to have Althea start the engine?" Janet asked, smiling at all of us like a doting aunt. She remained standing and counted off her charges. "Eleven," she announced. "When we start back I'll take another count. We must have eleven."

Off we went into the old historic part of town where the bus pulled up in front of an old frame house with Miss Laura's sign on a post in the yard near steps to the entrance. Janet tried to open the front door of the old house. It was locked. "Well ladies, we'll go around to the side door," Janet chirped, and we all followed, walking on a wrap-around porch. The side door, too, was locked. From inside a man suddenly appeared, unlocked the door, and bid us enter. Inside we arranged ourselves at three tables in one of three small dining rooms.

From the table where Janet was seated she said, "Are you admiring our table settings, ladies?"

"Yes," we chimed in chorus for at each place was a large embossed china plate, a flower-painted bone-china cup and saucer, sterling silver flatware, and a large white linen napkin. A bouquet of yellow and purple pansies graced the center of our linen-clothed table.

"Look around the room at the walls, ladies," said Janet. We obeyed and glanced around and observed the many artifacts decorating the pastel-printed walls. "Note the old, old photos in the aged oval wooden frames. That high shelf holding antique china plates. That beautiful framed hand-made lace and the mahogany view-box displaying antique figurines." Janet pointed as she gave us a viewing-tour of the walls and continued to talk to us like a teacher instructing her students.

I noted the lace curtains at a window near our table and how they privatized us from pedestrians and passing autos. The window's high sill was filled with vases of live flowers. Crocks of flowers graced all corners of the room.

My eyes scanned all this before a waiter in white apron and peaked cap arrived at our table. "Good afternoon, ladies," he said, bowing slightly and handing each of us a large weighty menu most difficult to hold. I read over the tastefully described entrées accompanied by a variety of teas. No other beverages were listed. After we placed our orders our preferred tea arrived in individual painted bone-china tea pots. Fruit salads sprinkled with shredded coconut and honey sauce and adorned with live orchids were served next, the large embossed china plates lifted simultaneously. We removed the orchids before partaking of the salads, of course. Hot rolls nestling in a printed-gingham cozy in a wicker basket followed along with stamped butter patties arranged on a small china plate. For the next course some of the women had ordered spinach quiche; I and others had ordered chicken salad. After eating this main course we chose from the dessert menu offering strawberry sundaes, chocolate mousse, and pecan pie. Well nourished, we boarded the bus again, Janet counting to eleven before we departed.

"Did you have a good time?" Jeff asked, lifting his eye glasses to the top of his head and looking at me with his blue eyes wide open, a crinkled smile on his unshaven face.

"Yes it was nice. But I ate too much, and once was enough. You were right. It definitely was not a man's restaurant. Too fancy. No male residents went. Only eleven females plus Janet."

"I didn't think it would be a good place for men, being named a tea house. Too many rhuderts and lollies. That's why I didn't go." He held up the little finger of his right hand in a feminine gesture. "By the way, I haven't been able to find my Barlow knife. If you see it let me know. I've looked everywhere."

I went on a search. First I looked in all the usual hiding places—under papers on his desk, in the guest bathroom under magazines he partially read while there, and on top of his chest of drawers. Finally I felt all the pockets of pants he'd been wearing. There it was! A hard lump in the side pocket of his green pants. "I found it!" I shouted.

"Where? Where did you find it?"

"In the pocket of your green pants," I answered smugly. "Right where you put it," I added and laughed.

"But I looked in all my pants pockets," he responded.

In the lounge that evening we saw the Summners, Greg and Shirley, having returned from summering in eastern New Jersey, and we welcomed them back. Immediately we noticed Craig spoke in a subdued tone of voice, and we were surprised not to hear his booming question about our health, his loud "HOW ARE YOU?" He still said, "How are you?" but quietly. When we asked him how he was he answered, "Better for having seen you." Rather nice, I thought to myself.

"I have a joke for you," he said and started right in. "A parson was visiting a dying parishioner in the hospital. The patient was desperately trying to tell the parson something and finally wrote a message on a piece of paper. The parson assumed his parishioner had a last wish and stuck the note in his pocket to read and fulfill later. He stayed until his parishioner died and then read the message. It said, "Remove your foot. You're standing on my oxygen tube."

It was the same joke he'd told us in the spring but we responded with anticipated laughter.

"I have a joke about a dying man too," Shirley said.

I was surprised because Shirley, of few words, rarely said more than to compliment me on what I was wearing. "You do?" I said. "I'd like to hear it."

"All right. A friend was visiting a dying man. Suddenly the dying man smelled an aroma coming from the kitchen. The smell roused him, and he said to his friend, 'My wife's baking my favorite cookies. Would you please go into the kitchen and ask her if I can have one.' The friend went to the kitchen and came back and said, 'She says you can't have one because she's baking them for your funeral.'"

"Oh no!" I said. "That's terrible!"

"But very funny," Jeff said, and we both laughed.

We stayed with them a while longer, and Shirley kept asking us to repeat everything we said. She, too, was losing her ability to hear. Nothing stayed the same!

After the Summners were called into the dining room we sat a few minutes with Grace Terwilliker before our table was ready. She seemed subdued, slouched in a chair, head bent, not holding up her hand and calling to the bartender to fill her glass. She wasn't even asking Jeff about his back pain. Her friend, Polly, sitting with her as usual, returned our smiles and answered our questions but was silent otherwise.

Don and Dorcas Sexton walking by stopped long enough for Dorcas to say, "I haven't made contact with Bea Burton at Pine Gardens yet but I plan to."

"Let me know when you do. We have good friends, the Hahns, who know both Bea and Nick. They live in Pine Gardens, too. We'll ask them for the same night and make a dinner reservation for an eight-top," I said, looking forward to such an evening. I really missed being with Chick and Betty, my friends for many years.

Shortly before Thanksgiving I decided to phone the Hahns. Betty answered. "Oh, Jeanie, you've been on my mind. I've been meaning to call you. Isn't it funny how we think of each other at the same time? How are you and Jeff? Do you still like it there at Sandycreek Terrace?"

"Yes, we do, Betty, and we're fine. How are you and Chick?"

"Chick had back surgery three weeks ago. He's getting P. T. and walking a little bit with a walker. He still has pain. But not nearly the amount of pain he had before the surgery. I'm doing a lot that Chick used to do." She laughed. "You should see me drive. You know I never used to drive much. Now I have to drive to the store and all around. I'm not used to that. I drive so slowly I make all the drivers behind me mad. But I can't help it. And Jeanie, I'm not having Thanksgiving dinner this year. I'm not able to do it with Chick the way he is."

"Of course you can't. Don't even think about it! You've had the Thanksgiving dinner every year for as long as I can remember."

"I know, and I enjoyed having it. Having all my friends. I'll have it next year for sure."

"Let us know if we can do anything for you. Anything, Betty."

After we hung up my mind went back through all the years I've known this fine couple. I remember a young Chick working for my father in one of his insurance and real estate offices. Chick was a fantastic real estate salesman. His great personality appealed to everyone and proved very beneficial when dealing with people having property to sell or wanting to buy a house or condominium apartment. He turned on his charm and instantly became their friend. I used to say he could sell the Brooklyn Bridge. He showed me a house I quickly bought in the suburbs of Pittsburgh, and then he sold it for me when I decided to move to Florida. He sold both my and Jeff's condominium apartments before we married. He sold us the single-family house we lived in and then sold before we moved into Sandycreek Terrace. Of course we spent time together socially all those years. Yes, Chick *and* Betty and I go back a long way.

Since Jeff and I weren't going to the Hahn's for Thanksgiving dinner we signed up to eat at Sandycreek Terrace, dinner being served from one to four o'clock. "When we go over for Thanksgiving dinner let's go as late as we can," Jeff said to me as we finished eating breakfast in our kitchenette the day before turkey day.

"I'd prefer that," I said. "I don't even like to eat as early as four. I wish holiday meals were served the same time as every other day, but I guess they schedule them early so dining room and kitchen staff can be home for a holiday meal. Makes sense." Then I said, "Thank you for breakfast, Honey." I gave him a smile, thinking again how fortunate I was to have a husband who liked to cook and didn't want me to do anything in the kitchen but clean up after breakfast and lunch. That was easy.

Jeff had had an opportunity to scan the morning newspaper, and I asked, "What's new in the news?"

He lowered his eyeglasses from atop his head and picked up the paper. "Another train accident. The autotrain again. Derailed. One person dead. One hundred sent to the hospital. I haven't had a chance to read the editorials. But I read one yesterday that I saved to read to you. One by that black editorial writer who always writes great articles. In my opinion. And there's one in this weeks' U S News and World Report. It's about the Bird Flu. I think you'd be interested in it."

"I would," I was quick to answer and realized again how much Jeff read. Most anything in print available to him. No wonder he was so well informed and had such a vast vocabulary. But of course he'd been a good student, learned *and* retained much in high school and college. Did some self-educating, too. And he used that knowledge and vocabulary when he talked. And he did talk a lot.

Reinforcing, I believe it was called. Use it or lose it, was the saying. I'd written an article titled *Use it or Lose it* long ago before it ever became an adage. Maybe I could have been the recognized originator if I'd done anything with the article. That was when I was working at South Mountain Restoration Center, a thousand-bed long-term care facility in south central Pennsylvania. I even talked to the Medical Director of the Center about my half-completed article.

"Sounds good," he'd said.

The fact that Jeff talked a lot pleased me. Some men talked very little, at least to women, and I was sure they'd be boring as the dickens. Yes, I was very fortunate. Jeff was talking now and I listened.

"Here's Dennis the Menace. Dennis is talking to his little friend. They're watching Mr. Wilson shoveling snow. Dennis says to his little friend, 'If you wanna learn some new words, just throw a snowball at Mr. Wilson.'"

After I laughed appropriately Jeff laid down the paper and said,

"Honey, how about not having a drink before we eat our Thanksgiving dinner tomorrow? Since it's so early to eat. And I get sleepy and worthless after I eat if I've had a drink before I eat. Do you think we could do that for once?"

"Sure. Let's abstain for a change."

At three thirty the next day we went over to the Club House and into the crowded lounge. Residents and guests were standing talking and drinking and waiting to be called to tables in the dining room. I was glad I'd worn my black ankle-length skirt and ornate loosely-knitted peach top as many of the women were wearing long skirts for the Thanksgiving holiday occasion. A number of the male residents wore ties with their dress shirts and sport coats. Even Jeff had worn a tie, surprisingly. Chuck was behind the bar three-deep with customers filling orders one after the other, mostly red and white wine in large stemmed wine glasses.

What happened next isn't surprising. Jeff looked at me and said, "Shall we change our minds and have a drink? It doesn't look like we're going to be served any time soon."

"Sure. Why not," I answered with a laugh. Why not? What was wrong with having a drink on Thanksgiving? Nothing.

A couple with whom we'd just become acquainted, Rebecca Stunkard and Calvin Colson, were part of the crowd and seeing us, came over to where we were standing. I recognized Rebecca's sweet face and curly white hair. Calvin standing behind her was tall, rather thin, had slightly bent shoulders and a constant smile in a pleasant unlined face. Rebecca said, "We just got here. If you're not eating with anyone would you care to join us?"

"Of course we would," we both acknowledged, pleased to have company especially on a holiday.

Calvin went up to the hostess desk and changed our table arrangements. No chairs were available in the lounge, and I said to Rebecca, "Why don't we go out on the patio. I see an empty table and chairs out there. The weather's nice enough to be outdoors."

"Fine. We have a guest with us," she said somehow managing to sort their guest out of the crowd, and the five of us walked out onto the patio and sat down with our drinks.

We were introduced to their guest, another Calvin. "Calvin's living in my daughter's apartment," Rebecca explained but failed to enlighten us as to how he happened to be at Sandycreek Terrace for Thanksgiving dinner and their daughter was not.

An hour and a half later we were seated in the dining room. For these special holiday dinners the menu was fixed, everyone receiving the same except for preferred beverages of coffee, tea, or sodas. Servers moved quickly from table to table, and Lorna as usual was rushing around taking beverage orders, clearing tables, setting up empty tables, and trying to pacify waiting diners. Lorna was not young although she moved even faster than much-younger quick-footed Emily in the Terrace. In fact, Lorna looked as old as some of the residents. She'd been hired a year after we arrived at Sandycreek Terrace and had recently been promoted to head server. A number of residents knew her because she'd been a dining room employee at a country club where they'd been members. When these residents heard she was coming to work in our dining room their comments were: "We're so glad Lorna is going to work here. She'll be a wonderful asset to our dining room." "You'll love Lorna. She takes a personal interest in everyone." "Lorna will work faster and better than anyone we have here." These comments turned out to be true.

Part-way through our meal the bag lady, having completed her dinner, walked through the dining room stopping at various tables soliciting bridge partners. As she was about to stop at our table with her male friend who still lived in a residential area across the street from Sandycreek Terrace, the Dining Room Manager approached her and said, "Not now. Not today. It's Thanksgiving." Then he had a server lead her and her friend out of the dining room.

"It's a shame, isn't it? How confused she is," Rebecca said, and we all agreed.

After Jeff and I reached our apartment I said to him, "Jeff, what's the situation between Rebecca and Calvin?"

"What do you mean?" Jeff asked and uttered a sound of relief as he took off his necktie, sport coat, shoes, and socks. I knew he much preferred to be comfortable in loose sweaters, knit sport shirts, and no ties, but at least he had dressed especially nicely and worn a tie for Thanksgiving.

"What I mean is, Rebecca and Calvin are always together. They don't live in the same apartment, do they?"

"No, they don't live together. They're listed with separate apartment numbers in the Sandycreek Terrace directory. They do seem to be very close. I don't know when or where they met. Maybe here, maybe before they came here. They moved in much before we did. So I have no way of knowing. I just always see them together."

"Like Betty Howe and Ralph Wilson, I guess. Maybe they want their own space. Still, everybody needs some body," I said, starting to sing *Everybody Needs Somebody*…"How about the couple in the apartment directly above Ruth and Stuart McKee? They've been living in that apartment together ever since we moved here, and I believe they moved in here together. I hear they're going to get married. Wonder what possesses them to get married now in their eighties? To each his own, I guess. Ruth and Stuart got an invitation to their wedding reception. I'm sure we won't get one because we don't really know them. After all, they can't invite everyone who lives here."

"They're going to make living together legal. This is like Peyton Place. Did you ever think of that? An old folks Peyton Place."

THIRTY-FIVE
HOLIDAYS

On the way to dinner one evening, Jeff and I had stopped and were looking through the New Year's Eve party sign-up sheets lying on the front desk counter-top when the receptionist looked at me and said, "I love your suit. Very smart-looking."

"Thank you," I said and smiled but didn't tell her it was a pants suit I'd bought at the Hospice Shop for ten dollars. A Talbot suit just my size appearing to have never been worn! The first time I'd ever bought anything in other than retail stores although I'd heard other women talk about shopping at thrift shops with much success. I always took clothes I planned never to wear again to the Hospice Shop, and that's the reason I was there the day I spied the fine-checked black and white Talbot suit. I was donating a red wool jacket with large shoulder pads extending too far over my shoulders and a pair of slacks too large around my waist and hips. I'd lost weight and was down to one hundred and ten pounds. My abdomen was fairly flat now, and I liked fitting into a size six

"We'd better sign up for the New Year's Eve party," I said to Jeff.

Since he had good vision and I poor, I pushed the stapled pages toward him. The sheets contained consecutive table numbers with four, six, eight, or ten lines for residents to fill in their names. Jeff leafed through the pages to find a table where people we knew had signed and said, "Here's a table for eight with Sarah Grant, Harry Scott, Tom Price, Irene Trenton, the Smiths, and guest written on the remaining two lines. Wonder who the guests are." He looked at me.

I shrugged and said, "I have no idea. Is there any other table where we might like to sit?"

Jeff turned page after page and finally said, "Many of the tables are filled. I find two tables with room for two more names but the written names belong to women. I'd prefer to have at least one other man at our table. Some of the four-tops on the last sheet are empty." He turned to me for a decision.

"Let's not sit with all women. Two other women will sign up in those spaces. I don't like to sit with just two other people at a four-top for a party." Suddenly I saw Irene Trenton walking toward us from the dining room. That tall pretty woman was always smiling. I stopped her and said, "Irene, we're signing up rather late for New Year's Eve. Who are the two guests signed up to sit at your table?"

She gave me a big smile. "No one in particular. Sarah called me from Virginia where she's having a book signing. She asked me to write in the names of the people you see there and write in guest in the last two spaces."

That left me in a quandary. It appeared to be Sarah's table, one she arranged from afar. But if she didn't request Irene to write anyone else specifically, surely we knew Sarah well enough to join that table. "Irene," I said. "Do you think it would be all right for us to write our names in those guest spaces?"

She hesitated then said, "I guess so. Yes, go ahead if you want to."

So Jeff erased the penciled in *guest* on the two spaces and wrote in *our* names. At dinner, thinking about the sign-up sheet, I said to Jeff, "It's quite noticeable how Irene Trenton and Tom Price arrange to be together. I wonder if Tom's wife, Elizabeth, knows of their relationship? Poor thing, spending all her days in Park Place so debilitated. But of course Tom has to have some fun."

"Life goes on. That's the way it is," Jeff hypothesized.

"And how about that Sarah calling Irene Trenton from Virginia and having her start a table and arrange for Harry Scott to sit with her?"

"His wife's dead. He's free catch," Jeff said, raising his eyebrows and then winking at me. So true but so obvious. I wouldn't have the nerve.

A fifty-five-piece band was presenting a concert in the auditorium of the public library in town one afternoon a week before Christmas. The

Sandycreek Terrace bus would transport residents to the concert if more than ten residents signed up, according to the announcement we read in the Weekly Newsletter. We decided to sign up as did twelve other residents. Jeff used his cane to walk to the bus parked at the entrance to the Club House and we chose seats after passing three occupied forward-most rows.

"My first ride in this new bus," Jeff remarked, testing his seat. "Quite comfortable," he said. Then he settled back, rested his head on the high back and closed his eyes.

Exactly fourteen residents were now seated. Althea, the beaming newly-hired driver, had helped residents board and now sat behind the wheel, triggered the huge door to swing shut, and proudly started the trip. In twenty minutes we arrived and filed into the library and into the auditorium. Since we were early, we had our choice of seats, and all of us went to the front two rows ten to twelve feet from the stage where a row of red poinsettias decorated the floor below. On stage musicians were tuning their instruments—a trumpet here, a clarinet there, a French horn mid-stage, a flute on the left. More instruments joined in, causing a cacophony to test our emotional stability. The discord reminded me of the long-ago nights I sat with my mother listening to warm-ups of the Pittsburgh Symphony Orchestra before its wonderful performances began.

In the row where Jeff and I sat Penny Ferris was sitting to my left and Rebecca Stunkard to *her* left. For some reason, Calvin wasn't accompanying Rebecca on this venture. The two women were talking, Rebecca speaking loudly so Penny who needed hearing aids but never wore them could hear her over the instrument warm-up. Rebecca's voice reached my sensitive ears as well, and I quickly realized the two women were discussing a third female resident, namely Lottie Yurasik. She was the vivacious resident who'd moved into Sandycreek Terrace about the same time as Jeff and I. I remembered the day she'd admired the top I was wearing and told me she intended to steal it and put it in her clothes closet. She'd impressed me as a friendly and fun-loving person.

To my left the conversation continued, and I heard Penny ask Rebecca, "She's not going with Alan Armstrong any more?" The inflection of Penny's low-pitched voice resonated with incredibility.

"No, no. That's past. Has been for a while. She's trying for Harry Scott now. Haven't you heard?"

"No. What happened to Alan Armstrong? I thought she was crazy about him," Penny said, obviously still disbelieving.

"She was. But he wasn't exactly fond of her. He tried to be courteous and kind. Had a terrible time getting rid of her."

Because Penny's voice was always alto and loud I had no trouble hearing her even though her words were directed toward Rebecca and away from me. Now I heard her say, "Is that right? What do you mean she's trying for Harry?"

"Well, she has her eye on Harry now. She's taking care of his dog. Harry was planning a trip up to Scranton, Pennsylvania, and he has this dog he's very fond of. He couldn't take it with him, and he wouldn't take it to the kennel. So he needed someone to take care of it while he was away."

Penny was hanging on every word, I could tell, and I also was listening to this story with interest. Only natural!

Rebecca said, "Somehow Lottie Yurasik found out Harry needed a dog sitter. Makes it her business to find out these things. And she offered to baby-sit the dog while Harry was away. I heard she actually begged Harry to take care of it."

"For goodness sakes. Trying to get on the good side of him, wasn't she?" Penny's words filled my ears.

"The same way she latched onto poor Alan. Not that Alan has a dog. He doesn't. But she was always doing nice things for him. She knows people like attention. But she gave him more attention than he wanted. Overwhelmed him. He got tired of it."

"Aggressive. She was too aggressive," Penny said, head bobbing up and down emphasizing her knowledge of romantic tactics.

I found this information amusing. It was fun to listen to this gossip, to keep abreast of the budding romances in this old folks' home. And my goodness, wasn't this just like high school, this gossiping? Or like college even? Did we revert to it when we were old or did it just never cease? And what about Sarah Grant? Two women vying for Harry Scott's attention. My, my!

The band director came to the edge of the stage, announced a musical medley, and the music commenced. It was loud. Several people moved to seats in the back of the room. I had to admit the music was a bit *too* loud but it was a band, after all. Bands were supposed to be loud. I'd never heard a band that wasn't loud. I thoroughly enjoyed the music and couldn't keep my feet from moving in time to the beat or my hands from marking time on my knees. Most of the pieces were Christmas carols, songs from *The Nut Cracker Suite, Babes in Toyland;* others were patriotic songs and marches. The band director introduced a second band director who led the band for two excellent renditions and then stepped aside and returned the baton to the primary director. Our clapping almost outdid the band in loudness. The music was non-stop for an hour and a half while I shifted my gaze from one instrument to another trying to isolate the sounds.

When the final clapping subsided and everyone rose to leave Jeff acclaimed, "Great playing!" as he reached into his wallet for a bill to place in the free-will offering-basket being held by a man at the rear door. We all exited and climbed back onto the waiting bus, Althea standing at the open door to lend needed assistance.

The day before Christmas we were packed and ready to head for West Virginia. Again I was thinking how nice it was for my daughter Mary Ann and her husband Steve to invite us to their house to spend the holiday. She'd phoned mid-November and asked us to come saying the trip would be our Christmas present from them.

"That would be fun, Mary Ann. I'd like that very much," I'd earnestly said but had to add, "After that horrendous flight back from the state of Washington I vowed I'd never fly again. I told you about that trip."

"But Mother, that was a long flight, and you had to change planes and didn't make connections. This flight will take less than three hours, and it's non-stop from West Palm directly into BWI."

It didn't take me long to realize one dreadful experience shouldn't keep me from making this special trip for the holiday. "All right, Mary Ann. I guess I can make an exception. Especially since it's Christmas, and we'd certainly like to spend it with you. And it's very nice of you and Steve to do this for us. But let me check with Jeff."

He had happened to come into the room at that very moment, and I'd held the receiver away from my ear and said, "Honey, Mary Ann is offering to fly us to their place for Christmas. As a Christmas present from them."

"Really? How generous!"

"Then I'll tell her we'll come?" I'd waited for his affirmation and gave her the good news.

"I'll have Daniel make the reservations. He flies a lot and has luck with Southwest Airlines. He'll be flying into BWI from Kentucky, and he'll try to get his flight and your flight to arrive at BWI around the same time. He can't come any sooner because the dance company is booked for their performance until then. Steve will be the one to meet you and Jeff and Daniel and drive you three here. His van is bigger and easier to get into than mine. You and Jeff would have a difficult time getting into my van."

"What about Lizzi," I'd asked.

"Oh, she'll be home from Grinnell a week before that. The college gives students a long vacation. I'll call you again before Christmas. A couple times before then."

So that's how it happened we were packed and ready to go to West Virginia the day before Christmas. I was wearing my old but not out-of-style fur jacket even the real animal would have thought was another mink, and Jeff was wearing a wool sweater under a wool sport coat. Apparently he'd never intended to travel north in the winter and hadn't kept any of his warm clothing. The man we'd engaged to drive us to the airport was due shortly. He'd taken us to airports a number of times before, and we'd found him quite reliable. We were ready early because Jeff was the kind of person who never wanted to be late, actually made a point of being ahead of time for any scheduled engagement or event. I, on the other hand, was the opposite before I married him. But I was learning and, quite truthfully, I was keeping up with him these days.

"Pack warm clothing," I'd told Jeff. "When I talked on the phone to Mary Ann a few days ago she said there was snow on the ground. And their house is always cold in the winter. I swear they keep it at sixty degrees. Of course it's a big house to heat, and their fuel bills must be horrendous."

To pack in medium-sized suitcases was another thing I'd learned from Jeff. "Pack lightly," he always told me. "Only one medium-sized suitcase a piece. Maybe one small carry-on in addition if necessary. No more. If you forget something, we can always purchase at our destination. There will be stores. No need to break our backs lugging heavy suitcases."

So I've learned. I pride myself on packing lightly yet having everything I'll need. I have yet a need to buy anything at our destination.

Jeff phoned the gate to advise security to expect our transportation and direct the driver to our entrance. Our man arrived, carried our luggage out to his large comfortable car, and we rode to the airport on I-95 in relatively medium traffic. While we waited for our plane we ate sandwiches frugal Jeff had prepared. That was another thing I'd learned about Jeff. He'd lived through the great depression as did I, but his father lost his great wealth and never recovered it. His family's house had burned to the ground, and they had to live in the hired man's house with little food or clothing for a whole year. He'd never forgotten how to save. *Waste not, want not.* And he never wasted anything or spent money unnecessarily. Yes, he clipped coupons to use at Publix Supermarket and Walgreens Pharmacy. By marking out any printing and then readdressing, he reused inserted envelopes from mail he received. He continued to buy those inexpensive but well-made clothes from that mail-order outfit called Haband, a far cry from Brooks Brothers. Jeff had no eye for fine quality and fashion and I couldn't convince him to care a hoot.

On the other hand, I confess, I, as I've said, have *too* much of an eye for those factors, too much for my own good and pocketbook, perhaps. I still didn't spend on cosmetics, fingernail polish, or hair-dos. A little blush-on and lip gloss was all. Savings from these items excused me for spending on top-notch clothes, I rationalized.

The plane was on time, the flight smooth, and son-in-law Steve met us at luggage, as prearranged, and greeted us warmly. Here we waited for Daniel for quite a span of time even though his plane was due to arrive twenty minutes after ours. Then all at once my tall handsome grandson appeared out of nowhere, was at my side, and was giving me a big hug and Jeff a big hug. A red and white tassel cap, one like I'd seen on a few others in the airport, encased his dark hair.

"I like your cap," I told him.

"My Santa cap? We exchanged Christmas presents at work. Janie picked my name and this is what she gave me. I like it, too."

"Is Janie your girl friend?"

He smiled at me. "No, Janie's just one of the dancers in the company."

Then remembering, I said, "Oh that's right. Your girl's name is Jessica."

"Yes," he said and smiled again. "We're living together now."

"Is that right? And how is that going?" I asked, amused and interested but not shocked because unmarried and living together seemed to be the norm these days with all generations, young and old. Didn't Jeff's son suggest Jeff and I just live together instead of getting married when, four months after his mother died, Jeff told him we planned marrying that next month? He did just that, and we didn't like the idea.

Daniel's answer was: "Fine! We're getting along just fine." Then he glanced to one side and said, "Oh, there's the luggage coming off carousel B. I better go retrieve mine"

He came back pulling a huge piece of luggage on wheels. Steve grabbed our two suitcases, and we walked out to the waiting SUV and rode to Martinsburg, West Virginia, chattering all the way. The sky was black and as we drove through residential areas we oohed and aahed at lighted Christmas decorations on houses we passed. Snow. I was looking for snow. It's been two years since I've seen snow, and I peered into the darkness looking for the white stuff. Finally I gave up. The snow Mary Ann promised me must have melted. But no! Just as we drove up to my family's house, there on the terraces of the back yard, glistening white in the van's headlights, I saw snow! There it was! Only patches of it but enough saved for me to enjoy.

After hugs and kisses from Mary Ann and Lizzi we were led into the living room to view the crystal-ornamented ceiling-high live spruce. "It toppled this afternoon," Lizzi said, giggling.

"Oh, no!" I exclaimed.

Mary Ann was quick to say, "No harm done. It fell against the window. Not one ornament was broken. The trunk wasn't firmly held in the tree holder. It's an old holder. We need a new one, like the one in the family room."

"I must see that tree," I said, knowing this house always had two trees. We left the living room to go to the large family room where, in a far corner, stood another large tree decorated with shiny colored balls, meaningful ornaments collected through the years, and colored lights glowing brightly. The smell of spruce filled my nostrils as I stood near the tree and inhaled deeply. Christmas in Florida with its decorated palm trees and *aromaless* fronds wasn't the same, couldn't compare with the holiday up north. Weather humid instead of crisp, and no children making snowmen and sled riding down snow-covered hills. My many memories of celebrated Christmases spent with parents and grandparents long deceased swept over me like a nostalgic blanket wrapping me in its warmth.

For dinner we had steaks Steve grilled on the patio, the steaks we'd ordered sent to them from Omaha Steaks, part of our Christmas present to this family. The next morning as Jeff and I were starting to eat breakfast Steve came into the kitchen after feeding the llama and five goats. He was speaking so low to Mary Ann we couldn't decipher what he was saying.

"Oh no," Mary Ann cried. "What did you do?"

"He's not supposed to be picked up," Steve said, his voice louder now. "I tried to feed him. He wouldn't eat,"

"Is he hurt? Did you examine him? Maybe he tried to get through the fence. I don't trust that new neighbor. Maybe he poisoned him if he was trying to get through the fence onto his property." Mary Ann's voice was high pitched, like an opera singer getting ready to hit the ultimate note.

"Mary Ann, I'm sure it's nothing like that! And he wasn't hurt. I checked him all over." Steve was saying.

With nervous fingers, Mary Ann removed the black ribbon tying her pony tail and shook her head several times causing her shiny auburn hair to spread over her shoulders. Then she pulled back her hair from her face and replaced the black ribbon tie. "We need the vet. But he won't come today. Not on Christmas day. My poor llama! What will we do?" she asked Steve, her voice shaking with concern.

"I'll give him an injection. It can't hurt. And I'll check on him every couple of hours. Relax, Mary Ann. We'll do the best we can."

At the breakfast table, Jeff and I had stopped eating to listen. "What kind of injection is Steve going to give the sick llama?" Jeff asked me.

"I'm sure I don't know. But being a physician, he'll administer something to help. It's a shame this had to happen and dampen the holiday."

"Why is it Steve and Mary Ann have these animals?" Jeff wanted to know.

"They were pets for the children. Another purpose in raising them is to keep down growth in some of the many acres on their property. Mary Ann has always liked animals. She brought home a lame stray kitten when she was little and used a tongue depressor to splint its leg. She used to ride horses quite well. English and western saddle."

When Daniel and Lizzi got up it was open-present time. Jeff and I opened gifts Kirk and Sally thoughtfully sent to this address so we'd have presents to open while others were opening theirs.

The five days passed quickly. Lizzi played the piano for us and also gave us a photo travelogue covering her semester as an exchange student in Manes, France. We understood from Mary Ann that Lizzi had spent one entire day in her room assembling photos and completing her France scrapbook to have it ready to show us.

Daniel turned out to be quite an extensive conversationalist and challenged Fritz and then me as we alternately won cribbage games. "You always did like to play games, Daniel," I said to him when we'd completed one of the cribbage games he and I were playing. "I remember when you and I played rummy when you were in grade school."

"I remember, too," he said, smiling. "I enjoyed playing rummy with you. Lizzi never wanted to play. She still doesn't care for most games although she likes scrabble."

Jeff had brought a copy of the first volume of his autobiography, and after the cribbage games, Daniel had picked it up and read some of it. "I like this book you wrote, Jeff," he said, smiling across the table where we three were still sitting.

Jeff said, "I believe you're the first person to read this labor of love. The order of one hundred volumes only just arrived at our apartment from the publisher the day before we left to come here."

During part of our visit while other family members were busy, Jeff read Frank McCourt's third book, *Teacher Man,* to me. I'd read his first book, *Angela's Ashes*, that I'd found in large print in Sandycreek Terrace's library. His second book, *'Tis*, Jeff had read to me at home. We both liked the first two books better than *Teacher Man*. Too much repetition there.

Needless to say, we were glad to have our heavy clothing since the house, as I predicted, was very chilly. Jeff wore three layers and I two the entire time. Before we left, the ill llama had partially recovered.

Thirty-Six
Harry

Back home in warm sunny climate, our winter duds unpacked and put away, Jeff slit open accumulated mail with his Barlow knife. "Phone bill, solicitations for contributions, and campaign literature. That's about all. Rhuderts and lollies,"Jeff said, casting the mail aside and glancing at his watch. "Guess we'd better get ready for dinner. Wonder what's on the menu for tonight?"

Now in the lounge seated at a round table, a bowl of mixed nuts in the center, Betty and Ralph greeted us. Betty looked elegant in a shiny green and blue brocaded jacket, silk threads interwoven throughout. Ralph's brown and white striped tie complimented his brown tweed jacket. "When did you get back?" they wanted to know. Then Betty said, "Did you have a nice time? We missed you. Come sit with us after you get your drinks."

At the bar Chuck had poured our drinks as soon as he saw us. "I see you haven't forgotten what we drink, Chuck," I said, giving him a smile.

"No Mrs. Metz. I never forget," he said, his blond hair longer than I remembered and scrambled over his head like he'd styled it with an eggbeater.

"What's new?" Jeff asked as we joined Betty and Ralph.

Before they had an opportunity to answer, I asked, "How did you celebrate Christmas here?" I was eager to learn how they enjoyed the holiday.

"Christmas Eve a group of young carolers from the Episcopal Church walked through the dining room and lounge while we were having cocktails. They ranged from little to tall. All ages. And they were led by their choir director. They weren't here very long. I imagine they had other places to go." As usual, Betty was talking in her sweet animated way while Ralph sat back in his chair with a smile on his face. She continued, "Then dinner on Christmas Day was served from twelve to four as it usually is on holidays." She reached over and patted Ralph's knee. "Ralph and I chose to go at four. A harpist played the entire time, I believe. Didn't she Ralph?" she asked, looking over at him and waiting for an answer.

"What was that, Betty?" he asked.

"I said, a harpist played the entire time during the dinner hours on Christmas Day. Isn't that true?" she repeated.

"I believe so," he said, still smiling.

Greg and Shirley Summners walked in and up to the bar. When Greg noticed us he said, "Back from your trip? How was it?"

"Just fine," Jeff and I answered in unison. "How have you been?" we asked.

"Fine! The better for seeing you," he answered.

Jeff and I had just started to help ourselves to the nuts and sip our drinks when Betty and Ralph were called to their table by one of the hostesses. "You'll forgive us, won't you?" Betty said rising from her chair, her thin bony hand grasping its back to steady herself, and adding, "We must have dinner together soon."

They had just left when I glanced up and saw Penny Ferris approaching, walking her slow slide. She stopped at our table and peered down at us. "When did you folks get back?" her alto voice questioned as she traveled on to the bar.

About that time, Jim and Jane Horner walked into the lounge. They hesitated when they saw us, and I said, "Come sit down," and motioned to the two seats just vacated by Betty and Ralph.

They sat down not saying anything, and since we were having a cocktail I said, "Are you going to get a drink?"

"No, we had one at home before we came," Jane said.

"How is everything with you two?" I asked.

"Not very good," Jane said, looking downcast.

Concerned, I asked, "Is something the matter?"

"Jim isn't well," she answered.

Both Jeff and I looked at Jim. He was smiling as usual, not appearing to be the least bit ill.

"I'm having kidney problems. Have to go to the urologist tomorrow. No matter what, I'm not going through kidney dialysis. That dialysis is a never-ending process, and I'm not going for dialysis three times a week. I'll just wait it out."

What I was hearing didn't sound good to me. I frowned, looked from Jim to Jane, and said, "I'm sorry to hear this."

Expressionless, Jane was sitting erect in her chair as she usually did and said, "Jim has only one kidney."

"Really!" I exclaimed, and Jeff made a similar comment.

"He donated one to our son," Jane explained. "We'd prefer you didn't say anything about this to anyone. We don't talk about it."

"Of course. We didn't hear you tell us," I promised her.

Jim was talking to Jeff and then looked at me as well. "I'm just going to continue my life as though everything is normal. No matter what the urologist has to say, I won't consider dialysis."

The conversation ended abruptly as a hostess approached and told us our table was ready. At the table I said to Jeff, "How wonderful of Jim to donate a kidney to his son. But of course what parent wouldn't do that for his son? I admire anyone who donates body organs. And being a physician, Jim would know all about kidney dialysis. I can understand why, at his age, he wouldn't want to go into kidney dialysis. I hope, whatever the problem, and it's probably cancer, I hope remission is a real possibility. That's probably what Jim's banking on."

Back in our apartment after dinner, Jeff picked up the remote control from the Florida room table and pushed the on-button. No picture, no sound. "Holy smokes! What now?" he emitted, frowning. He tried the button on the set itself. Nothing. He pulled the plug out of the wall outlet and put it back in. Still nothing. "Damn! What the devil's going on?" Then he managed to squeeze his arm behind the TV, pulled the plug from the set, shoved it back in, and looked up at me. "When did we have this repaired?" he asked.

"Several months ago," I told him, not remembering exactly.

"I guess we'll have to use the one in the den, if we want to watch anything. But you can't see that TV. The picture's too small. I hate to spend more money on this TV. It's pretty old. Guess we'll do without for awhile."

I shrugged. I'm not one to be glued to television.

The phone rang. I answered and heard Sarah Grant say, "I'm so glad you're going to be at our table for New Year's Eve. I was going to invite you to join us, and then I saw your names signed up for our table. I'm having the people at the table come to my apartment for eggnog after the party. At eight o'clock for a couple of hours until ten. Not until twelve. I'm asking everyone to think of a memorable New Year's Eve they spent in the past and tell about it while we have eggnog. So come prepared."

I smiled at the sound of Sarah's serious voice, like a lecturer. I replied, "We will, Sarah. And that's very nice of you to have everyone after the party. Parties here always end so early. And eggnog sounds great. May I bring something?"

"No, I'm just having a few cookies with the eggnog. That should be enough after we've eaten a big meal, don't you think?"

"Yes, of course. Telling about other New Year's Eves is a great idea. We'll look forward to it. Thank you, Sarah."

When we found our table in the Palace New Year's Eve I admired the table setting—a gold-colored lace cover spread over a black tablecloth and a live floral arrangement in the center. A toy horn and another toy were lying at each place setting. The other toy was a coiled inch-wide strip of colorful crispy paper attached to a wooden mouth-piece. I remembered this type of toy from the times I was a kid at birthday parties. With one of those crispy paper coils in hand, we kids would sneak up behind an unsuspecting kid and blow into the mouth-piece. The paper would unfurl, and a feather attached to the end would tickle the kid's neck.

Sarah Grant, posture erect and countenance stern as usual, was already seated at the table when Jeff and I arrived. Beside her was a woman we didn't know. Naturally, hostess Sarah would be first at the table. After all, she'd arranged the table-seating through a phone call to Irene Trenton all the way from the state of Virginia, an arrangement placing Harry Scott, now single, at her table. No doubt she'd e-mailed him in advance. Jeff was pulling out the chair on the other side of Sarah until I reminded him *that* seat should be saved for Harry. But Sarah was saying, "No Jeffrey, you go ahead and sit there."

So where was Harry? Where was *he* going to sit? When I looked surprised Sarah, lips pursed, explained, "Harry isn't coming. He's not feeling well. He's scheduled for surgery next week."

This most unexpected information made me give Sarah a second look, and it was true what Jeff always said about her. He always said, "Sarah looks like she just bit into a sour pickle."

Of course I had to say to Sarah, "I didn't know Harry was having surgery. I trust it's nothing serious." A statement, but I hoped she would interpret it as a question for an informative response.

Sarah seemed to realize that and said very solemnly, "He has a prostate problem."

So much for Sarah's well-laid plans.

Tom Price in his scooter and tall, smiling, Irene Trenton arrived next, and lastly and finally came the Smiths. Stocky Elaine Smith wore her short white hair in the *spikey* uncombed fashion I'd seen lately on female models in magazines. From the way husband Leslie leaned on his cane, the slow tedious way he walked, and then the way Elaine assisted him into his seat, I figured Leslie had had a stroke or similar medical problem sometime in the past. Twice throughout the party, he left the table and slowly walked in the direction of the bathroom, Elaine turning and anxiously watching for his return. No doubt that explained their late arrival, his frequent urination need.

When Leslie left again Elaine went to a nearby table to visit friends, and I noticed she, herself, had a slight limp. When Leslie returned I helped him into his seat, but Elaine quickly returned upon seeing Leslie back. Also throughout the party she devoted much attention to her husband, explaining the salad, the entrée‘, the dessert, and making pleasant conversation while he responded with one word or a nod.

I leaned over to Jeff and whispered in his ear, "Isn't it sad about Leslie, how much attention he requires?"

Jeff replied, "Yes. That's the way it goes. And if you don't laugh, you'll cry."

As we left the party, the single resident seated at Sarah's left (apparently invited in Harry's stead) said she wasn't feeling well and excused herself from going to Sarah's apartment. The Gathers, our neighbors down the corridor, were still sitting at their table when we passed on our way out of the Palace. They were complaining about the early ending of the party, so Sarah invited them for eggnog.

At Sarah's apartment, as promised, we enjoyed eggnog lightly laden with rum, cookies of various kinds, and also chocolate candy all served on an over-sized coffee table in her living room. We guests sat around the table, some on a large couch, others on chairs. At Sarah's request, Jeff began the telling of former most memorable New Year's Eves. That is, he was expected to. But instead of telling about a New Year's Eve, to my surprise he decided to talk about his most memorable Christmas Eve.

"It was a Christmas Eve during the Great Depression," he began. "After having our traditional oyster stew, I was still hungry. When I persisted in voicing my hunger my mother said all she had to give me was a banana. I said, 'All right,' and ate it quickly and went to bed. The next morning when my brother and I dove into our stockings, my brother brought out a banana. I had only the box of hard candy the Sunday school had given all us children. 'Where's my banana?' I asked my mother. She said, 'You ate it last night.'"

Everyone laughed and clapped. Then Sarah called on Daphnie Gather to tell her story. Not forewarned, she said she couldn't think of a New Year's Eve to tell us. Everyone else participated. Tom Price told about one New Year's Eve in New York City, and so did I as I was there in 1945 taking a course in Operating Room Technique and Management at the New York Hospital, part of Cornell University Medical Center. "Times Square was filled with soldiers, sailors, and marines, all of us cheering and making merry," I concluded.

After stories about past New Year's Eve concluded, Jeff's Christmas story prompted conversation about the Great Depression and those long-ago hard times most of us experienced. Sarah offered more eggnog but all declined. More for Irene would have been disastrous for, as it was, she'd already spilled some of her first cup on Sarah's handmade rug. Apparently she'd had too much to drink at the party. She'd been most apologetic, and Sarah had quickly cleaned the rug with a wet rag. Since a large quantity of eggnog was left, Sarah said, "Won't someone please take home this eggnog?"

Irene smiled, and I thought she was about to raise her hand, but Daphnie Gather intercepted and accepted. Sarah handed her a glass jar filled with the rich creamy liquid, and we all made our departure.

At home I said to Jeff, "Wasn't that nice of Sarah to have us all at her apartment? So we didn't have to go home at eight o'clock on a New Year's Eve? Somehow that just doesn't seem right. I guess we're past the age of staying up and seeing in the New Year, but going home from a party, any party, at eight just doesn't seem right."

"Guess we have to get used to it. That's the way it goes here. Nobody's as young as they'd like to be. Yes, it certainly was nice of Sarah. But she served too much! All that eggnog and those cookies and candy after we'd had such a large meal. And why doesn't she smile? She'd have a pretty face if she'd only smile."

Harry Scott went to the hospital for his surgery, and guess what? Guess who cared for his little furry dog? That's right. On the way back from my walk the next morning, I passed Lottie Yurasik walking out into the circle from our building, and sure enough she had a little furry dog on a leash. She didn't seem her usual energetic self, walking slowly, no makeup on a pale face, red hair uncombed. "Harry's in the hospital," she explained to me. "I'm caring for his dog while he's there."

I reached down and petted the little tail-wagging furry animal, all white and black. Then I drew back my wet hand when furry dragged Lottie over to a nearby bush.

In the lounge that evening as we sat with Rebecca Stunkard and Calvin Coldridge waiting to be called to a table in the dining room, a large young burley-looking man with uncombed hair walked into the lounge and up to the bar. I assumed he was a guest but he was alone, not accompanied by a resident. So I turned to Rebecca, nodded in the direction of the stranger at the bar, and said, "Do you know who that is?"

"Yes, that's Harry Scott's son. Here from Syracuse." Her twisted smile and raised eyebrows indicated to me that she agreed I had reason to question the likes of such a strange looking character.

I said, "So he's here to visit his father who's just had surgery? But I saw Lottie Yurasik walking Harry's dog this morning. I would think his son would walk the dog."

"You would think so, wouldn't you? But no, he stays inside Harry's apartment all day long," Rebecca advised, giving me another knowing look with raised eyebrows and a tilt of her head.

So Lottie was doing another good deed for Harry, having given up on Alan Armstrong, I supposed. I marveled how some residents, like Rebecca, for instance, found out so many facts about other residents. Perhaps because they communicated more with other residents, having lived at Sandycreek Terrace longer than we had. Now what about Sarah? I smiled to myself, wondering which woman handsome Harry preferred.

THIRTY-SEVEN
OTHER EVENTS

Jeff and I noticed that many more residents were coming to dinner later, fewer choosing to eat early. Apparently new residents and those returning from spending holidays elsewhere preferred to eat late thus causing an overflow of late diners. Because of this, late diners were required to wait in the lounge much longer to be seated for dinner, a number standing for lack of enough seats. Even though seating on the patio was available, the outdoor temperature was too cold now to sit there. The poor Food Service Manager was confronted with the problem of satisfying the number of residents becoming increasingly unhappy at having long waits and inability to sit down while waiting.

None of us residents should have been surprised to read a new notice on the bulletin board across from the front desk. In effect it offered those residents who came to dinner between the evening hours of five and five-thirty a special tantalizing entrée' such as lamb chops or filet mignon plus a free glass of wine.

When Jeff read the announcement he said, "So this is the manager's attempt to create a balance of residents throughout the entire dinner hour. Encourage more residents to come earlier. Presumably he expects residents who choose this early seating to be out of the dining room by six or six-thirty. This would allow late diners to have enough seats in the lounge while enjoying their cocktails and not have to wait very long to be seated in the dining room."

We walked into the lounge the first night this new system was in effect and found multiple residents standing, all seats in the lounge occupied as before. "What's going on?" Jeff asked Emmett Gorman standing near the piano, a scowl on his flushed face.

330

"Damn poor idea the manager has, encouraging people to come early by giving them a special menu and free wine. Someone told me there was a line out to the front door before five o'clock tonight. Now those residents who came early are all sitting in the dining room not leaving. Drinking their free wine and talking!" He clenched his fist and raised his arm causing the sleeve of his maroon sport coat to expose a large gold-banded watch. His eyes on the watch, he said, "I've been here an hour waiting. Lord knows how much longer we'll have to wait! I'm calling the Executive Director. He needs to know about this!" His voice was harsh.

After *we* waited an hour, Jeff said to me. "This isn't right. This new system is making us wait longer than we ever did. I'm going to send an e-mail to Ray Watson, president of the Resident Council. Give him my thoughts on this matter."

The situation was much the same the next evening. We paused briefly to talk to Emmett Gorman still irate about the wait. "Yes, I called the Executive Director," he said in answer to Jeff's question. "Didn't get much satisfaction. Wants us to give the new system a chance to work. A chance to work? Hell. It's not going to work! By George, something has to be changed! I won't let this rest!"

The Food Service Manager's new system of serving meals lasted two weeks and was then discontinued. It must have had a lasting effect on some residents because a considerable balance resulted. Some residents continued to come early, and a few late diners were choosing to come even later, thus partially easing the overflow.

One evening when the lounge seats were all taken and the temperature warmer we found chairs on the patio and sat with Betty Howe and Ralph Wilson. Again I marveled at Betty's appearance. She always dressed her slight ninety-one-year-old figure in lovely stylish clothes. She immediately started to talk saying, "We went to the Kravis Center this afternoon." Then her arm flew up over her head toward Ralph, almost hitting him and causing him to duck out of the way as she continued, "We saw *Tin Pan Alley*! It was absolutely marvelous!"

"How nice. I'm glad you enjoyed it," I said. Then when I asked how she was she pulled her printed scarf higher around her neck and said, "I'm having problems again with my skin on my neck and down my chest."

Her little eyes looked into mine, and her bony arthritic fingers flew to her scarf again, touching and patting it. "I'm going to a new dermatologist. I hate to give up my old dermatologist. He was so good. But his office is too far away. Now that I don't have a car. You know I decided to sell it. I have to use the transportation provided here, and they don't travel the distance to my old dermatologist. Down to Pompano where my dear dermatologist whom I've had for years has his office. I just hope this new doctor can help me."

Ralph said, "Is she talking about her dermatologist? I can't hear what she's saying."

As usual, Ralph Wilson's mumbling southern drawl was difficult for me to understand, even with my acute hearing. But I'd gotten accustomed to it, and it didn't annoy me as it had last year. I projected my voice because of his hearing disability and told him, "Betty's talking about her new dermatologist. She says she has to go to a new dermatologist because he's close by."

"I told her I'd drive her to her former dermatologist," he drawled.

Betty reached over and touched Ralph's arm, her blotchy bony fingers resting on his tweed jacket sleeve. "Ralph is so kind. But no, I won't let him drive that far. The traffic's so heavy."

I wondered again, as I had many times, was vision deficit more or less debilitating than hearing impairment? In some ways I believed hearing loss was worse than poor sight. Not to be able to hear what was said would leave an inability to respond, to communicate. I would hate to keep asking, "What? What did you say?" Or respond to a question inappropriately, like Ralph had that evening Jeff asked him to repeat his name, and instead he gave his apartment number.

He was not alone. A number of conversations I'd overhear in the lounge were humorous. Two females would be talking, and one would say, "Your name's Geoffrey?" The other would answer, "No, it's Jessie." Or a conversation between two other residents went, "You broke your arm?" The answer, "No, no one was harmed." Then, too, when I took my walks I was glad I could hear when a car was approaching from behind.

On the other hand, deprivation also resulted from poor vision. I met residents and then didn't recognize them the next time I saw them. I appreciated Jeff's telling them, "Jeanie's almost blind. She won't know you when she sees you again. She's not snubbing you. She just doesn't recognize you."

I'd started waving to everyone and smiling whether I'd met them before or not. And I did have some vision, thank goodness for that, even if my ophthalmologist, when I asked him, said I was legally blind when the chart reading was twenty eighty in my right eye and my left eye only able to see fingers at close range. To be deprived of two senses would be very sad.

After Jeff had served his homemade vegetable-beef soup, Keebler crackers, and oatmeal raisin cookies for lunch, I decided to get his opinion. "Which do you think is more debilitating, vision or hearing impairment, Jeff?"

Jeff looked at me across the kitchenette table and said, "The deciding factor is probably the extent of the debility. You do very well with your limited vision. No one would ever suspect how poorly you see. That's why I always let people know. So they won't think you're ignoring them. And I'm happy to read to you anything you want to hear."

"I know," I said, smiling at him and at his eye glasses looping his ears and circling his bald head. "And I'm very grateful, Jeff. I think of poor Victoria Watson with extremely poor vision. I'm sure Ray must help her in many ways, probably even helps her dress. She's always immaculate, her hair combed back in a pony tail, not one strand out of place. And tied with a ribbon or short scarf. Her outfits always match perfectly. And her stature is admirable, like a soldier walking in revue. Ray usually takes her hand and carries her drink."

Jeff said, "That little woman whose apartment is down the corridor from here is totally deaf. In the pool she swims laps like she's practicing for the Olympics."

"And how about that black Scotty dog she walks a couple times a day. When she sees me she always says something cheerful, usually about the weather. I understand her fairly well, but her voice is somewhat loud and her speech clipped and unclear. If she can't hear anyone talking, wouldn't it be difficult to continue to pronounce words correctly after a time?" I asked.

"I imagine it depends on how long she's been so deaf," Jeff answered. "Speech therapy helps some people. She may have had therapy."

Even with all the analyzing, I didn't have the answer as to which was more disturbing, loss of hearing or loss of sight.

With the end of that discussion we'd finished eating the oatmeal raisin cookies. "You like these cookies better than chocolate chip cookies, don't you, Jeff?"

"Yes, I do. And they're more nutritious. But as long as they serve both in the dining room and we're too full to eat them there, I'll continue to sneak both home because I know you prefer chocolate chip. You being a chocoholic." He grinned and winked at me.

"I wish we weren't prohibited from taking food home from the dining room. It's a sin to waste what we're too full to eat. To have it go back to the kitchen and be thrown out. Many of the residents take food home on the sly, like we do."

"I don't feel guilty. We pay for the food. And I'll continue to take zip-lock plastic bags to the dining room in my jacket pocket. I'm cautious. I doubt anyone sees me slip cookies and meat into the bags. Maybe a server does but they don't care. The bag of meat goes immediately into our refrig. Sometimes into the freezer."

I said, "I was told this policy exists because management is concerned residents will forget about food they bring home, and it stays in the refrigerator and is never eaten."

"And in time the food spoils, and if they do eat it, they'll get sick. That's what management's afraid of," Jeff added. "They probably have a point, considering the mental status of some of the residents."

"True," I said. "I was at the front desk the other day getting one of my nursing magazine articles copied to give to Amanda Murray when the phone rang. The receptionist answered and said, 'No, Mrs. Jenkins. This is Friday. No, it isn't Tuesday. That's right. It's Friday.' And then another time I was there signing up for the Symposium and a resident came along and told the receptionist she had a doctor's appointment the next day and didn't know how she'd get there. The receptionist said, 'You have to call transportation, Mrs. Howorth.'

"'But I never did this before. I should call transportation?'

"'Yes, Mrs. Howorth,' the receptionist said. 'Go back to your apartment and call transportation. The number is 456-1121. It's in the Sandycreek Terrace telephone directory. Call that number just like you did the last time they drove you to your doctor's appointment. Tell them the day and time of your appointment and your doctor's address, Mrs. Howorth. Transportation will ask you for all that information.'

The poor resident continued to stand there looking bewildered and then left.

"The receptionists do a great job. They're very nice and helpful to all the residents and very patient with the confused residents," Jeff said.

"There's probably another reason management doesn't want residents taking food home from the dining room," I said. "The appearance. The ambiance. Aristocrats don't carry doggy boxes out of a fine dining room. That's a fact. Management tries to keep up appearances." That said, we pushed back our chairs and left the kitchenette.

Kasey had phoned to ask if he might come and visit again. During his last visit, he'd commented on how much he enjoyed Dr. Tom Price and former Steeler star, Leo Badalato. "I like your residents. Dr. Price and Leo Badalato are neat guys. I have fun with them in the exercise room," he'd said.

For that reason, I'd decided to ask both residents to have dinner with us the next time Kasey came to visit, thinking the conversation would no doubt center around medicine and the importance of exercising. I'd phoned Tom first and he regretfully had another engagement, so I didn't phone Leo. I just let the idea drop.

Now Kasey was up from Davies, from Nova University for the weekend. Jeff said to his grandson standing in the living room in a sleeveless tee shirt and shorts, "I know you have studying to do for your medical courses, Kasey. Time for mid-term exams, isn't it? But before you get to that we have two tasks for you."

"Sure. What are they?" he said without hesitating, all the while running his fingers through his short blond hair standing straight up from the roots due to some goo he'd applied.

Jeff said, "First of all, this answering machine doesn't work. The light hasn't been on for over a week. The other is the TV. Hasn't worked since we got back from our ventures in Disney World. We had John of John and Matt, the maintenance men, take a look at it, but he couldn't make it work. Housekeeping was here for our yearly cleaning in our absence. We thought they'd done something to cause it to malfunction. Pulled a plug and put it in a wrong socket, maybe. But John said no."

Kasey stood listening, flexing his wrestling muscles, his short figure erect. His eyes were as blue as his grandfather's.

"Kasey," Jeff continued, "You fixed the TV the last time after John could do nothing. Put your magic to work again."

Kasey smiled. "I'll tackle the answering machine first." He lifted the powerless answering machine from the kitchen counter top. Then he looked at the free-standing electrical outlet where the answering machine cord had been plugged. After he unplugged the answering machine, he asked for a plug from an appliance.

Jeff picked up the waffle iron cord. "Here, try this plug."

"No power with this plug either," Kasey said. Then he pushed the red button on the wall outlet and inserted the answering machine plug again. "It's fixed," he said, grinning.

"By God!" Jeff said. "Is that all it took? How stupid can I be! I never thought to look at the wall outlet, at the red button. Didn't see it was popped out. Probably due to moisture of some kind. I must be getting old."

"No you're not getting old! I won't let you!" I told him.

"O. K. Now on to the television," Jeff prodded his grandson.

Kasey walked over to the TV in the Florida room, removed the plug from the wall and replaced it. Nothing happened. He reached behind the TV set, took the plug from the back of the set and reinserted it. Nothing. He shrugged. "That's what I did the last time. Worked then. Isn't working this time. I'm afraid it's the TV, Grandpa."

I suddenly came alive. "Didn't Frank's TV repair shop give us a warranty when they fixed it? A year's warranty? How long ago was that? When did we get it repaired?"

Jeff scratched his head. "I can't remember. I told you I'm getting so I can't remember things."

I went to the drawer where we kept papers that came with newly purchased appliances. With multiple papers and pamphlets in my lap, I leafed through them. "Here it is! I found it! I think I see the word warranty." I handed the pamphlet to Jeff to read.

"Ninety day warranty. The date of repair was October fifteen. What's today's date?"

"It's January thirteenth. The warranty's still good!" I answered, excited. "Is Frank's phone number on that sheet? Maybe we should call right away. The warranty probably runs out today."

Jeff picked up the phone and dialed. He listened and then gave our phone number to the recorded voice. "We'll have to wait until they call back."

Since I was putting clothes from the washer into the dryer, Jeff answered the phone when it rang the next morning. When he hung up he told me, "The repair man says our set's too old to bother fixing. Says it would be cheaper to buy a new one. Says if we shop around we can find a new one like ours for very little money. They don't sell TVs any more. Just repair them. He gave me names of places he recommends. I wrote them down."

On Monday, we bought a new television set. We didn't go to any of the stores Frank's repair man mentioned. Instead, in the morning paper, Jeff saw an ad by Jetson Appliances and apparently liked the information he read about televisions because that's where we went. As we entered the Jetson Appliance store we were surrounded by TVs everywhere we looked. A salesman approached us saying, "My name's Freddy. What can I show you?" Freddy was young, small in stature, and had a very pleasant voice.

"We're the Metz's, and we're in the market for a television, one with a large screen. My wife needs a large screen because of her vision. Show us what you have," Jeff said.

"Certainly, Mr. Metz. We have three models over here." Freddy led us to a front section of the store and stopped in front of one model. "This is a Sony. Forty-five inch screen. Has the controls underneath. It's a plasma model. And over on this wall..." His voice trailed back to us as he walked. "Is a Toshiba with controls along the side. Same width screen and also plasma. Both have non-glare screens."

We were stopped in front of the sets looking at them, and Jeff said, "Hold on. You're going to have to explain these features to me. I'm on the learning curve. Not in this business like you are."

"Yes, indeed, Mr. Metz. Plasma means the set is flat-paneled, allowing the TV to be wall-mounted or placed on a stand close to a wall. No tubes in plasma television sets. Electrified gas is used to produce the picture. A special treatment protects the screen from glare. The controls underneath give you a set that doesn't take up so much width-wise space in a room, if that's a feature you like. Either of these can be wall mounted."

From the smile on Jeff's face, I realized that feature appealed to him. "How much do these run?" he asked. "Costs an arm and a leg, I guess."

I held my breath, expecting the worst, and heard, "Three thousand ninety-eight. Actually, the Toshiba has been a floor model for a year."

"You mean it's been playing for a year sitting here on this spot?" Jeff inquired.

"That's correct." Freddy paused, coughed, then said, "So you can have it for a thousand less than the marked price."

"That's a good deal. If it's been playing for a year it must be a good set. Playing for a year and nothing went wrong. It's been tested." Jeff smiled and looked at me for agreement.

I was giving this some thought and had to say, "I don't think that's so good. It has a year less life than a new one. And the dials on the side make it bigger in width. Our Florida room is small to begin with."

Jeff frowned. "I still think it's a good deal. It's been tested."

Was Jeff comparing a TV with a car? He never bought a new car. Said year-old cars were road-tested. Freddy looked from Jeff to me and then said, "Let me show you this one." He headed toward the window and turned to point to a set on a stand. "This is our newest model. A Toshiba. Capable of being wall mounted or placed on a stand as it's shown here. Controls underneath and larger screen. Comes with stand." Again he looked from Jeff to me.

Jeff said, "And how much for this one?" He turned to me and said, "We better make up our minds soon. I can't stand much longer. Have to sit down."

"What about the glare feature?" I asked.

"It's non-glare. Just a minute," Freddy said and left to go to the desk in the center of the store. He was back in a few minutes. "You can have this one for three thousand twenty."

"Let's take it. I can't stand any longer," Jeff said.

As we walked to the desk to handle the paper-work I said, "Jeff, don't you want to go to any other TV store?"

"No, I've done enough shopping for today."

I knew his back must be paining more than usual. I was happy with the set we were buying. Then, too, with the new furniture arrangement we'd planned for the Florida room, this TV would work in just fine.

About three months ago, management had hired a new assistant administrator for Park Place to replace the former administrator, he being transferred to a facility in Durham, North Carolina, to become their Executive Director. As the Executive Director was orienting and rounding with Barbara Donnelly, the newly hired assistant administrator, he stopped when he saw me in the Club House. He smiled at me and then looked at Barbara. "Barbara, I'd like you to meet Mrs. Metz, a resident who's had lots of experience with nursing homes. Mrs. Metz has been a director of nursing of several large nursing homes and a state and federal surveyor of long-term care facilities."

Barbara gave me a broad smile, and I said, "I'm pleased to meet you." We shook hands.

That introduction by the Executive Director made me feel super good. Old as I was, I still liked praise. I guess one never outgrew the desire to be recognized for something significant, small as it may be. At any rate, at our Health Care Committee meetings that Barbara Donnelly now attended I noticed she addressed much of her report to me. I, in turn, felt free to add to her comments and ask questions, even anticipating her answers. I assumed she realized our conversation educated the committee members since none of the members had much knowledge of the healthcare field. The female members had been school teachers, stay-at-home moms, or secretaries. The two male committee members, one being the chairman, had held important positions in the business world, unrelated to the health field. I enjoyed the committee meetings, especially my contact with Dr. Tom Price and our short conversations, sometimes about new federal regulations for nursing homes, Medicare changes, and the cost of the new drugs Pfizer and Merck were marketing.

THIRTY-EIGHT
WALKS

When I awoke and went into the master bathroom each morning, I immediately pushed the button on the wall above the flashing red light that, through some electrical system, told security residents in our apartment were all right. As I had explained to Kirk, all residents were expected to follow the procedure of turning off the red light before eleven in the morning. If not deactivated by eleven, security would have concern and, having a master key, would come to the residence to check the status of the resident or residents. Therefore I purposely pushed the red button first thing every morning.

One morning at eleven I heard a knock at the door of our apartment. Before I had time to answer, the door opened. "Oh pardon me, Mrs. Metz," the man in a security uniform said. "You didn't turn off your light, and I came to see if you were in trouble."

Surprised, I quickly said, "We're fine. But I was sure I turned off the red light."

"Maybe you did," he said backing out the door. "Sometimes the system malfunctions. Sorry to bother you." And he was gone. But I was left trying to remember, to reconstruct my activities that morning. I was convinced I hadn't forgotten to turn off the light, wasn't getting incompetent or senile.

The employee from security had no sooner left than the phone rang. I answered and heard Tom Price announce his name and then say, "The very next time your grandson comes to visit, I'll be available to have dinner with you. I was sorry I couldn't join you the night you asked me to join you for dinner. But I'm looking forward to eating with you and your grandson. So just let me know when he's planning another visit."

"I'll do that, Tom," I said, glad he had called, solidifying our continuing friendship.

Faithfully every morning Jeff and I exercised, using a set of illustrated exercises we'd obtained from our former physician, the doctor who examined me in the emergency department when I sustained that TIA in July. He was the physician I feared would give me a hard time when he realized I was the patient who forsook him for another MD. But, as it turned out, even though he recognized me, he was exceptionally nice and was thorough with his physical examination.

Those exercises he gave us took approximately twenty minutes. Probably for this reason we didn't attend exercise classes given by Sandycreek Terrace's professional trainer, the Health and Wellness Coordinator. We figured we were doing well with our own exercises. In time we might attend those classes. Not the mild Sit and Be Fit program, but other more strenuous strengthening exercises. Right now we couldn't find time to get involved what with our writing, shopping, going to professional appointments and meetings on and off campus, our family visits, and personal business responsibilities. We and other residents often said, "How did we ever find time to work?" I believed others said this because they were busy attending many of the activities provided in Sandycreek Terrace. They weren't exercising on their own or writing, as we were, of that I was certain. Many residents didn't even own computers.

My walk and Jeff's bike ride before breakfast also afforded us exercise. I always took a walk unless it was raining, which was seldom, and unless it was a Sunday we went to church. Jeff encouraged me to walk every morning. "Good for you. Wish I could walk with you. But I ride my bike."

"You do," I said. "I never learned to ride a bike, you know. I've told you how my father would never allow me to have a bike because we lived on a busy boulevard. No place to ride a bike." I'd watched Jeff ride his two-wheeled bike and found it amazing how effortlessly he rode it and yet how painful it was for him to walk. I'd gotten accustomed to seeing him with a cane although at first I didn't want to believe it was a necessity. He'd hold it in his right hand and often took my right hand in his left. Never did he use it in the apartment.

The Rascal, his scooter, affected me differently. It didn't seem like a crutch, an assist, but rather a toy he enjoyed riding almost as fast as it would go. Five miles an hour, that is. As he rode over to the Club House for dinner ahead of me, I feared he scared poor little old ladies walking with canes and walkers along the corridor in the opposite direction, having had their dinners. At length, residents became accustomed to seeing him approach and were prepared for his advancing vehicle. After he passed them they'd smile and say to me as I followed on foot, "He's way ahead of you!"

To get back to the subject of my walks, I really enjoyed them in the mornings before the sun blinded me and before the humidity made it difficult to breathe. Even then, some mornings my hands felt damp from the mounting moisture in the air. Usually those mornings the air was still; other mornings a breeze fanned my face and rustled the palm fronds. The weather didn't seem to affect the birds. Hot or cool, perched on trees they chirped lively and then flew overhead into the distance.

I'd start my walk at the circle in front of our building and walk out onto the road where I'd pass six cottages, walk on down to the guard house, and pass two more cottages. That, I figured, was half a mile. So I'd turn around and retrace my steps. Usually I talked to God as I walked along. Some days I thanked Him for all my many blessings, naming them one by one. Other days I lumped them all together under one main heading and then went on to other thoughts such as an e-mail I intended to send to my granddaughter, an article I planned to write, and my concern about Jeff's increasing back pain.

Several residents would be walking their dogs on leashes. All dogs seemed to be fuzzy-haired and all were small as mandated by management's imposed twenty-five pound weight-limit. All were, that is, except Angel, a golden retriever. When her owner entered Sandycreek Terrace she was permitted to bring Angel because she was a trained therapy dog. Once a week, the owner took Angel over to the Health Center where the residents were enamored by the gentle friendly dog that talked to them and offered her paw.

I'd usually always pass Doris Jordan and her little white-haired schnauzer. Probably a great companion since Donald's death. Two male residents walked their little white-haired dogs, and both dogs wanted my attention, yipped and barked and strained at their leashes trying to get close to me. I'd often pass Raymond and Victoria Watson with their little well-behaved black-haired dog walking in step with its owners. Although Jeff and I both had had dogs as part of the family when raising our children, we said we'd never want the work involved in being dog-owners now at our age. For some elderly people pets were practically necessary companions, I realized.

During my walks, a few maintenance men would be riding around the premises or going to their work sites in modified golf carts. They'd pass me and wave and say good morning, and I'd return the waves and the good mornings. A golf cart slowed down as it passed me one morning. The driver, apparently having noticed I made a U-turn, called out, "Why don't you walk all the way around?"

"Because I don't want to be late for breakfast," I called back.

He laughed but I wasn't joking. I was giving him the real reason. Jeff knew how long my walk took and would have breakfast ready for us at the exact time I returned.

When I passed the last two cottages I often wondered about the residents who lived in the second cottage. Usually a different car was parked in the driveway in front of their garage. Some mornings a red sedan, then a black van, then a white sedan, and then a small white truck. Did the inhabitants give each vehicle a turn inside the garage?

When I returned home from my walk one morning I posed this dilemma to Jeff. "Jeff," I started. "Why does this one cottage I pass every morning have a different car parked in its driveway so often? The residents must own a lot of cars. Do you suppose they alternate cars and give each a turn in the garage?" Of course I was joking, but I was curious about the many cars. I waited for him to consider this situation.

He looked at me, forced his blue eyes wide open and elevated his eyebrows, as he sometimes did, and said very casually, "The cars probably belong to different caregivers."

Well of course. Why hadn't I thought of that? Many residents had caregivers, some twenty-four seven. The female resident at the end of our corridor had caregivers around the clock every day of the week.

My walks were also enjoyable because, in several areas on either side of the road, I could hear water running and splashing. I'd glance over and grab a quick view of a broad band of crystal water sparkling in the sun. It splashed down over steps of gray rock, and plummeted into a pond of moving darkness. Clusters of yellow flowers of various shades bordered its banks. Some days, traffic slowed my pace when I reached the guard house where a green hedge topped with blue flowers separated the lanes for in-coming and out-going vehicles. In a pond on the other side of the guard house near several cottages, I could see a seven-foot-high fountain constantly spouting sprays of whispering water into the air.

Back at the entrance to our building, I'd again pass the pond we always saw on the way to our car parked in a handicapped spot near the circle. This pond was a sight to lift my spirits. I'd stand close by and watch the silver streams of water flow over elevated granite-colored chunks of rock and cascade downward into the pool below. The panorama was enhanced by scarlet sage, water lilies, and low-growing green plants nestled in the earth around it.

Ray Watson came walking toward me one morning on the way to his car as I was gazing at the pond. "I'm admiring the pond," I said, explaining my reason for standing there.

He stopped by my side. "Used to be fish in there. In all the ponds on the premises. Management stocked the ponds with small fish. They were interesting to watch. Residents enjoyed them."

"What happened to the fish?" I wanted to know, having never seen a fish in that pond.

"No sooner were fish enjoying the ponds and residents enjoying the fish than snowy egrets were enjoying both the ponds and the fish. Thus ended the stocking procedure."

"What a shame!" was all I could muster, as the tall, handsome, stately resident walked on. He'd made an excellent president of the Resident Council during his term of office, now replaced by intelligent Tom Price. I'd noticed that Ray's wife, Victoria, seemed to be adjusting to her near-blindness as she was usually walking unaccompanied by Ray lately. I marveled at her determination to be independent.

Some mornings the weather was downright chilly, sometimes hot like the Sahara desert, other times quite pleasant. I listened to the radio's weather report while exercising and dressed accordingly for walking outdoors. I especially liked to walk the mornings the sun was just rising, and patchy white clouds blocked most of its rays, allowing a few to shine through. Other mornings, I'd look up at a blanket of blue, and then just below the blue I'd see a broad curtain of slowly-moving white puffy clouds penetrated intermittently by splashes of apricot radiating from the sun like a ball of fire rising behind. I'd stop and stare, beholding an unbelievable scene. An artist's dream!

Because of my morning walks, I also learned Mondays, Wednesdays, and Fridays were trash pick-up days for cottages. Those days, garbage cans sat at the end of garage driveways.

Our building had a trash room around the corner from the Greek fountain and the mail boxes. Inside the trash room stood eight large dark-green containers on wheels. Three containers on the right were designated for newspapers and other paper throwaways. On the left, two containers were intended for bagged garbage, one for plastic products, and two for empty cans and glass bottles. Unfortunately, not all residents or maids who disposed of items in the trash room adhered to the rules of what to throw where. At times, I'd see an improper distribution when I'd thrown away *our* trash. Then too, someone or ones of origin unknown to me did not break down cardboard boxes as instructed but rather placed large and small boxes on the floor by the paper-intended container closest to the door. Also on the floor appeared other objects such as metal brackets, closet shelving, and crocks with dead poinsettias.

One day I had quite a shock. I'd really never noticed the chutes positioned above the containers intended for bagged garbage. I always kept my eyes focused on where I was walking. But this particular day as I was leaving the trash room and walking past one of the containers meant for bagged garbage, down from above through the air flew a bag of garbage right past my head. With a loud bang it crashed into the container at my side. Nearly sent me off my pins! I screamed! Then I looked up and saw a chute and realized a second floor resident had just disposed of a bag of garbage.

Since the other containers didn't have overhead chutes, I decided to find out how second floor residents disposed of newspapers, plastics, cans, and glass bottles. On the second floor I found a trash room. It appeared quite large inside due to the absence of garbage containers. It had, however, more odds and ends of throwaways littering the floor. So much for my education of trash rooms.

Even with my exercising and walking, I realized my balance was still poor. It concerned me greatly. I talked to Jeff about it. "Jeff, when I get out of our car to go into a store, or anywhere, and a curb or a ramp confronts me, I just can't walk ahead normally. I have to hold onto something to negotiate the curb or ramp. A nearby pole, bush, or hood of a car. Or I wait for you to take my hand. Have you noticed? Well, I'm sure you have. I hate this! It isn't the independence I used to have. I've become an old lady trying to ambulate normally. I hate it!"

"That's the way it is. That's where we are in this life. We're not young any more. We have to admit it. We're not going to improve. But part of it's your vision, Honey," he tried to console me.

I decided I'd start to go over to the exercise room late in the afternoon when I thought no one would be using the bar. I'd practice the balancing routine the physical therapist had taught me after I'd completed eight weeks of P.T. to improve my balance. Therefore, about three times a week late in the afternoon I went to the exercise room located in the Club House. Sometimes one or two male residents were there using stationary bikes, tread mills, strengthening machines, rubber balls, weights of varying sizes, or other strengthening equipment. Often Ralph Wilson wearing a terry towel around his neck was working out on a stationary bike. We spoke, he coughing and asking how I was, and continuing to exercise his legs. Sometimes a guest of a resident, a young person like Kasey, came in to work out. The intensified noise was noticeable when the younger generation worked-out on the treadmill, bicycle, or strengthening machine.

A number of days Elaine and Leslie Smith entered the exercise room shortly after I did. I hadn't met them until New Year's Eve when we sat at the same table. With that little contact, I didn't feel I really knew them. Elaine was a titch too heavy, in my opinion. Her short hair stood up in spikes like on the head of a teenaged boy, and she wore a short coverall over her skirted bathing suit. Always she led Leslie across the room to a stationary bike. I'd hear her say, "Let me lower this for you. Someone taller than you used this bike last. Now see how that is."

Slowly Leslie would get a leg over the seat and sit down. "Now put your feet up on the pedals, Honey. How is that? Are you going to be all right?" she'd ask. As she'd start to walk away, she'd say, "I'm going out to the pool and swim a few laps. Your cane is here on the bar, Honey. Right behind you." She'd always repeat these instructions and point to the cane. "Don't forget your jacket. It's there on the bench." She'd point to the jacket. "I'll be back shortly."

He'd nod. She'd open the glass door leading to the pool some forty feet directly ahead and leave.

Each day at the bar I performed leg-stretching and balancing exercises and walked length upon length of the bar, toe touching heel, heel touching toe, while Leslie rode the stationary bike. Always, after about fifteen minutes, Elaine, now out of the pool and her blue printed bathing suit sagging and dripping wet, would open the glass door, lean in, and say to Leslie, "I'm going into the hot tub for a few minutes, Honey. Your cane's on the bar, and your jacket's on the bench. If you get off the bike, be careful. Move slowly."

I was truly impressed with the care Elaine provided Leslie, going through the same routine every day they came to the exercise room. What a devoted wife she was! I made a mental note to tell her so, to tell her how impressed I was. I'd do that the next time I saw her alone.

One day, in a matter of minutes after Elaine put Leslie on the bike and left to go to the pool, he dismounted, made his way over to a window, and stood there looking out toward the pool. When Elaine opened the door again, Leslie walked toward her with an unsteady gait. "Your cane, Honey. You forgot your cane. It's back there hanging on the bar. And your jacket. It's still on the bench," Elaine told Leslie.

I knew she didn't want to come in, dripping pool water on the carpeted floor, so I quickly retrieved the cane while Leslie was saying, "I can't see it."

I handed the cane to Leslie, went to the bench, picked up the jacket, and handed it to Elaine.

"Thanks so much. I really appreciate it, Jean," she said, standing there dripping wet and holding the door open for Leslie.

"No problem. Think nothing of it. Glad to do it," I said and went back to my toe to heel bar walking. Maybe I *could* do some good here, small as it might be. Before I left, I took the opportunity to weigh myself and was pleased with maintaining one-hundred-ten pounds. Then I picked up the clip board with the attached sign-in sign-out sheet and documented the requested information. This record indicated time spent by residents in the exercise room and validated expenditures for new equipment or repair of existing stock.

On the way home from exercising, I saw a woman approaching in the distance. I moved to the right side of the corridor to allow her to pass when she got closer. She moved to her left. I moved to my left to make room again for us to pass. She moved to her right. When we were a few feet apart she moved to the middle of the corridor and stopped. At this point I had to stop, too, as she was blocking further advancement on my part.

"I'm lost!" she exclaimed, frowning, her eyes darting about. "Which way is it to the Palace?"

"You're going in the right direction. Just keep on walking until you come to a corridor that goes to the right. Take that right and you'll be along side the Palace." She hesitated, seemed not to understand my directions. "Would you like me to go with you?" I asked.

"No, no. Thank you. Maybe I'll learn my way around here. I just came two days ago. Thank you very much. I'll be fine."

Two days after I arrived at Sandycreek Terrace I surely would have been going in the wrong direction, as confusing as this place was for me then. And I would gladly have accepted an offer such as mine. Now I was fully acclimated to our building and knew most of the residents who lived in the apartments I was passing. The wreaths on doors rarely changed. Nor did the artifacts placed on walks near the doors—a flowering plant in a crock, a ceramic dog, a painted Dutch bench, an umbrella stand holding different colored umbrellas.

I enjoyed looking at the courtyards between the apartments where low-growing anthurium with red flowers were planted and the white petals of taller lily plants opened during the day. Palm trees in each courtyard were various heights—Sabal Palms head-high and tall Chinese

Frond Palms reaching up and beyond the railings of second floor apartments.

In the evening when I walked back from the dining room lights shone in some apartments; others were dark. The apartment belonging to the deaf resident with the black Scotty dog was well lighted although I didn't see any movement inside. Never have I seen any resident through any of the apartment windows. Must be the way the rooms were configured or the lighting arranged. The ninety-six year old resident we drove home from the ophthalmology office must have gone to early dinner. Her apartment was dark. She'd been terribly frightened at the prospect of having eye surgery and then had learned her condition was inoperable, according to the glaucoma specialist. She hadn't been convinced and was going to seek another opinion.

I was now past the mail boxes and Grecian fountain rounding the corner and passing Jefferson's apartment. Again Frances Jefferson had changed the costume on their white goose ever-standing to the right of their apartment door. In December it was dressed like Santa Claus; for New Year's Eve, a black bow tie and black top hat were its adornment. Now it was wearing a blue and white checkered gingham cap and matching shorts, a tiny golf bag over its shoulder. In its cloth hands I saw a plastic golf ball. How clever!

Inside our apartment, Jeff said to me, "I saw Lynn this morning. He's resigning."

"Lynn? The employee who cleans the corridors and area around the pool? You mean he's leaving his job here? Why is that? I thought he liked working here." I'd seen him several times but never had a conversation with him. Just said hello. I knew Jeff had talked with him a number of times.

"Right. That's Lynn. He cleaned many areas besides corridors and the pool area. He's leaving because he says he has too many bosses here."

"What's he mean, too many bosses? He has only one, doesn't he? His only boss would be the Maintenance Supervisor. Isn't that right?" I didn't understand.

Jeff laughed. "The bosses he means are female residents. He claims too many of them are telling him what to do. Blaming him for not sweeping the walks in front of their apartments and leaving leaves on corridors where they have to walk with their canes. A risk, they say." Jeff laughed again. "Says he's going back to laying bricks. Bricks don't give him any lip."

"For heavens sakes," I said, laughing, too.

THIRTY-NINE
VALENTINE

As we sat in the lounge talking to Kathy and Carl Franklin, Kathy said, "I don't think we're going to be able to eat much dinner."

"Why is that?" Jeff asked, sipping on his Manhattan and chewing on a cashew he'd plucked from the bowl of nuts on the little table around which we four were seated.

"We went to our favorite ice cream parlor this afternoon. They serve the most delicious ice cream. We each had four different flavors. I like chocolate marshmallow with chocolate chips best, and Carl likes butter pecan over all the others," Kathy said, smiling and licking her lips.

I looked from Kathy to Carl sitting there grinning and nodding. He looked so well groomed in his suit, white shirt, and striped tie. "That sounds like fun. We should go there some day, Jeff," I said, turning toward him.

"We'll have to do that. Where is this ice cream parlor?" he asked, glancing across the table at the friendly couple.

"Next to Jetty's. Have you ever been to that restaurant? The ice cream parlor's right next to Jetty's."

Jeff nodded, and then Kathy said, "Tomorrow we're going on a cruise."

"Really?" I said. "Is it the cruise Janet planned for the residents? I've heard some of the residents talking about going on a two-week cruise to the Bahamas."

"No," Kathy said. "We like to go alone. That is, not with others from here. We'll be gone for just one week."

With that, a hostess approached and told the Franklins their table in the dining room was ready. I said to Jeff, "I think it's nice the Franklins are going on a cruise, don't you? It's the kind of a vacation Kathy can enjoy as well as Carl because caring for Carl on a ship will be easy, not like responsibilities she'd have at a resort or on a tour. He's not that confused yet. He'll follow her leads."

In a CCRC the size of Sandycreek Terrace with a varying census of approximately two-hundred-and-sixty residents, word of residents' illnesses, accidents, and admissions to hospitals and Park Place filtered through the facility like water seeping through Maxwell blend in a Mr. Coffee. In no time at all, most of the residents heard the news. One week after the Franklins returned from their cruise, Carl Franklin had been in the hospital for a five-day stay and was now in Park Place with a diagnosis of a second CVA.

Kathy, having gone to early dinner, was leaving the dining room one evening when we were entering. We stopped her to ask about Carl. "I'm going over to Park Place now to be with him while he gets fed through a tube." She pointed to her chest. "I do this every night," she said without her usual smile as she left us.

"What a shame. To have that happen to such nice people," I said to Jeff.

"That's the way it goes," he answered. "If you don't laugh, you'll cry."

On the fifteenth of January, sign-up sheets for the Valentine party appeared on the counter top of the receptionist desk in the lobby. Jeff and I decided to act early-on and form a table. In the lounge, I spied Jim and Jane Horner. We hadn't seen them for a considerable length of time, and I wondered about Jim's kidney problem and its status and if the cancer could possibly be in remission. Of course I would not bring up the subject. I walked over to them and asked if they'd like to join us at a table for the Valentine party.

"Yes, indeed," Jane quickly said. "That would be very nice."

"Sign-up sheets are already at the receptionist desk. I'll sign for both of us and invite another couple. Have you any suggestions?" I asked.

Jim was listening and smiling but letting Jane do the talking. She said, "I don't believe so. Anyone you care to include will be fine with us. Just don't get too many people. It's hard to talk when too many people are seated around one table."

"True," I said, and we went our separate ways. I followed Jane and Jim with my eyes and, as before, wondered how those two people happened to match up, he so short and thin and she almost taller and heavy. While he was a physician and they'd lived in Boston, what her career had been, if she had a career, I had yet to learn. Since I'd been in the working world many years, I found it difficult to get accustomed to the fact that many women here had never needed to have a career.

After we'd signed for the party, had dinner, and were home, I said to Jeff, "Who else should we ask to join our table for the Valentine party? I was thinking of Tom Price and Irene Trenton. Because Jim Horner and Tom are both physicians."

Jeff shook his head. "Irene told me the other day she's trying not to be paired up with Tom very much."

I responded to Jeff's raised eyebrows with, "I suppose Irene *does* have a point, being seen with Tom so much when his wife's in Park Place. Still, they seem to enjoy each other. Her first husband was a physician. That gives them something in common, I suppose. What career did her second husband have, do you know?"

"A contractor, I believe," Jeff said. "Why not invite the Jeffersons? They're fairly new, and they just moved into our building practically next door. I guess the first apartment they had for a few months didn't suit them. Frances is vivacious and bubbly even if her husband, Harold, *is* still trying to decide whether or not he's going to stay here. When I ask him how he is he always says, 'I'm still here.' Moving into a different apartment hasn't seemed to improve his attitude toward this establishment."

"But *she's* happy here," I said. "She told me the other apartment didn't have a view. This one's larger and nicer. Maybe Harold will come around." I could understand Harold's feelings. I still wasn't sold on being here. Just takes time. Lots of time.

"All right, I'll give them a call. Might as well do that right now while I'm thinking about it." I reached for the Sandycreek Terrace telephone directory and the phone.

Frances answered, listened to my spiel, and happily said, "Oh is there going to be a Valentine's Day party? I didn't know that. Yes, we'd love to join your table. Thanks for asking us."

I told her, "There's a party every month, Frances. Next month, St. Patrick's Day."

After we hung up I said to Jeff, "She says they'll be happy to join us. She didn't consult her husband. I don't know if he'll be happy or not but I'm sure she'll drag him along. He dresses rather conservatively. She often wears clothes like we wore in the sixties. Short dresses and skirts above her knees, sleeveless and bare-necked when everyone else is wearing a jacket and slacks. She's so tiny she can get away with it. Have you noticed how she swings her hips, almost dances when she walks?"

"No, I can't say that I've ever noticed," was Jeff's vague response.

I was surprised observant Jeff hadn't noticed when it was so obvious to me. She reminded me of a ballerina twirling on the lid of a music box. I dismissed the subject and said, "I think I'll invite Harry Scott, too. He's a nice sociable man and lonely without a wife. He has some medical background, and he and Jim Horner may enjoy conversing about that subject. Harry can choose his own partner. I'll tell him I'll add his name to our table on the sign-up sheet and after his name I'll write the word *guest*. Then he can decide whom he wants to bring. Sarah Grant, or Lottie Yurasik, or someone else. I'm not going to get tangled up deciding between those two women both running after him. I'm no match maker." I hummed a few bars of *Match Maker, Match Maker, Make Me a Match*.

"Good thought," Jeff said, winking at me with his baby blue eyes.

I still remembered the Hawaiian woman who'd joined Jeff and me as we were sitting on a picnic bench in a park near a lake on the Big Island of Hawaii. We'd talked to the native woman a bit, and then she'd stared at Jeff and said, "You have baby blue eyes!" So every once in a while I got a kick out of calling Jeff *baby blue eyes*.

Harry Scott and I talked on the phone quite a while when I phoned him. We'd talked a number of times before when his wife was in Park Place and after she died. He hadn't been pleased with the care she'd received in the skilled care unit. Now on the phone, he moaned, "I'm just recovering from a head cold, and I'm feeling down in the dumps. Things aren't going the way I'd like them to. Always something to knock me down. Last week I got rid of Bonnie's clothes. That was a hard thing to do." His voice cracked, and he started to cry.

"Oh Harry, I know how you feel. You and Bonnie had a good life together. It takes time. It takes time. I know." I tried to console him, and when he started talking in a clear voice again I said, "Would you like to join our table for the Valentine party? It's dinner, music, and a show. On the day itself. February fourteenth."

"Yes, I'd like that. February fourteenth, you say. What time?"

"Five o'clock cocktails. I'll sign your name on the sign-up list for our table. I'll write guest below your name, and you can fill in that space to your liking. How will that be?"

"Fine. That will be just fine. Thanks a lot, Jeanie."

I hung up and turned to Jeff. "Harry will be at our table. He seemed happy I called. But he's really sad. Still grieving for his wife. Said he just gave away her clothes."

"That's a hard thing to do," Jeff said. "Is he going to fill in a name where we write *guest*?"

"Yes, he is," I said. Or so I thought.

Wouldn't you know a week later Harry phoned. "Jeanie," he said. "Will you do me a big big favor?"

"Of course, Harry," I answered quickly.

"Oh, thank you so much. Will you write in a name for my guest? You understand why, don't you?"

I couldn't keep from giggling. Obviously he didn't want to write in either Sarah or Lottie's name, the name of either pursuing woman.

"Yes, I believe I do understand, Harry", I said.

"I don't care who it is. Just not either of those two. You know what I mean. Anyone else and I don't want to know who she is."

Before we hung up, I told him, "This will be fun for me, Harry." But actually it was not fun. I had my mind set on Diann Caldwell. This tall thin young-looking gal with short brown hair had first caught my eye at the bar one evening shortly after she moved in. She'd introduced herself as Diann, a name I wouldn't forget since my favorite secretary had had that name. Another encounter I had with Diann was on a Saturday afternoon when a number of us residents, Diann included, were viewing a movie in the card room before dinner. A technical difficulty with the CD was taking a long time to be corrected, and when Jeff and I decided to have a drink while we waited for the correction, I went to the bar to order our cocktails. Diann had followed me, signed for her own drink and insisted on signing for our drinks as well. She'd also carried Jeff's drink back to the card room. Probably in her early seventies, she was more capable of carrying two full drinks than I was, and I appreciated her kindness. A former architect, she'd made herself right at home at Sandycreek Terrace. In fact, she was now on Jeff's HMS Committee reporting on building and ground issues as only an architect would be able to detect. She'd started a Needlers' Club which I attended one time thinking I could knit an afghan as I had years ago. Such was not the case. Try as I might, I couldn't see to put a knitting needle behind a cast-on stitch, loop yarn from the ball of yarn around the needle, draw it through the cast-on stitch, and remove the cast-on stitch. So I stopped going to the meetings. All in all, I decided Diann was a great match for Harry.

I phoned Diann as soon as I hung up from talking with Harry. Since she didn't answer, I left a message on her answering machine asking her to return my call as soon as she came home.

She called back the next morning saying, "Sorry I didn't call as soon as I returned. It was eleven o'clock, and I didn't think you'd appreciate a call that hour of the night. I was down in West Palm at the theater to see *Guys and Dolls*."

How nice to be out that late away from Sandycreek Terrace seeing a great show! That's what I thought, but I said, "I called to ask you to join our table for the Valentine's party."

"I'd love to, but I'm already signed up with friends at another table."

So much for my well-laid plans! Now what would I do? I couldn't think of anyone else who would fit the bill.

It so happened that two evenings later Jeff and I were sitting at a dining room table with Gloria Semple, a resident we knew from church, her out-of-town male guest, and two female residents we didn't know. Gloria had arranged the table three weeks ago, inviting us by phone and then last week via a hand-written reminder-note placed in our in-house mailbox. The out-of-town guest was a Michigan man Gloria had met on a cruise she'd taken before Christmas. She'd come back from the cruise and told many residents, including us, she had a new friend who called her every week from Michigan.

"He'll be visiting me at Sandycreek Terrace. His reason for coming to Florida is probably to play golf rather than to see me," she'd said to us, but her enthusiasm belied her guarded comment. Then several days ago she'd told us, "I'm inviting you to dinner because, Jeff, you came from Michigan and my friend's from Michigan. And Jeanie, we're both Pennsylvanians. I'm inviting two other people who used to live in Michigan, too."

Now a party of six was seated at a table in the rear of the dining room. Gloria introduced her tall well-built white-haired male guest by going around the table saying each of our names in turn. One of the residents from Michigan had the guest's undivided attention.

Jeff was seated to my left, and I started talking to the woman to my right. "What is your name again?" I asked and learned it was Gertrude Campbell. "Just call me Trudy," she said. As we talked and laughed I found her to be very pleasant and congenial.

Meanwhile, the resident seated next to the Michigan guest was telling him of her former life experiences in Michigan, and I heard her say, "I really like people from Michigan!"

Gloria was listening to their conversation and interrupted. "You can't have him! Much as you like people from Michigan, you can't have him." Then she laughed and patted her guest's hand, and we all laughed.

The poor woman's face flushed, and she gasped, "Oh I was referring to Michigan people in general."

"Of course," Gloria said and changed the subject.

When Jeff and I got back to our apartment I swallowed my twice-a-day Preservision with Lutein and Os-cal with D, my after-dinner routine, and said to Jeff, "Gloria's quite taken with that Michigan man and he with her, it seemed."

"So it seemed. Seems like a nice man. She's a very happy woman since she came back from that cruise. That's nice. I'm glad for her. She deserves to have a life after caring for her husband for so many years." Jeff removed his jacket, put it on the back of a dining room chair, sat down, and took off his shoes and socks and shoved them under the chair.

I was accustomed to our dining room serving as a temporary clothes closet where Jeff routinely took off and deposited his uncomfortable apparel as soon as he came home. I figured he had a right to put his clothes where he wanted as long as we weren't expecting company, at which time I'd tidy the house some way or another. I said, "I remember before Gloria's husband died how she would bring him over from Park Place to the club dining room in a wheelchair so they could eat dinner together. That was so kind of her. And I'm quite sure she's the resident who was the subject or problem in the case study we discussed at the Ethics Committee meeting. I suppose she was under great stress when her husband was so ill. She's an entirely different person now. So happy with this new-found friend."

Jeff said, "I know how that can be to have an incompetent confused spouse, believe me. I had ten years of hell. It's no fun. Wears you down. And Gloria's still relatively young. She deserves to have some fun with a partner."

"Still in her seventies, I'm sure. You know, the woman sitting beside me at dinner was very nice. Fun to talk with. Maybe I should invite *her* to be Harry's guest at the Valentine party. What do you think?"

"Sure. Go ahead. Now what about a game of cribbage? You going to beat me again tonight?"

"No, it's your turn to win, and you'll get all the cards. Wait and see." I removed the cribbage board and deck of cards from the dry sink and placed them on the kitchenette table.

"I don't get good cards like you," Jeff joked as he sat down and cut the cards I just shuffled. I picked up my hand and stared at three fives and two kings! Lucky again! Mid-way on third street I was ahead by a whole street. Jeff leaned back in his chair. "Good grief! No sense in my playing! Let's take you to Lost Wages."

I laughed at his favorite name for Las Vegas. Then my luck changed. I got nothing but even cards, twos and fours and sixes, hand after hand. Jeff kept moving his pegs ahead until now he was ten pegs from the end of fourth street. His deal and he had enough to go out!

"See! I told you it was your turn to win. But I was so far ahead! How could this have happened?" I said, pretending to be shocked.

359

Next morning I called Trudy. She said, "I'd love to go! I really wasn't planning on going to the Valentine party, but I'd love to go with you." She sounded as though she really meant it.

"The Horners and the Jeffersons will be at our table and Harry Scott. Eight of us."

"I know the Horners and the Jeffersons. Horners live in my building and the Jeffersons used to live down the hall from me before they moved," Trudy said.

"Harry's a nice man. You'll like him," I assured her before we hung up.

That settled that. But it really didn't. The day after Jeff had erased the word guest and penciled in Trudy's name at our table on the sign-up sheet, he was at the front desk again to give the receptionist his minutes of the HMS Committee meeting to copy and distribute to committee members. While there he just happened to check the sign-up sheet.

I was working on a nursing article at the computer when Jeff walked into the den. He stood there looking at me and frowning. "Are you sure Trudy told you she wanted to sit with us at the Valentine party?" he asked me.

"Yes, of course. She said she'd love to join us. Why? Why do you ask?"

"Because her name is now with a different table."

"And whose name is on the line where you wrote Trudy's name yesterday?" I knew immediately it had to be either Lottie Yurasik's or Sarah Grant's name. One of them had erased Trudy's name and written in her own name in order to sit with Harry, of that I was sure.

"Lottie Yurasik's," he answered in an angry voice. Trudy's name is signed at a different table. "I'm making a call." He opened the Sandycreek Terrace directory, ran a finger down a page, picked up the phone, and dialed. "Trudy," he said, "We invited you to sit at our table for the Valentine party. Do you plan to sit with someone else at a different table?"

I could hear her negative answer and a laugh, but I couldn't hear what she was saying after that.

Jeff hung up and announced, "I'll take care of this! Very little makes me mad. But I am mad now! I'll see to this!" And he left, slamming the apartment door behind him and leaving me wondering what he was going to do.

I was still in the den on the computer when he returned. "Well, what happened?" I asked, swinging my chair around, all ears.

"Janet, the Social Director, was there about to make out the final seating list in bold print. I explained what happened. Harry just happened to be there, too. He said, 'Let it go. Let Lottie's name stay there.' Then Janet said she'd put both Lottie and Trudy at our table. I said, 'No you won't! I don't want Lottie's name filled in at our table. Put her somewhere else. At another table but not at ours!' I meant it, and she knew it! No one can change names after Janet makes out the final sheet in bold print. I'll check it this evening when we go over for dinner. Just to make sure."

As we neared the front desk before dinner, I was as eager as Jeff was to look at the final sign-up sheet. Not being able to see it clearly, I said to Jeff, "Well?"

He turned to me and said, "It's fine. It's the way we want it."

We'd ordered our dinner and were still sipping our cocktails waiting for our salads when Lottie Yurasik came past our table with several other residents. She stopped and leaned forward, "I apologize for what happened," she said. "Janet wrote in my name. I had nothing to do with it. I'm very sorry that happened."

She went on her way to join her group, and I whispered to Jeff, "She's blaming Janet. Janet wouldn't have done that, wouldn't have erased Trudy's name and replaced it with Lottie's." Or would she? Would Janet have moved the names if Lottie had told her both women had decided to change tables? Maybe so.

But Jeff was whispering, "Of course not. Lottie's lying through her teeth." He didn't have to whisper. Lottie was well out of hearing range.

"At least she apologized," I said. But how cagey she was.

A few days later, I bumped into Trudy. I was surprised and concerned. At dinner the night I'd met her I'd only seen her from the side and only in a sitting position. Now I saw she walked with a decided limp and had a heavy matronly figure. Not Harry's type. Nothing like Diann. He'd wonder at my choice. Darn that Diann Caldwell for having a prior arrangement!

The morning of the Valentine party, Jane Horner phoned. "Jim has a terrible cold and harsh cough. We won't be able to go to the party tonight.

I've called the social office and cancelled, but I thought I should call you, too, because you arranged our table."

I lamented, "I'm so sorry. I hope Jim recovers quickly. We'll miss you at the party."

"I just hope I don't contact it," she said and hung up.

At five o'clock, Jeff and I went over to the Palace where all parties were held, Jeff driving his Rascal, I walking. As we entered the party room we ran into Harry and the three of us located our table and found it still unoccupied. I sat between the two men. In short order, Jeff left to get us drinks at the bar set up in the back of the room. I told Harry, "The Horners cancelled because Jim has a bad cold. You know, Harry. I had a perfect partner for you tonight, but when I called her she'd made prior arrangements."

Harry shrugged, leaned close, and said softly, "Do you want to hear something ironic? Lottie Yurasik's in the hospital. She's having her appendix removed tomorrow."

I couldn't believe my ears. "Really?" I exclaimed. "That *is* ironic. But that's not serious. An appendectomy, I mean. They suck them out these days, don't they? They're not major surgeries like they were when I worked in the O.R. in the dark ages." I assumed, because of his medical background, Harry probably still had an interest and kept up with the latest in the medical field.

"She thinks it's her colon even though the doctors have assured her it's definitely her appendix. Nothing else. She wants them to do an exploratory while they're in there. She's certain she has a malignancy and it's metastasizing."

"Is she psychotic?" I asked.

"I don't know. She called me four times today before she went to the hospital. I might leave the party early and go to the hospital."

Just then, the Jeffersons, Trudy, and another couple arrived all at the same time. I was pleased Trudy knew the Jeffersons and the other couple Janet must have added to our table after the Horners cancelled. After a time, Trudy and Harry seemed to converse amiably. We all enjoyed a green salad laced with crab meat, lamb chops, potatoes Anna, snow peas, and an indescribably delicious melt-in-your-mouth chocolate dessert.

The musical show on stage was performed by the same group we enjoyed at the Anniversary party, a group that often performed on cruise ships, we were told. We were all captivated by the music, dancing, singing, and costumes of the six performing artists. Harry stayed the entire time, saying he would go to the hospital in the morning.

FORTY

NEXT

A week and a half later at six-fifteen, our customary time to go to dinner, we exited our apartment, I walking as usual, Jeff preceding me in his Rascal, not at top speed but continuing to drive faster than any other resident traveled in a scooter. He drove it like a farm boy traveling over farm fields in a John Deere Gator. And he continued to treat it like a toy, blinked its lights, and beeped its horn. Residents walking toward me said, "We just saw your husband speeding down the corridor. He's beating you by a mile!"

Another resident asked, "Why don't you ride with him?"

I laughed and replied, "I value my life too much to do that!"

Now at the front desk, I deposited the Satisfaction Report I'd completed that afternoon. Management had distributed these questionnaire reports several days ago, asking residents to indicate on a scale of one to six (six being the highest) their overall satisfaction with services provided by various departments. I'd given sixes to housekeeping and security, fives to maintenance and landscaping, and a four to food service. In the space provided for comments under food service, I'd indicated dissatisfaction because of hot entrees being served on cold plates and the unnecessary length of time for desserts to arrive after those orders were taken. Completed Satisfaction Reports would be mailed to a Kansas address where a disinterested tabulating company would send results to management at Sandycreek Terrace and to the president of the parent company.

Frances and Harold Jefferson were in the lounge, and I was reminded of how dissatisfied Harold was the last time we saw him, how he said he didn't know how long he'd stay. So I said, "How are you, Harold?"

He answered, "All right, more or less. That's the way it is with everyone here. Isn't that right?"

I smiled and made no comment.

Jeff parked his Rascal near the bar, removed his cane, and ordered us each a drink. When we were called to our favorite table in the dining room he carried his cane with him and leaned it against the wall near the table. We enjoyed this particular table where we could look out the window to the Jupiter Inlet, to the water and lights along the shore. One evening we saw an abandoned boat on a distant shore, probably washed there by the last hurricane. As we sat listening to the piano, sipping our drinks, and smiling at each other, I felt very happy, like I'd just won an Oscar. Pretty nice to be living like this. Temporarily, until we could get back to Pennsylvania.

My thoughts were interrupted by an unusual amount of activity occurring at a nearby table. We could see that several servers and the Assistant Dining Room Manager were there, and a number of residents were standing around the table. We heard, "Pull the cord! Someone pull the cord!" A scuffling followed, and we heard, "The Heimlich maneuver! Does anyone know how to perform the Heimlich maneuver?"

I knew how to perform the Heimlich maneuver! I pushed back my chair and started toward the table, forcing my way through the gathering crowd. By the time I got there, someone was already trying to perform the Heimlich. But he was reaching around the armed chair to grab her diaphragm after she'd slumped over the table. He hadn't gotten her in position to hold her and force out the food. In came a security employee and then a nurse from Park Place, all capable of handling the situation. I went back to our table and watched the E. M. Ts. arrive with a stretcher and carry the resident out of the dining room. Jeff and I finished our dinner in silence, not knowing the resident involved.

We'd been back in our apartment about fifteen minutes when the phone rang. I answered. "Mrs. Metz," a young male voice said. "Mr. Metz left his cane in the dining room this evening. Would you please tell him it's at the front desk?"

"Jeff," I called to him sitting at the kitchenette table shuffling cards in preparation for our cribbage game. "You left your cane in the dining room. It's at the front desk."

"Holy smokes! Did I forget that cane again? O. K. I'll ride the Rascal over now and pick it up. I'll be right back."

This habit of leaving his cane somewhere was happening more frequently, it seemed. Even in the apartment I'd hear him say, "Where did I put that cane when I came home? Have you seen it, Jeanie?" And I'd go on a search. I was getting accustomed to these searches, looking for his glasses or glasses case, his Barlow knife, and now for his cane.

When Jeff returned he said, "Many people were congregated at the front desk talking about the crisis. I learned that resident choked on a piece of meat. Seems the kitchen has orders to cut her meat in small bites before they serve it to her. Someone claimed they hadn't done that tonight. They're saying the Heimlich didn't work, or it wasn't performed soon enough. They don't think she was alive when the emergency medical techs carried her to their van."

Two afternoons later when I was walking back from the mail boxes I came upon Lottie Yurasik and McKee's next door neighbor who always talked about her two cats. We'd never seen the cats as they were house cats that never left her apartment. At any rate, the two women were standing talking there in the corridor. Since I wanted to ask Lottie how she was feeling after having her appendectomy, I stopped. The two gals were talking about Sarah Grant and the dinner party she was having this evening. Lottie had been invited but the owner of the cats had not. Jokingly I said, "She hasn't invited me. Should I be offended?"

Lottie shrugged, smirked, and spit out, "Of course not! I wish she hadn't invited me. Believe me, she's not one of my favorite people," and with that, the two gals laughed.

"How are you feeling since your surgery?" I asked Lottie.

She looked down at her legs and said, "I'm standing. Now I just have time to go get my shower," and she hurried to the elevator opening its doors.

Apparently she managed to shower and, at the appointed time, arrived at the table where stone-faced Sarah was entertaining. As we looked at the party table, we could see Harry Scott seated to Sarah's right, Lottie at the other end of the table, and other couples filling the seats in between, apparently following Sarah's seating arrangement. As we ate dessert at our table, we heard the strains of *Happy Birthday, Harry.* Jeff and I looked at each other, grinned, and joined in the singing. At home I said, "What do you think of Sarah hosting Harry with a birthday party and inviting Lottie to see them sitting side by side, enjoying each other?" I waited for Jeff to tell me he was just as amused as I was at Sarah's devious conniving and plotting to win Harry.

Jeff said, "Couldn't refuse an invitation to his own birthday party, now could he? Pretty foxy of our friend Sarah to have the party for Harry and invite Lottie Yurasik."

"Poor Harry. Isn't really interested in either one. Doesn't matter how old we get, some women will do anything to get a man. If I were single and desperate for a man, I'd use more sense. Use a different approach."

"And what approach would you use, Honey?"

"Not that kind. I'd just be myself," I said.

"Worked with me, Sweetie," he said, winking at me.

"You seem to forget, Honey. *You* made all the advances."

"You're right. But then, you're always right," he said, patting my hand and winking at me again. "I'm of the opinion Harry doesn't mind all the attention. He's a very social man. Likes to be around people."

The Jesieks moved into a cottage. Bill and Shirley Jesiek. Their small motor boat moved in with them, docked in the Inlet touching the shore of Sandycreek Terrace's eastern-most property. New residents were always noticed by seasoned residents, but some drew more attention than others. Bill and Shirley were such a couple, both diminutive in stature and girth. They were more self-assured and less aged than most residents, it seemed. Shirley exuded class and sophistication in her demeanor and uniqueness in her fashionable outfits. She wore dresses of silky fabrics in subtle colors of mauve, royal blue, and brandy that hung gracefully below mid-calf. Often a crocheted scarf of contrasting color was draped around her slim shoulders and arms. Sometimes she wore rather tight-fitting sweater-dresses, a gold chain circling her hips two inches below her waist. The sociable couple conversed easily with other residents. Although they spoke in normal tones about common subjects, other residents seemed mesmerized when the Jesieks talked, like constituents hanging on every word spoken by their beloved politicians.

Perhaps their boat afforded them such prestige, like a castle owned by royalty. They invited residents, one couple at a time, to join them for a ride on their boat in late afternoons. After such rides, the four boaters would come directly to the lounge to have cocktails and then go into the dining room for dinner together, smiling, chatting, and commenting on their excursion.

Old and seasoned as I was, I watched this activity with envious eyes, like a high school senior not getting an invitation to the prom, until finally one evening in the lounge Bill and Shirley invited Jeff and me to have a boat ride the following week. Until now I hadn't noticed Shirley's puffed eyelids. We accepted without hesitation. "Meet us at the dock at four-thirty," Bill instructed. "We'll have drinks as we ride along."

Two days before the boat ride I said to Jeff, "I think we should take something when we go on Jesiek's boat. Bill said we'd have drinks, so I think we should take something to nibble on. We could take that can of mixed nuts we've never opened, the one we received from Mary Jo for Christmas. Or we could buy shrimp. One of those round pre-packaged containers of shrimp with cocktail sauce." I looked at Jeff for his reaction.

He nodded. "I'll go to Publix and buy shrimp. That would be best."

The morning of the scheduled boat ride, Jeff didn't get out of bed when past-dawn light filtered through the bedroom blinds at seven, our usual rising time. "I didn't sleep well last night, and I feel like hell this morning. Think I'll just stay here awhile," he told me, voice dull and scratchy. "I don't believe I'll have any breakfast. Can you get your own breakfast this morning?"

"Of course I can, Jeff. You lie there and try to sleep," I said, getting out of bed. I not only prepared and ate breakfast but also lunch without Jeff who continued to stay in bed. In order to give him as much time as possible to rest, I decided not to disturb him until the last minute, give him just enough time to get ready for the boat trip. At three o'clock I dressed for the ride in white slacks and a red-printed long-sleeved shirt, also appropriate for dinner in the dining room. I reached into a drawer to get a sun visor. Then I woke Jeff and told him the time.

He sat up, blinked, rubbed his fingers over his forehead, and looked at his wristwatch. "Time to get ready for the boat ride, isn't it?"

"Yes. How do you feel?" I asked, looking at him with concern.

"Lousy. Tell you what. I'll get dressed and go down with you to the dock. But I can't go for the ride. Just couldn't make it, much as I'd enjoy it."

I frowned, studied my hubby. Sea-faring, boat loving man, he had to be sick to deny himself this pleasure. "I hate to go without you, Honey. I really do. If it were any earlier I'd call the Jesieks and cancel. But I think it's too late. Too late for them to invite anyone else. But why don't you just stay here, and I'll tell the Jesieks you're sick and can't go. No need for you to make the trip all the way to the dock when you feel like you do. Can I get you anything before I go?"

"No, thank you. I'm getting up and dressed and going down to the dock. I want to make an appearance and excuse myself."

No use trying to talk him out of it. I waited while he dressed in shorts and shirt and put a funky cap on his bald head. We went down to the dock, Jeff in his scooter, I walking and carrying the shrimp he'd purchased for the occasion, a package of crackers, and my windbreaker. We arrived at the dock first, then Bill, and no Shirley. After Jeff explained why he wasn't joining us, Bill helped me onto the boat, untied the ropes, and we sped out into the open water. "We're picking up Shirley at the launch. She had some errands to run this afternoon," Bill explained.

So that was it, why she wasn't on board. I leaned back and relaxed, enjoying being out on the water, the air fresh, the river smooth, and other boats passing at a distance. Before long, Bill came back where I was sitting close to a small table. He reached down and pulled open a drawer under a seat in front of me. "What do you drink?" he asked, lifting out a bottle of vodka.

"That's my drink. What you have in your hand," I said, pointing to the bottle. He poured the liquid into a plastic cup, handed it to me, and poured a drink for himself. I opened the package of shrimp and the crackers. "Help yourself," I said dipping a shrimp into the sauce and putting it into my mouth.

"There's more to eat in here," Bill said, pointing to the items in the open drawer. "Take what you want."

I was satisfied with the shrimp and crackers and didn't touch the cheeses, beef sticks, and other crackers I saw in the drawer. We rode along on the calm water, eating and drinking and saying little, Bill going to the controls from time to time. "It was very nice of you to ask us to go for a ride in your nice boat. We really appreciate it. I'm sorry Jeff couldn't make it," I said, trying to make conversation.

"We enjoy taking residents for rides. We feel we should share the enjoyment with the residents. We'll be going up north pretty soon."

"Do you take this boat with you?" I asked, trying to continue the conversation.

"No, no," he answered. "This boat's too small a craft to travel that distance. We have a large boat up in Massachusetts." He slowed the boat and steered it over toward a dock. "We're going to pull in here and pick up Shirley," he told me, bringing the boat along side a pier and tying it. As we idled there, he pulled a cell phone out of his jacket pocket and dialed a number. "Shirley," he spoke into the phone. "Who? Art? How did I get *you*? Well, how are you any how? Things going all right? Great! Talk to you later." He hung up just as Shirley, in windbreaker, sunglasses, and large brimmed hat, walked onto the pier. He climbed out and went to meet her and they walked back to the boat and climbed aboard.

Shirley immediately turned her attention to Bill. "I stopped at the lab for your test results, Bill. Your white count's extremely low. I'm worried, Bill. It shouldn't be that low. Something's wrong. They want you back again tomorrow. They want you back again tomorrow for another test."

She acted very concerned. How serious was this? They both looked so healthy. Bill didn't respond to Shirley's information but instead said, "I tried to call you when we were waiting for you, and I got Art by mistake. Dialed incorrectly."

"You did? You dialed Art in England? And he answered? How is he?"

"He's fine. Very busy, as usual." Bill sounded amused to have contacted Art but not concerned about making a call all the way to England. A natural occurrence to call England?

Now out on the water, Shirley greeted me as Bill poured her a drink. "Hello Jean. Have you found the hors d'oeuvres? Here are crackers and cheeses and nuts," she reached down into the open drawer and loosened the wrappings around the food items, not noticing or remarking about the shrimp I had brought and Bill and I had been eating. Again I noticed her puffy eyelids.

In no time at all we were pulling up to another dock and securing the boat along the side. "This is where we keep our boat when we're not going to use it for some time," Bill explained to me. "They take care of it for us. All the time we're up north, too. I checked the weather for next week. It's supposed to be stormy. So we'll leave the boat here for now."

It was starting to rain slightly when we climbed out of the boat, and as we walked toward their van parked near by I took the opportunity to say to Shirley, "You seemed worried about Bill's lab results. I hope it's nothing serious."

The rain increased in volume as we hurried along, and Shirley answered, "I hope not too. Bill has a serious heart problem."

I noticed she was limping. "Do you have trouble walking?" I asked.

"Sciatica. I've been getting ultrasound treatments. They're helping. At least I'm getting a little more sleep."

When we got to the Club House, Shirley and I hung our windbreakers in the cloak room and then went into the ladies' restroom. I saw Shirley was wearing a pants suit suitable for the dining room, and she complimented me on my red shirt and slacks. Then she combed her hair and applied lipstick, both comb and lipstick retrieved from a small purse she'd taken out of the pocket of her windbreaker. I glanced in the mirror, thankful my hair and lips needed no attention, in my opinion, as I'd brought neither comb nor lipstick.

Bill insisted on buying my drink at the bar. At dinner we had a pleasant conversation, residents stopped by our table to ask why Jeff wasn't with us, and, as we left the table Shirley said, "We'll go boating again when Jeff is better."

At home, I found Jeff in bed and crawled in with him.

The next morning he was nauseated, had diarrhea and lay on the couch in the living room. I placed the large pan he requested on the coffee table in front of the couch. Dry unproductive heaves wretched his body. I brought him a glass of ice water and put it next to the pan, filling it several times throughout the morning. There he lay all day. In late afternoon I stood near him, looking at him, at his face. "Tell me how you feel," I said, putting my hand on his forehead to feel if he had an elevation. It didn't seem so, but I stuck a thermometer in his mouth anyway. It registered normal.

"I'm just nauseated and weak because of this diarrhea. I'll be fine tomorrow. I just want to lie here and rest. You get ready and go to dinner."

I did as he told me, worried about him and trying to figure out what could be wrong. He hadn't vomited, no pain, no elevation, no upper respiratory tract symptoms, and the diarrhea had practically ceased. Just nauseated and weak. But, of course. He hadn't eaten for two days. Still, this malady mystery had me baffled.

I went over to the lounge where bartender Mandy started to pour our cocktails before I stopped her and told her I was alone. She was a new bartender, but already, after just a few days, knew what we drank. "Where's Mr. Metz?" she wanted to know.

"He's not feeling well tonight, Mandy. Thank you for asking. Where did you work before you came here?" I asked, looking into her dark eyes and at her olive skin and well-groomed black hair.

"My husband and I had a restaurant, and I tended bar there. Have lots of experience." She smiled, placed my full glass on a Sandycreek Terrace cocktail napkin, and pushed it toward me on the bar.

"I figured you had much experience from the way you remembered what we drank," I commented, signing the bar card.

"Tell Mr. Metz I hope he's better soon," she said just as Doris Jordan came up to the bar.

"You here alone?" Doris asked.

I nodded.

"Want to eat together?" she asked.

"Sounds like a good idea. Yes," I answered.

Conversing with her had always been difficult because of her hearing deficit but we easily carried on a conversation about our former profession. Then she said, "Our golf game at the country club course next to Sandycreek Terrace was fun this afternoon even though I didn't have my best drives."

"I used to play a lot of golf, but I don't have enough stamina to play any more. Do you have a low handicap?" I asked.

She laughed. "No, of course not. Not anymore. We play best ball and only nine holes, so we get finished fairly fast and don't have to hit the ball as often as we would if we played a regular game."

"Maybe I could play that much. But I gave my clubs to the pro shop at the club we belonged to before we came here. I still have a full set of clubs up in Pennsylvania. I'll probably never use them. They're there for anyone who visits and cares to play."

And so the conversation went throughout the entire dinner. Jeff and I should ask her to have dinner with us more often, lonely as she must be without her husband, I thought. What a beautiful tenor voice he had! She seemed to have adjusted well, however. But who really knew?

When I got back to our apartment Jeff was in bed, asleep. I read a nursing magazine with a magnifying glass and then crawled into bed beside him. "You home?" he asked. "Did you have a nice dinner?"

Although he was a light sleeper, I was surprised he was awake. "I thought you were sleeping," I said. "Yes, I had a good dinner. I ate with Doris Jordan. She was easier to talk to than at other times we've been with her. Maybe she has a new hearing aid. Do you feel any better?"

"About the same. I believe I did sleep a little."

The next morning I asked Jeff, "Can you eat any breakfast. I'll fix you whatever you want."

"No I can't eat a thing. I'll just stay here in bed for awhile."

Having no appetite was certainly something new for Jeff. He always had a good appetite. "I like food. I see food. I eat food," was his expression to describe his ability to eat. He always ate more than I and sometimes ate what I was too full to finish. Since he was too weak to drive to the doctor's, I wanted to call 911 and have an ambulance take him to the hospital emergency room.

He refused to allow me, saying, "I'll be better tomorrow."

Again I walked over to the Club House to eat dinner without Jeff, taking a large-print book with me. And again Mandy asked me how Mr. Metz was feeling as she poured my martini. I sat reading and sipping until the hostess came to seat me. The pretty young uniformed girl led me to our usual two-top by the window looking out onto the croquet court and further to the Jupiter Inlet.

When Jeff was no better the next morning, I said, "I'd like to call Dr. Gray. The trouble is you don't have any symptoms to report except nausea and weakness, and you did have diarrhea. He won't prescribe over the phone. He'll want to set up an appointment to see you right away, and you're too weak to drive and I can't drive. I can call Sandycreek Terrace transportation or I can call a cab."

"Forget it," he said. "I'll be fine tomorrow. Maybe I could drink a little ginger ale. I think we have a few bottles up on the top shelf of one of the kitchen cabinets."

"I'll go look," I said. I reached up and took three bottles out of the cabinet, opened one, poured a small amount into a glass and added an ice cube. "Here, you are, Honey," I said, handing it to him.

Then he looked at me and squinted his eyes. "Honey," he said in a concerned voice. "Isn't this your birthday?"

"Yes, 'tis," I answered with a little smile using Frank McCourt's lingo. "I'm now your senior. Older by six months. You have to listen to me. Obey your elder," I joked.

"I will. I always do. But I feel terrible. I haven't gotten you anything. I planned to get you roses."

"It's the thought that counts. Don't think another thing about it. I don't need anything. You just get better. That's what I want."

"Isn't today the day of the birthday luncheon? The day all residents who have birthdays in March are hosted to a luncheon in the dining room?"

I nodded. I hadn't planned to attend, feeling I should stay at home with Jeff.

"You go. Go and have fun. I'll be fine here without you. I insist," he said when I hesitated.

So I went, and I did have fun. Twelve of us March-birthday residents attended. Social Director Janet acted as hostess, of course, and distributed individual sheets of paper she titled *The Birthday* Post to each of us. Mine was dated with the year, month, and day of my birth. It listed famous people born on that date, popular music during 1920, and prices of milk, bread, new cars, gas, new homes, average income, and the Dow Jones average in 1920, all compared with today's figures. It also gave the

374

academy award winning movies of 1920. I must say the information was quite revealing. When we'd eaten soup, hot rolls, and a delicious chicken Caesar salad, the server approached our table carrying a large chocolate cake with white icing ablaze with many candles. At the same time, the Executive Director, Amanda Murray, two employees from the business office, and the Food Service Supervisor walked in and sang "Happy Birthday" to our group.

That evening, Jeff insisted I go to the dining room again without him. Even though he looked haggard and pale, he said, "I'm feeling some better. Had ginger ale again today and a piece of toast while you were at the birthday luncheon. But I still couldn't eat a meal in the dining room. You go and enjoy yourself on your birthday."

I went, but I really didn't enjoy myself. I didn't sit at our favorite table but rather in the middle of the dining room at a two-top and felt conspicuous sitting eating alone. And this was my birthday! March fifteenth and two-thousand-and-six already! How can time go so fast? But was this how it would be if I had no husband? Would I be like Doris Jordan and Penny Ferris, eating alone unless I asked someone to eat with me? Or someone asked me to eat with them? I shuddered to think of a future like that. But that time would never materialize because Jeff and I were going to die at the same time, in an airplane accident. That's what we'd agreed upon.

The next day, Jeff had an elevated temperature, perspired profusely, and then felt somewhat better. He still refused to have me call an ambulance to take him to the emergency department. He drank cold water and ginger ale but still ate nothing, and again insisted I go over to the dining room for dinner. "Keep up your strength," he told me.

So that evening I went to the lounge with my book again. Residents were getting accustomed to seeing me in the lounge alone before dinner and asked about Jeff. I explained, and they said, "A lot of residents are sick. It's the flu. Going around." Some said, "I was sick last week and the week before. It takes two weeks to get over it, sometimes three." I acknowledged their advice but was now confident Jeff's illness was not flu although I'd suspected it at first and taken precautions, washing my hands frequently.

At the bar Mandy asked, "Mr. Metz still not with you? He's no better? Here, you enjoy your drink," She filled a glass with ice, pouring vodka and then dry vermouth over the ice, rubbing a lemon twist over the rim of the glass, dropping it into the drink, and pushing the glass over the bar to me. I admired her immaculate black and white uniform and how her dark eyes smiled.

I carried my drink to a small round table in the lounge and was about to open my book when Rachel Hamburg came up to me. Her tiny figure, like a pixie, always amused me. Couldn't have weighed ninety pounds. My slight five-feet-three figure towered over her. Tonight she'd dressed in green slacks and a little green sweater trimmed with purple pansies. I listened to her craggy voice say, "I hear Jeff's sick. You come eat with Gus and me. We'll talk about Pittsburgh."

"Sounds good to me," I quickly answered, smiling at her small face, eyes holding my attention, light brown short-cropped hair brushed back from her forehead. Her craggy voice always projected, and I could recognize it a mile away. She'd come from old money, attended Ellis School for Girls, a private expensive elementary and high school and then Chatham College, an exclusive women's college, both schools located on Pittsburgh's Fifth Avenue. Then she'd met Gus, also of wealth, and married him, never using that wonderful education to foster a career. But she was a woman I felt comfortable with from the first time I'd met her. We kidded each other, understood each other, and talked about Pittsburgh although when she lived with her parents their home wasn't in the city itself but in Upper St. Claire, a suburb in Pittsburgh's South Hills.

A year ago, Jeff and I hadn't expected her to live. She'd been in Park Place for months on end with anorexia. Fed through a tube leading directly into her stomach because of her inability to swallow, she seemed never to improve. Every time Jeff and I saw her husband Gus in the lounge we'd ask how she was. He always voiced extreme optimism, "Oh she's getting better. She's getting better," he'd say. But she remained in Park Place receiving necessary care.

"Have they removed the stomach tube yet?" I'd ask.

"No, no. Not yet," he'd answer.

Gus himself was a walking miracle, according to Jeff who'd known him for some time. They were both boaters. Gus owned a yacht and then a sail boat and lastly a motor boat. Since Jeff had also owned boats in Jupiter, the two men had spent much time together on the river. But money hadn't spared Gus from multiple illnesses. Jeff said he'd had operations in New York, San Francisco, Greece, and Turkey, every operation in a surgeon's textbook. During Rachel's illness when Gus came into the dining room he ate alone, saying he was in a hurry each time we asked him to eat with us.

This evening Gus walked with a limp and leaned on his cane as he followed Rachel. "What's the matter with Jeff?" he barked in his usual way. He didn't wait for an answer but went to the bar to get Rachel her red wine. Jeff had once told me Gus never drank alcohol. He'd promised his father he would never take a drink, and he never had. So he brought Rachel her wine and nothing for himself. When we were seated at a table Gus kept the conversation flowing, asking me questions and giving me little time to answer before he asked another. A very nervous person.

As I left the dining room Mandy called to me from the bar, "Tell Mr. Metz I hope he's better soon."

I waved and said, "I will, Mandy. Thank you."

When I was near the front desk, I saw the Horners looking at a sign-up sheet. They saw me, and Jane, emulating concern, said, "Jeff hasn't been with you for several nights. We heard he was ill. What seems to be the matter? Is it a virus? What are his symptoms?"

I was attempting to explain when Jim leaned forward and listened intently with his hearing-deficient physician ear. "Time to have him be seen by his primary physician," he advised.

"I've been trying to do that, Jim. I've been prompting him to go but he's been so weak. And that's not like him. I've even tried to get him to go to the E. R. Wanting to call 911. But he's stubborn."

As I walked back to the apartment in a hurry to get home to Jeff, I scarcely noticed the beauty of the courtyards at night. Other times I frequently walked slowly or hesitated to admire the effect of in-the-ground lights, some casting beams up into the fronds of the varying heights of palm trees, or others spreading low lights on lilies or other flowering plants.

Now I was back at our apartment and to Jeff. He was stretched out in bed sound asleep. I tiptoed close enough to see if he was breathing. He was. He'd been sick for almost a week now. *Could* it be flu? "It's going around. Lots of people are sick, some for two weeks," I remembered residents saying.

I hadn't provided any nursing care. Should I feel guilty? There was no nursing to be done, was there? Jeff simply lay in bed, got up to go to the bathroom, and went back to bed or to the couch. He wasn't one to be fussed over. I did try to keep him hydrated, took his temperature, answered his phone calls, and worried only a little, not being a worry-wart. But even though he seemed somewhat better, was getting up and getting himself water and ginger ale and toast, always the independent person, he wasn't better, and enough was enough!

I went to sleep, realizing the weekend was facing us, and this illness, whatever it was, this mystery malady, had to be tackled tomorrow.

With this on my mind, I awoke early. Jeff was awake, too. In total seriousness, I said, "Jeff, this is Friday, and then comes the weekend. You *must* see a doctor today, not wait until Monday. No physicians are in their offices over the weekend. Can you drive? Could you possibly drive? Or should I see if one of the residents will drive you to Dr. Gray's office? Or call 911 to take you to the hospital? Sandycreek Terrace's transportation doesn't make trips to professional offices on Fridays."

"I know they don't. I don't want to go to the hospital and I don't think we should rely on a resident to take me to Doctor Gray's office. I'll drive if you go with me. I want you to go with me."

Why would he even be considering going alone or think he had to ask me to go along? "Of course I'll go with you. I wouldn't have it any other way," I assured him, giving him a hug and a kiss.

"I'll have some more toast for breakfast and more ginger ale. I should be well enough to drive."

I was on the phone, placing my call at eight-thirty, as soon as I knew Dr. Gray's office would be open. The answering machine said, "This is Dr. Gray's office. If this is an emergency, hang up and dial 911. The office is open from eight-thirty until five daily between Monday and Friday." I waited two minutes and dialed again. "This is Dr. Gray's office. If you're calling to make an appointment, click one. If …" I just hated those menus! I clicked one and heard, "Your call will be answered in the order in which it was received."

Finally a human voice! I explained the problem to the human voice who said a nurse would call me back. "This morning," I urged. "I'd like to have the nurse get back to me this morning." I was determined to have Jeff be seen today!

At eleven, a male nurse phoned and verified Jeff's symptoms I'd given to the human voice. "He can be seen by Dr. Wallace at three-thirty this afternoon."

"But we'd like him to be seen by Dr. Gray, his physician," I pleaded.

"Dr. Gray is booked solid today," the male nurse informed me. "Because he's going away next week. I'm sure you'll be satisfied with Dr. Wallace."

So we settled for a three-thirty appointment with Dr. Wallace. Or so we thought.

Almost two weeks prior to this week when evil struck, Jeff had been seen by Dr. Gray for his yearly physical. A urine sample showed a urinary tract infection. Needless to say an antibiotic was ordered to combat this infection and Jeff had been self-administering faithfully twice a day. I gave no thought to that. Totally unrelated. Surely the medication was curing or had cured the infection.

Now in the doctor's office expecting to be seen by Dr. James Wallace, in walked a female with below shoulder-length blond frizzy hair and wearing a white lab coat over an ankle-length brown printed skirt and ecru blouse. "I'm a nurse practitioner," she announced, sitting down at the physician's desk and opening Jeff's medical record.

"What seems to be your problem, Mr. Metz?" she questioned.

Jeff looked over at her and said, "I'm weak as a dog. I was nauseated and had diarrhea for two days. Dry heaves the first day. No appetite."

The nurse practitioner was looking at Jeff's chart, leafing through it, reading it, studying it. She continued with her questions. "You had a urinary infection? You were taking a medication Dr. Gray ordered?"

"Yes," Jeff answered. "I had to give a urine sample for my yearly physical a couple weeks ago. When the results came back they showed a urinary track infection. I've been taking a drug the doctor ordered for that."

She nodded, scrutinized him. "Stop taking it. Get up on the table. Let me listen to your tummy." Her stethoscope traveled over Jeff's bare abdomen after she pulled up his shirt and pushed down his pants. "You're allergic to the sulfa drug you were taking. Stop taking it. You would have needed to take it for only three days."

"Is that right?" Jeff said, getting up from the examining table and rearranging his clothes. "If that's so, I'm going down the hall and do more than have a word with that Dr. Gray," he jested.

"We'll get another urine sample and call you with the results in three days. In the meantime don't take any more of that medication. If you're not better in forty-eight hours, call us."

We left the office and climbed into the Impala. On the trip home, Jeff said, "I'll be damned! What do you think of that? All because of that medication! That nurse put her finger on the problem just like that! I have extreme faith in that nurse practitioner. I'll be better in two days!"

"I sincerely hope so," I said, not having total confidence. I'd wait and see. Truth was, Jeff improved almost immediately. No more sulfa! Keep that in mind!

Forty-One
Tom

Jeff and I were in the den, I at the desk top computer, Jeff at the lap top. For some reason unknown to me, Microsoft Word was misbehaving and I was getting more and more frustrated. The computer was changing my font on the monitor from sixteen to twelve and taking me out of bold. I needed sixteen and bold because of my poor vision. Then it took me from double space to single space. For no apparent reason! I'd hit no wrong key! My hands had been idle on the key board. Not my fault! No sooner would I correct this erroneous activity than all would recur. I started to huff and puff at the monitor.

"What's the trouble?" Jeff asked from his machine at the desk next to mine.

"This machine! This computer! I'm ready to throw it out the window!" I said, exasperated, my voice raised.

"What's the problem? Jeff asked again, looking over at me.

I started to tell him when I let out a scream. "Now this darn computer's writing over the words I just wrote! How can that be?" My Scot blood was heating up.

"You know how to correct that," Jeff said. It's happened to you before and I've told you how to correct it. Go to the bottom of your monitor and click on *over*."

"I don't remember this ever happening before!" In my anger, I looked at the bottom of the key board. "I don't see anything that says *over*. And this never happened to me before!"

"It has happened to you before, and you corrected it. Just listen to me. Look down at the bottom of your monitor and click on *over*. Just do as I say and you'll be fine."

"This never hap…"

"Do what I just said," Jeff said calmly, interrupting me and getting up from his lap top.

"I'm not allowed to talk! To tell you!" My voice was now an octave higher. Why wasn't I allowed to talk? Jeff talked far more than I ever did! I was furious!

Jeff was now at my computer, bending over me. His hand on the mouse, he moved the arrow to the bottom of the screen, to the logos written across the bottom of the monitor. He moved the arrow from left to right, and clicked on the bold printed logo *OVR*. The printing on the screen returned to normal. I gritted my teeth. I hadn't listened. I'd searched the key board instead of the screen. This further infuriated me. Without even thanking Jeff, I pushed back my chair and left the room to calm down.

An hour must have passed before I felt able to go back into the den. I stood next to Jeff working at the lap top. "I'm sorry I got so upset, Jeff," I said, wanting some reaction from him.

He turned in his chair and took hold of my arm. "Just remember I love you. That's all that matters. I love you," he emphasized.

"And I love *you*," I said, holding back tears.

A week later when Jeff and I were in the lounge before dinner I overheard Harry Scott say to Dr. Jim Horner, "Tom Price is in the hospital."

The words vibrated in my ears: Tom Price is in the hospital! A mistake. It's someone else. Surely Dr. Tom isn't in the hospital. Or if he is, it's for something minor. He doesn't get seriously sick. He's too valuable to the welfare of the residents of Sandycreek Terrace. Still I had this ominous feeling and hurried over to Harry, "Who did you say was in the hospital, Harry?"

"Tom Price. They called 911 last night and rushed him to the local hospital."

So I'd heard correctly. I shook my head and frowned. "What's his diagnosis?" I asked, fearful.

"No diagnosis yet. Probably his heart. They're taking tests."

I walked over to the bar where Jeff was waiting for Chuck to finish making our cocktails. Our bartender had poured bourbon over the ice in Jeff's glass and was adding sweet vermouth. I touched Jeff's elbow. "I just heard Dr. Price is in the hospital. I'd better pay Tom's wife a visit in a day or two. She'll be terribly worried."

"That would be nice of you to do that," Jeff answered.

I knew Chuck had to have heard my news about Dr, Price, and I rather expected him to act surprised but he made no comment. Of course an employee is instructed not to enter into conversations with residents unless directly addressed. None of the residents near us in the lounge were talking about Dr. Price. Apparently they hadn't heard the alarming news.

Several days later, I started my walk over to Park Place to see Elizabeth Price. From our apartment I walked along the corridor past Gather's apartment on the right, McKee's apartment on the left, the guest room on the right, and then the last apartment on the left now occupied by Harold and Frances Jefferson. The apartment was vacated by the house-bound resident when her daughter decided to take her mother up north. After passing the Grecian fountain across from the mailboxes, I continued on past more apartments and around the corner past the Palace, and into the Club House.

The receptionist at the front desk called to me, "Mrs. Metz, I have mail for Mr. Metz."

"I'll pick it up on my way back," I said to her and kept on walking. Arlene was at her desk in the beauty salon, and I waved to her before walking along the covered walkway and into Park Place.

Elizabeth's room was at the very end of East Wing. I knocked gently on her door and stepped into her room, not looking forward to this visit.

"It's Jeanie Metz," I said, rousing her from her drowsy state positioned immobile in her green upholstered recliner. Little blue eyes in her tiny face peered out at me like a bird looking out to a meadow. Paralysis prevented her head from turning.

"Tom's in the hospital," her weak voice told me as I sat on the edge of her bed and strained to hear and to read her lips at the same time.

"Yes, I know," I said, nodding, my voice emoting concern.

"He had tests, but no one's read them yet. The ones taken at the first hospital or the ones taken at J. F. K."

"So he was transferred to J. F. K. in West Palm? Did he have an MRI?" I asked.

I heard a weak, "No."

"A cardiac catheterization?" I asked, bending toward her to hear her answer. A physician's wife would know these terms.

"Yes. But no doctor's seen him. No one's read the test results."

He'd been admitted six days ago. Plenty of time for tests to be read and physicians to have seen Tom!

"Amanda Murray called the hospital this morning at eleven o'clock to find out about the tests. She told me the tests hadn't been read when she called. She said she'd call again this afternoon. But she hasn't called me." Elizabeth was talking slowly and softly.

I looked at my bracelet watch. Three o'clock. Then I looked over at Elizabeth again. No expression was possible in such an inert face, but I felt her concern as if it were my own. And bless Amanda Murray for contacting the hospital! "I'm sure Amanda will let you know as soon as the tests are read," I said, trying to assure her.

Then I strained to hear the next words uttered from lips scarcely moving. "How do they operate on the aorta?" She waited for my answer but a second and then said, "The arteries in his leg had surgery but they're small. How do they operate on the aorta?" She looked to me for an answer.

She would know the aorta was the main blood vessel in the body, the largest artery by far. Tom must have told her on the phone he expected to have surgery involving his aorta. He must have meant he'd have to have a blood clot removed or by-passed to let the blood flow to the heart.

"I haven't worked in the O. R. for years, but surgeons can do marvelous surgical procedures these days. Not like in the old days. Modern surgeons perform miracles, Elizabeth," I said, again trying to reassure her.

She was quiet for some minutes then valiantly changing the subject she asked, "What have you been doing lately?"

I told her about my phone call from my son, his plans to put a large addition to his old farmhouse, the one he'd bought years ago and renovated several times already. Almost before I'd finished, she started to describe the house she and Tom lived in when they were raising their family, how they left the concrete floor of the basement bare so the children could roller skate there. She directed me to one of several bulletin boards hanging on the walls of her room, the one behind the door leading to the hall. I was to view a photo of the house affixed to the board, the house she had just described. I beheld a very large white colonial-style house, dark-green shutters framing all windows, a grassy lawn and flowering shrubbery surrounding it. I exclaimed over it and then returned to the recliner to say good-bye to her.

"Thank you for coming," she said as always.

"It's my pleasure," *I* said as I always responded. And that brave little lady thanked me again as I took my leave.

I hurried home to tell Jeff about my visit with Elizabeth and found him working on his autobiography. "Do you have time to listen to this paragraph? See if you have any comments? Then I guess we'd better get dressed for dinner. Are we eating with anyone tonight?"

"Certainly I have time to listen. I always do. Fire away. No, we're not scheduled to eat with anyone tonight."

Jeff read more than a paragraph. He read what he'd written about the time he worked in the Heinz pickle factory in Holland, Michigan in order to pay for his college education. He read about his hands blistering from the hot brine even though he wore gloves, and how the blisters broke open and took a long time to heal. The scenario made me cringe. But I had a comment. "Describe the pickles. The story would be more interesting if I could visualize the pickles. How large? What color? Were they slippery?"

When Jeff read his story he always indicated punctuation marks using his own vernacular. At the end of an exclamatory sentence he'd say, "Scare mark." When a sentence ended with a question, he'd say, "Little button hook."

Those funny descriptions made me smile but also fully understand the intent of his grammar and message.

That evening in the dining room, we had a new server. His name was

Bud and we coached him on our culinary preferences. "We'd like crackers now before you bring any food. Not rolls. Please bring our rolls with our dinner so they're warm."

"Yes sir," he said.

"Can you tell us how the steaks are cooked? Can we order them charbroiled or Pittsburgh? Do you know what we mean?"

"Yes sir. I worked in a steak house before I came here."

"And we'd like to split a baked potato." Our preferred beverages were described in the same way, decaf coffee with milk, not cream, for Jeff and herbal tea, mint if available, for me, we explained as we ended our orientation.

The next afternoon, I poked my head in the back door of Amanda Murray's two-room office. Her LPN looked up at me from her charting, "Do you want your blood pressure checked, Mrs. Metz?" she offered.

"No thanks. I just came by to see if you have any news about Tom Price."

At that moment, Amanda Murray entered through the connecting door from her office, her presence always like a beam of sunshine. On hearing my question she sang out in her pleasant voice, "Nothing new, Mrs. Metz. Dr. Price says if he doesn't see a physician today he's coming home. We brought Mrs. Price over to this office this morning so she could talk to Dr. Price in the hospital. So she could talk on our speaker phone and not have to hold a receiver to her ear."

"How nice! And thanks for the no-information up-date," I said, trying to make a funny.

The next morning, Jeff and I performed our routine exercises, he in the living room, I in the bedroom. After that I donned my sunglasses and visor cap and left the apartment to take my mile walk out past the circle, down past the cottages, past the security gate-house, past three cottages, and back to the apartment. Jeff, in the meantime, climbed on his two-wheeled bike and rode around the perimeter. He always managed to return before I did and have breakfast well on the way. As we sat down to French toast, orange juice, his coffee, and my herbal tea, Jeff said, "I briefly brought up our e-mail this morning. You have one from Brother Krisher. Thought you'd like to know. I didn't have time to read it."

It tickled me the way Jeff addressed my favorite editor. I exclaimed, "I did!" To hear from editors always excited me. "What did he say about my article? Oh you didn't read it. Well, I'll look at it as soon as I finish eating. I hope it's about my glaucoma article, the continuing ed. course I submitted."

"Something about a thief, wasn't it?" Jeff asked, looking across the kitchenette table at me, eyebrows arched.

"Yes. I titled it *Living with a Thief.* A little of my history with the disease and then risk factors, symptoms, two types of the disease, medications, treatments, and surgeries. Enough to give nurses an education course with questions to answer to acquire one credit toward the twenty-four required over a two-year period in order to renew their RN license." I knew Jeff understood because I'd written six education courses before this one, and they'd been published in nursing magazines. The others were all about long-term care—levels of care in nursing homes, an effective director of nursing, inspecting and licensing long-term care facilities, nursing home abuse, the aging in place concept.

I was beginning to run out of current material, it being quite a while since I'd worked in the profession. Maybe this article would be my last. If so, how would I replace my writing hobby? How would I occupy my time? What could I contribute? I'd thought about getting material for another continuing education course. My idea was to visit an operating room, observe an operation and then write an article comparing a modern operation room and surgical procedure with one sixty years ago when I'd been O. R. supervisor. First I'd have to get permission from the hospital administrator. I'd talk about my idea to Mary Lou, the hospital supervisor whom I knew from Rotary. I'd ask her to introduce me to the administrator. Lately, however, I'd given up that idea because of my poor eyesight. I wouldn't be able to identify the instruments on the Mayo stand or the sterile supplies on the back table. I'd probably be able to watch the skin prep but not be permitted to stand close enough to look down into the abdomen. And would I have the stamina to stand for the duration of an operation? They often took three or more hours these days. An article like that would have been interesting, one Krisher would have grabbed, I was sure. What would he think if he knew this author, whose work he had been publishing, was eighty-six years old? I'd never tell him!

Jeff was now reading the *Palm Beach Post*, and he started to laugh. "Listen to this, Jeanie."

He always gets a kick out of misspellings, misplaced modifiers, humorous articles, and always Dennis the Menace. And he always laughed out loud making me smile. "Is it Dennis the Menace?" I asked.

"Yes. A magazine salesman is at Mr. Wilson's door. Mr. Wilson says, 'I don't need a subscription to your wild life magazine. The kid next door provides all the wild life I need.'"

"Oh that *is* funny!" I said, laughing with Jeff. "What's interesting in the news besides Dennis the Menace?"

"Teen pregnancy is on the rise. The United States leads many other nations in number of teen pregnancies. Different views on prevention. Looks like Sweden has less than most nations. They start sex education with children when they're in kindergarten. Maybe we here in the U. S. could learn from Sweden."

After rinsing the dishes and placing them in the dishwasher, I hurried to the computer and brought up Krisher's e-mail. Yes! Yippee! He wanted the article, could use the subject, and liked the title! But he said he recalled I had only a bachelors' degree, and for continuing education courses he required a higher degree, a masters or doctorate.

I had eighteen credits toward my master's in Health Administration from the University of Pittsburgh at the time I decided to retire and move to Florida. If I hadn't retired, I would have completed the required courses and would have my master's degree. I didn't have to retire, you know. In fact my boss whose office was next to mine on the fourteenth floor of the Pittsburgh State Office Building, one of my coworkers, and several of the inspectors I supervised pleaded with me not to retire. The choice was mine to make.

Choices were important. I'd made many in the past, some good, some not good at all. Everyone had to make them, and those choices determined what people did with their lives, whom they met, where they lived, and how they lived.

I was sixty-six years old then and undecided. Most people retired when they were sixty-five or younger. My decision was influenced by my friend Chick Hahn, a real estate salesman in Pittsburgh' east suburbs at the time.

He had clients who wanted to buy my house. He'd shown them many others, but mine was the one this couple wanted. No other. I should retire, I told myself. I was repeating salesman Chick's words, of course. And he was also urging me to go to a warm climate and have fun golfing, playing tennis, and swimming year-round before I was too old. I could write that novel I'd always wanted to write. First I'd read over the notes I took in those writing classes at Pitt before I started the required courses for my master's degree.

I erased those thoughts from my mind and continued to read the e-mail. Editor Krisher wanted to know do I have a nurse friend with either degree who would co-author?

"Listen to this," I said to Jeff coming into the den. I read Krisher's e-mail to him.

"Call Susan. Or send her an e-mail. She has her doctorate. She'd be happy to do that for you. To co-author."

"That's right. She's an RN with a doctor's degree in nursing. I'll bet your daughter would do that for me. I'll e-mail her. Thanks for the suggestion, Honey."

The next evening in the lounge, Jeff and I ran into Jim and Jane Horner. Since Jim was a retired physician I figured he might know something about Dr. Tom. "Have you heard any news about Tom Price?" I asked him.

"He's home."

"He's home!" I almost shouted. Why was this? Why would he be home?

"He was discharged. Congestive heart failure. He's on oxygen."

Jim waited for my next words.

My heart sank. Appalled, I said, "Oh that's terrible! My father died of congestive heart failure."

Face grave, Jim nodded, and with little more to say he and Jane walked on into the dining room.

I turned to Jeff standing next to me, "Jeff, did you hear that? Do you realize what that means? Poor Elizabeth."

Jeff nodded, expression serious. "Poor *Tom*," he said.

Repair of car ports, landscaping, and roofs was completed. The woodshop that had been frequented by a few male residents who had carpenter skills and enjoyed tinkering with wood projects had also been damaged by hurricane Frances. Rather than repair a damaged building poorly constructed in the first place, management had decided to have a new building erected in a different location. It was now on a side street near parking spaces designated for maintenance personnel. Being a new building, it attracted more male residents, Jeff among them, and the interested group formed a club known as the Vise Club. Club members convinced management to place a sign on the building that read *Vise Club* on one line and *Sawdust and Gomorrah* on a line below.

Of the roughly twelve members who belonged, some used the large new one-room building more than others. Jeff was delighted with the hard-wood flooring, shelving, counter space, and adequate wiring. He had Maintenance transport his many-drawer tool-chest filled with tools, nuts, bolts, screws, and what not to the shop early on. For days on end he biked over to the shop and sorted and sorted his supplies. Emmett Gorman, self-appointed chairman of the Vise Club, also spent much time in the shop and moved in his equipment including a brand new all-purpose miter saw.

All members were male, no females possibly considered. In my opinion the men had every right to have a club of their own although I'd heard rumblings from women. Apparently some felt no club at Sandycreek Terrace should be exclusively limited to one sex or the other. At any rate the all-male members of the Vise Club, proud of their new wood shop, decided to hold an Open House and requested the Social Director print news of the up-coming event in the Weekly Newsletter. For over a week the members prepared for this Open House and finally the morning of the big day arrived. It was more or less a success with about thirty residents arriving on foot, by car, and via bicycle. Emmett's wife had taken charge of refreshments—cookies, lemonade, and ice water—and had them delivered from the main kitchen. Guests partook of the cookies and drinks while admiring the shiny oak floor and built-in counter-tops located along two side-walls with electric outlets above. They also observed a free-standing band-saw, table-saw, and two drill presses.

Even though Jeff had treated me to a private viewing of the shop days before, I supported the Open House by going again and helping myself to a cookie and glass of lemonade. Jim Horner, one of the Vise Club members, was standing in the back of the shop and I cornered him to ask about Tom Price. He informed me, "I called him this morning. He's very depressed and starting to put his affairs in order. To make it easier for his family. His daughter's with him."

"I see," I said, heaving a sigh and wondering how long we'd have Tom among us.

The day after the Open House, Jeff took me shopping to buy a bathing suit so I could go swimming. I hadn't gone swimming for many months, using the excuse of not having a decent suit. Part of the reason, however, was lack of motivation, and a new suit just might inspire me. Aside from having a skirt ballooning out in the water in front of me, this only suit I owned had lost its elasticity and gapped around my thighs like droopy drawers on an old man. I hadn't bought a new bathing suit for some time because the ones I'd seen in department stores were all of the bikini type, and I wasn't about to parade myself in the near-nude with my wrinkles and sags. I needed a one-piece suit that would hide a few of the undesirables at least. The saving grace was that none of the residents could see as they once did, and none of them were bathing beauties.

The other day when I was doing my balancing exercises in the exercise room the Health and Wellness Coordinator walked in. I stopped her in her tracks and said, "I'd like to go swimming again but I need a bathing suit. I want one that covers me. Comes down my thighs a bit. Straight across in front." I tried to indicate the length by running my hand in a line across my upper thighs. "But I don't know where I can find one like that. All I see are bikinis."

"Oh you can find them, Mrs. Metz. Mrs. Stunkard was wearing one yesterday. A two-piece with the top coming down over the bottom part and resembling a pair of shorts. Very cute. I've seen others like you're describing in Targets and Anthony's."

So Jeff and I headed for Anthony's. As always, this store was advertising a sale. When I entered the store I saw bathing suits hanging on numerous racks, enough suits to outfit every woman in the state of

Florida. The display would bewilder even a frequent Anthony's shopper, to say nothing of poor me who never shopped in Anthony's. And they were marked twenty-five percent off! The salesgirl was busy sorting merchandise but I interrupted her to explain the style of suit I wanted to buy. She directed me to several racks. Amazed at the number fitting my requirements, I gathered up ten and took them into a dressing room. Five of them looked and fit just fine, according to my opinion as I looked at myself in the mirror. Now I had a problem. Which one should I take? As sometimes happened to me, I got carried away and decided to take three—green and blue printed, red and black flowered, and a solid navy with white trim.

The next morning I chose the green and blue printed suit, squirmed into it, covered myself with a terry cloth robe, slipped on a pair of sandals, and walked over to the outdoor pool. Jeff followed me on his scooter and drove over to the hot tub located along the side of the pool. No one was in either the pool or hot tub. Serious morning swimmers, of which there were two that I knew of, had been there earlier. The Health and Fitness Coordinator would have her aquasize class at ten o'clock. Several serious swimmers would swim laps in late afternoon. Guests used the pool all hours of the day. Because of my eyes and blotchy skin on my lower legs, I preferred to swim before the unfriendly sun was shining. From the supply provided on a nearby chair I took a terry towel and slipped off my robe. I placed both towel and robe on a chair and took off my sandals. Then I grabbed hold of the shiny railing leading into the pool and walked down the steps and into the heated water. I broke the water in front of me with my hands and walked the width of the pool from the three to the four-foot-deep water. Then I started at one end and swam the twenty yards to the other end, first breast stroke, then side stroke, then back stroke (my favorite), and finally free style, alternating strokes and stopping at each end before swimming back the length of the pool. About the third length of side stroke I was passing one of the ladders leading out of the pool, swam too close to the ladder, and whacked it with my right foot. Pain shot through my toes and one side of my foot! Surely I broke a toe! I was familiar with broken toes since I'd broken a toe three times in my other life. I continued to swim and walked home with no difficulty, deciding I hadn't damaged my foot after all. By mid-morning, I changed my mind. I couldn't walk without pain. No treatment existed for such a minor fracture, if my toe was actually broken, that is. Why was I such a klutz? I'd been doing so well, too. No colds, sore throats, abrasions, falls, bowel problems, back pain, and my intraocular eye pressure was controlled. All I could complain of was arthritis in my hands, my fingers stiffening if I didn't exercise them. Into each life some rain must fall, however.

FORTY-TWO
HOPE

My thoughts turned to Dr. Price and then to Elizabeth. She would know the diagnosis by now. How was she taking it? How depressed she must be! I felt obliged to go over to Park Place and visit with her. Maybe I could be of some help, converse and transport her mind for a few minutes to thoughts other than her husband's impending death.

Jeff was sitting at the lap top, deep into the first volume of his autobiography. In addition to the account of his job at Heinz pickle factory he'd read me parts of his childhood experiences where he lived in Holland, Michigan. Some were funny, some sad, some amazing. Especially interesting to me was his ambition and ability to start building a sailboat when he was in junior high and the fact that he finished high school at age sixteen. As he read this interesting autobiography to me I realized how well he wrote. Much better than I.

I interrupted him just long enough to inform him I was going over to Park Place to visit Elizabeth Price. He turned from the computer and said, "Are you going to be able to walk that far with that sore foot? Why don't you take the scooter? You know how to drive it."

"I'd like that very much, Honey," I said, grateful. The breeze cool on my face, I drove the Rascal over to Park Place, going along the corridors of our building, past the Palace, into the Club House, past the front desk and beauty salon, along the covered walkway between the Club House and Park Place, and into East Wing. Afternoon was the appropriate time to visit Elizabeth, after her caregiver had completed morning care and Elizabeth was left to face a long afternoon in her room alone. This was the time wise husband Tom had suggested I visit. I dreaded this visit and I sat in the parked Rascal a few minutes in the East Wing hall near Elizabeth's room wondering how to start the conversation. After I climbed out of the scooter I could see Elizabeth in her recliner. She was dressed in a black-and-white-checkered pants suit. As always I tapped on her door. I saw her mouth hello, watch me cross the room, ease myself between her walker and the end of her bed, and sit down.

"How are you?" I asked, looking into her little blue eyes.

"Things are not good," her faint voice told me.

"I know," I agreed and then softly, "Tom is very depressed."

"*We* are depressed," she corrected me. "Our daughter's with him. She is so wonderful. She made a pork roast and mashed sweet potatoes, but he didn't eat much. She's gotten bagged lunches from the dining room, but he doesn't eat that much." She talked so slowly and weakly I had difficulty hearing her and had to strain and sometimes pretend I understood when I just caught words, not whole sentences. Now I heard, "CPA, tax returns, Hospice papers signed.",

I shuttered at the finality of these words. "Has Hospice been to the apartment?" I asked.

"No care yet. He's much better today. I go over…"

Because of the long pauses and slowness of her speech I started to talk before she finished, thinking she'd said everything she intended to say. I said, "You've told me your caregiver takes you home every day. That's nice you and Tom can be together for a time." I watched her eyes flicker in sad acknowledgement.

Then, since she sat quietly I asked, "Can I do anything for Tom? Would he enjoy a box of chocolates?" I was thinking of the many unopened sealed boxes I'd received from my family on Valentine's Day and on my birthday.

"No," she whispered. "No, he's not fond of candy. A note would be nice. You could write a note and put it in his door. Two thirty-one."

How alert she was, giving me the number of their apartment. I nodded and said, "I was planning to do that, Elizabeth, and I will." I noticed the large bouquet of yellow gladiolas were no longer sitting in a tall vase in a corner of the room where I'd seen them when I visited last week. "Where are your pretty yellow flowers," I wanted to know.

"They died," she answered, moving only her lips, her body motionless in its black-and-white-checked pants suit, her feet in white socks.

The two plants on her bedside stand were still there sitting on either side of the photo of her grandson holding his tuba. The plants didn't seem too healthy. To her right, as usual, a small table held her telephone and magnifying glass on a white doily. I changed the subject and talked a bit about buying a bathing suit, a topic that made her smile. When I glanced at the clock on her wall it told me I'd been with her one-half hour. "Better go," I said, knowing she could only make her thin lips move just so long before she tired. As I rose from the side of her bed I said, "Promise you'll let me know if there's anything at all I can do for you."

"I will. I hope your foot gets better soon. Thank you for coming."

"You're very welcome. But it's my pleasure, you know," I answered and turned away and made my departure.

It had been a month ago when Jeff and I had walked into the lounge before dinner and heard music flowing from the piano without a pianist present. "Listen," I'd said to Jeff. "The piano's a player piano. I didn't know it was the kind that played tapes, did you?"

"Can't say I did. Can't say I know that tune, either," he'd answered as we'd walked on past the piano and over to the bar.

I hadn't known the tune, either, but was happy to hear music and glad to know we could enjoy music in the lounge and dining room without having to wait for Happy Hour every other Saturday for a hired pianist to play. Music livened the environment and made it more festive. I'd worn a new blue pants suit and matching jewelry I'd purchased at Patchington, and the music added to my uplifted mood.

Now the piano was playing every evening when we entered the lounge before dinner. One evening I'd asked Amelia at the bar how it happened we were enjoying piano music every evening. "Mr. Scott brought in the tapes, Mrs. Metz," she'd informed me. "He turned a switch to convert it to a player piano."

This evening as Jeff and I sat sipping our drinks and delving into the bowl of mixed nuts in the center of the lounge table, we were close enough to a group of residents to hear their conversation. "That piano's

396

too loud!" one of the female residents said. "You can't hear yourself think!"

"I agree," another female resident said. "I can't hear what your husband is saying. People here have trouble hearing as it is. The volume should be turned down. Way down."

"We don't need music! I'd rather not have any music. It was much more pleasant here before those tapes. Every other Saturday was often enough to have music," the first speaker said.

"Did you hear that, Jeff?" I asked my hubby.

"Yes. That's the way it goes sometimes. Can't please everyone."

Betty Howe and Ralph Wilson walked into the lounge and over to the table where we occupied two of four chairs. "May we sit with you?" Betty asked, smiling demurely and dressed in a stunning satin Japanese jacket atop black silky slacks.

"Of course, of course. Sit down," Jeff said, pushing a chair out from the table.

Ralph went to the bar for their drinks, and Betty immediately started to talk. "I hope you don't mind looking at my nose. I went to the dermatologist this morning, and he treated it again. I know it looks terrible. I can't cover it up like I can cover my neck with a scarf."

I giggled picturing her nose covered like a woman in a Turkish harem and said, "I don't notice it at all. You know I don't have good vision, Betty. But even so, I don't think people will notice it." I smiled at the little ninety-one-year-old resident, so thin she was. "Your jacket is positively beautiful," I commented.

"Why thank you," she said, smiling. "It's quite old. I purchased it when I was visiting in Japan some years ago." She looked over at the piano. "I wish that music could be turned down. It's much too loud. Ralph doesn't mind it, do you dear?" she said to Ralph who'd returned with their drinks.

"What did you say?" he asked.

She leaned toward him and patted his arm. "I said you don't mind the piano being so loud." Then she turned to us and added, "Ralph has a bit of trouble hearing, you know."

Of course we did know. Even with hearing aids he seemed to hear little. But I was surprised Betty thought the piano was too loud. I thought it was just fine, and I kept time with the beat with my feet. When I knew the song I sang it softly to myself.

Many residents attended the Executive Director's meeting the next afternoon in the Palace. Our neighbor, lively Frances Jefferson, came in and sat down beside me. "Harold's not coming. He's not feeling well," she explained to me and continued, "I just found out about this meeting from Ruth McKee when we were at the mailbox a bit ago."

I turned to Jeff and whispered, "The notice of this meeting's been in every Weekly Newsletter this month and in the monthly *Periscope*. Why wouldn't Frances know about it?"

Jeff grinned and shrugged. "That's the way things go," he said.

The meeting began and the Executive Director introduced the employee of the month, a housekeeping staff person, and presented her with a certificate. Next he introduced the resident of the month. She was a woman we hadn't met and we learned she'd traveled much and written a number of books. Accustomed to public speaking, she gave a short talk. After that the Security Supervisor explained the security system for the benefit of new residents and as a refresher for seasoned residents. The Executive Director then updated the audience on the current status of repairs of the damage caused by hurricane Wilma and also landscaping improvements. His talk was followed by a report of Park Place by Barbara Donnelly, the new Assistant Administrator. Alan Armstrong then stood and announced a meeting of the Resident Council to be held immediately after the meeting. Last week all residents had received a communication in their inner-facility mailboxes saying Dr. Tom Price had resigned from his office as president of the Resident Council and Vice President Alan Armstrong was now president.

The Executive Director was speaking again into the microphone and saying, "I'm going to end the meeting with the most important subject of our meeting. It has to do with piano playing in the lounge, a subject that has caused heated discussions, some almost coming to physical displays of differences." Laughter vibrated through the room. The Director smiled, cleared his throat, and continued. "It seems the music is too loud for some. Other residents thoroughly enjoy it, make requests, and sing along. Some people want to enjoy conversations and their dinners without noise. Others, who love music loud or soft, insist the piano continue to be played. Now you see what a problem we have."

A male resident rose and asked, "Can the volume be decreased?"

The Director retrieved his microphone and said, "Unfortunately, no, it can't."

Sarah Grant rose to her feet and projected her stern voice so all could hear. "This controversy over the piano arose some years ago. At that time, a blanket was placed over the strings to modify the sound. One evening some resident was cold, apparently, and took the blanket. We never saw it again."

Jeff and I both laughed out loud, and laughter from most present rang through the room. The Director's voice could be heard above the din, "The Resident Council has been made aware of the situation and is looking into the problem for a solution."

After the meeting, I cornered Sarah. "Why not get another blanket? Can't management afford one?" I inquired, half joking as I looked at her usual serious sour expression.

"The blanket was a special one. Made by the piano company. They don't make them any more. The blanket was of a particular weight and fabric," she further informed me. Then she turned to Jeff. "Jeffery," she said, always calling him Jeffery. "You're a member of a Rotary Club, aren't you? Do you have speakers at your Rotary Club?"

Jeff acknowledged, "Yes, at every meeting except those bi-annual meetings when we elect officers. Why do you ask?"

"I would like to be a speaker at your next meeting," she said.

"The Rotarian in charge of programs arranges the programs weeks in advance, Sarah."

"Well then, please give the Program Director my name and phone number and advise him I'd like to speak the next opening he has available. I'll talk about foster children and foster parents, of course, and our state social service program. Last week I spoke at the AAUW meeting, to the American Association of University Women, you know. The forty-five women who were there were very receptive to my talk but I only sold three books. I expected to sell twenty-four at least. I was very disappointed."

When we got home I said to Jeff, "Are you going to honor Sarah's request to speak at a Rotary meeting?"

"No I'm not," he answered. "It's against Rotary policy to solicit at Rotary meetings. I'm sure Sarah intends to attempt to sell her book after her talk. I'll tell her I talked to the Program Director and he told me programs have been booked months in advance. You know, if serious Sarah would just smile she'd be a pretty woman."

Another week had passed, and I hadn't visited Elizabeth Price. My toes were still somewhat painful when walking. That could have been my excuse for not going to see Elizabeth sooner but it wasn't. I'd just put off my visit. I dreaded to confront her again in her saddened state. Saturday I made myself go, walking determinedly over to the Club House, along the latticed walkway, and through the door into Park Place. When I approached Elizabeth's room I heard voices. Should I go in? Too late to turn back! A person on Elizabeth's bed called out, "Come on in."

When I neared the bed the figure in tan slacks and yellow jersey top sitting on the bed, legs outstretched, back against the foot board, smiled up at me and said, "I'm Kristine Bruni, Elizabeth's daughter, and this is Al Anderson." She turned and gestured toward a large middle-aged man sitting in a chair on the other side of the room.

"I'm Jeanie Metz. I'm so glad to meet you," I said, shaking her outstretched hand and smiling at her. Then I smiled at Elizabeth who was in her recliner on the other side of the bed and was acknowledging my presence with her little blue eyes.

Elizabeth's daughter said, "You're Jeanie Metz? Yes, yes, I know!" Her hands traveled through her short reddish-colored hair at amazing speed and she shifted on the bed and crossed and uncrossed her legs. She continued in a rather loud tone of voice, "I recognize your name. Dad has a list of people he wants called right away. And you're on that list with five stars after your name!"

I assumed the people on the list were to be called first in the event of his death and was truly impressed and honored to be included on the list. And with five stars! I hoped I indicated as much with an appropriate expression although death was not something to smile about.

"Dad and I have been very busy since I arrived. He keeps remembering things for me to do, things he hasn't gotten around to." Her fingers continued to comb her short reddish hair and her body was in constant motion. Was this body movement normal for her or was it caused by extreme nervousness due to her father's approaching death? She blinked her eyes and continued telling me, "I was sure he was leaving me two nights ago. We were lying in bed side by side holding hands and he said, 'I have just one more last thing for you to do.'

'No, Dad, this will not be the last thing,' I told him."

I glanced over at Elizabeth, eyes on her daughter, obviously listening to every word. "Yesterday Dad told me what I should be doing. 'Invest,' he said. 'Make some good investments.'"

Al, a very large man dressed in gray sport shirt and gray slacks, leaned forward in his chair across the room. "You watch those stocks, Kristine. You can make some good choices and some sad choices."

"I didn't do well with Red Hat," I ventured.

"Red Hat? I never heard of that stock," Al said, looking at me with curiosity. "When did you buy it?"

I had to think for a few minutes and then answered, "It must have been in ninety nine. A friend of mine bought it when it first went on the market but I waited too long. He sold his within a few days and made a killing. The stock dropped right after I bought it."

"Never heard of it," Al replied, shaking his head.

Kristine said, "Lucent. That was my downfall."

I interrupted, "I have that, too. I'm just going to hang onto it. Wait and see. Play a wait and see game."

"That's what I plan to do," Kristine said, shifting about on the bed and smiling up at me.

"How long do you plan to stay, Kristine?" I wanted to know.

"For the duration. I'm staying for the duration," she offered with a half smile. Dad said this morning to clear out a closet, go shopping, and buy some clothes. He'd pay for them, he said." She laughed. "That's what he told me. I only planned to stay for two days. I only have two tops." She laughed again and pulled at the sleeve of her yellow top, "This one and another."

After more chit chat about Costa Rica and where to shop in Jupiter I took my leave telling Kristine to let me know if Jeff or I could do anything to help. Pleased to have met her daughter, I waved to Elizabeth and told her I'd be back next week. I had chosen the right day and time to make my visit and now had the latest information about Tom's condition.

FORTY-THREE
DERMATOLOGIST

My legs some inches below the knees looked awful. Years ago I'd been a sun-worshiper. The desire to create that envied bronze-colored skin started when I was in nurses training. Along with my classmates, all of us in bathing suits, I'd climb up to the rooftop of the nurses' residence to lie on the solarium floor. This opportunity was afforded us during our three hours off duty mid-day those days we were scheduled a split shift. Not only then, but well into my sixties I continued to grab sun rays every chance I had. Now I was reaping belated *rewards*. Had I not lived so long this ugly result would not have occurred. Not that I planned to enter a beauty contest, understand. My concern was the worsening of the irregular round red marks a half-inch in diameter appearing under my skin and topped with keratosis. The keratosis was not a worry. I had those scaly areas of varying sizes on my arms and elsewhere, like rough wood one could make smooth with sandpaper. Heredity and age the causes. Not malignancy. I just had to live with and dislike the appearance and the unpleasant sensation under my fingertips. I was thankful slacks were in vogue so I didn't have to wear nylons I'd be required to wear to cover up my ugly legs if I wore a dress. Bare legs in Florida were a comfort necessity.

A year ago on recommendation and with a referral from Dr. Gray, my G. P., I had an appointment with Dr. Kane, a dermatologist. Actually, I had a number of appointments during which I was subjected to three biopsies, none of which was malignant, one site refusing to heal for over a month. I was also prescribed a local medicated ointment advertised to prevent any occurrence of cancerous growth. This I religiously applied for many weeks even though, in my opinion, I was not at risk for developing cancer. Neither cancer nor diabetes was in my family history.

I decided I needed a new dermatologist. Not Dr. Kane in whom I'd lost faith. I'd get an appointment just to obtain a topical prescription to prevent these ugly red areas from worsening or multiplying. A miraculous preparation. No biopsies! I was not cancer prone!

"So you liked Dr. Ronregus?" I asked Jeff. A month ago he'd been plagued with itching over his legs, arms, and back. I advised he not consult Dr. Kane because of my lack of confidence in him.

Our neighbor Ruth McKee had been going to Dr. Ronregus. "He's a marvelous dermatologist!" she raved. "Young. Very young and handsome." I'd also heard his name mentioned on the public broadcasting station.

"Yes I did like him," Jeff answered. "You know what I always said about dermatologists. I always said I'd never go to one. They never cure you, but they never kill you. They just keep you coming back, raking in the dough. Never have to make house calls. But yes, I did like this Dr. Ronregus. The stuff he gave me is helping a lot. He's just a kid. Handsome. Very pleasant."

"Then I'll call and make an appointment." I placed the call.

"I can give you an appointment at ten in the morning. September the eleventh," the pleasant female office-voice said.

"But this is April! I need to see Dr. Ronregus at least by next week," I exclaimed, shocked at the date she had indicated.

"I'm very sorry but the doctor is seeing no new patients until September."

I didn't answer immediately because I was recovering from the disappointing information. Finally, lacking rebuttal, I said, "Thank you very much," and hung up, not accepting a September appointment.

Later that week, I had a follow-up appointment with Dr. Gray because of an erratic blood pressure I'd been running. "I'm going to increase your Atacand from eight milligrams to sixteen milligrams," Dr. Gray said, looking up at me and then writing the prescription and noting the change in my medical record. "I want you to take your pressure daily and keep a written record. After two weeks you call me and give me a report."

"I'll do that, Dr. Gray," I responded then said to him, "Will you please take a look at these legs of mine again?" I pulled up my slacks for examination by this little doctor I liked and had been using as my general practitioner for six years. We were buddies now, I figured. He acknowledged my nursing background and we had a friendly nurse/physician relationship. When he prescribed new meds for me he often gave me samples.

Now he bent down and peered at my legs. "I referred you to a dermatologist about a year ago, didn't I?"

"You did. You referred me to Dr. Kane. Don't you think I need to see a dermatologist again?"

"You should. You didn't like Dr. Kane?"

My general practitioner was reading my mind. "Frankly, no. I tried to get an appointment with Dr. Ronregus, but I can't get an appointment until September."

"You can't?" He sounded as though he found that unbelievable, frowned, and said, "I'll give you a referral."

On my way out, the girl at the desk looked over the papers Dr. Gray had given me to give her and placed a phone call. When she hung up she glanced at me and said, "You have an appointment with Dr. Ronregus next Wednesday at seven-thirty in the morning."

I walked through the swinging door to the waiting room and over to Jeff sitting reading a newspaper. "Guess what?" I said, grinning. "I have an appointment with Dr. Ronregus next Wednesday."

He looked up at me and said, "How did that miracle occur? You told me you couldn't get one until September."

"Physicians have reciprocal agreements. They do favors for each other."

The day of the appointment with Dr. Ronregus, Jeff and I were the first people in the waiting room. I handed the receptionist my Medicare and Tricare cards and the medical information form I'd received in the mail and completed. Jeff and I took seats in two of the chairs lined closely together on three sides of the waiting room. I glanced around the walls at framed diplomas and degrees from various universities and medical schools and at paintings of landscapes while Jeff leafed through a magazine he retrieved from a center table. As well as multiple magazines neatly grouped, the center table also contained a freshly opened box of tissue and a small wicker basket filled with sample bottles of skin lotion. Before long, we were ushered into an examining room and I was instructed to sit on the examination table. To my right was a Mayo stand neatly set with two-by-two gauze, rubber gloves, containers of cotton balls and applicators, and several surgical instruments. I frowned at the equipment. No biopsy!

A dark-haired young man of medium height and weight clad in dark trousers, lab coat, white shirt, and tie walked in, shook my hand, and said, "I'm Dr. Ronregus." Then he glanced over at Jeff sitting in a chair in the corner of the room and, recognizing him, said, "How are you, Mr. Metz?" Back to me, he said, "Do you want a general examination or do you have a specific area you want me to examine?"

"Just my legs, Dr. Ronregus," I said, extending my legs. "I just need you to prescribe something to attenuate these red areas on my legs. No biopsies. They're not malignant. I'm plagued with keratosis everywhere but I'm not concerned with that. Just these sites on my legs."

He scrutinized my legs. "Yes, keratosis. The red areas don't appear to be suspicious of carcinoma. The information in your chart tells me you've been seen by another dermatologist. A year ago. Do you remember the name of the medication he had you apply? Was it a clear substance?"

I tried to think back. "I'm sorry, doctor. I can't remember. He took three biopsies, and none was malignant. But it took forever for one site to heal. Then he prescribed an application that was to prevent occurrence of carcinoma but I don't remember the name."

"A white creamy ointment?"

"Probably, but I'm not sure."

"Who was the dermatologist? I'd like to call his office. Get a little information on his treatment."

"Dr. Kane," I answered.

He left the office and was back in a few minutes. He was indeed young. Hardly old enough to have spent enough years getting his medical education. I liked his manner. He was spending time with me. Wasn't in a hurry. "Need to examine your legs again," he said, looking more closely now. "This one right here looks suspicious. I'd like to take a very small biopsy of it."

He looked me in the eye and I shook my head. "No biopsy," I said with conviction.

He left the room and came right back with a large text book. He opened the book, searched a minute, and smoothed a page. Then he came to my side and showed me a picture. "This is keratosis," he said, pointing to a colored drawing. "And this is basal cell and this is squamous cell carcinoma and this is melanoma." He pointed to each drawing and read the information under keratosis and squamous cell carcinoma. He put the book on his desk and stood in front of me. "A biopsy no larger than the head of a straight pin. I anesthetize the site first."

"The needle hurts," I said, frowning.

"This one won't. It's tiny."

"Twenty-five gauge." That was the smallest I'd ever used. A subcutaneous needle, one for administering insulin.

"Thirty gauge," he corrected me and held up the needle for me to see.

"I didn't know they came that small," I said, surprised.

"I think you should let him do the biopsy, Jeanie. Give you peace of mind," I heard Jeff say from his seat behind me.

I took a deep breath. Defeated, but knowing the sensible thing to do, I succumbed.

Mission accomplished, Dr. Ronregus held up a small glass bottle for me to see the tiny biopsy floating in a liquid preservative, probably formaldehyde, the chemical we used in the O.R. many years ago.

Five days later when the phone rang I answered. "I'm calling from Dr. Ronregus's office with the lab results of your biopsy," the female voice advised.

Glad to know the results were back. I smiled and said, "Oh good! Benign, isn't it?'

The female on the other end of the line said, "I'm sorry, Mrs. Metz. The report says squamous cell carcinoma."

"Oh no!" I said. "Are you sure?'

"Yes, Mrs. Metz."

"But I don't want this diagnosis, I said, still unconvinced, not believing.

"I understand, Mrs. Metz, and I am very sorry," she said, her voice sympathetic. In a second she went on to say, "They're often removed by radiation treatments."

"How many?" I wanted to know, glad she hadn't mentioned chemotherapy.

"Usually twenty or thirty sessions on consecutive days." Then, "Doctor would like to see you next Thursday. How does ten-thirty suit you?"

"Yes, I'll be there," I said, finally submitting to reality.

Thursday in Dr. Ronregus's waiting room Jeff and I occupied the last two available chairs and waited a half hour to be called into an examining room. Amazing how popular this dermatologist had become in a very short amount of time! Ruth McKee had been one of his first patients several months ago. I wasn't surprised at his popularity as I again looked at his handsome smiling face now approaching me, a welcoming hand extended as I sat on the end of the examining table again. After turning toward Jeff sitting on a chair in a corner of the room and greeting him Dr. Ronregus drew up his five-legged stool and sat down facing me. "To treat squamous cell sites we usually excise and suture and the healing is relatively quick and uneventful. Because of a location where the skin is thin and lacks underlying tissue excision is unadvisable as sutures won't hold and healing does not occur. So you understand?" he asked looking hard at me.

"Yes, I do," I answered, nervous and nodding.

"We can let it go for a year or two, try the application you've already used under Dr. Kane's care, or we can use radiation therapy and eradicate it now." He looked to me for a decision.

Almost at the same time Jeff and I said, "Radiation." I'd had enough of smearing ointment on my legs and seeing no improvement. Why would it eliminate the problem now when it hadn't worked in the past? "How many radiation treatments would I need?" I asked, eying my young dermatologist.

"I'll set you up for an evaluation with Dr. Gunsalus at the Martin Memorial Cancer Center. He'll be the one to determine the number of treatments. You can expect a call from the Center.

The Sandycreek Terrace lounge was crowded that evening, all seats at the little tables taken and residents standing. "Why is it so busy here this evening?" Jeff asked Mandy at the bar as she made our cocktails.

"Many of the residents went to the Kravis Center to see *Sound of Music* this afternoon and they're just getting back and coming in in droves."

"Let's take our drinks out on the patio," Jeff suggested, grasping his drink in one hand, removing his cane from his scooter with the other, and leading the way to the glass door opening onto the patio. With both hands occupied he waited for me to hold open the door.

One table remained empty. It was next to a table where the McKeess and Betty Howe and Ralph Wilson were sitting waiting to be called to a four-top in the dining room. Ruth McKee was holding forth in her usual manner with a voice like a loud speaker. I knew it irritated Jeff. She was saying, "I don't mind the piano most of the time. Some of the pieces have no tune. I'd like it if the selection was better."

"I don't care for the piano at all. It's much too loud all the time. Whose tapes are they?" Betty asked Ruth, her words barely audible compared to Ruth's.

"They belong to Harry Scott. I hear they're going to move the piano out of the lounge and over to the planting area."

Betty's words were barely audible, but we were able to hear, "Is that right? That's not very far away. If they do that, where will they put all the holiday decorations we always see there and enjoy? The reindeer, Santa climbing the ladder, the pumpkins, the Pilgrims?"

"I can't tell you," Ruth replied.

Jeff leaned over and whispered in my ear, "It's a wonder she doesn't know. She knows everything else."

"Now Jeff, behave," I said, shaking my head at him. She's a very nice person at heart. It's just her nature to want to be knowledgeable about everything. It's a good trait, actually.

When the four-some rose to go to dinner Betty paused at our table giving me an opportunity to tell her my dermatologist was sending me to Martin Memorial Cancer Center.

"That's where I go for radiation treatments," she said, resting her bony hand on our table. "You'll like Dr. Gunsalus and the therapists. Everyone there is so nice. They make you feel at home, relaxed, not a bit nervous."

I found that to be true. The day of the evaluation, the admission clerk questioned me politely and with apparent interest. In his spacious office, Dr. Gunsalus made Jeff and me feel immediately at ease as he offered us seats in comfortable upholstered chairs and talked to us in a slow friendly manner sitting behind his huge desk. Satisfied with the medical history involving my leg derma, he came out from behind his desk and visually examined the biopsy site. "Twenty radiation treatments should be the right amount," he said. "You'll come here for a treatment every day for twenty days with the exception of weekends. We'll keep close tabs on you. Your skin will get irritated but we'll give you something to alleviate that. I'm marking your leg with a pen. And now if you'll come into this other room we'll take a measurement. This will leave a circular mark on your leg. It outlines the radiation site."

I went into an adjacent room where a technician placed a clear thin disc on my leg over Dr. Gunsalus's pen mark and drew an outline on the disc. Back in Dr. Gunsalus's office I sat down next to Jeff and waited to learn the date of my first treatment.

In the Impala on the way back to Sandycreek Terrace Jeff said, "That's a lot of trips. Twenty. Every day except weekends for four weeks."

"I can't expect you to do all that driving. Drive every day, Honey. Why don't I take the facility transportation? It goes to professional offices."

"We've never done that. Taken the facility transportation. Not even to Publix or Walgreens," Jeff said, steering the car down U. S. 1.

"Other residents take the transportation all the time. I believe it goes to professional offices three days a week. I'll take it those three days, and you'll only have to drive two days a week."

And that's the way we worked it, giving me a new experience. In a designated notebook at the front desk, I signed up to ride the day of my first appointment and also called Security (the staff assigned to arranging trips in the facility vehicles) on Jeff's recommendation. He always made sure people had needed information even if it meant advising two or three times. I've finally gotten accustomed to this precaution of his as I've also been ingrained in his other worthwhile habits. "Stick with me," he'd say. "You'll learn something every day. Make a million." Then he'd chuckle.

After the first trip to the Cancer Center I always reminded the driver

I'd be riding the next day transportation was scheduled for professional offices. The first day of the following week I'd place a call to Security reminding them of the days I was to be picked up, just to make sure I wouldn't be forgotten.

Treatments went smoothly. Each day I entered the large building through automatic swinging doors, reported to the receptionist who greeted me by name, walked through another door past a nursing station, turned right, opened another door, walked down a short hall with tiny dressing rooms on one side, and entered a female waiting room. This room consisted of four chairs, a magazine table, and an ever-playing TV. Here I waited my turn, sometimes with other patients, some days by myself. Women receiving treatments for breast cancer were clad in slacks and hospital gowns. One rather young woman always wore a tightly-fitting printed cap encasing her entire head like our old white O.R. caps only attractive. Possibly she'd received chemotherapy prior to these radiation treatments and the chemo had caused loss of hair.

Each time I was called into the treatment room the technicians asked, "How are you today?" to which I said, "Fine, and how are you?"

One day a technician answered, "My son is home sick with mononucleosis." Of course I said I was sorry to hear that.

After being greeted I was instructed to lie on my side on a very narrow table, place my head on a not-too-soft small rectangular block, and bend my legs. A bed pillow was placed between my knees and a tight strap secured my legs to the table in a specific position.

"Now for my free ride," I joked as the table moved me under the huge radiation apparatus hanging from above like a large luminous light hanging from the ceiling over a patient's incision in an operating room.

Satisfied with the location of my leg under the apparatus, the technicians left the room saying, "Now comes your treatment." Protected from radiation rays, they performed a miracle, releasing rays to my leg's squamous cell site while I closed my eyes, fearing rays would hurt my diseased optic fibers. Then I listened to a humming noise and waited for the clicks. After I'd counted ten clicks they stopped and the technicians returned to the room.

"You're finished," they cheerfully said, releasing the strap and removing the pillow. As I climbed down from the skinny table and started to leave they called out behind me, "Have a nice day! See you tomorrow!"

After my treatment, I was seen by Dr. Gunsalus or another oncologist on Mondays, weighed on Tuesdays, had blood drawn the second Tuesday, and was seen by a nurse on Wednesdays. The first Thursday I was seen by a dietitian who said she'd see me the next Thursday to go over my diet until I informed her I was an RN and monitored my own diet. I was politely excused from taking more of her time.

The rides in facility transportation, a new white Lincoln Continental with blue Sandycreek Terrace logo on the side, afforded me the opportunity to become acquainted with the drivers, two females and one male, driving on designated days. The male driver was also on the security staff and wore one of the latest-acquired security uniform—dark green pants and matching-colored long-sleeved shirt adorned with Sandycreek Terrace logo on an upper sleeve. A badge was affixed to a breast pocket. The females wore black slacks and white long-sleeved shirts sporting the logo. They also wore white caps with black brims. Quite jaunty!

The slimmer of the two female drivers started a conversation with me one day when I was her sole passenger. She was divorced with three children and was about to get married, she said, to a man on the maintenance staff with whom she and her children had been living for five years. "He's finally asked me to marry him!" she exclaimed. "We're having a very simple ceremony," she continued, excited like a twenty-one year old planning her first wedding.

The trips in the Lincoln Continental also provided me with the opportunity to know some of the residents I hadn't previously met. One received treatments at a physical therapy office three times a week, another had a dental appointment one day, and a third, a check-up with her cardiologist another day. I was the only oncology patient, the only resident going to the Cancer Center.

For several weeks I'd been ignoring the increasing soreness of my left great toe. When podiatrist Dr. Sargent performed an extensive removal of an ingrown toenail of that same toe seven months ago he'd said further removal would probably not be necessary. The pain I was now experiencing was proving his prediction erroneous. Finally unable to ignore the pain any longer, I complained to Jeff.

"You better get it taken care of," he advised me.

"But I was hoping to wait until these radiation treatments were completed."

"Might as well get both problems taken care of at the same time. Be done with it," he said.

That made sense and I said, "Maybe I can get an appointment with Dr. Sargent after my radiation treatment on Wednesday, the day you drive me to the Cancer Center."

"Call and see what you can do. That sounds like a good plan," he said, scratching his arm, still having his eczema problem and applying the ointment Dr. Ronregus had prescribed.

I was able to get a podiatry appointment and that's how I happened to be sitting in the torture chair in Dr. Sargent's work chamber while he examined my toes. By then the laceration I'd sustained when climbing into my daughter's SUV in Kelso, Washington was practically healed. He noted it, however, and asked, "What's that from?"

"A laceration from foolishly trying to climb into an SUV like I was twenty-one again," I informed him.

"Was it sutured at our local hospital?" he wanted to know, still scrutinizing my wound.

"No," I said. "The accident occurred in the state of Washington. A physician in Longview Hospital sutured it in the emergency room. He had quite a time stopping the bleeding and approximating the edges. Put in thirteen sutures."

"Did a good job! Very good suturing job! I didn't think you had it done here. If you ever need any suturing on your legs or feet in the future, don't go to our hospital here. You come to us," he told me. I nodded but thought it strange for a medical professional to make such an adverse remark about a local hospital. Supposedly he had good reason and I tucked that bit of advice in my mental computer.

"This time I'll remove the nail, roots, and matrix. The procedure guarantees your nail will never become ingrown again. And this isn't going to hurt," Dr. Sargent said. "I promised you I wouldn't hurt you. See. I have a note right here in your chart telling me to inject you with lidocain the next time I remove your toenail."

I tried to relax while my podiatrist prepared dressings, instruments, and a syringe. "I'm going to scream when you inject that anesthetic. I told you to schedule me at the end of the day when no patients would be in the office to hear me scream."

I was joking as I'd done other visits and he knew it and came back with, "The walls are sound-proof. Scream all you like. But you won't need to because I'm not going to hurt you."

I gritted my teeth and squinted as the needle jabbed and liquid Lidocain infiltrated the tissues. I squelched a scream and whimpered over and over with the pain caused by more and more advancing anesthetic. "How much are you putting in? A quart?" I asked.

"Just a cc," he answered, looking up at me with concern. "You're doing fine," he assured me.

Surely this injection of Lidocain was worse than the actual cutting and removal of the toenail, wasn't it? I'd never know because, with the cc finally injected, I felt nothing.

"We're finished," Dr. Sargent announced, sitting back on his stool. I heaved a big sign and relaxed my clinched fists. "Now you watch while I dress your toe. So you can dress it just like I do. I want you to soak your toe twice a day in vinegar water. One ounce to a gallon of lukewarm water. Then apply a very small amount of Bacitracin ointment in this opening. Like this." He squeezing the tube. "Fold a two by two in fours like this and place it on the toe like this." He demonstrated. "Wrap a piece of adhesive around to hold it in place. After you soak your toe. Do this twice a day for a week and then come back."

I nodded at my instructor, gingerly slipped my foot into my sandal, and went to the desk to make an appointment for a week hence. When I walked into the waiting room Jeff scrutinized my bandaged toe sticking out from my sandal and asked, "How'd it go?".

"Terrible! It hurt!"

"Does it hurt now?" he inquired, getting up from his seat and taking my arm with one hand, his cane with the other.

"No, not at all. It only hurt when he injected the local. That's when it *really* hurt," I said as I got into the Impala.

Every day, twice a day, bless his heart, Jeff helped me dress my toe.

After I soaked it he applied the Bacitracin since I couldn't see exactly where to squirt it. He prepared the two by two gauze and tape and applied both. The second week Dr. Sargent instructed me to soak only once a day, continue with the Bacitracin, and secure the dressing with a seven-inch-long strip of stockingette folded back on itself. Those instructions were carried out for a week, and on the return visit my podiatrist said, "Your toe's healing nicely. No need to come back. The scab will fall off in time."

One day the second week into my radiation treatments when I boarded the Lincoln Continental for my return trip to Sandycreek Terrace, Betty Howe was sitting in the back seat. "Hello, Jeanie. How did your treatment go today? I've just been to my internist. My emphysema is worse. The doctor ordered a different inhalant. How many radiations treatments have you had so far?"

"This was my sixth. I'm not minding them at all so far. Nothing shows on my leg so far either," I said, settling back in the seat beside her.

"Your leg will get red and sore later. What is wrong with your toe?" she asked, looking down at my foot.

"I had an ingrown toenail removed. I call it a radical removal because the podiatrist removed the roots and matrix and said the job is permanent. I'll never have to have it removed again. *He* doesn't call it radical removal but *I* do. He made very light of it."

"Who do you go to, Jeanie?" she wanted to know.

"Dr. Sargent. He removed the same ingrown nail twice before, once ten months ago and then more extensively seven months ago. But not as he did this time."

"I go to him too. Many of the residents at Sandycreek Terrace go to him. He's the best in this area. Well, here we are back home," she said, as the driver stopped the car at the entrance to our building.

"Back home," she said. Would this ever feel like it was home to me? The word *home* just didn't fit somehow.

FORTY-FOUR
SUNSHINE

I'd been awake, turned over, and fallen back to sleep and into a wild dream when I felt Jeff's arm reach around my back and hold me close. I was safe, no longer living that horrid nightmare but safe in our bed with Jeff. Then his familiar hand caressed my breast. "Let's make love," he whispered.

After breakfast when Jeff had read the first section of the Palm Beach Post and was on the second page of the local news he said, "Listen to this! The family of the resident who choked on the piece of meat is suing Sandycreek Terrace. They're claiming the facility was negligent because the pieces of meat were too large for her to swallow and staff did not administer the Heimlich maneuver within the required time. The article says the attorney plans to investigate further by questioning staff and residents who were present at or near the incident and could serve as witnesses to determine actual attempts to revive Mrs. Harris."

"Oh dear!" I said. "I heard the meat was cut in fine pieces. People sitting with her were saying that. They *were* concerned about the Heimlich maneuver. It seems not all dining room staff are trained to perform the maneuver. They should be."

"Not all people have the same idea about size. A small piece of meat may not seem small to others. You cut your meat in smaller sized pieces than I do, for example."

"Jeff, I was near the table because I went up to perform the Heimlich. Remember? How do you think the attorney will obtain the names of staff and residents in order to question them? I wasn't at the table. I'm sure my name won't be mentioned. You don't think it will, do you?"

"I doubt it. The attorney will probably ask the Assistant Food Service Manager. He was there, wasn't he?"

"Yes he was," I answered and thought no more about it. I didn't realize he had seen me.

At my desk I flipped over my calendar from May to June and realized I was half way through my radiation treatments, my toes hurting but little from their swimming pool trauma, and my podiatry session a past memory fortunately. That evening after we'd completed a cribbage game Jeff asked, "Do you think we can make plans to go to the Shack?"

Was I hearing correctly? Make plans to go to the Shack! After last summer and my bouts of TIAs Jeff had led me to believe he opposed going very far from our physicians and local hospital. Too risky for me to be in an isolated place like the farming valley in Pennsylvania where I might spike another TIA or possibly a full blown CVA. Months ago we'd talked briefly about the possibility of going to the west coast of Florida for a few days to visit friends. But I'd thought even that had been wishful thinking. No more had been said. And that was before my appointment with Dr. Ronregus, before the biopsy diagnosis of squamous cell carcinoma and the need for twenty radiation treatments. Was Jeff serious about going now? That far? So late in the season?

The thought of going sent tingles up my spine. How wonderful that would be! To leave Sandycreek Terrace and all these close-proximity residents we see so often on the grounds, in the lounge, in the Palace. Like a commune. Many very old and debilitated. Many canes and walkers and scooters. How nice not to see the single red rose and white baby breath in the bud vase on the front desk reminding us of another death. A relief for awhile not to go out and come back in a gate of a facility where we all strived to live life to the fullest with what little time we had, bravely playing a game of survival until we died.

How exciting to drive along the interstate out of Florida, through Georgia, then South Carolina where we'd stay overnight in our favorite motel in Santee. Stop in North Carolina and see some of our children, his and mine. See the Shenandoah Valley, the Blue Ridge Mountains of Virginia, and finally Pennsylvania! Climb to the top of Sidling Hill

Mountain then drive down, down, down five to ten percent grades twisting to the right and to the left for five miles past dense trees and clumps of pink laurel. How thrilling to suddenly behold a fertile valley of farm lands spread out in front of us! See once again my plowed field and unpainted barn, over one-hundred-years old. Drive in a lane, cross a wooden bridge, and park. There it would be! The Shack. I'd smile at the sight of it, still there, waiting. We'd enter and look around to see everything just as we'd left it! Back we'd be, to live with familiar furnishings, touch the player piano, smile at my children, relatives, and friends in the framed photo collages. Let my mind linger on the antique kerosene lamps on the mantle, lamps that once lighted my grandparents' red brick farmhouse before electricity came to the valley. Observe the boot lasts hanging above the mantle decorating the stone fireplace. Admire the stained glass pieces hanging at the dining room windows. Finally climb the stairs to the bedrooms and touch the woven antique throw on the cedar chest filled with old worn handmade quilts.

Suitcases unpacked, we'd sit on the screened-in porch, grassy green meadow spreading out to the creek bank beyond. We'd watch a squirrel run up and down the giant trunk of the black walnut tree and breathe in the refreshing breeze stirring its leaves. We'd smell the meadow's fresh-cut grass Ron mowed before he stayed for the dinner we'd eat there on the screened-in porch.

On Sundays we'd attend the small white-frame country church with its thirty parishioners where a lay minister preached and eighty-year-old Gladys Ford sang a solo (always a familiar hymn) while Terry played the ancient piano. We'd drive to the little post office and sit on an old wooden bench to wait for the mail to be sorted by the one and only employee, the female post master. We'd join the local crowd the day of Homecoming and watch the parade along the mile stretch of the village street.

Was it possible? Dare I hope? At the thought, excitement ran through my blood along with plasma and white and red corpuscles. But I still had two weeks of radiation therapy. When would Dr. Gunsalus want to see me again after my last treatment? And when would Dr. Ronregus require a return visit? Quite possibly in two weeks or a month or two months, leaving no time to make any trip anywhere. So don't look forward to this, Jeanie. Don't ask for disappointment.

I needed to squelch my hopes and voice my fears to Jeff. "Honey, it would be wonderful to go to the Shack. But I'm afraid Dr. Gunsalus will want to see me again, maybe in a month or two after the radiation treatments are completed. Maybe even Dr. Ronregus will need to have me come back."

Jeff had returned to reading his *U.S. News and World Report* but after my comment he glanced up and said, "We won't come to any conclusions now. When will you next see Dr. Gunsalus?"

"A week from this Monday. I'll see him then. This Monday I see a different oncologist."

"Good. Ask him when you next see him. You're mended otherwise. Feet and toes. Your eye pressure's stabilized. I think you're doing just fine. If we go we should make the trip worthwhile," he said, giving me a big smile.

What did he mean by *worthwhile*? *More* than a few weeks? Surely he wouldn't think it wise to stay longer and be thirty miles from an acceptable hospital. That distance didn't take into account the time it would take 911 to travel to the Shack and then to a hospital. I took a deep breath and asked, "How long do you think we'd stay?"

"Until mid-September probably," he replied, and back to his magazine he went.

I smiled to myself, jubilant to hear the long length of time he was considering. Now to convince the physicians I didn't need to be examined until fall.

When reading about resident activities in The Weekly Newsletter I picked up from our intra-facility mailbox the next afternoon I noted with great interest Dr. Tom Price was a patient at Shands Hospital. Had his condition worsened or was he there to receive treatment? At least his daughter Kristine would get a rest, be able to go back home to take care of pressing matters. Three days later when Jeff and I attended the in-house movie one of the residents said, "Has everyone heard that Tom Price died?"

My chest tightened. I didn't want to hear this. I turned to Jeff, "How, in such a short time, in just two years, could I feel so close to a person?" I asked.

Jeff patted my arm. "Death is part of life. It's in and out."

"That's what happens here," I said, tears welling in my eyes.

Jeff responded, "It happens everywhere."

No vase with a red rose and baby's breath was on the front desk. Apparently Tom had requested that ritual not take place. A headline in the Palm Beach Post read *Doctor for the Needy Mourned.* His photo and a fitting article followed. A memorial service was being held in a local church. No commemoration at Sandycreek Terrace.

On my next trip in the facility car to the Cancer Center, I rode with a resident who quickly introduced herself and said, "Isn't Tom Price's death a catastrophe? Our place won't be the same without him. He did so much for the residents. Worked with management for our benefit."

"Yes," I agreed. "And represented our facility and other CCRCs at the state capital trying to eliminate the need for us to pay increased maintenance fees by fighting the possibility of legislatives passing a bill that would increase taxes levied on CCRCs." I was talking from the back seat to her gray head in front of me.

The resident said, "I didn't understand why there was no recognition of his death at Sandycreek Terrace, as well known as he was and because of all he did. I know his wife. My husband was in Park Place a long time before he died and I visited her there when I visited him. We became good friends. I went over to see her yesterday. She covered her face. Wouldn't look at me. I asked her, 'Do you want me to leave?' She nodded."

With that information I was glad I hadn't gone to see Elizabeth yet. I'd wait a week.

We had dinner that evening with Gus and Rachel Homburg. They were planning their usual trip to an island in a Canadian province. "Are you two leaving for Pennsylvania this summer?" Gus asked.

"We're thinking very seriously about it," Jeff said, cutting into his prime rib.

"How long do you stay?" Rachel wanted to know as she took a sip of wine.

I waited for Jeff to answer. To my delight he said, "Probably mid-September if all goes well."

When we returned to our apartment we sat down in the Florida room to have our usual game of cribbage. "Your turn to deal, Jeff. You're on a winning streak," I said, handing him the deck of playing cards.

"I believe the gods of the cards are favoring me at last," he said, dealing six cards to each of us.

I opened my hand. Two fives, two kings, a two and a four. A winner! I kept a poker face.

Jeff looked into his hand and said, "Not great. I need a cut,"

"I'll give you a wonderful cut. I always do," I promised.

"That's no cut. Can't you do better? I said I needed a cut!"

I smiled. The cut was good for me. A five! We played out our hands, each moving two pegs. Jeff looked at my cards, now face up on the table. "Holy smokes! Look at your hand! That's one of the biggest hands in cribbage! Did you pray to the gods of the cards? Did you tell them not to give me a good hand? Just look at my hand!"

"It is pretty sad, isn't it?" I said, laughing at his miserable cards as I moved my peg forward twenty-four counts.

"You keep this up and you'll double skunk me tonight," he moaned.

"I need to, I'm so far behind." I skunked but didn't double-skunk him.

The next morning I brought up the e-mails on the desk-top computer while Jeff went to chair his Housekeeping, Maintenance, and Security Committee meeting. My cousin had sent me her last information to include in the Scottish family genealogy we were compiling. I had partially completed a family tree and had written a paragraph or more about each of the twelve siblings born to our great grandparents. Now I realized I had information about their children and families. With this final heritage e-mail from my cousin I intended to complete this genealogy project before we went north. I was daring to think of that trip as a reality.

Another e-mail, one from Jeff's son Fred, was directly under the one from my cousin. As soon as Jeff returned from his committee meeting I told him, "Jeff, you have an e-mail from Fred."

"What does he say?" Jeff asked, immediately interested of course.

"I didn't read it. I left that for you to do. I'll bring it up."

Jeff stood behind me seated in front of the monitor and we read the message together. "What do you think of that!" he said, chuckling. "My grandson's getting married! Our grandson's getting married," he corrected, changing the pronoun. Jeff always wanted me to know his family was also mine and I appreciated that. "They're getting married in Holland, by George. My home town! Now isn't that something! Why would they pick Windmill Island? Well, I guess that's their choice, but it seems an unlikely place for a wedding. When is the twenty-first of July? What day of the week?" Jeff turned to his desk and looked at the wall calendar. "A Friday. It's a Friday."

"You'd want to go, wouldn't you Jeff?" I was sure he would.

"Yes, of course. We'll be up there. We can drive over to Holland in a day or two. Maybe go the week before and bum around. Visit friends. Go to a Rotary meeting. The museum."

I was glad Jeff liked to drive. At eighty-five he still had excellent vision, good reflexes, didn't tire, and his back never bothered him when he drove. Another thing. He didn't mind when I reminded him his turn signal was still clicking or once in a long while gave him a heads up when I saw the red brake lights of the car directly in front of us and he wasn't slowing down. When he drove in the left lane, which he usually did, and a car pulled in front of him and slowed down making him apply his brakes and shift out of cruse-control he still didn't swear. Most men would. In his relaxed driving manner he still just said, *"Friend"* although he meant the opposite. Best of all, he continued to reach over with his right hand and hold my arm at times. Yes, for the most part, he still drove with his left hand only.

After a lunch of Jeff's home-made chicken soup, I made up my mind to visit Elizabeth. I walked my usual route to Park Place and paused at the door to her room. Her chin almost touching her chest, her curly hair white like Queen Ann's Lace and matching the white of her anklets, she appeared to be asleep as usual. Again I could hear Tom's words telling me, "Talk to her. She's not really asleep." I knocked on the door and walked in.

"Elizabeth," I said. "It's Jeanie Metz."

She looked up. "Yes, I know who you are. Come in. I'm glad to see you. How are you?" she said, her voice soft and low.

I perched myself on the edge of the bed facing her. *"I'm* fine. Tell me how *you* are." She looked sad, dejected. I waited.

"I can't believe it. I can't believe it."

"I know. It's hard to believe. He was a fine, stalwart man. So active, always busy," I said.

"Always busy," she repeated. "Too busy. He shouldn't have worked so hard. I miss him."

"I know," I said, patting her hand. "He lived a very worthwhile life. He contributed so much to so many."

"Yes, he did," she acknowledged. Then her little blue eyes on me she said, "You always look so pretty. You look good in that purple color. It becomes you."

I strained to hear her words and glanced down at my purple shirt. It was the first time I'd worn it, ordered from a Haband catalogue. "I ordered this shirt and a pink one like it out of a catalogue from Jeff's favorite shopping outlet," I told her. "I've never done that before, ordered from a catalogue. I always shop at *my* favorite stores, stores where salesgirls help me with size, colors, and price tags. But Jeff insisted I look at Haband's women's catalogue and find something. Mostly to please him, I chose two permapress shirts. When they came I had to iron them because they were so wrinkled. But they fit fairly well, much to my surprise."

She smiled and murmured, "It looks very nice on you. Becomes you."

To make more conversation, I told her, "I'm finally getting my physical problems resolved. The excision of my ingrown toenail. That foot I banged into the ladder of the swimming pool is healing. And I'm receiving radiation for the squamous cell carcinoma on my leg.

"Things always seem to occur in threes, don't they?" she murmured."

"It looks like we'll be going up to Pennsylvania in a few weeks," I told her.

"How nice. How long will you stay?" she asked.

"Probably until mid-September. Would you like me to write to you?" Would someone read my letters to her if I wrote?

"Would you send me cards? I'd like that very much."

"I certainly will," I promised, realizing picture post cards would be just the right communication. Something she could see. I'd send one from North Carolina, one from Pennsylvania, and then one from Holland

Michigan. One of Windmill Island where Jeff and I would be attending a wedding. Little did I know she'd never receive the cards. She died before I returned.

I'd stayed my allotted time, always leaving after a half-hour visit when I noticed Elizabeth was beginning to tire from talking.

"Thank you for coming. I'll be thinking about you and your trip," she said as I left.

I'd rounded the nursing station and was passing the physical therapy department when I noticed Kathy and Carl Franklin coming toward me, Carl with a walker faltering along with Kathy by his side. Carl was but a ghost of his former self. He'd been a tall man, nicely built, straight of stature, rather handsome, and always pleasant and attentive. Now this thin, stooped, gaunt man looked haggard and didn't recognize me as I stopped to talk to them.

"Come into his room," Kathy invited. I turned around and walked at their pace until Kathy stopped at a door. The three of us entered the room and Kathy showed me a painting on one of the walls. It was her painting of their former residence, a lovely house on a green lawn surrounded by shrubbery and trees.

"That's beautiful, Kathy. I'd forgotten you were an artist," I remarked.

She smiled. "It's our former home. I brought it over here from the apartment for Carl to enjoy."

"I've missed seeing you," I said to Kathy, thinking of the time she had pinched me on the bottom and been so terribly embarrassed, apologizing over and over. "We should have dinner together some evening."

"That would be nice but I eat early and quickly and then come here while Carl gets fed through a feeding tube. And I stay until he goes to bed for the night."

I walked back to our apartment feeling very sad for Kathy and Carl. Carl had never seemed totally alert, probably a stroke some time in the past with partial brain damage, and then another stroke eight months ago, requiring his admittance to Park Place. At least they'd had that cruise together.

When I got back to our apartment Jeff had just returned from his monthly Vise Club meeting. "How did the meeting go?" I asked him.

"Only six of us were there. Emmett Gorman, self-appointed chairman, wants Maintenance to notify all residents they need to be cautious when handling the electrical equipment. Hell, not enough men use the woodshop to worry about that. Those of us who do frequent the shop know all about that equipment. Next thing you know, management will want members to buy insurance to cover possible accidents. I told Emmett, 'Keep management out of the woodshop. We don't need them nosing around. It's our shop. Members that use it know how to be cautious.'"

"Who uses the woodshop besides you, Jeff?" I asked.

"Emmett hasn't used it since he installed his equipment. Craig's airplane's still hanging from the ceiling, never touched. He's been in and out of the hospital, too weak to come to the shop. Jim Horner putters around making a footstool for his wife. I use it more than anyone else."

"How are your bird houses coming along?"

"My bird houses for blue birds? I've finished eight of them. I'm going to take them with us up north. Give a couple to Mary Jo and Mel, one to Martje, and two to Kirk and Sally.

"That's nice. I'm sure they'll appreciate them."

"I'll finish them off at Mary Jo's. Sand them down and lacquer them."

FORTY-FIVE

ACCEPTANCE

The very next day we learned Horace James was in Park Place. We didn't happen to see Patricia James or anyone who could tell us the reason for his admission. A week later, however, both Horace and Patricia were in the lounge. As Jeff and I stood at the bar ordering our pre-dinner cocktails, Patricia immediately walked up to us and said, "Please don't say anything to Horace about his having been in Park Place. He doesn't remember he was there."

To Jeff I said, "Another set-back for Horace. And for Patricia. She'll need to lead him now more than she has in the past."

"No doubt," Jeff responded.

The next morning I had an e-mail from my cousin Gina. She was one of my five first cousins on my mother's side of the family and, unlike cousins on my father's side, was the only one who owned a computer. Three years younger than I, she and her husband Fred lived in Wayne, New Jersey. We corresponded via e-mail throughout the year when the spirit moved us and always at Christmas. In years past we'd visited back and forth, and after Jeff and I married we'd visited them at their home in Wayne one time. Since we'd discontinued our small family reunions a year ago, I hadn't seen her. We had always enjoyed each other's company and had similar ideas about life in general.

I reread her e-mail and was pleased to learn she wanted to meet us somewhere in Pennsylvania and spend a weekend together. That would be after we made our trip north and were at the Shack. I was to choose the spot. Since I knew she and Fred enjoyed visiting old towns and delving into history, I chose Gettysburg. The Dobbin House, built in 1776 and located on the route to the Civil War battlefield, would be a perfect place to stay, I decided. I remembered having candle-light dinner in its underground tavern where servers were dressed in colonial costumes. The ambiance was enchanting and romantic. Sleeping quarters were available in several old houses a few steps on either side of the Dobbin House. If the oncologist gave me the answer I needed on Monday, I'd call Gina.

I'd decided to lengthen my morning walks to two miles and was no longer walking a half mile and retracing my steps but continuing on past all the cottages. The security employee in his golf cart would no longer have to ask why I didn't go the entire distance. This new route led me onto the curved bridge over the Venetian pond with its three fountains and along a route leading past the Club House and Palace and down the corridors back to our apartment. I enjoyed this walk as it took me on a curving walkway past golden-mound hedges topped with little yellow flowers, on past the pigmy date palm to the Crimean lily plant with flowers like clusters of milk-white sticks that could only grow six inches high before they drooped and descended another six inches. Then I came to the leathery-leaved ornamental croton, crepe myrtle, and blue-flowered plumbago. On either side of the road leading to the Club House tall stately royal palms stood at attention. At the circle in front of the entrance I always admired the lower-growing palms and magnolia. Then the sweet little pink and white impatiens lined the beds on either side of the walk leading to the automatically opening glass front doors.

The last Monday of my radiation treatments at the Cancer Center arrived. This was also the day for my examination by Dr. Gunsalus. He came into his office dressed in a lab coat over a white long-sleeved shirt, tie, and dark trousers and asked in his usual jovial manner, "How are you today, Mrs. Metz?" Then he took a seat across from me sitting there waiting after my treatment.

"I'm just fine, Dr. Gunsalus," I answered, smiling at him. "My leg's getting a little sore as you can see." I lifted my leg and he came over and elevated it further for a better view.

427

"It looks all right. The way it should look by now after the number of treatments you've had. Are you applying Aquaflo?"

"Yes I am," I answered. Then I took a deep breath and said, "I have a question I need to ask you." He looked at me quizzically as I said, "Will you need to see me after my last treatment which is Wednesday?"

"Yes I will in about a month. You can make an appointment as you leave here Wednesday."

I took another deep breath, crossed two fingers, and cupped them in my other hand. "Is that absolutely necessary? I was hoping to go up north to Pennsylvania for several months this summer, and we'd like to leave fairly soon."

"You were? Where in Pennsylvania?" he asked, smiling. "I went to medical school in Pennsylvania. Love that state!"

He sounded truly interested, and I said, "It isn't anywhere you would know. It's in farm country. A valley surrounded by mountains east of Bedford and west of Chambersburg," I mentioned two towns he just might know.

"I know that area. Lovely country! How soon were you planning to go?" he asked, leaning forward.

"In about two weeks," I told him, knowing I had scheduled appointments with my cardiologist, my neurologist, and my dentist, all marked on the calendar for the next two weeks.

"I shouldn't need to see you until you come back. If you have a problem in the next two weeks, you call. I'll be here every day the next two weeks. Just call. Otherwise, when you get back to Florida call and make an appointment to see me. And you have a great summer," he said, rising.

I was elated. We shook hands and walked out of the office together. The nurse stopped me before I'd taken two steps. "I need to weigh you today, Mrs. Metz. I won't be here Wednesday. Hop up on the scale." I mounted the machine. "One ten. You're doing fine." she announced.

I felt like telling her *she* wasn't doing fine with all those pounds she carried, but I restrained myself. As I was pushing open the last swinging door, Dr. Gunsalus called to me from behind the nurse's desk, "Have a good time in my favorite place in Pennsylvania."

"I will," I answered, giving him a big smile. When I stopped at the reception desk the clerk said, "I'll call for your ride, Mrs. Metz." By now I was a seasoned patient, like an inmate about to be released for a day out into the community.

Back to Sentinel Building and hastening to our apartment, I opened the door and called to my hubby. "Jeff, are you here?"

"I'm in the den, Honey," he called back.

I hurried there and he'd turned around from the lap top to learn what I had to say. "I don't have to be seen again by Dr. Gunsalus until fall! Isn't that great?"

"Yes it is, Sweetie. Now we can start making plans to leave." He grinned at me.

I went over to him, put my arms around him, and gave him a kiss, almost knocking off his spectacles perched on top of his bald head. "You don't have any more commitments before we leave, do you?" he asked, looking at me wide-eyed.

"Well yes, but they're all in the next two weeks. My cardiologist and a pacemaker check. The neurologist. And the dentist is last. My dental appointment's two weeks from today. Just for a routine cleaning and check."

"Holy smokes!" Jeff chuckled. "You keep all those guys in business. Good thing we have Tricare. I'm sure glad we finally got what was promised years ago to us retired military. I told you legislatures have had it for years."

"I have to call Dr. Ronregus's office to make sure he doesn't want to see me again. I'll talk him out of it if he does," I giggled, leaving the den and going to the Florida room to make the call.

After that successful call I called Gina. She expressed delight at my choice. We set the date for the weekend after Jeff and I arrived at the Shack, and then I called the Dobbin House. Another wonderful reason for going up north!

The next morning Jeff tried out our new waffle iron using Jiffy corn muffin mix to make the waffles. I could smell the marvelous mix cooking before I entered the kitchen. "These are delicious, Jeff," I exclaimed after chewing a bite-sized piece spread with orange marmalade preferable to syrup, in my opinion.

"Thanks, Sweetie. They *are* pretty good," he said, cutting off a second generous piece of his waffle smothered with butter and maple syrup. "I guess we made a good buy with that waffle iron. After we eat, I'm going to start a list of all the things we need to do before we leave for the Shack. After I read the morning paper. And we need to have a little talk, too."

I detected a serious note in his voice and, not wanting to wait, asked, "A little talk about what, Jeff?"

"Finish eating and then we'll talk," he instructed.

So I had to wait while we drank our orange juice, ate our waffles, and took our morning pills always stored on the kitchenette table. We hadn't quite drained our coffee and tea cups when Jeff leaned back in his chair and began, "This trip we're taking. We're going to have a great time at the Shack, at Gettysburg with your cousins, and in Holland, Michigan visiting friends and attending my grandson's wedding on Windmill Island. I can drive long distances without any difficulty. But I don't know if I'm going to be able to do that much longer. Maybe not next year. This may be our last long trip." He paused and looked across the table at me.

"I understand," I said. And I did understand. I knew how fortunate we were that he could still drive long distances. But I didn't want to think about the time when he wouldn't be able to drive. I looked at him, waiting for him to continue.

"You've been fine for quite a while. No TIAs. But I've told you before how concerned I am about being so far away from competent medical help. All our physicians are here. If we need care we should go to physicians who know us, not some strange doctor. Not a Dr. Turbanhead. Not the kind of physician my cardiologist daughter says is on the staff of many small hospitals."

I snickered remembering Mary Jo saying, "You don't want to wake up in a strange hospital and see Dr. Turbanhead looking down at you."

"Another thing," Jeff continued after raising his coffee cup and swallowing his last mouthful. "The Shack has steps. Steps we have to climb to go to bed. Then back down in the middle of the night to go to the bathroom because the bathrooms are downstairs. I don't know how long I'm going to be able to climb stairs. How long are you going to be able to climb stairs? They're hazardous. What if we should fall?"

I drew a deep breath. I'd heard all this before and it was true. But I didn't want to hear it, to believe the risks involved.

Jeff rubbed his hands together and went on. "We're isolated at the Shack. Neighbors are not close."

"We can call 911 if we have an emergency," I said weakly, squeezing my eyes into slits, concentrating on rebuttals.

He sighed. "Now, Jeanie, you know how long it would take for 911 to get to the Shack and then to get to a hospital." He paused, rubbed his hands together again. "Food. We have to go thirty miles for an order of food. And when we get it home we have to carry it in. Up patio steps and up porch steps. Those groceries are heavy. Neither of us is supposed to lift anything heavy. You have osteoporosis. My orthopedic doctor said nothing over five pounds. We lift over five pounds all the time when we're at the Shack."

"And when we're here," I had to say because it was true. I took another deep breath, shifted in my seat, and waited, saying nothing more.

Jeff looked at me and reached over and took hold of my hand. "Here at Sandycreek Terrace we have everything. If we get in trouble all we have to do is pull a cord. You just used the facility transportation. You know how convenient it is. And I hope that will never be. But if I can't drive we can be driven to a store to buy food and necessities." He released my hand and took off his glasses from atop his head and laid them on the table. "I know you run the sweeper at the Shack and clean the bathrooms in between the times Charlene comes to clean. You wash all those dishes from all the meals. More when Ron eats with us. Here, Marigold comes in once a week and cleans. Here we eat breakfast and lunch in our apartment and the dishwasher washes those dishes."

"I do those tasks gladly at the Shack. I like the exercise. I need the exercise." I said this emphatically and meant it

He ran his hand over his head and focused his eyes on mine again. "I know you do, Jeanie, but I don't like to see you work like that. Also we get yearly all-inclusive apartment cleaning and carpet shampooing here. We never have to make dinner. We have a lovely dining room to enjoy. And we can take advantage of many activities and attend a great party every month. We've made nice friends. What more could we ask?"

"Nothing," I said. I knew he was trying to prepare me for the inevitable. We weren't ever going to make another trip to the Shack after this trip. He wanted me to accept that fact. I was to realize we couldn't ask for a better place to live than Sandycreek Terrace. He wanted me to be satisfied and thankful. I leaned back in my chair and took another deep breath. We *were* in a fine place. I had to agree that all Jeff said was true. I should accept Sandycreek Terrace as my permanent home. Could I? Yes, I had to. I shouldn't think I had to leave for four to six months every summer to get away. For years I'd enjoyed those months and other times at the Shack. I should be satisfied, more than satisfied to be financially able to live in a wonderful place like Sandycreek Terrace at my age. My parents and grandparents had had nothing to compare to this when they were old.

From the kitchen I looked out to our dining room, the living room beyond, and then the Florida room and patio. My eyes scanned our well-made furniture, familiar pictures, bone china dishes, Jeff's unique saki bottles, the étagère filled with Jeff's treasures from Japan and mine from Africa. Tears filled my eyes. I looked over at Jeff, my sweet concerned husband. I tried to smile. "You're saying this is the last time we'll be going to the Shack, aren't you?"

"It probably will be, Honey. We can take short trips, a short cruise or two. Maybe even fly up north and be at the Shack for a week or two with a rented car. We'll have to see. He pushed back his chair. "I guess there's not much more to say on this subject. We'll make our big trip in two weeks. Have a great time! How's that?" He rose and gave me that wink I loved to get from him. A wink meaning he loved me.

As long as I was with Jeff, did it really matter where we lived? I pushed back my chair too, got up, cleared the dishes from the table, stacked them in the dishwasher, and turned off the kitchen lights. As I passed the painting of the Shack hanging on the Florida room wall, I stopped. It was that painting my son and his wife had given me, painted by an artist known to my daughter-in-law. I gave it my best smile and whispered, "We'll see you soon."

That evening we had plans to eat dinner with Jane and Jim Horner and Betty Howe and Ralph Wilson. The lounge crowded, we found a table for six on the patio and sat there sipping cocktails while waiting for our table in the dining room. Betty set down her glass, looked over at Jeff and me, and asked, "Are you two going away this summer?"

"We're going up to Jeanie's Shack for three months, Jeff answered.

"When are you going," Jim wanted to know, smiling as he always did, it seemed to me.

"In two weeks," I answered and took a sip of my martini.

"That soon?" Betty exclaimed, her bony fingers flying to her neck to arrange her scarf.

Directly across the table from Jeff, Jane sat in her usual position, shoulders squared in an exaggerated manner to relieve the back pain she'd previously explained. She asked, "Where in Pennsylvania is this place? You did tell me once this place of yours is in Pennsylvania, didn't you?"

"Yes," Jeff said. "Do you know where Breezewood is? It's where the Pennsylvania Turnpike, interstate route 70 to Baltimore, and old interstate route 30 intersect." He drew lines on the table with his fingers to indicate routes and directions.

"I know where that is," Jim said.

"All right. From there you go five miles east on route 30 to state route 915 north. Then go five more miles down steep eight to ten percent grades and hair-pin curves into a farming valley. Lots of small farms surrounded by mountains. Beautiful country!"

"What's the name of the town?" Ralph asked in his southern drawl, coughed, and cleared his throat.

"Actually it's a village. Nothing there except a post office, a Presbyterian church, and a smattering of houses. About two hundred and fifty people. No store. No gas station," Jeff said, chuckling. "The village is called Wells Tannery."

"Sounds wonderful!" Jane said just as a hostess came to seat us in the dining room.

We had stepped into the lounge from the patio when, directly in front of us, white-haired server Lorna hustled from the dining room toward the lounge. On her outspread palm above her head she was carrying a dark-brown tray filled with empty cocktail and wine glasses. All of a sudden she was sprawled on the tile floor! The sound of smashing glass filled the room. On the floor some feet from us, the tray she'd been carrying was spinning and pieces and splinters of broken glass were scattering everywhere.

Residents near by gasped while a server and a hostess rushed to Lorna's side.

"Don't move her!" a resident screamed.

"Call 911!" another resident shouted.

"No, no. I'm all right," Lorna uttered weakly, trying to get up.

The two employees helped her to her feet while residents who'd been sitting in the lounge started gathering up pieces of glass from the floor. Lorna limped over to them and cautioned, "Don't, don't! You'll get cut! I'll get them." She picked up several large pieces then left and came back with a broom and dust pan.

We six had stopped in our tracks to witness the accident and now followed our waiting hostess to our table. We sat quietly for a few minutes, dazed by the scene we'd just witnessed. Then Betty said, "She's always in a hurry. Lorna is always in a hurry. She works faster than any of the other servers and she's three times their age! Why does she do that? Why doesn't she slow down?"

Jane said, "She worked like that at Long View Country Club where we belonged before we came here. She was a waitress there for twenty years. You can't slow her down. That's the way she is even at her age." Jane folded her hands. "She's a grandmother, you know."

"Really?" I said, amazed, my eyebrows raised.

"She's quite a gal," Jeff said as he opened his menu. "Maybe we should decide what to eat." He looked around the table and smiled.

At that point we all studied the typed menus inserted in dark blue leather covers. "I'm having the mustard herbed pork tenderloin," Jeff announced. "I guess you're having the blackened grouper, Jeanie?" He turned toward me.

"Yes, that's my choice. You know I'd rather have fish than chicken or pork." I picked up the stemmed glass filled with ice water and drank a small amount.

"What's this farfalle a la vodka?" Betty asked, pointing to the third entrée' on the menu.

Jane looked over at her. "Must be a pasta. They always have one pasta. Who would order that when there's a choice of pork, chicken, or grouper? I think I'll have the pine nut-crusted chicken breast. What about you, Jim?"

And so the meal continued with conversation about upcoming events, Lorna's fall, and a resident who'd been admitted to the hospital two days ago, a neighbor of the Horners. "Didn't turn off her red light in the bathroom by eleven," Jim said. "So security called on the phone, got no answer, and went over. They found her unconscious in bed. 911 revived her but she's still not responding that well, I understand."

Our meal completed, we all rose from the table. A server had gone for Jeff's Rascal, and Betty came over and hugged me. "Send me a card from up north, Jeanie. I'd like to hear from you. Let me know how you're doing."

"I will," I promised, giving her a squeeze in return.

On the way out of the dining room we passed a four-top. No surprise to see Gus and Rachel Homburg, but there with them was Harry Scott and Lottie Yurasik. I'd heard Harry had gone down to Ft. Lauderdale last week to visit a friend for a few days to get away from constant pursuit by Sarah and Lottie. Now who had called whom for dinner tonight? None of my business, I guess.

The next day Jeff answered the phone when it rang and called to me, "Jeanie, You're wanted on the phone. An attorney by the name of Wallace wants to talk to you."

An attorney? By the name of Wallace? Our attorney's name was McCain. Why would any other attorney be calling me? I picked up the phone.

"Am I speaking to Mrs. Jean Metz?" the male voice asked.

"You are," I answered.

"This is Richard Wallace, attorney representing the family of Mrs. Harris, a former resident at Sandycreek Terrace. Your Food Service Manager gave me your name as a possible witness of the choking incident occurring in the dining room of your facility on June the eleventh of this year. Would you please verify this?"

I frowned, swallowed. I didn't care to be involved in this case. "I didn't attend the dinner party. I wasn't seated at the table with the guests," I said.

"But you were in the dining room at the time? You did leave your table and you were one of the residents near Mrs. Harris at the time she was choking? The Food Service Manager explained that you are a nurse and probably came to the table to assist. Because you would know how to perform the Heimlick maneuver. Can you verify this information?"

My mind raced back to the incident. What he said was true. "Yes. But I did not perform the Heimlich maneuver. Someone else was attempting it and I left and went back to my table." I hoped what I was saying would release me from any involvement in the case.

"Nevertheless I believe you would be a valuable witness. Your knowledge as a nurse and observation of attempts to revive Mrs. Harris. They weren't successful, as you know. You could explain why. I intend to send you a letter in the mail informing you of the case, requesting your participation, and stating the place, date, and time of the trial. Of course I'll want to talk to you briefly prior to the trial. I'll notify you of this brief meeting. Let me express my thanks in advance. Now have you any questions?"

I needed to get out of this! "Yes," I said. "When exactly do you expect this trial to take place? In two weeks I'm going out of state to Pennsylvania for the summer months. I'd like to be excused from this case. I truly don't think I can be of any help."

"That might present a problem. I expect the case will go to trial in less than two months. When I see how it's shaping up I may not need you. But then again I may. In either event I'll be sending you the afore mentioned letter with return receipt requested which will require you to send, by return mail, your Pennsylvania address and telephone number in order for me to send you a subpoena if necessary. Simply answer the letter in writing when you receive it."

As soon as we hung up I called to Jeff. "That was the attorney representing Mrs. Harris, the resident who choked in the dining room that evening. He thinks I'd be a valuable witness. I tried to get out of it."

"Didn't you tell him you wouldn't be available? You'd be out of state?"

"Yes, and hopefully that will excuse me. But he's sending me a letter requesting my Pennsylvania address and phone number in case he has to subpoena me. I'm not liking this one bit!" I told Jeff as I walked into the den where he was working on his autobiography.

436

"I wouldn't worry about it. He won't make you come to Florida all the way from Pennsylvania," Jeff tried to assure me.

The next week the in-house mailbox contained an invitation for me to attend a VIP Tea being held in the lounge the day before we were to leave. RSVP was requested by the Social Director. When I phoned Janet to accept the invitation she gushed, "I'm so happy you're able to come. We've only sent invitations to a few of the residents. There'll be a guest speaker."

Curious, I asked her, "How did I happen to be selected to attend?"

"The thirteen residents we've invited are those who have visual impairments. I'm sure you'll enjoy the speaker. She's very knowledgeable in the field."

So that was it. With all my years of visual problems, treatments, and surgeries, I doubted the VIP Tea would be of interest to me. What could I hope to learn from the guest speaker? Then it occurred to me Amanda Murray just might attend the Tea because of her position, her interest in all the residents in independent living quarters, and their needs for assistance and their problems, health wise and otherwise. As promised by the editor, I had just received copies of the nursing magazine containing my continuing education course on glaucoma. The article was well presented with drawings depicting the normal eye and one with open angle glaucoma. I was pleased with it. I always gave Amanda Murray's staff my nursing magazines after I read them but I intended to give Amanda her own copy of this current issue containing my article. I could take the copy to the Tea and give it to her there.

Because I was so busy packing the day before we were to leave, the same day as the VIP Tea, I was late getting to the lounge where the Tea was being held. The guest speaker was already wrapping up her speech and answering residents' questions. I did have an opportunity to interject with several comments of my own concerning glaucoma.

After the Tea while bartender Mandy, in the role of waitress, was picking up empty teacups, saucers, and dishes speckled with cookie crumbs, I approached Amanda with the nursing magazine. I pointed to the title in the left-hand corner of the cover and said, "You'll find my article on page eleven."

"Oh Mrs. Metz! You've had another article published!" She beamed at me and then opened the magazine to page eleven. "Why it's on glaucoma! I'll be interested in reading it. You know what I'm going to do?" she said, eyes flashing. "I'm going to make copies and give one to each of the VYP residents. They'd be very interested in reading it."

"I'd appreciate that," I said. Janet was standing beside Amanda listening with apparent interest and smiling at me. I'd changed my mind about her. She was a very vivacious person, catered to the residents, and was a perfect Social Director for elderly people. She needed a condescending personality to relate with many of them, I'd decided. "I guess this would be a good time to say good-bye," I said to both of them.

"Oh you're leaving, Mrs. Metz! How soon are you leaving?" Amanda Murray asked.

"Tomorrow," I answered, grinning, unable to contain my enthusiasm at the prospect of leaving.

"Tomorrow? Then let me give you a big good-bye hug," Amanda said, putting her chubby arms around me and squeezing. "Send me an e-mail, won't you? We'd like to get an e-mail from you. And I'm going to make copies of your article for the residents."

I left the other residents gathered in groups conversing and walked back to the apartment in good spirits. But not just about hitting the road tomorrow. I had a good all-encompassing feeling deep inside about Sandycreek Terrace, the staff, and the other residents.

I'd keep in touch via e-mails with Amanda Murray and send postal cards to Elizabeth. Even to Betty Howe and Jane Horner. Betty and Jane were true friends. I liked Rachel Homburg, too. A fun Pittsburgh buddy. I considered Ruth McKee, our across-the-corridor neighbor, sober and irritating as she could be sometimes, a true friend, too. She meant well and provided me with helpful information. I knew she and Stuart would respond if we ever needed anything in a hurry, or not in a hurry. Then there was our Saturday afternoon movie group, eight of us who always ate together at a large table in the dining room after attending the movie in the card room. The Gathers, the Walters, Sarah Grant, and Gloria Semple. Sarah was such an interesting enterprising person even though Jeff described her as a sour puss.

Now I wondered, would Sarah's book become a best-seller? And Gloria Semple, a long-time church acquaintance, interested in a Michigan man who visited her at Sandycreek Terrace and made her come alive again a year after her husband's death. Would anything come of that relationship?

And what about the piano? How would that problem be solved? In favor of those who liked to hear it playing every night or those who didn't? The law suit. Would the jury decide in favor of the family of the resident who choked or find Sandycreek Terrace blameless? Had insufficient measures been taken to save her? Was the meat the fatal cause or did the resident have a heart attack perhaps? And wasn't I lucky to be up in Pennsylvania and probably not have to testify? I'd pray that I wasn't called. Surely I wouldn't be.

I suddenly realized I'd miss all these people with whom I'd become more than acquainted. I'd miss getting dressed in my Patchington clothes to eat in the fine dining room with its lavish menu, food served by courteous and friendly young men and women. I'd miss looking out over the blue water of the inlet and talking to Jeff while we enjoyed our dinners together. In advance of dinner I'd miss the cocktail hours, sitting and chatting with friends, and listening to the piano. I'd miss the weekly bulletin and monthly *Periscope*. I'd miss the Symposium, the monthly meetings with the Executive Director presiding, the monthly parties, and mornings swimming in the heated pool. And I'd be dying to know which of the two pursuers, Sarah Grant or Lottie Yurasik, was making inroads with Harry Scott.

When we returned I'd relax. I'd be happy knowing Jeff was contented. No steps, no heavy lifting, less back pain, and his scooter to ride where he couldn't walk.

Wasn't I blessed to have another summer at the Shack? Three whole months! And I'd make the most of it. Yes, much as I loved the Shack, the familiar surroundings, and country living, lovely Sandycreek Terrace with its secure protective environment where I shared my life with Jeff was where I belonged at my age. It was my home.